From a young age, Tilly Tennant was convinced that she was destined for the stage. Once she realised she wasn't actually very good at anything that would put her on the stage, she started to write stories instead. There were lots of terrible ones, like *The Pet Rescue Gang* (aged eight), which definitely should not see the light of day ever again. Thankfully, her debut novel, *Hopelessly Devoted to Holden Finn*, was not one of those, and since it hit the Amazon bestseller lists she hasn't looked back. Born in Dorset, she currently lives in Staffordshire with her husband, two daughters, three guitars, four ukuleles, two violins and a kazoo.

ALSO BY TILLY TENNANT

THE VILLAGE MIDWIFE SERIES
The Village Midwife
Christmas for the Village Midwife
Family Ties for the Village Midwife

THE VILLAGE NURSE SERIES
A Helping Hand for the Village Nurse
A Family Surprise for the Village Nurse

THE LIFEBOAT SISTERS SERIES
The Lifeboat Sisters
Second Chances for the Lifeboat Sisters
A Secret for the Lifeboat Sisters

AN UNFORGETTABLE CHRISTMAS SERIES
A Very Vintage Christmas
A Cosy Candlelit Christmas

FROM ITALY WITH LOVE SERIES
Rome is Where the Heart is
A Wedding in Italy

HONEYBOURNE SERIES
The Little Village Bakery
Christmas at the Little Village Bakery

STANDALONES
The Summer of Secrets
The Summer Getaway
The Christmas Wish

TILLY TENNANT

New Dreams for the VILLAGE NURSE

Bookouture

BOOKOUTURE

First published in 2024 by Bookouture, an imprint of Storyfire Ltd.
This paperback edition published in 2026

1

Copyright © Tilly Tennant 2024

The moral right of the author has been asserted.

A CIP catalogue record for this book
is available from the British Library.

PB ISBN 978-1-83618-869-8
EB ISBN 978-1-83525-576-6

Printed and bound in Great Britain by
Clays Ltd, Elcograf S.p.A.

Papers used by Bookouture are from well-managed forests
and other responsible sources.

Bookouture
An imprint of Storyfire Ltd.
Carmelite House
50 Victoria Embankment
London EC4Y 0DZ

An Hachette UK Company

The authorised representative in the EEA is Hachette Ireland
8 Castlecourt Centre
Dublin 15 D15 XTP3
Ireland
(email: info@hbgi.ie)

www.hachette.co.uk
www.bookouture.com

To Paula – a brilliant nurse and friend.

CHAPTER ONE

It was close to a year since Ottilie Oakcroft had first arrived in the quaint and picture-postcard-pretty Lake District village of Thimblebury. She'd arrived full of sadness, but even then she'd fallen in love with it so quickly she'd hardly noticed it happen. She loved the people, the ramshackle collection of lovely cottages, the history, the beauty of the surrounding countryside and the new life it had given her. And she loved her job, caring for its residents, best of all. Caring was something she'd always felt born to, a calling she'd never been able to ignore, and never had she felt more valued for this than she did in her new home.

Mostly Ottilie worked from the tiny office that doubled as her treatment room at Thimblebury's only surgery, but sometimes a patient would need a house call. Their GP, Fliss Cheadle, often complained that she didn't have time for them, but Ottilie secretly liked to go out on visits to patients, if only because she got to breathe in the fresh, clean air of the hills that surrounded the village, and remind herself of how lucky she was to live in the most beautiful place on earth.

Today was one of those days. Her house call was so close by she hadn't bothered getting into her car. Instead, she'd walked the lanes of the village while a sweet breeze set the trees swaying gently. Over the hills, the racing clouds cast shadows that changed the light, the emerging sun making them emerald one moment and disappearing behind the clouds to turn them black the next. She'd been greeted warmly by every local she'd encountered. They all knew her now – she was like the newest member of a vast, ungainly, slightly dysfunctional but ultimately wonderful family. Though she'd never have imagined her current love for the village even a year ago, now she couldn't imagine living anywhere else.

'There… that's healing nicely.'

Ottilie had just finished inspecting Mrs Smith's burned hand and was applying new dressings.

'Thank you.' The old lady beamed gratefully. 'It's been a right nuisance.'

'I should imagine so,' Ottilie said as she fastened the bandage and began to put away her equipment. 'But I don't think it will be long before you'll be able to take off the dressing and wash it again. Far be it for me to tell you how to cook, but maybe you'll think twice before you get that old chip pan out now. Get yourself a nice air fryer or something – something a lot safer – please.'

'Oh, but they don't taste the same. I've always done them in a chip pan. You can't beat home-made chips in a chip pan.'

'I bet you could at least get one with a proper lid? I'll tell you what – I'll ask around to see if anyone can spare one for you.'

'I'd rather keep my old one. It's the first time I've ever burned myself on it.'

'Yes, it might have been, but you did it in style. It's lucky the oil didn't catch more than your hand when you spilled it.'

Ottilie studied the old lady thoughtfully for a moment. Tact was needed here. Her patient was close to ninety. Sprightly, yes, and still sharp, but it was obvious she was getting to the stage in her life where she wasn't quite as fast as she used to be, nor as strong. Ottilie suspected the old lady had dropped the pan because it had been too heavy for her. And she'd been lucky that the only real damage had been done to her hand.

At the end of the day, however, Ottilie could only give her opinion on whether Mrs Smith ought to be wheeling out that antiquated deep-fat fryer every time she wanted chips; she couldn't stop her from using it. All the same, she made a resolution to track down something safer and more modern and to drop it in anyway in the hope she might be able to persuade her patient to swap.

'I know chips aren't very good for me,' Mrs Smith continued, 'but at my age, I don't see the point in stopping eating them.'

Ottilie smiled. 'They're only bad for you when you decide to throw them and the oil you fried them in all over your kitchen and yourself. Just promise you'll be more careful from now on, and I don't see any reason why you shouldn't have the odd plate of chips if you want them. You know you could come to the community kitchen and get a dinner from time to time. I don't think I've ever seen you there. We'd do chips if you asked us nicely, and it's nice to have someone else cook for you on occasion, isn't it?'

'Oh no, I don't go. It's for people who've got no money, isn't it? Well, I'm not rich, but I have enough for what I need.'

'It's for anyone who wants to drop in, really. I think you'd enjoy it. Why don't you come down later? I'll be doing a shift in the kitchens tonight, and it would be lovely to see you there.'

'Are you? I didn't know you volunteered there.'

'When I can. I don't always have as much time as I'd like, but I try to do a bit.'

Ottilie wasn't exaggerating. She spared time as often as she could to the meals-for-residents scheme that provided weekly get-togethers for those who were alone or unable to eat as well as they ought to. Once a week, the village hall would be filled with trestle tables, laughter, conversation and good food, and anyone who needed it was welcome, but that wasn't the only project she was involved in. It was fast becoming a running gag with

Heath – the man who'd shown her that second chances at love did happen; the one person who wasn't part of the village who she dearly wished was – that he'd have to make an appointment with her PA to see her before long.

There was the mum and baby group – ostensibly handed over to her friend Stacey once off the ground, but Ottilie couldn't resist getting stuck in whenever she had a spare moment. And there was another loneliness project, inspired by Flo, Heath's grandmother, and one of her elderly patients whom she'd grown close to and who would never have admitted to being lonely but often was. Ottilie had organised a buddy system so that village volunteers were allocated someone vulnerable or lonely to befriend and visit. And all those things were without the extra mile she went for her patients, like Darryl and his mum Ann at Hilltop Farm, where she called every morning before work to make sure he'd taken his insulin.

Then there was her membership of Thimblebury's film club and (newly in a bid to push her boundaries) the wild swimming group that went out to splash about one morning a month at one of the local lakes.

She barely had time to draw breath, but it was a long time since she'd been this happy. She felt she owed Thimblebury so much that it was only right and fair she did what she could to make it a better place, to make others as happy as being a part of the village had made her.

'Right…' Ottilie fastened her bag and got up. 'I'll pop back next week. You've got a hospital appointment lined up to see the specialist at the burns unit too? It'll be up to them to give you the final all-clear, but I can't see why they'd be unhappy with your progress.'

Mrs Smith nodded. 'Yes, the letter is somewhere. Thank you, Nurse.'

'And don't forget, we'd love to see you at the kitchen tonight.'

'I'll think on it.'

Ottilie bid her a last goodbye, strongly suspecting that Mrs Smith had already decided she wasn't going to be at the community kitchen that evening. It was her choice, of course, and Ottilie understood how pride stopped some people from seeking out the things that would make their life easier and more fulfilled, even if it sometimes frustrated her that those same people could be so much better off if they swallowed their pride and took advantage of them.

Stepping out onto the lane again, she drew in a lungful of sweet air. There were green buds on the trees in people's front gardens, and the sight reminded her that spring was just about upon them.

The walk back to the surgery took less than ten minutes.

Lavender, their receptionist, looked up from her computer. 'Some woman's been on the phone asking about you.'

'Oh…' Ottilie shrugged off her coat. She noted her next couple of patients waiting in the seating area. 'Who was it?'

'Didn't give her name. Sorry, Ottilie.'

'What did she want?'

'Didn't want to leave a message either.'

'Right… a patient maybe? Might have been something a bit personal they didn't want to discuss with anyone else.'

'Could have been. It was a bit weird, though. I can't think of a regular patient who wouldn't want to at least say who'd called or leave a number for you to call back.'

'So she didn't leave a number?'

Lavender shook her head and Ottilie shrugged. It was strange, but she was too busy to worry about it now. If it was important she supposed they'd call back. More likely, it was some sneaky sales rep from a drug company or medical supplier she didn't currently order from trying to get in to see her through the back door. She certainly couldn't think of any other reason for the secrecy. Thimblebury surgery already had their approved suppliers, but that never stopped new ones from trying to steal the business.

Ottilie went round to the back of the reception desk and looked over Lavender's shoulder. 'Who's first?'

'Mrs Icke.'

Ottilie could sense Lavender's mental eye-roll because she was feeling it too. Mrs Icke was one of her more cantankerous patients. She had a condition that Ottilie liked to call selective deafness – she pretended not to hear things when it suited her, usually when she was being told something she didn't like.

Lavender opened her desk drawer and pulled out a chocolate bar. 'Here,' she said, passing it to Ottilie. 'Picked you up a treat to soften the blow. If you're very good, I'll bring you a cup of tea to go with it.'

Ottilie grinned as she took the bar. 'My favourite. You know you're the best receptionist there's ever been, don't you?'

'I try,' Lavender said with a grin of her own. 'We've got to get through the working day somehow, right?'

As Ottilie started for her room, she noticed Mrs Icke getting up to follow her without waiting to be asked and stifled a sigh of resignation. Lavender looked ready to say something but Ottilie shook her head. It wasn't worth bothering, and she was more or less ready anyway. For now, at least, her tea and chocolate would have to wait.

Fliss was already in the kitchen at lunchtime heating some leftover stew at the stove. Ottilie could smell the rich sauce on the air. The surgery team always ate together in the hour they closed the doors to patients – it was an old-fashioned practice in some ways, but one Fliss was insistent on. She said it fostered a sense of belonging amongst her staff and that it was a well-needed daily recharge, and Ottilie had never seen any reason to argue with that.

'I've made enough for all of us,' Fliss said. 'Lavender's got bread.'

'Sounds lovely.' Ottilie sat down with a weary sigh. 'I've got some cream cake in the fridge if we can fit it in afterwards.'

'I might be tempted to skip the stew then,' Fliss said with a light laugh. 'How was Mrs Icke today?'

'She was the usual Mrs Icke. Thank goodness there's only one of her.'

'Everything else has been all right then?'

'Yes, pretty much standard.'

Lavender came in with a set of keys. 'All locked up. That smells amazing.'

'One of Charles's recipes,' Fliss said. 'The secret's in the wine.'

Lavender sat down next to Ottilie. 'Do you two put wine in everything?'

'Do you know…?' Fliss replied as she turned off the stove. 'I do think we might. It would explain how we get through so much of it.'

'You get through so much of it because you drink so much,' Lavender said briskly. 'Don't forget I've been round your house and seen you both in action.'

'Which house?' Fliss asked vaguely. 'Mine or Charles's?'

Ottilie laughed. 'Does it matter? Whichever you're at, you're just as bad.'

Lavender accepted a bowl of stew. 'I'll never get used to the fact that you two don't live together. After all, you've been married for donkey's.'

'God, we could never do that!' Fliss put a bowl in front of Ottilie. It was thick and rich, with generous chunks of potato and beef. 'I keep telling you, I think every married couple ought to live apart. It makes for a far better marriage. We've both always hated the idea of living in each other's pockets.'

Ottilie could think of many good reasons why most married couples took the more traditional route when it came to living arrangements – namely the cost of running two houses – but she didn't say so. Fliss and Charles had their ways, and clearly it suited them. In fact, Ottilie would have been pushed to name a happier couple, so perhaps there was something in it. Not that she'd have dreamed of such an arrangement with Josh, the husband she'd lost sixteen months previously. She tried not to dwell on that now, though. There would be quieter moments, private moments to remember and be sad. This wasn't one of them.

'Actually,' Fliss said, 'we've booked a lovely trip with some vouchers my sister-in-law gave us. A winery tour in Sussex.'

'Oh, don't tell me you're actually taking time off!' Ottilie said with a laugh.

'I know, insane, isn't it?' Fliss replied. 'Even I need the odd weekend.'

'So we'll be getting emergency cover?' Lavender asked.

'Yes, but it won't be for a few months yet, so I wouldn't worry about it.'

Lavender slurped at her stew and made a face of appreciation. 'I can't remember the last time you went on holiday.'

'Neither can I,' Fliss agreed, 'though it's hardly a holiday. We are both looking forward to it, though. A bit of quality time together and all that.'

Ottilie grinned. 'Plus wine.'

'Yes, my one true love,' Fliss replied. 'And Charles isn't too bad either!'

As they all laughed, the sound of the phone ringing in the reception reached them. Ottilie shot a questioning look at Lavender, but Fliss intervened.

'Everyone knows not to phone at this time of the day, so if it's a patient they'll call back, or they can press the button and go to the emergency line.'

Ottilie enjoyed their lunches but she'd never been comfortable with that arrangement. However, it did seem to have worked for the surgery over the years, so she didn't argue. Instead, she went back to one of the best beef stews she'd ever eaten and thought no more about it.

There'd been time for a quick drink and a change of clothes at home that evening, and then Ottilie had headed straight back out to the community kitchen to help with the cooking. It was yet more work, but she'd been looking forward to it all day. There was a camaraderie, a sense of pulling together and of doing good that was addictive – not to mention how much she enjoyed simply socialising with the other volunteers.

Ottilie was the last to arrive and work had already begun. Her friend, Stacey, tossed an apron over to her as she walked into the kitchen.

'Come on, slacker. I've peeled half a sack of carrots already and you've only just waltzed in.'

Ottilie grinned. 'Sorry, boss.'

Everyone else greeted her with a little more decorum, but no less warmly.

The kitchen was part of the village hall and fitted with steel units and white tiles. It was too small for so many of them, but they always managed well enough. The important thing about this venue was that the hall where the dining tables were being set up by Magnus and Geoff from the village shop and post office was big enough to comfortably seat their regulars and anyone else who might want to stop by. Everyone was always welcome and nobody was turned away, no matter how full or busy they got. It was a philosophy of friendship and nobody was judged for using the service.

Working tonight was Janet – the founder and organiser of the kitchen – along with Stacey, Ottilie's new best friend, Magnus and Geoff setting up the dining room and Heath's grandma, Flo. Ottilie and Heath had got together four months previously – a romance that very nearly didn't happen, but one that Ottilie was happy to report, after many setbacks, did. Happy because she was in love when she never imagined a second chance at something this good could be out there. When she'd lost her husband, Josh, she'd felt as if her life was over. But then she'd come to Thimblebury and she'd met Flo, and through Flo she'd met Heath, and suddenly she'd had happiness and hope again.

'Where do you want me?' she asked Janet as she tied her apron.

'I know it's a horrible job, but I don't suppose you could cut some onions?'

Ottilie nodded and went to get the sack. 'I've got plenty of tissues in my bag at least.'

'Put a spoon in your mouth,' Flo called over.

Ottilie stared at her as she came back to her workstation and hunted in the drawer for a knife.

'It stops you from crying,' Flo said.

'Don't fall for that,' Stacey called over. 'She tried to tell me that once – it didn't work. I think it might have made things worse, actually. And all I could taste all night was rusty spoon.'

'It does work!' Flo shot back. 'My old mum swore by it. She never cried once cutting an onion.'

Stacey wagged a carrot at her. 'I don't know about your old mum, but it certainly didn't do me any good. I mean, a spoon in your mouth? How's that meant to work? It makes absolutely no sense.'

'You don't need to know how it works. Plenty of things work even if you don't know how.'

Ottilie decided the best course of action was to humour her. She'd seen what a riled Flo could look like before and she wasn't about to wind her up now, even if Stacey delighted in it. And so she pulled out a teaspoon and held it up.

'Will this one be all right?'

Flo nodded. 'You'll see.'

Whether it was purely a placebo or whether Flo's strange and archaic remedy actually worked, Ottilie couldn't say, but as she began to chop, sucking on the spoon as she went, her eyes didn't even so much as water. The downside to Flo's less than scientific triumph was that it also prevented her from joining in the gossip. She'd just decided that she'd rather cry and be able to chat than persevere with the spoon when the door to the community centre's kitchen opened and Heath looked round it, chestnut hair curled at his collar where it was getting a little longer than usual and his soft brown eyes full of mischief.

'This is where you're hiding, is it?'

'I'm not exactly hiding,' Flo said, and Ottilie had to hold in her laughter again, because she was fairly sure Heath was talking to her. They'd arranged to meet later that evening, but perhaps he'd found himself at a loose end and decided to come over early.

'Hello, Gran,' he said, going over and giving her the sweetest kiss on the cheek.

Ottilie watched, smiling, tummy doing cartwheels of anticipation. She was hoping her kiss would be rather less sweet and a bit more spicy, but that would have to wait because as much as she craved it, she wasn't going to embarrass everyone else in the room with such a display.

Four months had gone by since they'd sort of unofficially got together. They'd taken it slowly – Heath certain that was what she'd needed and Ottilie sure of the same for him, an unspoken agreement by them both. Slow and steady, and slowly and surely, Ottilie was falling for him.

Things had been tentative at first – though she'd had no doubts about Heath, she'd had doubts about her own emotional state – but there were signs that things were growing more serious. Ottilie had tried not to think about that too much because if she gave herself a moment to consider it, she might frighten herself away. She'd given her heart completely once before and had lost everything. Lightning couldn't strike twice like that, she told herself, and to find otherwise would be more than she could bear.

Thimblebury now felt like home too, properly and forever. While Heath was still living in Manchester, Ottilie had no pull to the city she'd once called home. Everything and everyone – other than Heath, but he drove over often enough – she needed and wanted was here.

'Go on,' Flo said, waving Heath away and going back to her tea. 'I know you're not here to see me.'

'Of course I am,' he replied gallantly. 'The fact that I get to see Ottilie is a bonus.'

'Gawd.' Flo shook her head impatiently. 'You must think I fell off a Christmas tree. I think it's more likely the other way round.'

'If it is, you only have yourself to blame. You did try to get us together after all.'

'I did no such thing!'

Ottilie and Heath exchanged a grin. Flo could deny it until the alpaca of Daffodil Farm came home, but they knew the truth. She *had* been matchmaking, and she'd done a terrible job of hiding it. And she hadn't been the only one, as Ottilie was forcibly reminded when the name of one of the other matchmaking culprits was shouted out.

'Magnus!' Janet called through the kitchen doors into the main hall. 'How's it going out there? Are you and Geoff nearly done?'

'Nearly!' Magnus called back.

Flo looked at Heath. 'As you're here, you could give them a hand.' She narrowed her eyes. 'Why are you here, anyway?'

'We've got plans,' he replied, looking at Ottilie.

'Not for ages,' Ottilie reminded him. 'I did say I had to do a couple of hours here first. In fact, as I recall, I said I wouldn't be able to spare much time tonight at all…'

'I know, but can I help it if I want to see you whenever I can?'

'Be still my heart,' Stacey cut in from across the room. 'Please, God, or Cupid or St Valentine or whoever, please find me a man who will drive all the way from Manchester just to watch me cut onions while I suck on a spoon.'

Heath grinned. 'So Gran's got you doing the old spoon thing?'

'Oi!' Flo huffed. 'Even Ottilie has admitted that it works!'

'She'd never dare say anything else to you, Gran.'

Just then Magnus put his head around the door. 'All done in here. Geoff and I will head home if you don't need anything else. We'll pop back later to help clean up.'

While Janet thanked him, Ottilie turned back to Heath.

'Looks like that's you off the hook then. As you're here, we ought to find something for you to do.' She nodded at a hook on the back of the kitchen door. 'There's a spare apron. Make yourself useful – there's peas to shell.'

'That's served you right,' Flo shouted over.

'It did backfire a bit.' Heath grinned and went to get the apron. 'But I suppose I walked right into it.'

'That you did,' Flo replied.

Ottilie showed Heath where the bags of peas were. They were both smiling. Ottilie's face ached from it, but she couldn't stop. She was also pleased to see Heath getting stuck in. Since they'd got together, he'd been supportive of her community projects but he'd always shied away from getting involved. Ottilie understood – he was busy and he didn't live locally, so it was more difficult for him to get there – but it was nice to see it now. She was aware of him as he stood at her side, and it was so distracting she could barely concentrate on her onions. But that was lovely too. Right about now, life was as perfect as it had been for a long time.

CHAPTER TWO

The restaurant was stone-built, nestled in the skirts of one of the Lake District's many hills. They served fairly traditional but upmarket versions of pub classics – hearty steak-and-ale pies, smoky salmon and parsley potatoes, meaty lasagne, and good old scampi and chips. Ottilie had checked out the reviews online. The interior was warm and mellow, the low ceilings festooned with fairy lights, giving it a magical grotto sort of feel, the furniture old and solid and the floors heavy stone. People seemed to be raving about it, which would explain how difficult it had been to get a booking. She could almost taste the salmon she planned to order, and it set her tummy gurgling in anticipation.

Night had already fallen, which had disappointed Ottilie, because she couldn't see the majesty of that hill, or its cousins, as she and Heath drove the road out to it. She'd marvelled at the sights of her new home on the day she'd arrived – the greens and russets of the towering hills, the stark contrast of the grey rocks peppering their sides; the dark slants of the valleys and the way the light shimmered through racing clouds over the vast lakes, a different light for every hour of the day; the random patches of wildflowers on roadside verges and the heavy trees that dipped over roads and riverbanks – and since that day, ten months earlier, she'd never been able to get enough of them.

They'd driven past this place a few weeks before, and Ottilie had said how much she'd like to try it, but this was the first table available. That day, they'd taken Flo out to Kendal to get her favourite mint cake, and the hills had been wreathed in cloud, brooding and magnificent. Ottilie loved the Lakes in any weather, but there was something all at once mysterious and a little bit scary that she loved when it looked like that.

It hadn't always been so. In her previous home she'd always felt low when Manchester was grey with rain. And not long after her arrival in Thimblebury, a freak storm had flooded her house and it had been one of the worst things that had ever happened to her, but out of adversity came joy. That flood had shown her the very best of her community, and she'd felt so incredibly loved and wanted it had flicked a switch inside her. She'd liked Thimblebury well enough when she'd first arrived, but after that – after her friends and neighbours had rescued her from financial ruin, and made her house better than it had been before the flood, all because they simply wanted her to stay – she'd felt as if this small, insignificant village in the great lakes of England was lodged in her soul and would be until she died.

Heath pulled up in the car park and turned off the engine. 'We're a bit early, but they have a nook where we can get drinks while we wait for our table to be ready.'

'I don't mind that.'

'I didn't think you would. I honestly thought it would take us longer to get up here. Gran said Geoff had told her about a rock fall or something, but I suppose that was wrong.'

'It's good actually…' Ottilie was suddenly troubled. There had been a thing nagging at her, something she'd wanted to talk to Heath about but hadn't dared yet bring up. She didn't even know why she was nervous about it. He knew all about her past with Josh – she'd kept no secrets – and he knew how in love she'd been with her husband.

When she'd first started to date Heath, it was almost as if she was cheating on Josh, even though he was no longer alive. It had taken some time to come to terms with that and change the narrative, and now she wanted to talk to Heath about something she needed to do for Josh, it was almost like things had switched. Now, to bring Josh up, to need to do something for him felt like she was somehow cheating on Heath. It was crazy, Ottilie knew that, irrational, but when had a notion being irrational ever stopped her from feeling it just the same?

'It's good because there's something I want to tell you, so the extra time somewhere quiet might—'

'This sounds serious.'

Ottilie reached for his hand. Hers was cold and clammy where only moments before it had been warm. Those nerves again. Inwardly, she chided herself. Heath would understand – what was there to be nervous about?

'Do you want to tell me now? Is it a thing we shouldn't be discussing in public?'

Ottilie gave the most reassuring smile she could, though she felt far from reassured. 'It's not that...' She drew a breath to steady herself. 'It's Josh's birthday next week. Well, it would have been. It would have been...'

Her eyes glazed with tears. Damn it – she hadn't wanted to cry. She didn't want it to look to Heath like she'd loved Josh more than she loved him. It was different – she loved them differently but equally, but could she make Heath see that? She didn't want to make him feel like the consolation prize. Sure, of course, there was no argument that if Josh had still been alive she'd be with him now, but he wasn't. She'd never expected a second chance at a love this good, but it had come to her anyway and she didn't want to ruin it. But...

Heath pulled her across the gap in the seats and into his arms. 'You should have said before. I had no idea.'

'Of course you didn't. It's my fault. I didn't want to bring it up, but he would have been forty, so it feels significant, you know. And I think I'd like to go to Manchester to see his grave. And maybe visit some of his family too. And I just want you to know about it, because I don't want you to find out I was in Manchester from someone else.'

'Why would that matter?' he asked, pulling away to look at her.

'Because I won't be seeing you while I'm there. I need to do this alone, you know? And I don't think it would be good for either of us to spend time together on such a weird occasion. You understand, don't you?'

'Yes! Completely! But – and hear me out before you give an answer – do you really want to do this alone? We're a team now, right?'

Ottilie nodded slowly.

'And so we're there for one another. I know this will be a tough thing for you, and I get it – if you're going to see his family, then you might want to do that alone, but you don't have to be alone for all of it. What if I come to Josh's grave with you?'

'Why would you…?'

'I don't know.' He shrugged. 'It just feels like I ought to. It feels like a way to support you through this. And maybe…' He paused. 'I don't know… like maybe I feel as if I ought to say a word. Kind of get his approval, you know. Sounds daft, doesn't it? Now that I've said it that sounds daft. Forget it.'

'It sounds lovely,' Ottilie said through the tears she hadn't been able to hold back. 'It sounds exactly like the sort of lovely thing you'd do for me. But I couldn't ask you to do that.'

'Why not? You don't want me there? Because if that's it, then I understand—'

Ottilie shook her head. 'It's not that. It's… It would be weird for both of us. I don't know how I feel about it.'

'OK,' he said after a long pause. 'Sleep on it. Let me know, but the offer is there. I realise this is going to be hard but I want to be there for you, in whatever way you need me to be there. If you need me to stay away, then I can do that too. All you have to do is ask and it's yours.'

'I don't deserve you.'

'I don't know about that, but I know you deserve my best, and I always want to give you that. You make me want to try harder to be better every day, and I owe you everything for that. I *am* better because of you.'

Ottilie buried her face in his shoulder and tried to stop her tears. 'Thank you.'

He lifted her face gently to his and kissed her. 'There's nothing to thank me for. I'm the thankful one. Now… do you want to go in and get that drink? Because if you'd rather stay out here and talk more in private, or if you don't feel like going out at all now and you want to go back home, we can—'

'No, I want to go in. Let's have a nice evening; I don't want to ruin it.'

'You wouldn't. I wish you'd told me all this before, though. If I'd known, I would have… well, I don't know, but I feel as if I've been heartless not to have considered that this type of milestone would come up. You should have said – I wouldn't have suggested we go out. I'd have stayed away and given you space.'

'I don't want you to stay away and I don't need space. You're right – we should be there for one another.'

Ottilie paused. She was so lucky to have found Heath, and she couldn't let herself take him for granted, not for one minute. She didn't want to lose him.

'I'd like it if you came to the cemetery with me next week. I think it would be good, and you're right, I'd appreciate the support. But maybe not the rest of the stuff.'

'Anything you want.'

'You're sure you really want to do this?'

'Absolutely.'

Ottilie took a long breath and sniffed hard. 'I can't believe I've ruined my make-up before we've even set foot in the place. People will think we've had a massive bust-up in the car park.'

'Let them think what they want – what do we care? And you look gorgeous whatever your make-up is doing.'

'You have to say that.'

'Yes, I do, but I don't have to mean it. And I do mean it. Ottilie, to me you're perfect, and I never want you to feel anything less than that.'

She nodded, unable to express the same in quite such an eloquent way. She only knew that the more time they spent together, the more she wanted to be with him. He was quickly becoming a part of her life that she couldn't do without. And it scared her. Once, Josh had been that, and then she'd lost him, and it had almost ripped her in two. She didn't know if she had the strength to go through that again. She prayed she'd never have to.

CHAPTER THREE

Stacey bounced her new grandson, baby Mackenzie, on her knee. He was drooling over a fist rammed into his mouth, podgy cheeks aflame. Ottilie reflected vaguely on how good Stacey looked today. She wore a denim dress, belted at her trim waist, and knee-length boots. She'd been telling Ottilie how she'd travelled to a neighbouring town where there was a decent salon to have her hair cut shoulder length. Ottilie was in awe – it was a style she'd never be able to pull off, a chic, shaggy kind of haircut that really framed her face and made her look very cool. Stacey was a grandmother in name, but she was only in her late forties and looked younger than that, still gorgeous and still fun. Ottilie had never understood how she'd been single for all the years since her husband had left her to bring up daughter Chloe by herself.

As she jogged Mackenzie on her knee, he grizzled. 'This is the first time he's been quiet all day. I'd be tempted to say Chloe's being a drama queen, but this time I can understand why she needs a break.'

'She's doing so well, though.' Ottilie smiled at Mackenzie as she offered him a teething ring.

'Better than I ever thought she would,' Stacey agreed. 'Considering how down she was on the idea of motherhood at the beginning—'

'Quite near the end too,' Ottilie said, and Stacey gave a light laugh.

'True. But she's smitten with him now. I always knew she would be, but I never expected her to take to it so well. She copes better than I ever did with her.'

'So what's she doing today?' Ottilie asked, her gaze going to a playpen where two toddlers looked as if they might start to fight over one of the toys. She was wondering whether she might have to go and break it up when their mothers noticed and did the job for her. She didn't know why she'd even worried. Everyone here was perfectly capable of handling their offspring.

The notion made her a little melancholy. She'd have liked being a mum, but at almost thirty-six, she was afraid that ship was about to sail. Would her grief have been either easier or harder to bear if she and Josh had done the family thing before he'd died? She'd have the child she felt she was missing out on now, but she'd be raising that child alone, having to heal not just her own soul but theirs as well. It would be a big responsibility. As it was, she'd only had herself to worry about, and that had been hard enough.

'She's taken a bus into Bowness to meet… *someone*.'

Ottilie looked up at the stress on the word. 'Someone as in… someone? Someone significant?'

'It's hard to tell. She can be a bit secretive. But if it's a lad, then she's not likely to tell me about him at this stage. And I suppose it's good for her. I think she felt as if her life was going to end when she had Mackenzie – there'd be no dating or going out or anything – and even though she understands Mackenzie has to come first, I don't feel it's right to deny her those things at her age. I mean, what were we doing at eighteen? We were having fun. You're still a kid, aren't you?'

'I suppose so.'

'I know I was wet behind the ears; I don't know about you. That's why I fell in with Chloe's useless git of a dad. If I'd been a bit older, had more about me, I might have saved myself all that heartache.'

'But you got Chloe, so it can't all have been bad.'

'I did, and of course she means the world to me. But what he put us through…' Stacey shook her head. 'I'd never wish that on anyone.'

'Was he…' Ottilie glanced around the room. There were five other women there with their children. It was a quiet session at the recently reinstated parent and baby group. Stacey had taken it on for Ottilie, who mostly had other work to do, and kept saying how much she was enjoying it. Even so, Ottilie had wanted to pop in during her lunch break to see how she was. She'd noticed Stacey seemed keen to do this and to take the lion's share of the childcare for Mackenzie so that Chloe could have that normal life, but Ottilie wondered whether she was doing too much.

She lowered her voice, uncertain whether this was an inappropriate question considering the timing. 'Was he…?'

'You mean did he hit me?'

Ottilie gave a tiny nod.

'No. He might as well have, though, because he couldn't have hurt me any more if he had. He did just about everything else. Abusive, hurtful, drinking, messing around with other women, and you've seen the size of this place – that's quite a feat.'

Ottilie looked around the room again and silently wondered if it was anyone she knew.

'She left the village, in case you're wondering,' Stacey said. 'In fact, she left with him.'

'Ah.' That explained it.

'So at least I don't have to see them every day playing happy families.'

'Has he got any other children? Did he have any with her?'

'Not that I know of, but I haven't heard from him in about seven or eight years, so he might have done.'

'He doesn't stay in contact for Chloe's sake?'

'She won't have him. To be fair to him, he tried, but she told him to sling his hook. Even at that age she could see what he was and what he'd done. You'd have to get up early in the morning to get anything past our Chloe.'

'I suppose I can see why she was so upset when Mackenzie's dad left her.'

'Literally holding the baby. Yes. Me too – which is why I never gave her a hard time about it. Who was I to lecture when I'd screwed up myself.'

'It wasn't your fault.'

'You say that, but sometimes I think it was. I could have been stronger, stood up to him. He got away with too much, and he thought he was untouchable. He made our lives a misery because I let him. Never again.' She shook herself and looked up with a vague smile. 'It's not like I'll need to worry about that anyway the way my love life is going – or the way it isn't going…'

'Would you have another man? I know you've said before you'd like a bit of romance, but would you have someone properly in your life again?'

'Did you think you would before Heath came along?'

'Not really. I suppose you can't answer that until you meet the right man, can you?'

Stacey nodded. 'I haven't met anyone yet who makes me feel that way, but right now I'd settle for being treated well and having a bit of fun, you know?'

'Yes. Did you sign up for that dating—'

Ottilie didn't get to finish her question. From across the room there was an ear-piercing squeal. Both women spun round to see one of the toddlers in the playpen trying to pull the other one around by the hair.

'Oh, here's trouble,' Stacey said, handing Mackenzie to her and racing over to help sort the ruckus.

Ottilie watched her. In her arms, Mackenzie seemed to sense a less competent adult and was gearing up to cause a ruckus of his own. He grizzled and whined, and Ottilie had to get up and start walking up and down, feeling a bit desperate and knowing he could probably sense it.

Oh, please don't…

Ottilie had once been nicknamed the patient whisperer by one of the consultants she'd worked for in Manchester, but if they could see her now, the moniker would definitely not stretch to baby whisperer.

'Let's go and see what's out of the window, eh?' she said, marching over to try and distract him.

Outside, the skies were a heavy gunmetal grey, the wind whipping around a bunch of daffodils that had sprung up in the grass next to the drystone wall that surrounded the community centre. Ottilie was ready for summer to arrive, and she was happy to see their sunny faces as a reminder that it wasn't far away.

'Look at the flowers, Mackenzie. Aren't they pretty? And there… some big trees…'

Ottilie turned to see Stacey at her side. Everything seemed calm again, and she held out her hands to take Mackenzie back, gazing out of the window at the same time.

'Wind's getting up. Come on, Mackenzie… come to Nana. Let's have my bestest boy before the wind blows him clean away…'

'I've realised why you have Mackenzie way more than Chloe does,' Ottilie said, smiling. 'She can't get near him for the fuss you make over him.'

'That could be true, but at least I'm self-aware! You know, I might have had more children if Chloe's dad hadn't done the dirty on me. I suppose I always sort of felt like I wasn't finished.'

'So Mackenzie's sort of a consolation prize?'

'God no, he's the star prize!' She hugged him again, and he squirmed to get free. 'Aren't you, my little prince?'

Ottilie was still smiling as she checked her watch. 'I ought to get back to work. Full clinic this afternoon.'

'Won't Fliss be offended that you didn't have your usual lunch with them?'

'I don't think anyone had brought anything much in today,' Ottilie lied, not wanting Stacey to know the real reason she'd missed out on lunch with Fliss and Lavender at the surgery was because she wanted to check up on her.

'Oh,' Stacey said, 'I hope you weren't thinking you'd get any decent food here – unless you're a fan of mashed banana and Cow & Gate milk.'

Ottilie laughed lightly. 'Tasty as that sounds, maybe I'll give it a miss.'

They bid each other goodbye, and Ottilie was still laughing as she went to pick up her coat and bag from a hook by the door. She'd grown to love Stacey over the few months she'd been in Thimblebury. She was kind and funny and humble and hardworking, and she deserved so much better than the cards life had dealt her. Ottilie hoped one day she'd see Stacey get her reward because it really sounded as if she'd been waiting far too long as it was.

CHAPTER FOUR

The following morning Ottilie's car had struggled up the muddy path to Hilltop Farm, so she'd given up and left it down at the bottom, choosing to walk up to the farmhouse. Ultimately, it would probably be a more efficient way to get there, even if in reality it was slower.

Hilltop was another one of her home visits, though this one was daily and in more of an unofficial capacity. It was more run-down than Daffodil Farm where Victor and Corrine lived with their family and a herd of alpaca that were almost like family too. But where Victor and Corrine had a large family and a mostly happy and warm home, poor Ann, now the sole owner of the farm since her husband died, had a more isolated and lonely existence, made more difficult still by the fact she struggled to care for Darryl, her grown-up son who had severe learning difficulties.

As she walked, she sent a quick text to Lavender.

Really sorry but I might be a couple of minutes late this morning. Up at Hilltop with Darryl. If you could stall the first couple of patients I'd love you forever. X

Lavender sent a thumbs-up emoji to show she'd got the message. Ottilie guessed that she might be too busy to reply with anything more.

. . .

Ottilie knocked once at the front door of the farmhouse and then let herself in. Ann and Darryl were used to her visits now to check on them and knew exactly what time to expect her, so they'd started to leave the door open with the invitation to let herself in. And the visits really were to check more than anything else. Ottilie wanted to make sure Darryl took his diabetic medication – he'd often been difficult about that in the past – and besides, she enjoyed chatting to Ann.

Ann was at the stove cooking bacon. The smell filled the air of the low-ceilinged kitchen and set Ottilie's stomach gurgling.

'Morning!' Ann called over to Ottilie. 'You're just in time!'

'Someone's very lucky today!' Ottilie said to Darryl, who was poring over the train book she'd bought him the previous year. It was always open at the breakfast table whenever Ottilie arrived.

Darryl looked up with a goofy grin. He was almost twenty-one now, too big for his skin, all elbows and knees and hair. He wore a permanent look of anxiety, but that was only an outward thing. Ottilie knew him well now and knew that inside he was content with his life, however constrained it might seem to others.

'Ottilie!'

'Morning, Darryl. Had your insulin?'

He nodded and then bent right back to his book.

'Everything all right this morning?' Ottilie went over to Ann at the stove.

'With Darryl? Yes, good as gold,' Ann said, smiling. 'Apart from that, my bank account is still empty, but what can you do about that, eh? We've got a roof and we've got food, so I've stopped complaining about the rest.'

Ottilie gave a sympathetic smile. She'd seen Ann's struggles first-hand over the past few months and she admired her stoicism in the face of them. That didn't stop her from feeling desperately sorry for her, though. 'He's had his medication?'

'No fuss today. Probably because he knew you were coming. He's been so much better since you started to call in of a morning. Want a sandwich?' she added.

'Not sure I have time, though it smells amazing.'

'I can give you one for the road.'

'It's all right. I can grab—'

'Don't be daft! It'll only take me a minute. Can you stay for a cup of tea?'

'Sorry, but I've had to walk up today, so it might take me a bit longer to get to work, so I'd better not.'

Ann nodded as she flipped the bacon over. 'That reminds me, not sure if you're interested, but I've come across an old bike in the barn. Wondered if it might be of use to you for your visits.'

'Where did that come from?'

'Oh…' Ann's head went down. 'We used to go cycling, me and Jim. When he died, I couldn't face going on my own. It's not rusty or anything – though it might need a bit of a clean – but you're more than welcome to it. It's the least we can do for all you've done here with Darryl.'

'Won't you need it?'

Ann shook her head. 'I doubt it. Don't have time to go cycling, even if I wanted to, and it's not really the same now.'

'Darryl doesn't like cycling?'

'No, he struggles with his balance. And I don't like to go on my own these days, mostly because I don't like to leave him. He used to be a lot better when his dad was alive, but as you know…'

Ottilie nodded. She'd already heard the story. Things had taken a turn for the worse when they'd lost Ann's husband – the farm had got into financial difficulties, and Darryl had struggled to come to terms with his new fatherless life. And poor Ann, who was grieving herself, had been forced to cope with all that on top of her own loss.

'I haven't been out on a bike in years,' Ottilie said.

Ann slid the bacon from the pan onto a slice of bread. 'Well, the offer's there if you want it. Don't want any money for it.'

'You must have something.'

She shook her head. 'Wouldn't hear of it. Could you use it? If you took it off my hands, you'd be doing me a favour really, because I could do with the room in the barn.'

Ottilie was tempted. Having a bike would save taking her car out on calls. It would save money on petrol and having to drive out to get it so often. Thimblebury didn't have a garage, so the nearest one was on the road out of the village, and it was a pain sometimes to go up there when she had so much else to do. It might be fun, too, to whizz around on a bike. She pictured herself in a flapping navy coat and a white cap and a basket on the front with her leather treatment bag in it, like someone from a fifties TV drama, and the mental image made her want to laugh. Heath would find it hilarious, no doubt, too.

'I might take you up on that,' she said finally. 'Thank you, that's so kind. I couldn't take it with me now, but perhaps tomorrow?'

'That's all right – give me a chance to clean it up a bit for you.'

'There's no need.'

Ann put a lid on the sandwich and took it to Darryl, tapping him lightly on the arm to let him know his breakfast was there. Then she cut some more slices from a loaf and began to make a second sandwich. 'Do you have sauce on your bacon?'

Ottilie shook her head. She decided it was pointless to argue because Ann would probably clean the bike anyway.

As Ann made her sandwich, Ottilie went over to Darryl.

'How are you this morning?'

Darryl looked up from his book, his mouth full of bacon and bread. 'I've had my insulin.'

'Yes, that's good. What are you up to today?'

'Cleaning the barn with Mum.'

'Ah, that explains the bike. Is there a lot to clean up?'

He looked a bit perplexed and then to his mum, seemingly to seek the answer to Ottilie's question.

'It's not too bad,' Ann called over, 'but it's been a job that's needed to be done for a good while. There's an old car Jim was putting back together which I'll probably sell. Would have fetched a lot more if he'd finished it, but still.'

'What sort of car?'

'I don't know – I never took an interest. One of those old and collectable types. I had wondered if Dr Cheadle might be interested. Her husband's into all that old stuff, isn't he?'

'I don't really know.' Ottilie took the sandwich Ann had made and wrapped for her with a grateful smile. 'I could ask her when I get to work if you like.'

'Would you? I don't know her all that well. Not sure how to approach her with a question like that. She's a bit…' Ann shrugged.

'A bit what?' Ottilie asked.

'A bit scary.'

Ottilie laughed. 'Really? God, is that how she comes across?'

'Don't you think so? She's so stern and always seems like she's in a rush to be somewhere else.'

If Ann made a habit of trying to catch Fliss Cheadle during her off-duty hours to ask health-related questions, then she could well believe that. Fliss made no secret of how annoying she found it to constantly be on call even when she was trying to go about her daily life.

'Don't you think so?' Ann asked again. 'I'd be nervous to work for her.'

'No, she's lovely when you get used to her. Underneath that scary tiger exterior is a fluffy kitten.'

Ann looked doubtful.

'Honestly,' Ottilie said.

Ann turned off the stove and winced.

'Are you all right?' Ottilie asked.

'I've got this pain in my back. It's nothing… Flares up every now and again.'

'What kind of pain?' Ottilie asked.

'Oh, it's here…' Ann rubbed at a spot more on her side than her back.

'Any other symptoms?' Ottilie asked gently. 'Can I have a look?'

'I felt a bit weird this morning,' Ann said. 'Nothing too bad.'

Ottilie put a hand to the spot, but she couldn't feel anything. 'What kind of weird?'

'I don't know… I can't really describe it.'

'No fever or sickness?'

'No… I mean, I'm not sure. I'm exhausted and feeling a bit strange. What do you think it is?'

'I don't know. Are you otherwise well?'

'It only started this morning. Like I said, I felt a bit weird but haven't been sick or had a fever or anything. Should I go to see Dr Cheadle? I suppose I could ask her about the car at the same time.'

Ottilie gave a wry smile. 'See how you get on this morning and if anything develops, you probably ought to make an appointment. Not sure about the car sales, though – she might not appreciate that during your consultation. If you're really worried, or you think you're deteriorating quicker than she can see you, then you can phone me and I'll get you an emergency slot.'

'You're so good to us,' Ann said. 'Thank you, I will.'

'Right… I'd better go.' Ottilie held up the sandwich. 'Thanks for this – I haven't had breakfast yet, so this is going to go down nicely.'

'You don't eat properly' Ann said. 'It's a wonder you don't fade away.'

'With these hips?' Ottilie laughed. 'I've got enough padding here to see me through an apocalypse!'

'Don't be daft – you have a lovely figure. I wish I still looked like that.'

'You do – you're too hard on yourself. Anyway, I must dash. I'll see you tomorrow morning.'

'And we'll have the bike ready for you,' Ann said.

Ottilie bid a distracted Darryl goodbye and closed the door of the farmhouse behind her.

She was about to unwrap her sandwich and eat it on the walk back to her car when her phone bleeped a notification. It was a text from Lavender, and it was then she noticed she had half a dozen missed calls from the surgery receptionist that she hadn't heard come through because she'd been talking to Ann. Perhaps there'd been a problem putting off her early patients. With a vague frown she dialled the number, but there was no answer.

Weird. Lavender always answered during surgery open hours, and if she had to leave her desk she usually took the phone with her.

Ottilie opened the text and froze as she read it. And then she started to run down the hill, sandwich and mud forgotten as she raced to her car.

CHAPTER FIVE

Fliss had already left by the time Ottilie arrived at the surgery. Lavender was back at her post on reception, making frantic phone calls and clearly struggling to hold back tears.

'Ottilie!' She looked up from a call she'd just ended. 'Thank God you're here!'

'What do you need me to do?' Ottilie asked briskly, shrugging off her coat and dropping it and her bag on the nearest empty chair.

'I'm trying to cancel as many non-urgents as I can. I won't be able to get them all, and some will still turn up, but we'll just have to deal with that when they do.'

'If they're within my remit, I might be able to see some of those. What about the urgent appointments?'

'We've got a locum doctor on his way from the agency, but it's going to be at least an hour before he gets here. But he won't be up to speed with any of our patients, so we still need to cut this afternoon's clinic to make it as small as we can because he'll obviously take a bit longer with everyone than Fliss does.'

'Right.' Ottilie went to look over Lavender's shoulder at the clinic lists. 'I'll start cutting some of mine so it will make room for some of Fliss's to go on my list.'

'Why don't I phone yours and you go through Fliss's to see who's on there and who you're qualified to look at?'

'OK, that makes more sense.'

Lavender pressed print on a list while Ottilie went over to

the printer to wait for it. Her head was in a whirl, but there was no time to reflect on the madness of the morning's sudden handbrake turn, or to get any real detail from Lavender about what had happened. All she knew was that Fliss had had to run to Charles's house and that whatever had made her go must be very bad for Fliss to abandon her clinic. Lavender must have known more, but until they'd sorted this situation, it would have to wait.

They spent the next hour phoning as many people as they could get hold of to ask them not to come to the clinic or to change their appointment or to see Ottilie instead of Fliss, and by the time they'd finished, Ottilie was starving, having abandoned her sandwich in the rush back down from Hilltop Farm. She hadn't had a drink that day either, but there wasn't time to do anything about it. And there was still no time to find out exactly what had happened that morning, because patients had started to arrive and Ottilie had to either see them or help Lavender explain why they couldn't be seen.

People demanded to know what the reason was, and as Lavender and Ottilie assumed Fliss wouldn't want the villagers knowing her personal business – and because they didn't know all that much themselves – they couldn't tell them, and the secrecy hardly helped. It wasn't until someone had rushed in wanting to know why there had been an ambulance outside Charles's cottage all morning that Ottilie realised the cat would soon be out of the bag whether Fliss liked it or not.

It was a relief to finally close for lunch, though lunch itself was to be a sombre affair. Without Fliss's larger-than-life presence and the banter they usually all shared, Lavender and Ottilie ate the food she'd left in the fridge when she'd thought she'd be there with them. Lavender took a moment to fill Ottilie in on the drama that had unfolded while she'd been up at Hilltop Farm.

'It all happened so quickly,' Lavender said as she made a pot of tea. 'One minute it's business as usual, Fliss laughing and joking about trying to book a holiday to Austria and almost booking Australia instead, and the next she's running out, white as a sheet.'

'And you don't know what's wrong with Charles?'

'No, but it must be bad for her to take off like that. I've tried to call her but I'm getting no reply.'

'So what did she say exactly?'

'That he was being rushed to hospital and she didn't think she'd be back today. I'm guessing she had a good idea what was wrong with him or she wouldn't have been so certain about that. I really hope she returns my calls later because I don't know what to do about tomorrow's sessions.'

'So who's this locum? I thought he was meant to be here by now?'

'I didn't book him so it must have been Fliss at some point. I've no idea when she sorted it out – must have been from wherever she is with Charles. First I knew of it was a call from the agency to say he'd been booked and was on his way.'

'Do you think that means she's expecting to be off longer than just today?'

Lavender stirred the tea and then slotted the lid on the pot. 'I never thought of that. I suppose it's a good guess. I wish we knew.'

'I'm sure she'll be in touch as soon as she can.'

'Do you think we ought to phone the hospital?'

'Which one? Depending on what's wrong with him he might be at any number of centres.'

'I suppose so. I hate feeling so helpless. I'm not even sure we're doing the right thing keeping the surgery running. Do you think we ought to close?' Lavender asked.

'But what about the patients?'

'Well, if they're urgent we can see them, but we can't do a lot else, can we?'

'But the locum can. He'd be able to refer on and prescribe when he gets here.'

'*If* he gets here. That was hours ago and there's still no sign.'

'Could you call the agency?'

Lavender brought the teapot to the table and sat down. 'I was in such a tizzy when they phoned that I didn't take a number for them. I couldn't even tell you what the agency is called – totally gone out of my head.'

'Let's see how this afternoon pans out. I think all we can do now is tread water until help comes or until Fliss calls to tell us what she wants us to do. I'm sorry I'm not more help, but I've never been in this situation myself.'

'It's not your fault.'

'I know, but still…'

The doorbell to the front door of the surgery rang down the hallway. Thimblebury surgery occupied an adapted house complete with a front door and tiny garden. Lavender always locked up for lunch so the staff could sit together and not be disturbed, and usually she refused to answer the doorbell if it went during that time. But today she leaped up.

'Might be our locum,' she said, hurrying out of the kitchen.

A few moments later Ottilie heard voices travelling down the hallway. Lavender was talking to a man and he was inside. It was a safe bet that she'd been right – their temporary doctor had arrived at last.

The door to the kitchen opened.

'Ottilie, this is Dr Stokes…'

Ottilie stood up and offered her hand.

'Call me Simon,' he said. 'Pleased to meet you, Ottilie.'

'Ottilie's our nurse,' Lavender said.

He looked from one to the other. 'Your nurse… like the only nurse? Surely there's more than you two here?'

'It's a very small surgery,' Ottilie said. 'There are other people who come and go – a community midwife and mental health team and such, but for the most part, it's just us and Fliss. Don't usually need anyone else.'

'Blimey!'

Simon rubbed a hand over close-cropped black hair. His brown eyes were so dark they were almost black too. Ottilie would have put him at around her own age, perhaps slightly more towards forty. His features were even and pleasing, and they had a kindness about them that shone out the moment they crinkled into a smile. His skin was a warm tone, but covered in freckles that made Ottilie think he might have come from somewhere hot and sunny.

'I don't know whether to be impressed or pitying.'

'Oh, you can pity us today,' Lavender said. 'It's been one hell of a morning. I thought they'd assigned you first thing? They'd told me at nine you'd be here within the hour.'

'No…' He shook his head. 'Perhaps they'd assigned someone else first who couldn't make it for whatever reason. I've literally just had a call and then driven straight out.'

'Where have you had to come from?' Ottilie asked.

'Liverpool.'

'That's a fair drive.'

'You don't sound Scouse,' Lavender said.

'I'm not.' He smiled but didn't offer anything else.

'So are you only with us today?' Lavender continued.

'I've been told I'll be here for the rest of the week at least. I've booked a hotel not far outside the village.'

'Ah, so you won't have to commute from Liverpool every day,' Ottilie said. She shared a look of concern with Lavender.

She guessed they were thinking the same thing: that things must be very bad if Fliss planned to be off for the rest of the week.

'Have you done GP work before?' Lavender asked.

At this he offered a disguised but unmistakably exasperated look.

'Sorry,' Lavender said. 'Of course you have or you wouldn't be here.'

'Don't mind us,' Ottilie said. 'We're usually better than this, but it's been a stressful morning and we're worried about our own GP. She was called home for some emergency and we think it must be very bad.'

'Understandable,' he said. 'So, do you want to show me where I'll be working from and get me this afternoon's list?'

'We're not ready to start yet,' Ottilie said. 'We've got ten minutes or so until lunch is over.'

He stared at her as if she'd spontaneously grown a second head.

'I know,' she said. 'I couldn't get my head around actual breaks when I got here either. There's tea in the pot if you'd like one.'

'That's kind, but I think I ought to get my bearings before you start letting patients in. If you could show me where the treatment room is…'

'Yes, of course…' Lavender glanced at Ottilie before turning back to him. 'I'll bring a drink through to you.'

'I don't need one, thank you.'

'But there's—'

'No thank you,' he insisted. 'And I don't drink tea or coffee anyway. For the past year it's been boiled water, but that's another story,' he said as he followed Lavender out of the kitchen.

Ottilie tried to catch the rest of the conversation, her interest piqued by his last statement, but it was too muffled once they were beyond the heavy kitchen door for her to make it out.

But she wasn't curious for long – at least, not about Dr Stokes. Her mind went back to their own, their much-loved Fliss. She hoped everything was all right there, but she was very much afraid that it wasn't.

She unlocked her phone and dialled Fliss's number. It was in vain, because there was no answer. She'd expected as much, but, not knowing what else to do, it had seemed worth a try. Poor Charles and poor Fliss. Fliss joked about him all the time and pretended he drove her mad, but for all her banter, she adored him. Ottilie wished for the best, as if she could manifest it, because she knew what it was like to lose a husband too soon, and she wouldn't wish that on her friend, not for anything.

CHAPTER SIX

Just after the last patient of the day had left, before Lavender locked the front door and Dr Stokes got his coat on to leave, Fliss walked into Thimblebury surgery. At the sound of her voice, Ottilie looked up from the computer where she and Lavender were trying to work out what to do with the following day's patients.

'Good afternoon,' she said, and although it was her usual robust tone, the sight of her drawn, pale face and swollen eyes told a different story.

From nowhere, the urge to hug her swept over Ottilie, and where she might have tried to restrain herself, today she acted on it. Whether it would be welcomed or not didn't matter because she couldn't help herself. Fliss had never been a hugger and obvious displays of affection weren't in her nature, but she allowed Ottilie's arms to envelop her for a moment before pushing her away with an expression that was something like regret.

'I'm all right,' she said briskly. 'It's Charles in hospital, not me.'

'What happened?'

'Heart attack.'

Ottilie sucked in a sharp breath, and Lavender's hand shot to her mouth.

'Oh, Fliss…' Lavender murmured. 'How is he? I mean…'

'Not dead, if that's what you mean,' Fliss replied. 'But he's been better.'

'Oh, Fliss, I'm so sorry.'

'Never mind. At least he knew what to do as soon as it struck. I've trained him well, it seems. I would say with our lifestyle that I might have had a bit of a premonition about this sort of thing, but that would be a lie. I see cases of heart disease every day, and I warn enough people of the consequences of an unhealthy lifestyle, but somehow, when it comes to me and my own, I never thought it would happen.'

'Thank goodness you were able to act fast.'

'That was all down to Charles. I'm only glad he managed to call for an ambulance and didn't mess around phoning me here and asking silly questions about it.'

'That was lucky,' Ottilie said. She'd seen enough heart attack victims during her career to know that many of them wouldn't have been able to speak or function, let alone phone for an ambulance. From that perspective he might well have saved himself.

'Wasn't it? Anyway, I came in to see if everything is all right here.'

'You shouldn't be worrying about us,' Ottilie said. 'We're fine.'

'Still, I thought I'd better check. And to let you know that I won't be in for a few days.'

'Yes, the locum said he'd been contracted for the rest of the week.'

As Ottilie said this, Dr Stokes walked in, coat on and satchel in hand.

Fliss shot him a shrewd look. 'You're covering for me?'

For a moment, he looked taken aback. Ottilie could see how her tone might sound a little confrontational, but her briskness was never rudeness, only practicality.

'Yes. I think… Dr Cheadle?'

'Fliss.' She stuck out her hand for him to shake. 'And you are…?'

'Simon Stokes. How's everything with you? I believe your husband is…?'

He hadn't been present for the explanation Fliss had given to Ottilie and Lavender, and so Fliss briefly filled him in on the basics while he pulled a sympathetic face.

'Do you think you might be off longer than this week?' he asked finally.

'It's hard to say,' Fliss replied. 'Possibly, but I won't know until I get more information from his consultant. Can you be available for longer if it's necessary?'

'I think so. I don't have anything else lined up, and I'm still applying for permanent roles.'

'Good.' Fliss nodded thoughtfully. 'I'd rather have someone who knows the ropes here than keep getting new people in every five minutes. Makes it easier for my staff for one thing.'

'Not for the patients,' he said with a wry smile. 'You were missed. Apparently, if a doctor isn't you, they can't possibly be a proper doctor.'

Fliss gave a tight smile. 'They'll get over it. I can't always be here for them.'

Ottilie wondered whether her flippant comment might carry more weight than she was letting on, because Fliss would always want to be there for her patients and would never suggest otherwise. Of course, she joked about them and about being asked to examine people in the village shop and such, but the reality was that she loved the people of this village. Being their GP carried a special sort of responsibility that she took very seriously.

'Right, if you're all coping, then I'm going to head back to the hospital to see Charles. I'll pop in tomorrow morning.'

'There's really no need,' Simon said.

'No, you need to think about yourself and Charles,' Lavender agreed. 'We've got it under control.'

Fliss gave a brief nod. 'Thank you. I'll see you tomorrow regardless.'

She turned to go.

'Give our best to Charles, won't you?' Ottilie said.

'I would,' Fliss said, turning back to them, the first hint of new tears in her eyes, 'but he's not conscious. As soon as he's out of intensive care and awake, I'll be sure to pass on your good wishes.'

Ottilie exchanged a look of sorrow with Lavender. Fliss had never said he was so poorly, and she'd been so calm and collected Ottilie had never thought to ask. Now she felt guilty and miserable for not having realised sooner that Fliss was putting a very brave face on a terrible situation. At that moment, she couldn't think of the right thing to say, and so she said nothing, and by the time something had come to mind, Fliss had already gone.

Heath wrapped his hand around Ottilie's as they walked from her house to Flo's. A damp fog blanketed the village, heavy droplets caught on cotton-wool air that felt thick enough that they'd have to chop their way through it. Evening was fast approaching, but it was heartening to Ottilie, who always loved summer best, that it came a little later every night. Warm, bright summer evenings were just around the corner, and she was looking forward to spending them with Heath in her beautiful Lakeland home.

Thinking of all the things they could do, and all the places she hadn't yet seen that they would visit, lifted her spirits, because, try as she might to be positive, she was troubled and afraid for Fliss and Charles. Fliss had texted her (and presumably Lavender) since her visit to the surgery before they'd closed up and had said that Charles was stable and as good as he could be and that they shouldn't worry about her – and could they make sure that the locum was available for emergency out-of-hours care? And for ever-practical Fliss, that last point was probably the main reason for texting at all.

Stable was good, wasn't it? Ottilie thought so, but there could never be any complacency in cases like this. Years of nursing had told her that much. Was Fliss more worried than she let on, or should they take comfort from her apparent hope? Ottilie and Lavender had discussed it as they'd locked all the doors of the surgery, but neither of them felt certain of anything. Lavender had all the usual horror stories to share, of relatives who'd dropped down dead instantly, and though Ottilie hadn't wanted to hear them, she had to admit she had plenty of her own.

'It'll be all right, you know.' Heath squeezed her hand.

Ottilie looked up at him. God, she was glad not to be going through this alone, as she might once have been forced to do. She was glad to be able to share her fears with him and she was grateful for his quiet encouragement.

'I hope so. I just feel so helpless.'

'It doesn't sound as if she wants your help.'

'But she must need it.'

'That might be true, but from what you've told me, I don't think saying that to her is the way to go about things. She sounds proud. Not one for admitting a weakness.'

'But in a situation this horrible anyone could be forgiven for a bit of weakness. She must know that.'

'I'm sure she does, but that doesn't change the sort of person she is. I'm sure she'll ask if she needs it.'

'I'm not.'

'You say she's super practical, right?'

'Yes.'

'So then she's practical enough to admit when it makes sense to ask for something she needs.'

'I suppose so.'

Ottilie was silent for a moment as their boots echoed on the lane. There was still a little traffic, the odd car moving through the village as people came home from late shifts at work, but the rush hour – such as it was in Thimblebury – was over and the roads were quiet. Most people were in their homes sitting around tables for evening meals or visiting friends or relatives, as she and Heath would be doing when they got to Flo's house.

'So what's this spare doctor like?' Heath asked. 'Has it been difficult today working with him?'

'Actually no, he's good. Seems to know what he's doing; more or less hit the ground running.'

'Makes life easier for you then.'

'Loads. It's stressful enough so at least that's one thing we don't have to worry about.'

'Where's he worked before?'

'Don't know. He hasn't said, though I get the impression he's been out of the country even though he's based in Liverpool now.'

'What makes you say that?'

'Little things he says. He's applying for jobs, but he's too old to be newly qualified, and he's too good to be an agency locum, so I think he must have been out of the workplace – or the health service here, at any rate – for a while. I wonder if he's trying to get back into it after a sabbatical.'

'I suppose that makes sense. It's a good thing he's working out because it sounds as if you might be stuck with him for a while.'

Ottilie nodded. 'I remember…' She drew a breath and started again. She'd wanted to say something about Josh, about how she could empathise with Fliss because she knew what that fear was, how bereft Fliss would be if she lost Charles, but this was Heath, and if she wasn't careful he'd start to feel as if he was playing second fiddle to a dead man. She checked herself more and more often whenever she wanted to talk about Josh. Heath had never said anything to make her feel she ought to, but she did it all the same.

Oversensitive, Stacey had said when Ottilie had aired her fears about it, and perhaps she was right. Ottilie only knew how she might feel had things been the other way around.

'I think I might start a collection of some sort,' she said instead.

'For Fliss?'

'Yes.'

'What would you do with the money?'

'I don't know, buy a gift to show her the village is thinking about her. Like flowers maybe.'

'Sounds like a waste of money to me. She doesn't sound like a flower sort of woman.'

'No, I don't think she is, but it's a token, isn't it? It's not about the flowers but about what they're saying. I'll talk to Lavender at lunch tomorrow to see what she thinks, but I bet she'll be up for helping me to collect.'

When they arrived at Flo's house, the front door was already open.

'Saw you coming down the road!' Flo shouted from the sitting room.

'I'll bet she did,' Heath said, grinning as he closed the front door and followed Ottilie down the hallway.

'Behave,' Ottilie whispered, trying not to laugh. 'That's your grandma you're talking about.'

'Yes it is, and I know only too well what she's like.'

'What's that?'

Flo appeared at the doorway, arms folded across her chest.

'I said it's lovely and light in here,' Heath said, Ottilie trying not to giggle. 'Because you've got all your lights on. A bit like Blackpool illuminations.'

Flo rolled her eyes as he kissed her on the cheek, and then Ottilie did the same. She and Flo had a strange and new relationship since she'd started to date Heath – no longer just the local nurse and not quite a surrogate granddaughter, but an odd ground somewhere in the middle. There was an uncertain affection on both sides, something beyond the friendship they'd started to cultivate after Ottilie's arrival in Thimblebury, but not quite family.

As soon as Ottilie's bottom had hit the armchair in Flo's living room, the questions began.

'What's this about Doctor Cheadle being off sick today? I heard there was an ambulance outside her husband's house. Do you know why? You must know why.'

Ottilie didn't see the point in keeping Charles's heart attack a secret any longer, and she didn't think Fliss would be keeping it a secret now either. It was only a matter of time before it became common knowledge, because enough people knew enough fragments of the truth to be able to share and piece them together.

'She's not sick, Charles is. That's why she's off.'

'Oh. What's wrong with him?'

'Heart attack.'

'Is he dead?'

'No,' Ottilie said patiently. 'He's sick.'

'I'm not surprised.' Flo folded her arms and gave a supremely knowledgeable look. 'The way they drink, the pair of them. Surprised it hasn't happened to one of them before now.'

'That's not exactly helpful, Gran. You're supposed to say how sorry you are to hear it.'

'To Ottilie? It's not her who needs to hear how sorry I am. Doesn't make any difference to her, does it? She's not ill. And

I'm not sorry. He should have looked after himself better. His wife's a doctor – you'd think if anyone knew how to look after himself, it would be him. And they say it's old people bogging down the health service.'

Ottilie's cheeks flared. She was fond of Flo, and usually she could take her rantings with a pinch of salt, but this was a step too far.

Heath glanced at her and then shot his gran a warning look. Not that Flo noticed.

'She needs to lose weight as well,' she continued. 'Or she'll be next. And she had the nerve to send me for tests for my heart.'

'If you recall, I asked her to do that!' Ottilie stood up. 'I'm going to… Sorry… Just getting some air…'

She marched down the hallway and out into the cool evening, swallowing breaths to control her temper. She didn't want to fall out with Flo, and she knew it was only idle gossip, but Fliss was suffering and she was a loyal friend to the people of Thimblebury. She didn't deserve to be the subject of cruel, unthoughtful comments like Flo's. It was as if Flo was enjoying it.

'Ott…'

She turned to see Heath at the front door.

'I'm all right. It's been a weird day, that's all.'

'I know. And Gran gets it now. She wants to say she's sorry; she didn't know it would be so triggering for you.'

'Triggering? So that's her word, is it?'

'Well' – Heath gave a wry smile – 'I'm paraphrasing. But she does realise she's out of order.'

'I'm sure it's nothing Fliss wouldn't admit herself. She's always said she knows they drink and eat far too much, but nobody asks for illness, do they?'

'Of course not. We're all guilty of that "it'll never happen to me" mentality from time to time.'

'Exactly.'

'Come in. Half an hour and then we can go back to yours.'

'We don't need to do that. Just give me a minute.'

'You're still mad?'

'No; I'm not mad. It's… My brain is all over the place. I need a minute to get it in order. Go and talk to your gran; I'll be in shortly.'

He was silent for a moment, making no move to go inside.

Ottilie sent him a silent question.

'It's about more than Fliss and Charles, isn't it?' he asked, and she let out a sigh.

'I can't get anything past you, can I?'

'I haven't forgotten it's a weird time for you right now.'

'Josh's birthday's coming up. I didn't want to keep going on about it, but…'

'So I'm right.'

She nodded. 'It's just another thing, and it doesn't seem important at all when something like Charles's heart attack happens, but yes, it's on my mind. In the most horrible way, I just want to go to the cemetery and get it over and done with. Is that awful? Because it feels awful. I feel so guilty, but that's how it is. I want to remember him, but it hurts, and I don't want you to think…'

'Hey, we talked about this. We're together but that doesn't erase him from your life. He was here before me, and that's fine. Sometimes I feel shitty, because I wouldn't wish what happened to him on anyone but I am grateful to have you, and I know I wouldn't have you if he'd still been alive. So if anyone ought to feel guilty, that's a big tick for me right there.'

'Who knew this whole second-go thing would be so hard?'

'If it's any consolation, you don't need to have any guilt where Mila is concerned. My toxic ex can stay in my past where she belongs.'

'I suppose it's one less complication, and God knows we have enough of those.'

'Maybe, but we're worth it, aren't we?'

Ottilie nodded. 'I hope so.'

'Only hope? So you don't know how crazy I am about you? I haven't demonstrated it enough already? Jeez, what do I need to do?'

She couldn't help a quiet laugh now. 'I don't know. I think I get it. I'm sorry if I'm sometimes a bit unsure. And I get so scared…'

'I'm not going anywhere.'

'That's what Fliss thought about Charles only twelve hours ago. And now look at them.'

'OK, I don't intend to go anywhere. How's that? I'm afraid it's the best I can do.'

'I know it is, and that's what scares me. I keep telling myself that lightning can't strike twice, but the thing is, it can. It does.'

'It's less likely.'

'But still possible.'

Heath walked the path to take her in his arms, and she let her head sink into his shoulder. His shirt had got damp from the mist; she could feel the fabric sticking to her cheek as she listened to his heartbeats. Safe, solid, strong. It gave her comfort to hear them, to know he was alive and real and present in her life. This thing with Heath was still so new, and yet she couldn't imagine a day when she wouldn't want to have him close.

'I get it,' he said, kissing her head. 'You know that I do. I can't tell you what you want to hear; I wish I could. All I can do is let you know that I understand and that you don't have to keep it from me. Whatever you're feeling, however scared or doubtful, even if you think it sounds crazy, come and talk to me.'

'I know, and I want to. I'll try, I promise.'

'It's not a promise you need to make to me but to yourself.'

'Yeah, I know that too.' Ottilie pulled away to look up at him. 'Is your gran watching us from the window?'

He laughed. 'Yes. She thinks if she pulls the curtains open just a crack we can't tell. Bloody nightmare she is.'

'She's just Flo. I suppose we can let her off that.'

'You think you can go back in? Half an hour and we'll head back to yours.'

'Yes. I wasn't really mad at her anyway.'

'You could have fooled me.'

'No, I wasn't. I just have a short fuse right now.'

'It's understandable.'

As Ottilie turned to go back to the house, she noticed the curtain moving at the front window. Perhaps Flo was only trying to gauge how much she might have ticked off Ottilie. Poor Flo – she wouldn't have meant it. Ottilie decided she must try harder to be more tolerant. She had the feeling she was going to need all the patience and tolerance she could muster over the next few weeks.

CHAPTER SEVEN

When Ottilie let herself into the kitchen of Hilltop farmhouse the following day, there was no smell of cooking breakfast. Darryl was sitting at the table with his beloved train book, but he didn't have his usual mug of blackcurrant cordial – his only drink of choice and something that Ottilie was trying very hard to wean him off, if only for the insane things it did to his blood sugar – and he was alone.

'Good morning.' Ottilie frowned as she looked for signs of his mum. 'On your own this morning?'

He looked up from his book, but his usual recognition at the sight of Ottilie wasn't there this morning either. 'Yes.'

'Where's your mum?'

He gave a vague shrug.

'Ann?' Ottilie went to the door that led to the living room and called through. Getting no reply, she went to the foot of the stairs and shouted up. 'Ann? Are you up there? Just letting you know I'm here!'

From upstairs there was a muffled reply.

'Shall I wait down here?' Ottilie shouted. 'Is everything all right?'

She had no reason to believe any different, and yet she'd never been to Hilltop Farm and found Ann absent from wherever Darryl was. She watched him like a hawk, bending over backwards to cater for his every whim. To find him at the breakfast table without breakfast and without her was the thing setting Ottilie's alarm bells ringing.

She went back through to Darryl, recalling bits of the conversation she'd had with Ann the previous day. She hadn't been feeling quite herself – had her situation worsened?

'Has your mum got out of bed yet?'

'No.'

'Have you had your insulin?'

He shrugged, which Ottilie took to mean that he hadn't but he didn't want to let her know that because he often made a fuss about having to take it. But she didn't want to give him a double dose by mistake. She could check his blood sugar, but she could just as easily get the answer from Ann.

Making a snap decision, Ottilie went back to the stairs and started to climb them. With the way the last few days had gone, she wasn't about to risk putting anyone else in danger.

'Ann…?' She tapped lightly at the first door, unsure if it was the right one. 'Ann… are you in bed? Is everything all right?'

'Ottilie…'

Ann's voice was small but coming from beyond the door.

'Can I come in?'

'Yes. Sorry, I…'

Ottilie pushed open the door and peered around it. Ann was in bed, lying on her side with her blankets pulled up around her chin.

'I feel rotten,' she said.

'You don't look so good.' Ottilie made her way over and perched on the edge of the bed, putting the back of her hand to Ann's face. 'Bit hot.'

'My back… it hurts so much. Is Darryl…?'

'He's fine – he's downstairs at the table. I'll make him some breakfast. Has he had his insulin?'

'I don't know. I didn't give him…'

'That's all right – don't stress. I'll see to him. I'm going to phone the doctor to come up and see you.'

'No, I'll be up in an hour or so—'

'You won't, Ann. He'll be able to tell us better, but I'd say you're going to need some antibiotics and a bit of bed rest.'

'I can't stay in bed – I have too much to do on the farm, and Darryl—'

'Don't worry about any of that. We'll get you some help. You need rest or you'll end up being out of action for a lot longer.' Ottilie gave her a reassuring smile. 'I'm going to make a phone call downstairs, make Darryl some toast and then I'll be right back up, OK?'

Ann gave a weak nod, and Ottilie left her to phone the surgery, thankful that she'd been here to catch this before it got a lot worse.

After a long conversation with Simon, the cover GP, Ottilie had tried to persuade Ann to let her call an ambulance to take her to hospital, but Ann wouldn't hear of it. Ottilie wasn't entirely convinced she needed one either, but as Simon was busy in clinic and wouldn't be able to make a house call for a few hours, he'd decided it would be the safest option. In the end, Ottilie had been forced to leave Ann, with some very detailed instructions for her and Darryl if things should take a turn for the worse – though how much of it had gone in with either of them was anyone's guess – and a promise that the doctor would be up as soon as his morning clinic was done.

At lunch, Ottilie drove Simon up to Hilltop. It seemed easier than trying to direct him around an area he was new to, and she knew Darryl would feel less stressed to see a familiar face alongside one he didn't know.

'These aren't roads designed for healthy suspension,' Simon said, grimacing as they jolted over a pothole.

'I hate to break it to you, but there's a possibility that any minute now my wheels will start spinning and we'll have to abandon the car and walk the rest of the way to the farm too.'

'Yeah, I forgot how much I hated the countryside.'

Ottilie laughed lightly. 'You can't mean that. Surely nobody could hate the countryside.' She threw him a sideways glance before turning back to the road. He wore a wry smile.

'No, I don't suppose so,' he said. 'At least when the sun is shining and it's all green and lovely you can't. But in the winter.'

'It's spring.'

'Is it? I wouldn't have noticed if you hadn't said.'

Ottilie laughed again.

'How long have you lived here?' he asked.

'Not quite a year.'

'So you came for this job, or did you want to move here anyway?'

'The job mainly, but I did want a move out of Manchester. I saw this advertised and it looked like the perfect fit.'

'And is it?'

'Yes. I'm happy here and I love the work. How about you? Is Liverpool home? You don't have much of an accent.'

'I was born in Essex but, a bit like you, moved up to Liverpool for my first GP post. I met my wife there. She was studying there.'

Ottilie carefully noted the suddenly melancholic tone of his voice. What did that mean? They were no longer together? Or something sadder, more like her own situation? She wondered whether to ask, but then the wheels of her car started to slip, and she decided to pull over before she got well and truly stuck, unable to move up or down.

'That's it, I'm afraid. We're going to have to walk the rest of the way.'

'You need a tractor,' he said, getting out of the car.

'I definitely need to invest in a sturdier car,' Ottilie replied. 'An old jeep or something. But it's a lot of money and I manage well enough for now.'

They began to walk. It was steep and she noticed Simon was soon a bit breathless. Simon looked far from unfit – in fact, he had a good physique from what Ottilie could see – but these hills could defeat even the hardiest sportsman if you weren't used to them. Ottilie had grown used to going up and down to Hilltop over the past few months and found it challenging but not quite as strenuous as she had in the beginning.

'Who looked at this hill and thought "I really want to build a house up there"?' he panted.

Ottilie turned to him with a smile. 'I know what you mean. But I suppose if you can build anywhere around here, you might as well have the views. I mean' – she turned and swept a hand across the vista – 'look at that. You can't say that's not amazing.'

Simon turned to look. Sunlight and shadow were racing across patchwork greens of fields, sectioned up with darker strips of hedgerows and stone walls, hillsides dotted with houses and trees, the lines of valley floors struck across them. They stretched out as far as the horizon.

'What's that water?' he asked, pointing to a glittering basin.

'Um, I think that's Windermere.'

'OK,' he said, turning back to the hill. 'It's not so bad. Still not happy about this climb, though.'

'You get used to it.'

'You do this a lot then?'

'Every morning, more or less. Darryl – Ann's son – has quite complex needs, so I call in before I come to work to make sure everything is OK. It's only because of that I found Ann in bed.'

'What kind of needs does he have?'

'Mostly learning difficulties, diabetes, occasional seizures, though Ann says he hasn't had any of those for a long time. Certainly not since I started to visit.'

'And you have to come up every morning? Isn't that within a social care remit?'

Ottilie turned to him with a wry smile as they started to walk again. 'You're in Thimblebury. We're miles from anywhere, with a population smaller than some inner-city schools. Social care availability is limited around here. Besides, Darryl has got used to me now and he trusts me, so it seems easier to carry on as we are. It doesn't take that long – usually, anyway – it just means me leaving the house half an hour or so before I would ordinarily.'

'Well, I applaud your dedication.'

'Thank you. And I applaud yours right now – you're doing a sterling job of climbing this hill.'

'Is that sarcasm?'

'Of course not! Wouldn't dream of it.'

'Because I'd like to remind you,' he replied with a smile of his own, 'that I may only be temporary cover, but I'm still the GP.'

'Yes, Doctor.'

'That's better. I knew it was a bad idea to have you calling me Simon – all sorts of dissent going on left, right and centre.'

'You'll know for next time.'

'I will. Never had any of this in Botswana.'

'Botswana? Is that where you've been?'

'Got back about three weeks ago. I was there for a year.'

'Working as a GP?'

'On a voluntary basis, yes.'

'Wow, that's impressive.'

'Not really. I've always felt I had a moral obligation to give back. You know, I'm lucky enough to have been born in a country where I was afforded the time and space and finances to pursue a career that pays me well and is good to me. I need to somehow repay that… Well, at the risk of sounding like a raging hippy, I like to think of it as a karmic debt. It's only dumb luck that you and I were born here – we could just as easily have been born in a place a lot less kind to us.'

'What did your family think about you going off for a year?'

'They were fine about it. We're not that close anyway really.'

'And your…' Ottilie wanted to say wife, but that doubt crept in again. He'd been so sad when he'd talked about her. And were there children? He hadn't said so. 'So you were pretty free to do what you wanted?'

'As a bird,' he said. He nodded at a wide metal farm gate. 'Is that the way in?'

'Yes.'

'Thank God. If I go much further you're going to have to find me some oxygen.'

At the front door, Ottilie knocked briefly and pushed it open, as she did every morning. Darryl was still sitting at the same spot at the table, empty crisp packets littering it and three more mugs with the unmistakable purple stains of blackcurrant juice. Simon gave them a critical once-over. Darryl started to smile at the sight of Ottilie, but it froze halfway to his face when he noticed she wasn't alone.

'Who's that?' he asked her.

'This is Dr Stokes. He's come to see your mum. Is that all right?'

Darryl gave a sullen nod.

Simon strode over and held out his hand. 'I'm pleased to meet you, Darryl. I've heard lots about you.'

Darryl looked at the outstretched hand and then at Ottilie as if for reassurance.

'It's fine,' she said. 'I've been telling Dr Stokes how much you like trains.'

At this, Darryl seemed to brighten. He held up the book Ottilie had bought for him. 'Here,' he said. 'There's loads in here.'

Simon went to look over Darryl's shoulder as he flicked through it, pointing to each glossy photo and reading out the name of the train.

'That's very cool,' Simon said. 'Listen, I'm going to take a look at your mum. Why don't you find the page with your absolute favourite train and show me when I come back down?'

Darryl's head went down and he began to rip through the pages with a feverish excitement.

Ottilie smiled at Simon. 'Nicely done,' she whispered. And then in a louder voice: 'I'll show you where to go.'

At the top of the stairs, Ottilie called out, 'Ann… it's me. I've brought the doctor to see you. Are you awake?'

'I thought I could hear you…'

Ann's voice came from beyond the bedroom door. Ottilie pushed it open. Ann was still wrapped up tight in her blankets, her face flushed, but she seemed more lucid.

'The ibuprofen helped a little bit then?' Ottilie asked. 'You seem brighter.' She turned to Simon. 'This is Ann. Ann… Dr Stokes.'

'Oh,' Ann said. 'Where's…'

'She's off right now,' Ottilie said, not wanting to get into it. Clearly gossip from the village took a little while to get up this far, and Ann had probably been in no state to follow it even if that wasn't the case. 'Dr Stokes is filling in. He's brilliant, so don't worry, you'll be in safe hands.'

'You're staying, though?' Ann asked uncertainly.

Ottilie nodded. 'Of course. I'll be just here by the door.'

Ottilie watched as Simon gently encouraged Ann to sit up on her pillows and started to question her. She had to be impressed. He had a bedside manner as pleasant as he seemed to be. She'd enjoyed their walk up to the farm, and she'd been intrigued enough by what few details he'd shared of his life to want to know more. She'd been worried about his cover for Fliss, but she was beginning to realise that she needn't have been – she could see he was capable and gentle and very thorough. As long as the surgery could keep him for however long Fliss had to be off, they were going to be absolutely fine.

CHAPTER EIGHT

It was already going dark as afternoon clinic wrapped up, but Ottilie had promised to get some help for Ann, who had been given antibiotics and reassurances by Dr Stokes but was still panicking about the work that needed to be done on the farm.

Her first thought had been Victor and Corrine at Daffodil Farm. They were the closest thing to farming neighbours Ann had and were always brilliant in a crisis. Ottilie recalled how much she'd relied on them when her house had been flooded the previous year, and how they'd been her saving grace. She'd tried the landline but had got no reply, and Victor famously (or infamously, depending on your viewpoint) refused to have a mobile phone because he'd lost so many of them over the years. As Corrine didn't have one either, and because Ottilie loved to visit them anyway, she decided to go up there straight from work. If she was lucky, she'd get a slice of Corrine's divine fruit cake and a cup of tea, and if she was even luckier, she might get to visit Victor's alpaca herd.

It was the third hill she'd climbed that day, and as she made her way up to Daffodil farmhouse, she decided that if she didn't sleep like a log that night then she might need a doctor's appointment herself because there had to be something wrong with her.

Corrine was already standing at the front door as Ottilie pushed open the gate.

'I saw you come over the top there,' she called. 'I was saying to Victor only yesterday we hadn't seen you for a while.'

'Yes, sorry about that. Things have been a bit hectic.'

Corinne gave a grimace of sympathy. 'I heard about Dr Cheadle. Such a shame. How is her husband?'

'Still quite poorly,' Ottilie said, following Corrine inside and closing the door. The kitchen was warm and welcoming, a spicy sweetness hanging on the air. 'We're all hoping for good news but we haven't had it yet. I'm going to call later to see how she's doing.'

'Give her our best wishes, won't you? And you – how are you doing?'

'Good,' Ottilie said. 'Apart from the things that come to test us all, I'm good. How's everything here?'

'Oh, about the same. I've had the all-clear from the hospital so that's good, isn't it?'

'Completely clear?'

'Yes. Cancer free. I can't quite believe it myself, if I'm honest. Keep thinking I misheard the doctor, but that's what he said.'

'That's brilliant!' Ottilie gave her a hug. 'I'm so pleased for you.'

'It's a relief, I can tell you that much.'

'I bet Victor is thrilled.'

'I think so.' Corrine showed Ottilie her finger. 'He got me this, so I suppose that means he's happy. Hasn't bought me a ring in forty years. I don't know what possessed him to get this – hardly practical for scrubbing the stone floors in here, is it?'

'Oh, that's gorgeous!' Ottilie lifted it to the light. The ring was gold, a ruby set into a shoulder of modest but pretty diamonds. 'He wants to show you he loves you and he appreciates you. I say don't knock it.'

'I'm not. It's just not like him to be all sentimental.'

Ottilie smiled. She could well imagine what a health scare like Corrine's could do for a couple. When Corrine's skin cancer had first been diagnosed, Victor had freely admitted to Ottilie that he was terrified of losing Corrine. 'Well, I think it's beautiful.'

Corrine held up her hand and took a moment to admire it, and Ottilie could tell that despite her protestations, she was rather in love with her new jewellery, and perhaps even more with what it represented.

'Anyway.' She shook herself. 'I'm about to make a pot. You'll have tea, won't you?'

'Don't need to ask me twice.' Ottilie took a seat at the table.

'I've been baking too, if you want cake.'

'I thought I could smell fruit cake. Ah well, if you're forcing me, then I'd better take a slice.'

'Right. Won't be a minute.'

Corrine went over to a cooling rack on the worktop, and it was then that Ottilie noticed the freshly baked brick of fruit cake. 'So have you come to visit us or the girls?'

Ottilie laughed. 'A bit of both.' 'The girls' was the nickname they gave to their alpaca herd, and it was a running joke that when Ottilie came to visit them she really only wanted to see the alpacas. It was only a bit true, in that no visit ever felt complete without a walk to their enclosure on the top field. 'I've actually come to beg a favour, if you can spare the time.'

'Oh?' Corrine cut into the cake. 'This is still a bit warm and a bit crumbly – sorry about that.'

'That sounds amazing,' Ottilie said. 'I'll take your cake however it comes. So you know Ann at Hilltop?'

'Yes, of course. Is she all right?'

'Not really. I mean, it's a temporary thing, but she's got a nasty infection and she needs a week or so of decent rest, but she's panicking about the farm. I know you and Victor are busy with this place, but if you or your daughters and their other halves can spare the odd half hour here or there to go and help her, I think it would make a huge difference. Only day-to-day stuff, enough to keep things ticking over. I'm sorry to ask; I know you have a lot on. I thought I might ask one or two others as well, but I came to you first because you'll know farming, and other people won't so much.'

'Of course we'll always do what we can for a neighbour. Do you need someone to go over today?'

'Whenever you can would be brilliant.'

'And she has all that extra worry with her lad, poor thing.'

'Exactly. So any support for her would be amazing.'

Corrine put a slice of cake in front of Ottilie just as Victor came in, bringing a blast of cold winter air in his wake.

'All settled in… Oh, hello, Nurse!'

'Hi, Victor. How are you?'

'All the better for seeing you. You've come up at the right time as well. Just had a new delivery.'

'Of what?'

'A new girl, of course!' He took off his hat and sat at the table expectantly. Corrine didn't need to ask – she simply put a slice of cake in front of him too.

'You've had a new alpaca? A baby?'

'No, a rescue. Some daft wench over at Ullswater thought she could rear one in her back garden. Soon realised it wasn't that simple and was looking to get rid.'

'So you've taken her on? What's she named?'

He grinned at Corrine, and she gave a mischievous one in return. 'Ottilie.'

Ottilie laughed. 'Seriously? Was that her name already, or have I been greatly honoured?'

'Oh, we've named her. Both said it straight away, as soon as we saw the photos.'

'Hmmm…' Ottilie took a bite of her cake. 'So what you're saying is, I look so much like an alpaca from Ullswater that it was the only name you could give her. I'm not sure how to feel about that.'

'No,' Corrine said, 'she reminds us of you.'

'Isn't that the same thing?'

'She were trying to be kind,' Victor said, laughing, 'but if you want to have it that way, yes.'

Aside from Victor and Corrine, their alpaca herd were some of the first creatures Ottilie had met on her arrival in Thimblebury the year before. She had fond memories of that time and still had a soft spot for the animals. 'Can I go and see her?'

'If you want to go up tonight, we'll have to be quick; it'll be dark soon.'

'Maybe we should wait for a better time then.'

Victor looked vaguely disappointed but nodded agreement. 'Might be for the best. I've only just settled her in.'

'It's exciting,' Ottilie said. 'I've never had an alpaca named after me. Never had anything named after me. Nobody can ever spell my name to name anything after me!'

'Well, now you have. You'll have tourists leading an Ottilie up and down the fields come the summer.'

Ottilie smiled at them both.

'We heard about Dr Cheadle.' Victor reached for the teapot to fill his mug. 'A bad business.'

'Yes,' Ottilie said. 'It's been stressful.'

'Is he going to be all right?'

'We don't really know yet. We'll know more in the next few days, I expect.'

'Ottilie wants to know if we can spare half an hour to go and look in on Ann at Hilltop. She's not well and needs some help.' Corrine got up and filled the kettle to boil again.

Victor nodded. 'I expect we can do a bit here and there.'

'I was hoping you'd be able to,' Ottilie said.

'I'll give her a knock in a bit,' Victor said, and Ottilie gave a grateful smile.

As she reached for her tea, a notification came through on her phone. She pulled it out of her bag to see a text from Stacey.

How are you doing? How's the new doc? X

'Sorry…' Ottilie began to type a reply. 'Don't mean to be rude but I need to quickly reply to this…'

'Don't mind us,' Corrine said.

Fine, holding up. No news on Charles yet. New doctor very good and a nice guy. X

Good. So I hear. Not bad to look at either?????

Ottilie had to smile at the leading row of question marks in Stacey's reply. She had clearly already been told Simon was handsome. And now that she thought about it, he was. Not her type, but she could appreciate good looks as well as anyone, and he'd been blessed in that department with dark hair and dark eyes, broad shoulders and quite an attractive gravelled tone to his voice.

Her reply would need to be longer and it would have to wait until she'd left Victor and Corrine. Perhaps she'd call on Stacey on the way home for a chat and fill her in on the latest gossip.

Ottilie sent Stacey a brief text as she left Daffodil Farm. Victor had insisted on running her down the hill in his old Land Rover before going over to check on Ann and Darryl. Stacey had replied quickly, happy for Ottilie to call. She had lasagne in the oven and enough for an extra plate anyway, and so the arrangements to stay for dinner had been made with Ottilie barely noticing.

But when she arrived, she realised gossip would have to wait as she walked in to see Magnus and Geoff already in the kitchen.

'We were just talking about the next film club,' Geoff said, getting up to give Ottilie a brief kiss on the cheek, Magnus following suit. 'We're struggling to know what to show this time. I think we should go with an old classic. I thought *Kramer vs. Kramer*.'

'I've never seen it,' Ottilie said.

'It sounds depressing,' Stacey put in.

'It's desperate,' Magnus agreed. 'I'd have to miss film club for the first time ever if that was on.'

'You've never even given it a chance,' Geoff said. 'You never give my films a chance.'

'I do. Wasn't *On Golden Pond* yours? And it was bloody miserable!'

'Well, what do you want?' Ottilie asked Magnus. 'Could we find something somewhere in the middle?'

'*Priscilla Queen of the Desert*.'

Geoff rolled his eyes. 'Talk about cliché! We're gay but we don't have to be camp!'

'It's a brilliant film!' Magnus said in a sullen tone. 'Whether you think it's camp or not makes no difference.'

'We're not putting it on. Can you imagine Flo sitting down to watch that?'

'Flo hates every film we show anyway, so why worry about that?'

'He's got a point there…' Stacey handed Ottilie a glass of wine.

Ottilie hadn't intended to drink, but now that it was in her hand and in the face of the argument about to erupt between Magnus and Geoff, perhaps it wasn't such a bad idea.

Geoff rounded on Stacey. 'Whose side are you on?'

'Nobody's. Is it actually your turn to choose?' she asked.

'It's Lavender's, but she said she was too busy to think of one.'

'Perhaps she ought to try again, if only to save your marriage…' Stacey shook her head and turned to Ottilie. 'How's it gone today then?'

'Oh, you know, there's not much to say other than what I texted you. The locum is lovely, seems to know what he's doing and is settling in very fast. We couldn't have asked for better in the circumstances. And I'm waiting to hear from Fliss.' She checked her watch. 'Visiting time ought to be over soon, so I expect she'll message with an update.'

'You'll let her know we're thinking of her, won't you,' Magnus said, and Geoff nodded.

'It's an awful shock.'

'Absolutely.' Ottilie put her wine down to take off her coat.

'And as soon as you hear some news you must let us know.'

'I will,' Ottilie said.

'So you haven't been home yet?' Stacey asked.

'No, I've been up to Daffodil Farm. Had a quick cup of tea with Corrine and Victor.'

'Ah. And they're well?'

'I think so. Corrine was showing me this stunning ring Victor had bought for her.'

'Really? I didn't know he had it in him.'

Ottilie smiled. 'I think he wants to show her how much she means to him.'

'Lucky cow,' Stacey said.

'They've had a new alpaca as well.'

'Don't they have enough already?' Geoff asked.

'This one's a rescue apparently.'

'What have they called her?'

Ottilie's smile became a bit more sheepish. 'Would you believe they've called her Ottilie?'

Stacey clapped her hands together. 'That's brilliant!'

'I'd like to see,' Magnus said. 'I bet she's cute.'

'I thought you said they were smelly long-necked sheep with delusions of grandeur,' Geoff cut in.

'That was a joke,' Magnus said hotly.

'It didn't sound like a joke.'

'If you can't tell a joke from a serious observation, then you're in trouble.'

'It looks as if I can't. I married you after all…'

Ottilie frowned at Stacey, who let out a sigh and signalled for Ottilie to follow her into the living room.

'They've been driving me mental for the last hour,' she said in a low voice as she and Ottilie moved away from the bickering. 'Don't know what's got into them.'

'Poor you. Where's Chloe and Mackenzie?'

'Well…' Stacey took a breath and sat down. 'She's taken him to meet this person she went to meet the other day.'

'She told you that?'

'Not in so many words, but I sort of worked it out. It must be serious because she doesn't take Mackenzie out on her own, and certainly not on the bus into another town.'

'Aren't you worried about her?'

Stacey blinked. 'She's an adult; I can't tell her what to do. I don't know that there's any cause to worry yet, and she'll have to get used to taking Mackenzie out eventually, so she might as well start now.' Stacey took a thoughtful sip of her wine. 'Do you think I ought to be worried?'

'Of course not – I was only asking. But you thought it was a boy last time you mentioned it. So it seems a bit quick for her to be introducing him to Mackenzie if it is.'

'I know, but I suppose being upfront isn't a bad thing. There's no point keeping him a secret and then her getting down the line with this lad and really liking him, only for him to dump her because she didn't tell him she had a baby. Right?'

'I suppose so. I can't say I know a lot about this sort of thing.'

'If I'm being honest, I'm jealous that she's found a fella already and I can't get anyone interested.'

'You don't know that.'

'She might not have, but neither have I, and I've been waiting a lot longer.'

'Perhaps you ought to start driving around the neighbouring towns trying to pick one off.'

'Don't even joke about it,' Stacey groaned. 'It's crossed my mind. Kidnap a tourist – nobody would miss the odd one.'

'Oh, Stacey…'

'I know – modern women aren't supposed to be so needy, are we? I don't care about modern. I am needy!'

'You're not, you're brilliant and gorgeous and funny – and you should hold on for someone who deserves you. I'm not going to tell you to be patient because I realise it must be hard, but he is out there, and you will find him.'

'Hmmm. So this new doctor then… he's good-looking?'

Ottilie gave a little laugh. 'He's very good-looking.'

'And what's his story?'

'I'm not entirely sure. He mentioned a wife but like he wasn't with her now.'

'Like he didn't bring her with him or like he's divorced?'

'Like… well, like she isn't around any longer.'

'You think he's widowed?'

'I sort of got that feeling.'

'How old is he?'

'I'd say close to forty-ish.'

'I might have to make an appointment to see him for my ingrowing toenail.'

'Don't you go making appointments just to gawp! Poor bloke's got enough on his plate.'

'Who said anything about gawping? I'm deeply offended you'd think such a thing of me.'

Ottilie laughed again as she sipped at her wine. 'It's a genuine medical emergency then?'

'Of course.'

The door to the living room opened. Magnus and Geoff came in.

'What are you two whispering about in here?' Geoff asked.

'I'm surprised you noticed we were gone,' Stacey shot back. 'Too busy taking potshots at each other.'

'We weren't.'

'We were a bit,' Magnus said ruefully. 'Sorry, Geoff.'

Geoff sniffed and turned back to Stacey. 'Well, it was rude of you to go off and leave us. We're guests.'

'You're not; you're my brother. Doesn't count. And Magnus is as good as. The only official guest we have to be polite to here is Ottilie.'

'Hey…' Ottilie held up her hands. 'Don't drag me into this!'

'Button it, lady – consider yourself dragged.'

'Ottilie…' Magnus cut in, making himself taller, as if he was suddenly above all the petty squabble and idle banter. 'So you were going to tell us more about the new GP.'

'He's not really our new GP; he's only a very temporary cover.'

'I've heard he's very nice.'

'He seems it.'

'I heard he's been out of the country.'

'Yes, he's spent the last year in Botswana doing voluntary work.'

'Has he?' Magnus looked impressed while Stacey looked far more attentive now. 'That's very interesting, isn't it?'

'Yes,' Ottilie said, wishing she hadn't given that snippet away.

'Is he staying locally?' Stacey asked, and Ottilie was beginning to wish everyone wasn't quite so interested. She didn't want to give away things that Simon might not appreciate, but she didn't want to be all secretive either – because that often made people even more curious.

'He has a hotel outside the village for the next couple of days, but then if he stays any longer than that, he says he's going to have to commute from Liverpool.'

'Every day?'

Ottilie nodded. 'To save money, I suppose.'

'That's a long way,' Geoff said.

'It's a bit of a distance,' Ottilie conceded, 'but for someone like him, it's all part of the job. He must be used to being sent all over the place – doctors often are.'

'Still, isn't there somewhere in the village he can stay while he's working here?'

Stacey raised her eyebrows. 'Yes, how about that massive luxury hotel… Oh, wait, there isn't one, is there? Not even a piddly B&B.'

'But there are people with spare rooms,' Magnus said.

'And there are guesthouses in nearby towns,' Stacey continued, 'so presumably if he'd wanted to stay nearby, he could have done. Maybe it suits him to commute and Ottilie just mentioned the expense, so…' She glanced at Ottilie. 'And maybe he has someone in Liverpool he wants to get back to every night. We'd have to find out, wouldn't we?'

Ottilie could see where all this was going. Everyone was desperate to know more about Simon, and they probably all wanted Ottilie to dig and report back to them. It wasn't going to happen, though. It wouldn't be appropriate, for a start, not given their working relationship, no matter how temporary it was.

Geoff frowned at Magnus. 'That's your problem. Can't keep your nose out of anything.'

Magnus frowned in return, and it felt as if their argument was about to resume. Ottilie watched carefully. What was going on here? Ordinarily they were a loving and very harmonious couple; she'd never seen them like this before, but she'd noticed them bickering more than usual the last few times she'd been around. She hoped it would blow over, because she was fond of them both and hated to think of them splitting up.

'While I think about it,' she began as a way to distract everyone, 'is there anyone who can spare an hour to go and check in on Ann at Hilltop Farm?'

'Why, what's wrong with her?' Stacey pulled a cushion onto her knee and leaned on it as she looked up at Ottilie.

'I can't tell you that,' Ottilie said.

Stacey rolled her eyes. 'I know, patients have to have secrets.'

'But she could do with some help and she's happy for me to ask one or two people.'

'I hardly know her,' Magnus said. 'She never comes to the shop.'

Geoff turned to him. 'Is that a reason to deny help? Doesn't seem very neighbourly to me.'

'She's not our neighbour,' Magnus shot back.

'Of course she is! What does it matter? We're not meant to give to charity unless they're right next door to us, is that what you're saying?'

'No! I'm only saying she wouldn't come down to help us if we asked for it—'

'*She* isn't asking; Ottilie is.'

Stacey sent a pained look Ottilie's way and mouthed an apology. Ottilie looked at her watch. She hated to see them so at odds too, and though she felt guilty for abandoning Stacey with them, it felt like a good time to leave them to it, despite the offer of dinner. The following day was going to be another busy one and it was already getting late.

'I'm sorry, I'd better go,' she said, though only Stacey noticed. 'Thanks so much for the wine.'

'Any time. I'll see you out.'

'There's no need.'

Stacey glanced at Geoff and Magnus, and her expression of despair was almost comical. 'Oh, yes, there is! I might even come with you!'

CHAPTER NINE

The headstone still looked new. It was far newer than the ones on the row behind it but had started to look older than those that shared the same row. Ottilie stood and looked at it and was overwhelmed with guilt. It wasn't only because she was here with Heath, but for so many other reasons.

Instinctively, she'd slipped her hand from Heath's as they'd arrived, and so she felt guilty for that, because it must have hurt him, and she felt guilty that she was even holding someone else's hand in front of Josh's grave. She was filled with shame that she hadn't been to visit it more often. There were flowers laid there, but until now, none of them had been hers. She'd found it difficult to get away from her commitments in Thimblebury to come here – or so she'd told herself. Those excuses had been white lies to ease that nagging guilt. In reality, she hadn't been here because she simply hadn't been able to face it.

There was a deeper, nameless guilt too. Was it because she was still alive, forging ahead with a new life in a new place while Josh hadn't been given that luxury? Would it have seemed to him she'd far too readily grasped the chance to start again? That she'd forgotten him too quickly – although she still thought of him every day – that she'd left him behind with far too much ease?

Today would have been his fortieth birthday. In the years leading up to his death, they'd talked about what they'd do to celebrate. Go on a cruise, perhaps hire one of those houses on stilts on some Thai beach, maybe throw an old-fashioned family party at a local pub. He'd always hankered to see the Northern Lights, and that was meant to be her anniversary gift to him, only they never got that far. Josh had died before then, and nobody had gone on the holiday Ottilie had booked as a surprise.

So here she was, the day they'd talked about for years, and there was no cruise, no house on stilts, no family knees-up. There was only Ottilie standing here with another man, looking at his grave.

Heath kept a respectful silence as he stood at her side. He was good at this sort of thing, Ottilie had noted. Knew when he should offer comfort and when to back off. Even before they'd become a couple she'd noticed that about him.

She recalled the day he'd found her sobbing on the floor of her house when she'd heard Josh's killer had been arrested, and how brilliant he'd been. He was sensible enough to be here with Ottilie and not see her past with Josh as a threat. She'd admitted she still loved him – because how could she have fallen out of love with a man who wasn't here to fall out of love with? – but Heath had taken that information like a proper adult, and she wasn't sure she'd have been able to do the same if it had been the other way around. He was good for her and she knew it, and she was certain Josh would have seen it too, but none of that helped her feel any better.

As she wiped away her tears, she glanced up to see Heath watching her carefully. He offered a pained smile.

'I'm all right,' she said.

'You don't have to pretend for my sake.'

'I know. I mean, I'm obviously not all right, but I'm all right enough.'

'Do you want me to leave you alone for a minute?'

Ottilie considered his question. Did she? On the one hand, she could say what she needed to Josh better without Heath there. But on the other hand, she didn't want to keep secrets from Heath, not even that one. And she appreciated the strength that she absorbed whenever he was close. Right now, she needed it. The time for falling apart had passed, but it didn't mean that standing in front of this stone was easy.

'No,' she said finally. 'Stay, please. I won't be much longer.'

'Stay as long as you want to.'

Ottilie shook her head. 'There almost doesn't seem like any point. He's not there really, is he? Now that I'm here, I don't even know why I've come. It's nobody's birthday – how can a man who isn't here have a birthday?'

'You don't mean that.'

'I'm not sure if I do or not, but it's how I feel looking at his grave right now. It makes no difference to him if I come or not.'

'It makes a difference to you – that's what matters.'

'Then that's selfish.'

'Ottilie…'

Heath's tone had a note of concerned warning in it. She was spiralling – she felt it, and he could see it. It used to happen a lot in the early days. Perhaps it was selfish to have come, but perhaps the only way she was ever going to completely move past this tragedy was to be selfish. Perhaps she could only be selfish, and perhaps Josh would have understood that too. Josh wasn't here, so everything she did that concerned him and his memory was for herself in some way. Visiting the grave, seeing his family… it was all for her really. She'd go and sit with his parents later because she wanted them to think she still cared. It wasn't for Josh – he couldn't give a fig now. She was here now because she felt that forgetting him made her a bad person – Josh didn't care about that either. Josh would have known that she hadn't forgotten him; there was no need for any big show as far as he was concerned. So all of it had to be for her.

'There's a little café at the gates,' she said. 'Let's go and get a hot drink.'

'You're sure? You don't want to stay a bit longer?'

Ottilie shook her head. 'I think, just for today, a bit of selfish might be OK.'

Heath had gone off to see a friend, giving Ottilie time and space to visit Josh's parents. It had been a lovely but emotionally draining few hours, and by the time she and Heath met for a late lunch she was exhausted.

'I'm sorry I'm going to be rubbish for the rest of the day,' she said as they followed a waiter to their table.

'Don't be daft. I wasn't expecting us to be going on a pub crawl. It's fine – you don't have to apologise to me. I knew what sort of day it was going to be.'

'And yet you still came.'

'Of course. You'd have done it for me. You'd have done it for anyone.'

'Even so, it must be a bit miserable for you.'

'Would you stop that – I don't want you to think about that again. I'm here with you and that's enough for me. I want to be here.'

Ottilie took a seat at the table they'd been shown to. The restaurant was a decent mid-price Italian that was considered a reliable bet by locals for a good bowl of pasta. The walls were dotted with black-and-white photos of Italian scenes: rolling Tuscan hills, glorious churches, terracotta-roofed villages and clifftops bordered by sparkling seas. Some of them were photos of people in fashions of days gone by. Ottilie had been here before and often wondered if they were the ancestors of the current owners. In fact, she'd eaten here often with Josh, but when Heath had suggested it she hadn't the heart to say so. He'd seemed so pleased with his choice, eager to see her pleased too, it would have been cruel to deny him that little triumph. And as days went, hers had been sobering but his hadn't exactly been a picnic either. They both deserved better.

'It's nice in here, isn't it?' Heath said as he poured them both a glass of water from a jug already on the table.

Ottilie nodded. 'Good choice.'

'I remembered you'd said you liked Italian food.'

'I do. I love it.'

He was silent for a moment. He seemed eager to please but wary of saying the wrong thing. Ottilie hated that he might feel that way.

'It's nice to be in Manchester,' she said.

'Really? Because we…'

'I know we only came because of Josh, but I've actually enjoyed being back here more than I thought I would. I love Thimblebury, don't get me wrong, but Manchester is home. It's where I'm from so it's always going to be important.'

'I'm glad.'

'I'll come to visit you more here. It doesn't seem fair now that I think of it. You always have to come to Thimblebury.'

'I don't mind; I like Thimblebury.'

'I know. And I don't really have so much of an excuse to stay away now. After all, they got the guy who killed Josh – not that I had to worry in the first place. It was a weird time, I suppose.'

Heath seemed to pause for longer than was necessary before he asked the next question. 'Bound to be. It looks like this conviction is going to stick then?'

Ottilie reached for her water. 'Faith seems to think so… You know, Josh's old colleague Faith.'

'Oh, yes, you did mention her. So that's good. Does it make you see it all a bit differently?'

'I'm not sure,' Ottilie said as she stared into space. Did it? She'd waited to hear that news for so long she didn't know how she felt about it now. Materially, what difference could it make to her life? It wasn't going to change anything. But knowing that there was finally some sort of justice for Josh, she couldn't deny there was a certain satisfaction in that. It was a closure of sorts, but closure only sparked those feelings of guilt again, because closure was halfway to accepting and forgetting as far as she could tell.

Shaking herself, she forced a smile for Heath. 'I'm suddenly starving.'

'That's good. Have whatever you want – my treat.'

'No, I don't—'

'Don't argue. I knew you'd make a fuss. Let me do this please. I've been pretty useless to you for most of today, so let me do this much.'

'You've been brilliant, not useless!'

'I've felt useless.'

'You're here and that was all I needed from you. Thank you for coming.'

'Ottilie, I live in Manchester. It was hardly a trek for me to be here!'

'You know that's not what I mean,' she said with a smile.

Heath reached across the table for her hand. 'It might not be the right time to say this, I realise, but I don't think I can keep it in any longer.'

Ottilie held back a frown.

'In fact,' he said, 'I'm sure you already know it.'

'Do I?'

He nodded. 'But I want to say it, just for the record, so there's no doubt, because I haven't been brave enough to say it before. Ottilie, I lo—'

'Heath!'

They both looked up at the sight of a woman marching towards their table. She was blonde and curvy, with the sort of polished glamour that would make someone take a second look on the street. Heath yanked his hand from Ottilie's as if he'd been burned. She looked sharply at him, but his eyes were wide, fixed on the newcomer.

'Bloody hell!' the woman cackled. 'Fancy seeing you here!' She looked at Ottilie, and then her sardonic gaze went back to Heath. 'I take it this is your new model. I might have known you wouldn't stay single for long.'

Heath cleared his throat, suddenly seeming to find his voice. 'What are you doing here?' he asked with such frost in his voice that Ottilie turned to him in surprise. She'd never heard that from him before, not even when they'd been at loggerheads over Flo when they'd first met. No, it wasn't just coldness; it was clear contempt.

'I fancied an Italian,' the woman said. 'It's a free country, isn't it?'

'Alone?'

'Why? Are you still mad at Dwight?'

'I've got no feelings for your new boyfriend either way. I'm only making conversation.'

'As a matter of fact, he's parking the Merc.'

'Right.'

The woman looked from him to Ottilie and then back to him. 'So you're not going to introduce me?'

'No.'

She ignored him and turned to Ottilie with a saccharine smile. 'I'm Mila. Heath's wife.'

'Ex,' he corrected her.

'Still, the wife bit's what matters. We made vows.'

'It's a shame you didn't think about that when we were married,' he muttered.

She ignored him again. 'And you are…?'

Heath shushed Ottilie in a way she didn't like. She was going to decide whether she would answer, not him.

'Mila…' he said in a deliberate tone, 'much as I'm enjoying our catch-up, is there any way you could possibly go and eat somewhere else? I don't know, like maybe the Shetland Isles? As far away as you can would be perfect.'

'Sorry, got a meal booking. How's Flo these days? Still flying around on her broomstick, or has that mental village of hers finally burned her at the stake?'

Heath shot off his chair. 'I'm asking you nicely,' he growled. 'If you can't eat somewhere else then go and sit down – preferably where I can't see you.'

'So she's dead?' Mila asked. 'You're touchy so I'm guessing so.'

'No!' he snapped. 'Not that it's any of your business!' His gaze travelled to where the waiter was showing a tall, well-built man with a shaved head to a table across the room. 'Looks like Dwight's all parked up. Don't you think you'd better go and join him? Don't want him getting the wrong idea.'

Mila threw back her head and laughed. 'About us? Please!' She waved at the man, who frowned slightly, and then the moment of clarity hit. He sidled over and took Mila by the arm to lead her away with the briefest nod at Heath. At least one half of the couple seemed to have some sense.

'Wow…' Ottilie said in a low voice as she watched them go to their own table. 'So that's the infamous Mila.'

Heath grimaced. 'Sorry, but do you mind if we go and eat somewhere else? I know you like this place and…'

'God, no!' Ottilie grabbed the coat from the back of her chair. Given what had just passed between Heath and his ex, there was no way they could stay. And besides, secretly she was relieved not to have to go through with the pretence that this wasn't a regular haunt for her and Josh. Somewhere else was fine with her.

CHAPTER TEN

They'd gone on to another restaurant that served more general Mediterranean cuisine. It was pleasant, if a bit more generic and a bit more of a chain type of place than their first choice. They'd enjoyed their meal and managed to pick the mood back up, but both were very obviously ignoring the massive Mila-shaped elephant at the table. Ottilie didn't want to bring her up because the memory of the sour looks that seemed close to hatred were still vivid, and she didn't like to see them on Heath's usually gentle and handsome face. She was afraid that asking about what had happened at the Italian might bring that expression back again. Presumably, Heath simply didn't want to talk about the ex who'd caused him such misery and had tried to rip off his gran, which was fair enough. Ottilie didn't know whether this was because seeing her had opened up all sorts of old wounds, or whether he hadn't wanted to make Ottilie feel uncomfortable, or whether he simply did hate her that much now. The history he'd given of their marriage was always sketchy, and Ottilie had never pushed for more because she'd heard often enough how it had scarred him, but after today, she couldn't deny that she was burning with curiosity. Because the thing about hatred that strong was that it often came from a place of passion. Hatred like that came from a place of deepest, violent hurt.

Almost everyone who knew about the marriage had told Ottilie he'd been deeply in love with her and had struggled to let go. What Ottilie had seen today ought to have reassured her that he *had* let go, but it had almost done the opposite. It had seemed to Ottilie that it was about more than Mila trying to rip him or his gran off. He'd hated her too much. If there were no feelings left, he wouldn't have cared. He wouldn't have let Mila get under his skin; he'd have shaken off her taunting and they'd have moved on, but Ottilie didn't get any sense of that happening. Not only did it now feel important to know more, but she desperately wanted to.

It was dark by the time Heath drove her home. She was off work the following day and wondered if he might suggest they spend the night together at his place in Manchester, but he didn't. Ottilie got that – she was certain it was out of respect for the primary reason she'd come to Manchester, but she was afraid that his meeting with Mila had something to do with it too.

The image of the woman came to Ottilie's mind as they drove the darkened motorways out of Manchester. Physically, she was a bit like Ottilie: on the curvy side but not big, a bit girl next door but with far more make-up and an expensive-looking haircut. The designer goods were very much in evidence, where Ottilie had never cared for brands. From an entirely physical point of view, she could see why Heath had been attracted to her. But that was where the similarities ended. Mila was far more confident than Ottilie could ever be – she had to be to have marched into the restaurant like that and bowl up to the man she'd treated so badly without a care in the world and not an ounce of conscience or remorse. At least, she was showing neither of those things as far as Ottilie could see. In fact, she'd seemed to enjoy the trouble she'd caused.

She glanced across at Heath, his silent attention on the road. What had their marriage been like? She'd heard the gossip and she'd heard his account, but what had it really been like? He'd once loved Mila, that much was evident, because the sort of betrayal and loathing on his face that day couldn't have come from anywhere else.

And then Ottilie's mind wandered to the moments before Mila's arrival. Heath had been about to tell her something, and Ottilie thought she might know what it was. She'd been desperate to hear it too. Those three words. She felt them, and she felt certain he did too, but as yet they hadn't been said out loud by either of them.

Did it make any difference to them that nobody had said it? Did it matter as long as they both felt it? Ottilie wanted to believe that it didn't, but she'd always felt there was an intention in the saying of it, a promise. To say those three words was to tell the other person that they were important and wanted and that their happiness was everything. And even if they knew it, as she and Heath did, saying it out loud was different. It was an affirmation to be sent out into the universe.

She looked at him now, eyes fixed on the road, seeming to be as deep in thought as she was, wondering whether the moment had passed them by. It felt that way. She could say it, but it would sound like an afterthought, or perhaps a prompt – either way it didn't feel like the right time. She could have asked him, but to hear him say it then would have felt hollow, as if she'd forced his hand, and surely it had to come from a place of conviction for it to mean anything. It had to come from his heart to hers, without prompting, without pressure, and it had to be pure and natural. That's how she'd always seen it.

Despite thinking all this, she still wanted to hear it, and the temptation was there to instigate a return to that conversation. And something about that moment – the thing left unsaid – felt like a turning point, for reasons she couldn't even see. For good or for ill? That was the question.

'How are you doing there?' Heath kept his eyes on the road as he spoke.

'All right. I was wondering the same about you.'

'Me? I'm all right.'

'That's good. Only I thought… you seemed a bit quiet.'

'Not really. I was giving you a minute's peace, that's all. You've had a stressful day; I thought you might have had enough of me jabbering on.'

'I like to hear you jabber on.'

'Oh.'

'So feel free to jabber.'

'See, now I can't think of anything to say.'

'There must be something you want to talk about.'

He glanced briefly her way now before turning back to the road. 'Is this about Mila?'

'If you like. I'm not going to force you to talk about it, but I wonder if it would help.'

'I don't need to. As soon as she was out of my face she was forgotten.'

'Really? You can put her out of your mind that easily? Because I don't think I would be able to.'

'That's because she didn't do the things to you that she did to me. Let me tell you, if she had you'd be only too happy to put her out of your mind. I was annoyed when I first saw her. It's just my bloody luck she'd turn up today of all days, the one time I take you out in Manchester. Honestly, I'm starting to wonder if Gran might have a point. I might be better off living in Thimblebury. At least I won't run into her there.'

'You'd go to those lengths to avoid seeing her?'

'It's not quite like that. There is another very persuasive argument for moving to Thimblebury.'

Ottilie flushed. They'd joked about it, and she'd never taken any talk of him joining her there seriously, but she'd made it clear that she wasn't about to leave the village she'd grown to love, and so there would only be one ending if they stayed together. It wasn't quite a declaration of love, but if there was even one atom of meaning in what he was saying now, it was as good as.

'But yes,' he added, 'I would go to those lengths to avoid her.'

In an instant the bubble had burst. Ottilie was dropped back to earth with a thump. A little about her, but mostly about Mila. Just as Josh was her past and would always be a part of her present and future, it seemed that in her own way, Mila would be the same to Heath.

'I won't stay tonight if it's all right with you,' he said.

'Sure, whatever.'

There was a beat of silence.

'You're upset?' he asked.

'What makes you say that?'

'Because I didn't want to stay. You sounded upset.'

'I'm not.'

'It's for your sake. I thought because it was Josh's birthday…'

'I know.'

'Do you?'

'Yes. But you could stay if you wanted to. If that's the only reason you're not, then it's…'

'I just don't think it would be a good idea. I think you need some space.'

Ottilie gave a small nod. Perhaps she did need some space, but it still felt a bit too much like a rejection for her to be happy with the arrangement. She couldn't help but feel as if he was using Josh's birthday as an excuse because he didn't want to stay over.

'Will I see you this weekend?' she asked.

'I'm sure we'll do something. We normally do.'

'OK.'

Ottilie laid her head back on the seat rest and closed her eyes. This new love business was far too confusing at times. Sometimes she longed for the days of settled marriage with Josh, not only because she'd loved him and missed him, but because there'd been none of this uncertainty. She'd known where she was with Josh; she never had to second-guess his motives or forensically examine something he'd said. There was no complicated past, no skeletons waiting to jump out at her. Maybe one day it would be like that with Heath, but that day felt like a long way off right now.

CHAPTER ELEVEN

Despite her difficult week, Ottilie had a spring in her step as she headed over to meet Fliss for a walk on the shores of Windermere. In fact, more than a spring – it was a skip. She was due to meet Heath later that day for dinner, and she was hopeful they'd be able to clear the air properly, back to normal; and Fliss had phoned saying Charles was home. Not at his home – of course, they famously lived in separate cottages which supplied endless gossip to the villagers – but staying with Fliss, where she could keep an eye on him. Reading between the lines – as in, gleaning from what Fliss didn't say rather than what she did – Charles had been blessed with the luckiest of escapes. Perhaps if his wife hadn't been an incredibly experienced GP and hadn't spent years sharing her knowledge with him, he might not have recognised his symptoms so quickly and he might not have called for help in the nick of time. Others who lived so far from an ambulance station and who weren't quite as aware might not have been so fortunate.

But Fliss had sounded cheerful on the phone, far more positive than she had since her ordeal had begun. That alone was enough to lift Ottilie's spirits. She was so fond of Fliss it filled her with joy to know things were moving in the right direction at last. And it would have been comical a few weeks before to hear Fliss talk of healthy lifestyles and getting out into the fresh air more – even her patients recognised that she never took her own advice where healthy living was concerned – if not for

Ottilie recognising how much Charles's close call must have scared them both. Certainly enough for Fliss to even discuss going out for walks.

That Sunday morning was cold, a frost lingering on the hills and mist wreathing the valley floors, but the sun was doing its best to burn through, giving it a magical sort of light. Ottilie had grown to love days like this since her arrival. She was often out early, up at Hilltop Farm before work, and the view from up there on such days was something else. She'd often have to stop for a moment on the path to admire it, and just as often she'd spare a thought for Josh and wonder what he would have made of it.

Ironically – though it would save them time – Fliss had offered to drive them both to Windermere instead of making the hour or so's hike there to start their walk. Small steps, she'd said, laughing, when she'd told Ottilie the plan; she couldn't be expected to turn into Sherpa Tenzing straight off the bat.

What Ottilie hadn't expected when she arrived at Fliss's cottage was to see Lavender making her way up the path to the front door.

'Morning!' she called, wondering why she hadn't realised before that Lavender would be invited too. Perhaps what was more surprising was that Lavender had accepted the invitation – she was another resident of Thimblebury who more often than not squandered chances to explore the glorious landscape that surrounded the village. In the time Ottilie had lived there she'd never known Lavender to go walking.

Lavender turned around, hand poised to knock, and smiled. 'So you've been summoned too?'

'Not summoned, exactly. There was definitely some cajoling involved. But to be fair, I'm always up for an excuse to go for a walk.'

'I wish I could say the same. I ought to be, but I'm always too bloody busy.'

Lavender had a box of chocolates under her arm, and Ottilie dug into her bag and held up one of her own. 'Snap.'

'Great minds think alike, though I can't help wondering if we ought to have brought something a bit healthier over.'

Ottilie laughed. 'They'd have binned it if we had. Perhaps they'll both pace themselves.'

Lavender raised her eyebrows, and Ottilie's laughter grew.

'OK, we can't expect immediate miracles.'

Whether Fliss heard them talking or whether it was pure coincidence, the front door opened and she stepped out.

'Morning, you two!' she said briskly. 'This is odd, isn't it? Feels like it ought to be a work morning but somewhat surreally we've replaced the surgery with my front garden.'

'Doesn't it?' Lavender said. She looked at the door with a vague frown as Fliss pulled it closed behind her to join them on the path.

'Charles is asleep,' Fliss said in answer to her obvious confusion. 'I hope you don't mind if I don't invite you in just yet. Perhaps when we've had our walk he'll be awake and more open to visitors.'

'It'd be nice to see him,' Ottilie said. 'But only if he's up to it.'

'I'm sure he will be. His recovery is actually going remarkably well. I hadn't imagined he'd be back on his feet so quickly, but he gets tired easily these days. I'm sure that will remedy itself in time too.'

The drive over to the lake was short but boisterous. Ottilie was pleased to see Fliss in high spirits, although she allowed Lavender to do most of the talking – and a lot of it was focused around what had been happening at the surgery in Fliss's absence. Ottilie sat in the rear seat and enjoyed their back and forth, only prompted now and again to chip in with some agreement or expansion of something Lavender had said. She was more animated when the conversation turned to the locum GP, Dr Stokes.

'He's not you,' Lavender said emphatically.

'It might prove confusing if he were,' Fliss said, laughing, as they crested a hill, rising above the early mist where it was so bright she was forced to pull down the car's sun visor.

'But he's been very good,' Lavender added.

Ottilie leaned forward. 'He's brilliant actually.'

Lavender twisted to look at her. 'Someone's a fan.'

'Not like that,' Ottilie said, flushing. 'I'm only saying I've seen him working first-hand and he's wonderful with patients. He's good at his job – even you can't argue with that.'

'I never said he wasn't. I only meant it's not the same as it is when Fliss is there. He's good for a temp.'

'And he seems like someone with a lot of integrity,' Ottilie continued. 'I like him – he's easy to work with.'

'Hmmm…' Fliss was suddenly thoughtful. 'That's interesting,' she said finally, her eyes fixed on the road. 'Very good to know.'

The sun had finally broken through as they parked up and began their walk. The route Fliss had chosen – starting at Wray Castle and along to Blelham Tarn – was new to Ottilie, and she suspected it was new to Lavender and Fliss too. She'd chosen well, though, because the clear, crisp brightness of the early spring weather only added to the stunning beauty of their surroundings.

Wray Castle was an odd little place, and they took half an hour out of their schedule to take a proper look at it. It was curious and quaint and lovely, and Ottilie wasn't surprised to hear that it had actually been built by a Victorian rather than someone far earlier, because it looked like a toy castle, exactly like the sort of thing a wealthy Victorian would build. She was surprised and quite excited to learn that it had also hosted a very young Beatrix Potter and must have played a part in her love for the Lakes.

From there they made their way to Blelham Tarn, which was so untypical of the district, with a quieter, gentler beauty, but beautiful nonetheless. The water was calm and blue, and Ottilie could see acres of plant life beneath the surface, not to mention the forests of reeds along the banks. She held her breath as she spotted a kingfisher dive into the water and tried to make out what birds might be making up the cacophony of song, though there were far too many to recognise even one, even if she really knew how to.

'I feel as if I've missed out all these years,' Fliss said as they stopped to rest halfway around the tarn. 'How entitled of me to have all this on my doorstep and yet never take the time to come and see it.'

'You're busy,' Ottilie said. 'We all are. Life gets in the way often.'

'Far too often…' Fliss's gaze was on the distant hills, indigo and emerald and gold and amber in the sun, pensive, as if her thoughts weren't really on their beauty after all.

A movement caught Ottilie's eye as something splashed into the water. Another kingfisher? She turned her gaze to the spot, hoping to see it emerge from behind the reeds, but her thoughts weren't really there either. Fliss was right – life got in the way far too often to enjoy simple pleasures like this. She wished she'd learned that lesson while Josh had been alive because, though they'd been happy, it seemed now that in one way or another they'd always been too busy to make time to enjoy moments like this together, and she made a pact with herself right there and then that she wouldn't let that happen with Heath.

She was brought back to the moment by the sound of a deep sigh from Fliss.

'Actually…' she began slowly, 'there's a reason I wanted to see you both today. Apart from enjoying this lovely morning,' she added. 'I hadn't quite decided what I was going to do, but I've had plans hatching in my mind for a while now. I was hoping to get your opinions on it, but as our walk has gone on, I've realised I don't need anyone else's opinion. I think I'd already made up my mind, but I was too scared to say so.'

She looked at Lavender and Ottilie in turn, and her smile was so sad and yet so resigned that Ottilie couldn't imagine what she could possibly be about to say that was so bad it would make such a smile.

'I've decided…' Fliss hesitated, and then, as if it hurt to look at them, she turned her attention back to the distant hills. 'I've decided to take early retirement.'

'What?' Lavender's eyes widened.

Fliss turned to her now, something shrewder on her face. 'Don't tell me it's a complete surprise. I'm not getting any younger—'

'You're not old!' Lavender cut in, and Fliss held back a frown.

'Almost sixty-three. Not old, but not getting any younger either. Neither is Charles. We both work hard and we don't have nearly enough time to do the things we'd always said we would. His heart attack was a timely warning that we don't have all that many years left. I choose to see it as a positive thing, a reminder that it's time we both put ourselves and each other first.'

'Just like that?' Lavender's voice was thick and there were tears in her eyes. Ottilie might have felt that way too, but she had such empathy for Fliss's position that although she didn't want her to go any more than Lavender did, she understood that it was a positive step, one that Fliss and Charles deserved. Hadn't she herself been thinking that she ought to dedicate more time to Heath? How many times had she cursed that she'd never done it with Josh? Of course Charles's close call would make Fliss do the same.

'I understand it might seem sudden,' Fliss said. 'But I can assure you it's not. Just because I haven't mentioned it, doesn't mean I haven't been thinking about it. In all honesty, it's been at the back of my mind for some time, even before Charles's heart attack, but every time it came to the fore I put it on the back burner and got on with things. *Next year*, I kept telling myself, *think about it again next year*. But what if there isn't a next year? If Charles's illness has made one thing very clear, it's that there are no guarantees of a next year.'

She glanced at Ottilie, a glance loaded with understanding. Ottilie gave a tiny nod.

'Can't you go part-time?' Lavender asked.

'Lavender,' Ottilie cut in, 'it sounds to me like Fliss has made up her mind. And we all know that part-time in a job like that is never really part-time.'

Fliss nodded slowly. 'I'd always be thinking about the surgery even when I wasn't there. I'd need a partner, and I'd be worried about continuity of care if there was more than one doctor seeing a patient. I'd end up going into work even if it wasn't my turn.'

'You'd be bored if you retired now!' Lavender insisted. 'I know you – you'd last two minutes before it started to drive you mad!'

Fliss was quiet, her gaze on the hills again. 'I must admit that had crossed my mind too.'

'Then why don't you take on a partner and carry on with reduced hours? We'd make sure you didn't do more than you were meant to…' Lavender looked at Ottilie for support. 'Wouldn't we?'

Ottilie shrugged. 'Yes, but ultimately it has to be Fliss's decision.' She turned to Fliss. 'I haven't known you anywhere near as long as Lavender, but I think I know you well enough to know that you might be tempted to make your decision based on what you think we want, but this time you can't. You have to think of yourself and Charles and what's best for you both. Obviously I'm on the same page as Lavender – I'd miss working with you and I would wish you to stay – but I'm not going to say so.'

Fliss gave her a small smile. 'Thank you. Shall we walk some more? Perhaps a bit more oxygen to the brain will make things seem clearer. I must admit, I hadn't expected quite such a strong reaction to my announcement. And I know what you're saying, Ottilie, but it is making me question my decision.'

'I can see why, but if you think it's right, then please don't.'

'But I wonder if there might be another option. You said the locum is very good and he's looking for a permanent position.'

'Yes, but…'

'I don't know whether a part-time role would suit him, but I suppose it can't hurt to ask.'

'You mean take him on as a partner?' Ottilie asked as they began to walk the path again.

Fliss smiled. 'Let's not get ahead of ourselves. But I wonder whether he might be persuaded to join our team.'

Ottilie turned her gaze to the tarn, catching a diving flash of dazzling blue-green. That elusive kingfisher again? She couldn't allow herself to be too hopeful, but if Fliss was determined to spend more time with Charles but she wasn't ready to let go of the surgery just yet, perhaps drafting Simon in was the perfect solution. Whether he'd be on board with the idea was another matter entirely.

CHAPTER TWELVE

As she did every work morning, Ottilie knocked and pushed open the door to Hilltop farmhouse to check in on Darryl and Ann before she went on to the surgery for her clinic. This time, she was pleased to smell bacon on the air, a moment later seeing Ann at the stove.

'You look better!' she said.

Ann turned with a smile. 'Good morning. I'm feeling much better. Thanks to you and Dr Stokes. He is lovely, isn't he?'

'Yes,' Ottilie replied.

'Want a cup of tea?'

Ottilie nodded and sat at the table. Darryl was in his usual spot, and he was engrossed in a book. Ottilie glanced at it but then did a double take. It wasn't his usual book – the train encyclopaedia she'd bought for him that he pored over every day – but a new book. It contained photos of trains, but Ottilie could tell straight away they were different.

'Morning, Darryl,' she said. 'New book?'

He looked up. 'Yes.' He held it up to show her. 'It's got trains in it.'

'I can see that. It looks good.'

He nodded briefly and then turned back to it.

'Have you had your insulin this morning?' she asked.

When she got no reply, she looked up at Ann, who nodded.

'That's good,' Ottilie said. 'So everything seems nice and calm here this morning. It's good to see you up and about, Ann.'

'It's good to be up and about…' Ann put a mug of tea and a plate of bacon sandwiches down in front of Ottilie.

'A sandwich too?' Ottilie smiled. 'I'm being spoiled this morning.'

'Well, it ought to be a lot more than that, considering all you do for us.'

'Oh, it's nothing – only doing my job.'

'That's what Dr Stokes said when he came over last night.'

Ottilie held back a frown. 'He came over last night? After surgery?'

'About seven. Said he'd been doing some overtime at the surgery and wanted to see if we were all right before he headed home.'

'But home for him is Liverpool! God knows what time he got back!'

'Is it?' Ann mused. 'Well, that's extra kind of him. And he brought this book over for Darryl. Said it was one of his favourites as a boy and he'd searched it out because he thought Darryl might like it.'

'Looks like he does,' Ottilie said. 'That was nice of him.'

'Darryl wasn't sure at first, but I think he likes him now. He's anyone's for a train book.'

Ottilie smiled. 'That's true.'

'It's a shame Dr Stokes won't be with us for long; it's not often Darryl takes to a man. He's very wary, you know. Feels safer with women.'

'We've still got Dr Cheadle, and she's a woman.'

'Yes, but even so, I think it might have been good for him to build up some trust with a man, you know? There's been nobody since his dad and, well… if I'm honest, Darryl and his dad didn't always understand each other. His dad could get impatient and Darryl got frustrated; they didn't communicate well, even though they loved each other.'

Should Ottilie mention that Simon might well be staying in Thimblebury? She quickly decided not to. The matter was far from settled and she didn't want to get Ann's hopes up. Besides, if Fliss decided to offer him a part-time position and continued to work herself then Simon wouldn't always be the GP who visited on the occasions when they needed one. He'd clearly made an impression on them, though. And he was starting to make quite an impression on Ottilie too. Nobody had asked him to come and check on Ann before he'd gone home but he'd done it anyway, and he'd taken the time to search for a book he'd known Darryl would like. She was beginning to hope that Fliss would offer him a permanent position and that he'd say yes. She liked him more and more with each day she worked alongside him.

Darryl lifted the book to his face and almost squealed with delight.

'Must have seen a good one,' Ann said with a fond smile.

'Must have done,' Ottilie agreed. She drank her tea. It was a bit hot, but she could see she wasn't needed here and there was plenty to do down at the surgery. 'If you two are OK I'd better get off. Thank you for the sandwich.'

'I thought you probably haven't had breakfast yet.'

'As always, you're spot on.'

'Would you…?'

Ann was suddenly shy and she hesitated.

'Yes?' Ottilie picked up her sandwich.

'Would you mind taking something to Dr Stokes? He's there today, isn't he?'

'Yes.'

Ann went to the fridge and took out a plastic container. 'It's some millionaire's shortbread,' she said, flushing as she handed it to Ottilie. 'I gave him the last bit of one yesterday and he said it was delicious so I made another one.'

'I'm sure he'll love it,' Ottilie said. 'That was a lovely thing to do.'

'He's been so kind to us, and I know he'll be leaving soon, so…'

Ottilie smiled as Ann flushed again. It seemed the charming and handsome and very kind Dr Stokes had been weaving his magic spell here too. He seemed to do that everywhere he went. Unless Ottilie was very much mistaken, Ann was a little bit in love with him.

'I'll make sure he knows where it came from,' Ottilie said as she waved them goodbye and headed off to work.

The lunchtime tradition of eating together that had been instigated by Fliss had fallen by the wayside in her absence. Simon mostly stayed in his consulting room and ate whatever sandwiches he'd brought with him while he caught up on paperwork, and while Lavender and Ottilie still got together in the kitchen, more often than not, they also ate food they'd brought in from home for themselves. Lavender had agreed that with only two of them contributing it just wasn't the same and didn't seem worth it.

Lavender was already in the kitchen eating a salad when Ottilie arrived, her stomach growling after her clinic had overrun by a good twenty minutes.

Lavender looked up from her plate. 'What happened?'

'Mrs Icke.' Ottilie flopped into a chair and Lavender grinned.

'You should have phoned through to me – I'd have cooked something up to get rid of her.'

'You'd have needed the three-minute warning to shift her today,' Ottilie said wearily.

'But she's so deaf she wouldn't have heard it.'

'She's not deaf, though, is she? She's selectively deaf. Hears well enough when it suits her.'

'Fliss is in,' Lavender said.

Ottilie sat up. 'Here?'

'In with Simon.'

Ottilie detected a triumphant little smile. Lavender was trying to keep it from her face, but she wasn't doing a very good job.

'Now,' she said, a note of caution in her tone. 'Just because she's in with Simon doesn't mean we've won that battle.'

'So you admit you want her to stay too?'

'Of course I do, but I don't want it if it isn't what she really wants. I'd hate that.'

Ottilie reached for the teapot and touched a hand to it. It wasn't exactly piping hot – Lavender had probably made it twenty minutes before when they were supposed to have broken for lunch – but she was so thirsty it would do.

'But it's a good sign she's gone in to see him.'

'It might be nothing to do with her retirement plans. She might be keeping abreast of progress for one of her patients. She might be signing some paperwork for the agency. Who knows? We're jumping to a big conclusion.'

'But you know Fliss – she doesn't mess about. When something needs doing she gets on and does it. I wouldn't be surprised if she didn't go home and talk to Charles about it straight after she'd been with us and she'd have made her mind up within the hour.'

'Usually, yes, but she does have other things to think about. Like Charles.'

Lavender smiled. 'I see what you're trying to do there. And I get it. You don't want to be disappointed, and you don't want me to be disappointed, and I appreciate that. Let's see, eh? With a bit of luck we'll know by this afternoon.'

'What makes you say that? Surely Simon's got to think about it too, even if Fliss is talking to him about it right now.'

'Yes, but you're pally with him. You can get his early reaction, can't you?'

'No pallier than you.'

'Oh, you are! He's always popping into your room for a chat.'

'About patients, yes!' Ottilie said with a little laugh.

'It's more than I get.'

Ottilie poured some tea. 'Lavender, he comes to reception as often as he comes into my room.'

'How do you know if you're in your room?'

'Because…' Ottilie paused. 'I just do.'

'I'm telling you he doesn't.' Lavender had a sudden wicked gleam in her eye. 'I think he fancies you.'

'Don't be daft.'

'He's all smiley when you're around.'

'He's like that with everyone. He's just a nice guy. I was up at Hilltop this morning and he'd been there with a new book for Darryl. Nice guy with everyone – it's as simple as that.'

'If you say so.'

Ottilie took her lunch from her bag, trying not to be annoyed at Lavender's teasing, and then noticed the plastic container with Ann's millionaire's shortbread in it. She hadn't been able to see Simon that morning to pass it on. Seeing it now reminded her that she needed to do that before he left for the day.

'Do you think Fliss will pop in after she's done with Simon?' Lavender asked. 'Maybe I should reboil the kettle just in case.'

'I would imagine so, assuming they're done before afternoon session starts.'

'She'll have to be done because Simon will have patients to see to.'

'Maybe not with much time to spare, though.' Ottilie narrowed her eyes and regarded Lavender over the rim of her mug before taking a sip. 'You want to know what's gone on, don't you?'

'No,' Lavender replied, looking sheepish anyway. 'I only wonder if she'll have time to say hello. Anyway, don't pretend you don't want to know because you absolutely do.'

'And I'm sure we'll find out in good time.'

Lavender folded her arms and grinned at Ottilie. 'Spoilsport. Play the game with me, would you?'

Ottilie couldn't help but grin in return. 'You're terrible.'

'I know, but you love it. I bet I'm the best doctor's receptionist you've ever worked with.'

'You're the only doctor's receptionist I've ever worked with.'

'Hey, I'll take the small victories.'

Ottilie shook her head, still smiling. 'Daft sod.'

She was about to say more about it when her mobile began to ring.

'Sorry, got to take this.'

Lavender's smile faded. 'Looks serious…'

'It's Josh's old workmate,' Ottilie said as she hurried from the room.

Out in the surgery garden it was chilly, Ottilie's skin erupting with goosebumps. This garden had been witness to some intense conversations since she'd been employed here, and Ottilie had a feeling this was going to be another one.

'Hi, Faith. How are you?'

'Good. How's everything there? Still loving the country life?'

Faith sounded cheerful. It was a good sign. Ottilie allowed herself to relax a bit.

'It's great, actually. Lovely.'

'Those Sunday walks must be nicer than they are around here.'

'I can't say I go on that many. Too busy most of the time.'

Ottilie waited through a pause. Was there something in particular Faith had called for? They'd promised to keep in touch at the beginning, but contact had tailed off. Ottilie had started to feel that Faith only called when something was happening with the efforts to convict Josh's killer, and perhaps Faith felt that too, the calls dropping off because she felt they were unwelcome.

'Anyway,' Faith said finally, 'I wondered if you'd had a letter yet about the trial date?'

Ottilie frowned. 'Trial date? I didn't even know there was one.'

'I thought you might not. So much for the grinding wheels of justice, eh? More like ground to a halt. In that case, we've got a date. I was wondering if you had plans to come to the trial. I mean, I get it if you'd rather not… and of course, you're quite entitled if that's what you'd prefer. But I thought… well, I'd make myself available if I could, like while you're here.'

'There's no way of knowing how long I'd need to be in Manchester for, though, is there?'

'No, I suppose not. We might get an idea of how long it will last once we're up and running. But you have family to stay with, don't you?'

'I also have a job here and I don't know how easy it will be to get away from that. When's the trial?'

'Next month. That's if it doesn't get delayed, of course, and it's not like that never happens.'

Ottilie was aware of her heart suddenly beating in her ears. Did she want to face the man who'd taken her husband's life? Could she really be in the same room as him and be OK? She'd always imagined she would stand before him and make certain he knew who she was, because she wanted him to squirm with his guilt, but now that the reality was close at hand, she wasn't sure she could do it.

'I expect I'll get the letter through soon,' she said, fighting to gather her chaotic thoughts. 'I'll see what Dr Cheadle says when I do. I think that's the best way.'

'Sounds sensible to me. Listen…' Faith paused again. 'I'm sorry I've been a bit… well, I'm sorry if you think I've forgotten about you. I haven't; it's…'

'I know,' Ottilie said. 'It's OK. I appreciate you keeping me up to date, but it's weird, right? When we speak like this we're dragging up a tough time we'd both rather forget. I don't blame you – in many ways I feel like it's harder for you than it is for me.'

'You were Josh's wife.'

'Will always be Josh's wife, but I'm not still doing the job that killed him. I've made a new start and it's OK. In fact, though I feel guilty for saying it, it's good. I love it here. I miss him, but…'

'And there's… Is there anyone…?'

'Anyone else? No.'

The denial had come out before she'd even processed the question and Ottilie couldn't understand where it had come from. But she didn't want to tell Faith about Heath. Faith would think it was too soon; she'd disapprove. She'd wonder how Ottilie could move on so fast, how she could say she was devastated by Josh's death and yet be in a relationship with someone else. And the fact was, Ottilie had real, deep feelings for Heath, perhaps even close to what she'd had for Josh, but she could never admit that to Faith. Not now, at any rate, and perhaps never, even if she eventually came clean.

'Right, of course not. Sorry, I didn't mean to offend you. I only meant—'

'You didn't; it's totally fine. I suppose it's a natural question to ask. It's been almost eighteen months, right?'

'Exactly – that's what I meant. People do start to think about it after that sort of time, don't they? Not that I know, of course. But it's what I heard. But I suppose everyone's different.'

'Listen, I'm sorry but I have to—'

'God, of course, you must be at work. I'll let you get on. Just wanted to keep you in the loop.'

'Thanks, that's really good of you. I don't know what I would have done without you since it happened.'

'Take care of yourself. And let me know what you decide.'

'I will. See you soon.'

Ottilie ended the call. With a deep breath, she pocketed her phone and headed back inside. Lunch break was almost over and there were patients waiting to be seen. There would be a time to unpick the tangled knots of her thoughts, but this wasn't it.

CHAPTER THIRTEEN

Another weekend was fast approaching. Ottilie's week had been strained, with news of the trial from Faith and having learned Fliss hadn't yet decided whether she was going to retire or not, or whether Simon was going to stay.

'All right, Ottilie,' Geoff said cheerfully from behind the counter. 'Want your bread rolls? We were getting low so I thought I'd put some up for you just in case.'

She put her milk on the counter. 'Yes, I'll take them as you've saved them for me.'

'Sounding a bit weary there. Long week?'

'Kind of,' Ottilie said, forcing a smile for him.

Ottilie got out her reusable bag, and Geoff took it from her to pack her groceries. 'Have you seen much of Flo this week?' he asked.

'Not really. It's been one of those funny weeks where I don't seem to have had time to see anyone. Why?'

'No reason. Only that she came in yesterday and didn't seem quite herself. I mean, she can be a bit cranky, but she seemed worse than usual.'

'Oh, you know she can be up and down,' Ottilie said, trying to believe her own words but a vague concern crept over her. 'I'll call later, though. Thanks for mentioning it.'

'I'd call, but I think she opens up to you a bit more. You know, because of you and Heath.'

'Of course.'

Geoff looked a little mischievous now. 'And how is that going?'

'Good,' Ottilie said as neutrally as she could. Perhaps, on a different day or in a more positive mood, she might have been more enthusiastic. The truth was, her relationship and her new troubles with Heath had been on her mind more and more of late. There was all the weirdness around Mila, which they still hadn't put the time aside to fully address, and the fact that he still hadn't said those three little words to her. People could be in love without having to say it – she knew that well enough – but that coupled with everything else was unnerving. Her doubts were growing daily – was her relationship with Heath really as strong as she'd believed it to be?

'Only good?'

'Very good.'

'So we might hear wedding bells soon?'

'God, no!' Ottilie spluttered. 'It's way too soon for that!'

Geoff's face fell. 'Could you hurry up? It's ages since we had a decent wedding round here.'

'I'm sorry to disappoint you, but it might be a bit more ages. We're…' She paused. What were they? She still wasn't entirely sure she knew. 'Taking it steady,' she said finally.

Geoff nodded. 'Very sensible.'

Sensible was a word she often heard in the same sentence as her name. That was her: sensible Ottilie Oakcroft. Sometimes she wished she could be something more exciting, but she supposed she could only be what she was.

Ottilie left the shop, wondering if she ought to check in on Flo on the way home. It might be nothing, but if there was a problem, she knew from previous experience that uncovering it early was a good idea where Flo was concerned.

She was tired and she wanted to get home, but if she was going to see Flo without Heath (and she had a feeling that would be more productive), then she was going to have to do it immediately because she had an entire weekend full of Heath planned.

The sun was already sinking below the horizon as she took the path to Flo's cottage, the temperature dropping rapidly. There would be a frost, and the sooner she was at home with her fire on the better. Just one more errand, she told herself, and then the evening was all hers to ruminate on what the week had brought.

The knock echoed down the lane. A minute later, Flo opened up. She looked tired but still managed a smile.

'I wasn't expecting to see you tonight! I thought you'd be coming over with Heath this weekend.'

'I was. I mean, I am. I was just passing and thought I'd call in to see how you're doing.'

Flo gave a keen look. 'Just passing, eh?'

Ottilie laughed. 'All right. I can't get anything past you, can I? I wasn't passing, but I was sort of around and I did want to see how you were doing.'

'You could have done that with Heath.' Flo nodded for Ottilie to follow her down the hallway.

'I know,' Ottilie said as she went in and closed the front door, shutting out an ochre sunset. 'But sometimes it's nice for us to have women chats, you know. You can't talk about the same things when there's a bloke around.'

'That's true. What's on your mind then?'

Ottilie found a space to sit in Flo's cramped living room. Not cramped because it was small – although it was – but because of the countless ornaments and souvenirs that littered every surface. Flo always said she was a collector, but Ottilie would have called it hoarding. Still, she knew that Flo had a story for every piece and that everything was important; Flo wouldn't have kept it otherwise. She might have been a bit of a hoarder, but there was still a system.

'It's not so much what's on my mind as what's on yours.'

'Mine?' Flo looked up sharply as she settled on the sofa. 'Why would there be anything on my mind? Has someone said something?'

'No. I'm only saying, if there was anything on your mind I'd be all ears if you wanted to talk about it.'

'Nothing on my mind,' Flo grumbled. 'I suppose you want a cup of tea now you're here.'

This was Flo's way of saying she'd be upset if Ottilie didn't stay for tea, and so she nodded. 'I'd love one if there's a cup going spare.'

Flo pushed herself up again and went to the kitchen. Ottilie could hear the sounds of the tap being run to fill the kettle and then it being set to boil.

A moment later Flo returned. 'You've opened a can of worms, you know.'

Ottilie blinked. 'What do you mean?'

'Heath's ex-wife. She saw you out with him, didn't she?'

'How did you know that?'

'Because she wanted to know about you, that's how. No shame, that woman. I can't believe she dared to phone me after everything she's done. I can't believe I even gave her the time of day but she caught me off guard. Don't worry – it won't happen again. Next time I hear that voice I will put the phone down.'

Ottilie shifted awkwardly, unsure why she suddenly felt so unsettled by the notion that Mila had been asking about her but knowing that she did all the same. 'What did she want to know?'

'Oh, I didn't tell her anything. Fool me once and all that. Was a time I might have fallen for it, but not now.'

'She didn't come here, did she?'

'No, no…' Flo waved away the notion. 'Only on the telephone.'

Ottilie wanted to ask if Flo thought that would be the end of the matter, but it was obvious by the accusation that she'd opened a can of worms that it was far from the end. She had the worrying feeling that it was only the beginning. Was this the reason Flo had been so tetchy with Geoff?

'Did it upset you to hear from her?' Ottilie asked. 'Only last time she was trying to get money from you.'

Flo didn't reply. Instead, she went back into the kitchen and Ottilie heard her making the tea.

'So what time shall I expect you and Heath tomorrow?' she asked when she came back in with their drinks. 'Will we be going out anywhere? Let me know in plenty of time so I can look for my mac – it's given out rain.'

'Um, I don't know. Heath hasn't mentioned plans. I could ask him to let you know.'

'You'd have thought he'd have the brains to do that himself. Gets that from his mother.'

Ottilie was well acquainted by now with the fractious nature of Flo's relationship with her daughter-in-law, so she let the comment slide. Any chance to get a dig at Heath's mum was a chance Flo grabbed, sometimes even at the expense of the grandson she adored.

'Flo… I'm sorry, I know you don't want to talk about her, but…' Ottilie paused. Was this a good idea? 'Should I be worried?'

'About what?'

'About Mila.'

'Oh, no!' Flo threw her hands into the air. 'God, no! Heath thinks the world of you!'

'It's not Heath I'm thinking of. I've heard things about Mila. She can't really be as bad as she sounds, can she?'

'She'd see you for the sap you are a mile away – best to keep well clear.'

Ottilie frowned. 'What's that supposed to mean?'

'Don't get me wrong, everyone around here loves you to bits, but you are a bit wet.'

'Thanks!' Ottilie huffed. 'I don't even know what to say to that.'

'Trust me, if she comes knocking, don't open the door.'

'She can't be that bad! You're making her sound like Al Capone!'

'Hmm…' Flo put her cup to her lips and slurped a mouthful of tea.

Ottilie watched her. She knew Mila had tried to con her and had caused plenty of trouble during her marriage to Heath, but was she really that bad? And she had a new man now. Then again, she had phoned Flo asking about Ottilie. Why? Curiosity? Perhaps. Perhaps Ottilie could give her the benefit of the doubt. Plenty of women would be curious about their ex's new partner, wouldn't they? If not, what could she possibly want from Ottilie? It wasn't like she had money or anything else Mila might want.

There was Heath, of course. What if Mila had never got over him?

No. Ottilie shook off the thought. That would be insane. They'd been divorced for ages, so why would anything happen now? And there was no way Heath would take her back even if she did want him. Would he? Her mind went back to the restaurant where they'd bumped into her, and she remembered the pure hatred on his face, and she thought now, as she'd thought then, that nobody could hate like that without caring. Was he really over her?

'Is Dr Cheadle back yet?' Flo asked, breaking into Ottilie's thoughts.

'Not yet.'

'I doubt she'll come back,' Flo returned sagely. 'She's not getting any younger.'

'She's not that old.'

'Still… What about that new man?'

'Dr Stokes?'

'Is he staying? Lavender says he might.'

'Lavender would,' Ottilie said wearily. Of course Lavender had been gossiping all over Thimblebury about him. 'I don't have a clue. I don't even know whether it's been discussed.'

'Lavender says it has. Says they were in there today talking about it.'

'If they were, it's more than I know. Fliss could have been signing his agency timesheet for all anyone knows, Lavender included.'

'Is he foreign?'

'No.'

'Only Lavender says he's only recently come to England.'

'He's only just come *back* to England.'

'Oh. So is he any good?'

'Brilliant, actually. I think Thimblebury could do a lot worse than him offering to stay. But he drives in from Liverpool every day so I don't know how feasible that would be long-term.'

'Couldn't he buy a house here?'

'He could try, but knowing how little there was for sale when I was buying I don't think it's quite as simple as that. I suppose he could move a bit closer if it was worth his while.' Ottilie sipped at her tea. 'You're very interested in our locum doctor all of a sudden.'

'I like to know who's going to be looking after me in my dotage, that's all.'

'It might well be Fliss, so I wouldn't worry about it yet.'

'Lavender says she wants to retire.'

Ottilie let out an impatient sigh. *Bloody Lavender…*

'That doesn't mean it's set in stone. She talked about it – that's all.'

'I don't expect she can manage nowadays. At her age.'

'She's not that old!'

'Hmm. Everyone says the new man is very young.'

'I think he's about forty, so not especially.'

'He looks young.'

'I suppose he must be lucky then.'

'Good-looking too.'

'I suppose so, if you like that sort of thing.'

'Must be nice to have him decorating the place all day long.'

'What do you mean – decorating?'

'You know, must be easy on the eye. Nice to look at.'

Ottilie held back another deep frown. 'I don't think what he looks like has anything to do with it. He works hard and we'd have sunk without him when Fliss went off.'

'Lavender fancies him.'

'Lavender never said anything to me like that.'

'I can tell. And I'll tell you who else fancies him… Magnus does. Geoff doesn't like that at all.'

'How do you know that?'

'Geoff told me.'

'Did he?'

'Not in so many words…' Flo folded her arms. 'But I can tell what he meant. And Stacey. Fair fainting over him, the whole village… Can't see it myself.'

'Neither can I,' Ottilie said firmly. 'I mean, he's a lovely man and, yes, I can appreciate he's handsome, but that's as far as it goes for me.'

Flo gave a slow, silent nod, as if she was mulling over Ottilie's statement, and then seemed satisfied. Ottilie wondered if she'd been somehow concerned that Heath might get shoved aside for Simon. It sounded silly, but then again, Flo had been hugely invested in her grandson and Ottilie getting together. In fact, she'd done her best to engineer it from the moment she'd met Ottilie.

'I'm more than a bit partial to Heath,' Ottilie added. 'And no handsome new doctor will change that.'

'I never thought it would,' Flo said, a defensive edge to her tone.

'I know. But I'm saying it anyway.' Ottilie gave a conspiratorial smile and leaned in. 'So Magnus has a thing for him?'

This seemed to cheer Flo no end. Her troubled frown turned into a grin. 'Oh, you don't know the half of it!'

Once Ottilie had phoned Heath and told her about Faith's news, he arranged for them to spend that Sunday in a spa. He'd said she'd earned it, and he hoped it would help her relax, but Ottilie could tell his heart wasn't in it when he arrived to pick her up. Her misgivings hadn't been helped by the fact that they'd been meant to spend the entire weekend together, but he'd been forced to cancel their Saturday plans, saying he was snowed under with work. Somehow, Ottilie couldn't help but feel this was an excuse, though she tried not to see it that way. But was it more than that? Was there a problem? Was it a bigger deal than she wanted to believe?

'What's wrong?'

He kissed her vaguely as she got in the car. 'I could ask you the same thing.'

'Nothing's wrong with me except trying to work out what's wrong with you.'

'I'm fine.'

He turned the key in the ignition, and Ottilie closed her mouth, swallowing back any further interrogation. His tone told her he wasn't in the mood to discuss it, but if he was trying to convince her there was nothing going on, he was doing a terrible job. Something had happened. Was it to do with Mila? She cursed herself. Why was it her mind always went there lately? Why was she so fixated suddenly on Heath's troublemaking ex? Stupid Ottilie. She was spiralling, and she was heading to a bad place if she didn't get a hold on this and sort it out.

The spa hotel was an hour away. As they drove in, however, she was beginning to think it might be harder work than a spa day was ever meant to be. She'd sensed an edge in the car, a strange atmosphere that had made conversation more awkward than it had ever been between them. She couldn't tell if it was Heath's fault or hers, but it was there just the same.

'This looks lovely, doesn't it?' Ottilie grabbed his hand as they walked towards the vast row of white columns that heralded a grand entrance. The venue was a renovated stately home, beautiful and elegant, with perfectly manicured grounds and a pristine gravel path that crunched beneath their feet. Some would say it was a bit too clinical, especially compared to the wild and wonderful garden of Wordsworth Cottage, Ottilie's home, but if it meant some desperately needed pampering and relaxation, Ottilie could cope with that.

'What's first?' she added. 'The pool? Oh, have they got a sauna? They'll have a sauna, right? And a hot tub? What about one of those hydro things? You know, the ones that massage you? Have they got one of those?'

'Are you thinking of doing them all at once?'

Ottilie let out a little laugh. Things had been strained on the drive over, but perhaps she'd sensed tension that hadn't really been there. Perhaps it had come from her rather than him. She still had things on her mind, but she was optimistic, now they'd arrived, that today would go a long way to helping ease that stress.

'But what do you fancy doing first?'

He turned and raised a saucy eyebrow, and her laughter grew.

'I mean in the spa,' she chided.

'You want to do it in the spa? I don't think the manager will be happy about that. And as for the other customers…'

'Stop it!' Ottilie shoved a playful elbow into him. 'You know what I mean.'

'Do I?'

'Yes, so stop teasing me.'

'OK, OK… I've booked you a massage first. And then I thought maybe we could get hot stones or… whatever you like.'

'Facial? I could do with some tightening up.'

'Tightening up? What are you talking about?'

'You know, a bit of nip and tuck, a bit of smoothing here and there.'

'Don't be daft. I mean, have a facial if you want one, but to me, you're perfect as you are.'

'Well, I love that, but I'm still going to have one if I can. How about you?'

'You think I need a facial?'

'No, silly. I mean what treatments do you fancy?'

'I don't know… I expect I'll spend some time in the pool and maybe do some reading. Have a nice lunch with my best girl, you know… that sort of thing.'

Ottilie pulled him into her. 'So where is she?'

'My best girl? I don't know. I'm sure she'll turn up at some point.'

'Cheeky.'

'You wouldn't have me any other way.'

'You're right, I wouldn't.'

. . .

While Heath checked them in, Ottilie browsed a list of treatments. He'd already booked a massage for her, and she'd told him she wanted one or two other things too, but there was also a bit of her that didn't want to be separated from him, even for the short time her treats would last. This was meant to be a couple's day after all, so what kind of couple's day was it if they weren't doing anything together? So she decided against the facial but would suggest they went for a sauna or perhaps a dip, and then got lunch.

Then they stowed their belongings in a locker and got changed into fluffy robes and slippers, the fabric wrapping around Ottilie like an embrace, her cares instantly lifting from her. She felt a ton lighter, and as she emerged from the changing area to find Heath waiting for her, she could see the same look on his face too, despite the fact he'd insisted that the day was for her to de-stress, not necessarily for him. Judging by the way his brow had cleared, he'd had his own burdens, whether he'd admit to them or not. Ottilie wasn't surprised – everyone did. If he got as much from this day as she did, then it would be a day well spent.

'I'm so up for this,' she said as Heath offered his arm and they made their way to the sauna.

'Me too. It's weird, isn't it? You think you're relaxed when you go home after work or whatever, but you're not really relaxed. You need something like this to properly let go, but you don't even realise that until you get it.'

'Absolutely. Let me tell you, I haven't felt relaxed when I've got home from work this week. It's been a hell of a week, in fact.'

'Oh? Anything I should be worried about?'

'Oh, the usual. By which I mean, not usual at all, but only the stuff I've already told you about. But honestly, that's more than enough.'

'I can imagine. Same here. But that's what today is about.'

'Well, I love it. Thank you so much for booking it.'

They spent an hour alternating between the sauna and the plunge pool, sleepy in the first one and exhilarated in the second, and by the time they'd done there, Ottilie's skin was tingling and she was already more relaxed than she'd been in months. She went off to her massage and Heath went to the pool to do some lengths and wait for her. The massage finished the job that the sauna had started, and by the time she found him sitting on a lounger poolside with the latest Lee Child novel, she was about ready to take a nap, and she told him so.

'It's lucky we don't have a room booked,' she said as she sat next to him. 'If we had, I'd have been tempted to go and get forty winks.'

'You could have done.'

'But I wouldn't have wanted to waste a single minute of this lovely treat.'

'I think it's lucky we don't have a room booked as well.'

Ottilie clicked her tongue against the roof of her mouth but she was smiling. 'You're terrible.'

'You're gorgeous – can I help myself?'

Laughing, she ran a hand through her hair. 'I've done sauna, plunge pool and massage, and you think I look gorgeous? I must look as if I've been dragged through a hedge by my legs.'

'You do. I wouldn't say it if it wasn't true.'

'Yes, you would.'

'Maybe.' He grinned. 'But I mean it.'

Ottilie leaned in to kiss him. She'd never been a public kissing type of woman, but just this once, she didn't care who was watching. Pressing his lips to hers, he took her breath away, and she had to agree that it was a good thing they didn't have a suite reserved because they'd have been in it, and there wouldn't have been much relaxing going on.

'Want to swim?' he asked, pulling away, his eyes still locked onto hers.

'I suppose I could fit in a length before lunch.'

'I told you we don't have a room booked…'

Ottilie let out a saucy giggle. 'I don't even know what to say to that!'

'Sorry, I couldn't resist it. Seriously, though, we could have a quick dip and then see about getting some food. I'm feeling peckish.'

'Me too. I haven't looked at the menu yet. Have you?'

'No, but I hope they have the salmon on. It's really good.'

Ottilie's forehead creased into a vague frown. 'I didn't realise you'd eaten here before.'

'Oh, yeah…'

Heath shifted on his lounger, and something in his expression was suddenly guilty. Or was that in Ottilie's imagination? Why would he be feeling guilty? Weren't they having the loveliest day? Hadn't they both been fancying the pants off each other, only moments before?

'Oh…' Ottilie paused, struggling to piece something together that made no sense. 'So you've been here before? I thought this was your first time too.'

He nodded slowly. 'Yeah. Ages ago.' He rose from the lounger, shed his robe and walked towards the pool. 'Coming?'

The crease in her forehead etched a little deeper as she watched him get into the water. He'd never told her he hadn't been here before, but at the same time, when he'd booked it, if he had, surely he would have said so? It was a natural thing to do. If it had been the other way round she'd have told him before they arrived. There was no reason not to. Unless…

She followed him to the steps and got into the water. He was already swimming towards the deep end, and she struck out after him. He got to the end and turned to face her, ready to go again, but she held out a hand to stop him.

'When did you come here?' she asked.

'A few years ago, I think. Does it matter?'

'No, I just think it's weird you didn't mention it earlier.'

'I didn't think it made any difference. We're still having a nice day, aren't we? I knew we would because I knew it was nice. I wouldn't have brought you if I hadn't known that.'

'You might have done. It's never stopped you before – we try new restaurants neither of us have been to all the time.'

'I never thought it was an issue. I don't know why it is – why are you suddenly so hung up about it?'

'I'm not. It feels like you are.'

'I'm not either.'

Ottilie didn't want to ask the next question, but it seemed to have a life of its own, because it came out anyway. As soon as it had, she wished she'd been able to stop it.

'Did you bring Mila here?'

He didn't answer, and that was enough to tell her the truth. She watched him swim back to the shallow end.

It didn't matter. He'd had a life before her, in exactly the same way she'd had a life before him. He'd had Mila and she'd had Josh. It didn't matter, did it? He was bringing her to a place he already knew about. But why not tell her that? Why the secrecy? And why this place? She'd never take him to a place she'd been with Josh, not deliberately. Yes, there'd been that one restaurant in Manchester, but that had been his suggestion and she'd not had the heart to rain on his parade. And they hadn't ended up eating there anyway because Mila had turned up.

Mila – the queen of raining on parades, it seemed, because, try as she might not to let it bother her, Ottilie suddenly hated that Heath had brought Mila here long before he'd brought her. And perhaps she could have forgiven it if he'd been upfront. Was she being unreasonable for feeling this way?

She swam back along the length of the pool, trying to shake her doubt and irritation. He'd done a lovely thing for her – that was the only thing that mattered, wasn't it? It wouldn't be fair to ruin it over some petty, irrational jealousy that made absolutely no sense. It wouldn't be fair to either of them, because until this point, she'd been having a great time.

'I'm hungry,' Heath said as she reached him for the second time. 'Let's go and eat, eh?'

Ottilie wanted to argue. She wanted to talk more about what had just happened between them. She wanted to let it go. She wanted to forget it had ever been said, and that she'd ever had these feelings. She didn't know what she wanted or how to feel. She could only nod.

'OK.'

But she knew she'd sit across from him in the dining room and she'd look at the menu and wonder how much of it he'd tasted with Mila in her seat. How many times had they been there together? Was it a regular thing or a one-off? Was it significant? Did it hold special meaning for them? Had he proposed there? Had they rented a suite and made love there when they hadn't been able to contain themselves? Ottilie hated herself for dwelling on things that she knew didn't matter. He wasn't there with Mila now; he was there with her. He'd parted from Mila and she knew there was no love left, so why did she feel this way about her discovery? There was no reason or logic to it, but still she couldn't help it.

As she watched him go to retrieve his robe from the lounger, she had a sudden yearning to go home. The shine had gone from the day and she didn't know how she was going to get through the rest of it. But she was afraid to ask, because she knew where that would lead and she didn't want to go there. He'd be hurt, and she'd seem unreasonable, and they wouldn't be able to understand each other's points of view and it would get horribly messy. It might even be their first full argument. It might even be the beginning of the end. Despite this, she cared for Heath and she didn't want to lose him before they'd even had a chance. No matter what it took, she had to make this right somehow.

She climbed the steps to get her own robe, a sudden chill and goosebumps on her dripping skin. Heath watched her, his own robe now wrapped around him. As she pulled hers on too, he reached for her.

'Listen… I'm sorry. I should have told you.'

'It doesn't matter—'

'I can see it does. I didn't think it was a big deal but I was wrong. I only brought you here because I knew it was a nice place and I knew you'd like it. I should have searched for somewhere else.'

'It's lovely…' Ottilie was shivering.

'You're cold?' He frowned.

'I'm fine. Must be all the in and out of the water and whatnot.'

He pulled her into an embrace, her cheek pressed against the softness of his robe. It smelled of the outdoors, though Ottilie suspected that was the soap powder because there was a faint tinge of the unnatural about it, not like when she dried washing on her line in her little garden in Thimblebury, where it was all fresh air and mountains.

'Forgive me?'

'There's nothing to forgive.'

'Why do I feel as if that's not true?'

'I'm sorry.'

'You have nothing to be sorry for. I'm the idiot. It never occurred to me until now that it might even be an issue me coming here with Mila.'

'That only makes me feel worse.' Ottilie looked up at him. 'It makes me feel stupid for my reaction, like it's totally out of proportion. If it didn't even occur to you then that means I overreacted to something that meant nothing.'

'You didn't!' He let out a sigh. 'Ottilie, if it matters to you then it matters. I should have seen it – I'm the stupid one, not you.'

'If I ask you something, promise it won't…' Ottilie shook her head. 'Never mind.'

'What? You can't start that conversation and then just drop it.'

'I can because it's silly, and I already know the answer.'

'What did I just say? If it matters to you then it matters. That applies to anything, no matter how small or silly you're afraid it might be. So ask me.'

'I don't want to. It's insulting and you'd have every right to be annoyed. I'd rather leave it.'

He bent to kiss her again. There was no lust this time, only confusion and worry and sadness and an attempt to reassure her that he clearly wasn't convinced he could pull off. All the sudden uncertainty and doubt they now both felt was in that kiss. It was almost a kiss to gauge her reaction, to see how far she was willing to forgive the huge mistake he must have now felt he'd made. Ottilie had done that, and in the kiss she offered in return there was remorse.

She told herself it didn't matter, just as she'd done before, but it would never be true. And in the back of her mind the question still lingered, the one she was too afraid to ask. He'd told her about Mila, about how difficult his life with her had been, that their relationship had been toxic and doomed from the start, and yet he'd once admitted that he'd loved her so much he'd struggled to let go, even when he'd known how bad she was for him. So the question was this: despite what he said, did the fact he'd brought Ottilie here today mean on some level he still thought about Mila? Did he sometimes wish he was still with her? Did he still love her?

Ottilie was afraid of the answer but even more afraid that she might never know.

CHAPTER FOURTEEN

The day had been strange and difficult after Heath's admission. Ottilie had tried hard to let go of it, and she suspected Heath was overcompensating for his mistake – at least, the one he thought he'd made, though she felt that for her to call it a mistake was unfair – and it only made things worse. They'd forced jollity and affection over lunch, and thank God salmon wasn't on the menu. In the afternoon Ottilie had decided it might be a good idea to give him some distance and so had booked herself into some extra treatment sessions while he went into the gym.

As she lay with her eyes closed, having lotions and potions applied to her face, she ought to have been more relaxed than ever, but her mind was teeming. She and Heath had been seeing each other for four months now, and yet she was reminded on a daily basis – and never more than this day – that four months was still very new and uncertain. She'd taken for granted when Josh had been around how easy married life was. Not easy in the sense that they never argued or that they never encountered difficulties, but easy in the sense that they knew each other's souls in a way that only years together can do. She'd look at Josh and she'd know what he was thinking. She could see when he needed company and when he needed alone time, when he needed consoling and when he needed to brood. She knew the things that would hurt him if she did them, and he understood her in exactly the same way. Sometimes they thought exactly the same thing at the same time and an explanation was seldom needed.

She couldn't remember them getting to that point. It had seemed like a natural progression too subtle to notice, and yet it must have been exactly like this with Josh in the beginning. Looking at things now with Heath, it also felt like it would be a long time before she got to that point with him, and the mechanics of that journey were laid out so plainly that she felt daunted by it. Could they do this? She had no doubt that she wanted to go the distance with Heath, but wanting and achieving were two very different things.

Ottilie had also wanted to ask him whether he knew Mila had been trying to contact Flo again. He hadn't mentioned it, though she realised now that him not mentioning it didn't mean anything. It would have been a difficult conversation, but far easier than it would have been before Mila had thrown her shadow over their day. It would seem as if Ottilie was on a special vendetta, out for some kind of character assassination rather than genuine concern for Flo's well-being. And it *was* genuine, as was the need to understand how Mila still fitted into Heath's life. No matter how he denied it, how many times he told Ottilie that he didn't think about her, the fact was she had a past with him which inevitably still had some effect on his present and would probably continue to influence his decisions into his future. That much was obvious, even if Heath chose not to believe it.

Ottilie was also convinced that their encounter at the restaurant wasn't the last time they'd ever run into her. If nothing else, it seemed Mila would make sure of that. Her enjoyment of the moment, of Heath's obvious discomfort, of causing such emotional chaos had been written all over her face that day. And from what Ottilie had heard, she wasn't the sort of woman to give that sort of sport up easily.

They'd chatted all the way home in the car, but for all the good humour, it had felt forced. Heath had come inside for a drink but didn't stay long, announcing that he had an early start in the morning and needed to get a good night's sleep. So Ottilie kissed him goodbye and was left to watch television alone, trying to follow the plot of a thriller, but really her mind was taking her back over and over the events of the day, more and more mortified at her own behaviour and more confused about Heath's with each visit.

Ottilie had just made her morning call to Hilltop Farm and was pleased to see Ann making good progress and all calm with Darryl. It was also exciting to have the promised bicycle ready for collection. She'd taken a sneaky turn around the farmyard on it and was looking forward to picking it up later after work and going out for a ride. And she was still munching on a doorstop of toast with jam Ann had made from her own strawberry crop when she arrived at the surgery and Lavender almost leaped over the reception desk to greet her.

'Fliss is in with Simon again!'

Ottilie crammed the last corner of toast into her mouth. 'Is she?'

'She was here really early.'

'How do you know?'

'Because she was here when I got here, and I was early.'

'Hmm…' Ottilie dropped the greaseproof paper her toast had been in into the bin behind the reception desk and leaned across to look at a patient list showing on the screen. 'Well, whatever it is, I'm sure we'll hear about it later.'

'How can you be so calm about it?'

Ottilie looked up. 'There's no point in being anything else, is there? What are we meant to do? Listen at the keyhole?'

Lavender grinned. 'There's an idea!'

'You're welcome to try.' Ottilie laughed lightly as she unbuttoned her coat. 'I'll wait until Fliss or Simon are ready to tell us. It might not even be anything to do with us anyway.'

'It is – I feel it in my bones.'

'You want to see a doctor about that,' Ottilie replied as she went through to her own office. She could still hear Lavender laughing as she closed the door and switched on her computer.

Ottilie was in no doubt that Lavender had a point – Fliss was in early, and they knew she'd been deliberating her future at the surgery. There was a good chance that this morning's meeting was a follow-on from that, but though Ottilie was dying to know as much as Lavender was, there was no point in speculating.

The clinic had been a gruelling one and it had overrun, as it seemed to do a lot these days. Ottilie could have sworn Lavender was sneaking extra patients onto her list and not telling her, because the flow seemed to be never-ending. Much of it was blood-pressure checks, breathing tests, diet progress, wound dressing and other routine things that Ottilie could do with her eyes closed, but now and again one of her patients would throw her a curveball, making an appointment for a routine thing and then dropping something more challenging into the visit. This morning she'd been invited to examine some unexpected haemorrhoids, and a bunion so big it needed its own extra shoe. She'd no sooner seen Mrs Icke off than Fliss popped her head around the door.

'Are you free for a moment?'

'Of course!' Ottilie went to give her a brief hug. 'How is everything? How's Charles doing?'

'Really well actually. The cardiologist is pleased, though he's complaining like mad that I won't let him go back to work yet.'

'That sounds good then. So… I'm guessing this is not a social call?'

Fliss stepped into the room and closed the door behind her. 'Nothing gets past you, does it? No, it's not. Well, there is a social element to it and there is business too. It's sort of all connected if you like.'

'Right.'

'I've come to a decision about my retirement.'

'I thought as much.' Ottilie offered Fliss a seat, but the GP shook her head.

'I won't keep you. Much as I want to tell you all about it I am aware that now's not the best time. I've mentioned it to Lavender and she's amenable, so I wanted to ask if you could come also. I was thinking about cooking dinner one evening this week. The soonest everyone is free. If we must discuss it, we might as well do it over some good food.'

'That sounds good.'

'So when are you free?'

'For something this important I can be free any night you like. Has Lavender got a preference?'

'Lavender says her diary is fairly empty too, and Simon will stay behind if needs be. In fact, they're both free tonight if you are?'

'I mean, yes, but does that give you enough time to cook?'

'I was thinking Italian. I've got what I need in for a rustic pasta dish, if you don't mind slumming it.'

'It'll hardly be slumming it if you're cooking,' Ottilie said with a smile. 'Tonight sounds brilliant. Might as well get it off your chest as soon as you're able, eh?'

'Then we'll all know where we are going forward, won't we? Seven suit you? Don't want to keep Simon here too late as he'll be driving back to Liverpool afterwards.'

'Seven is perfect. I'll see you then.'

. . .

Ottilie had finished work later than she'd meant to. She hated turning up to dinner at someone else's house empty-handed and had been hoping to throw together some kind of dessert or side dish but was now running out of time. In fact, she'd be lucky to get a shower and make herself look presentable in the time she had left. Rifling through the cupboard produced a bottle of red and a box of chocolates that she had spare, and at this point they'd have to do.

She'd just put them out to take and was heading up to shower when her phone started to ring.

'Hi. How's your day been?'

Heath sounded like he was in a good mood. Ottilie was glad to hear it after their strange day at the spa, but while she didn't want to put him off, she was in a bit of a rush.

'Good,' she said briskly as she raced up the stairs, phone to her ear. 'Interesting, actually.'

'Oh?'

'Fliss has made up her mind.'

'About her retirement?'

'Yes. She's invited us over to talk about it.'

'You and Lavender?'

'And Simon.'

'Simon?'

'The locum who's been covering for her. Dr Stokes.'

'Oh, right! What's it got to do with him?'

'Well, I'm not sure yet. There was some talk of asking him if he wanted to stay on. It makes sense, as he's already used to the surgery now. And he's looking for a permanent job. Or rather, I think he still is.'

'And the patients of Thimblebury haven't managed to put him off yet?'

'Doesn't look like it. I mean, I'm only guessing this is how it will go – I have no idea yet. I might be on the wrong track completely.'

'Right.'

There was a pause. Ottilie was about to explain how much of a hurry she was in when he spoke again.

'I wanted to clear the air.'

'Does it need clearing?' She sat on the side of the bath. 'What for?'

'Yesterday at the spa… I didn't mean to… It was wrong of me not to tell you I'd been there before.'

'Heath, I thought we'd cleared this up. It's OK.'

'But it wasn't OK, was it? And don't say it was because I could tell. I should have said something yesterday but… I don't know… I didn't want to mess it up or make it worse by saying the wrong thing. Can I come over?'

'Tonight?'

'I could be there in an hour and I wouldn't keep you up late. I just want to—'

'I'm sorry. I'm going over to Fliss's.'

'Is that tonight?'

'Didn't I say?'

'You said you were going over but you didn't— I didn't realise it was tonight.'

'Yeah. I mean, I could put them off, but…'

'God, no. This can wait.'

It didn't sound like it could wait. And now that he'd brought it up, Ottilie realised she wanted this conversation as much as he did, but she'd committed to something else now, and it was too late really to change it without upsetting Fliss and putting everyone else out.

'I'm sorry. But Fliss is cooking, and Simon has stayed behind from surgery, and—'

'No, I get it. I said it could wait.'

Did Ottilie detect the merest hint of impatience in his tone? Or was that in her guilty imagination?

'Maybe I could phone you back when I'm done there?'

'It might be late.'

'It might be, but I could if you think it would help.'

'I think…' He paused again. 'I think I'd prefer to do it face to face. It feels too easy to mess up on the phone.'

Ottilie frowned as she picked the lint from a towel. What was it he needed to say that he could possibly mess up? She was filled with a sudden dread. Surely he wasn't thinking of ending things? Had their misunderstanding caused that much damage? Surely not?

She shook the notion. He sounded calm enough, if a bit awkward. He didn't sound like someone who was about to dump her.

'What do you mean?'

'I mean it's easier to get crossed wires, isn't it? It's easier to mistake someone's tone.'

'We could FaceTime?'

'Still…'

'How about I let you know when I'm home and you decide if it's too late to FaceTime or not?'

'Maybe. But it could wait until I see you.'

'I don't think it can. I don't think you can put ideas like this in my head and then make me wait.'

'What does that mean?'

'Heath… what's so bad you need to say it in person?'

'Nothing!'

To her relief, Ottilie could hear humour in his voice now.

'God, nothing bad!' he repeated. 'I just think we need to clear the air. I owe you some explanations, and I'd rather we talk them through in person. Honestly, that's all it is.'

Sometimes it felt as if they were going backwards. Instead of being more certain as time went on, Ottilie was more confused. She longed for that day when they'd be as comfortable as she'd been with Josh, but she had to wonder, as she tried to work out now what exactly was going on here, whether that day would ever come.

'I…' He stalled again, and once again Ottilie was thrown. 'I get it – you need to be there tonight.'

'Sorry, but I do. I wish I could…'

She was about to say she wished she could get out of her commitment with Fliss, but actually, why would she say it when it wasn't true? Why did she feel the need to placate everyone all the time, pretend their needs were more important than hers when they weren't? People-pleasing Ottilie. Safe, reliable Ottilie. Here she was again, and she wasn't going anywhere in a hurry.

'I could see you tomorrow if you want.'

'It's OK; I've got a lot on. We're meant to be going out Thursday anyway, aren't we? Let's leave it at that, eh?'

Ottilie nodded, and then realised he couldn't see it. 'Yes. If you want.'

Ottilie said goodbye and went back to her shower. She was still unsettled and unhappy with the way they'd left things, but there was no time to think about that now.

CHAPTER FIFTEEN

Rustic pasta had never smelled so good. Ottilie arrived at Fliss's house at the same time as Lavender and she could smell the herbs even from outside the front door. They both held up their bottle of red.

'Snap,' Lavender said. 'You can't go wrong with red when you're coming to Fliss's house.'

'Has it been in the fridge?'

'Of course!'

'Mine too. Is it just me who finds that cold red thing weird?'

'It's weird. She's weird, but she's our weirdo.'

Ottilie smiled and knocked. 'I wonder if Charles will be eating with us.'

'Me too. I hope so. I like Charles and it feels as if we haven't seen him in ages. Too much excitement for him, right?'

'Us? You might be, but I'm definitely not!'

A moment later a smiling Charles opened the door.

'Speak of the devil!' Lavender kissed him lightly on the cheek.

'And he shall appear – yes, I know. Hello, Lavender.' He turned to Ottilie. 'Hello, Ottilie. Both bang on time, of course. And of course, we're not. Fliss is still cooking, so I thought I'd better rise up from my sickbed to get the door before she finished the job the heart attack didn't manage. Come on in. Simon's already in the sitting room.'

'How are you doing?' Ottilie asked as she and Lavender followed him inside.

'I'm no expert, but I appear to be doing very well,' Charles said. 'Or so I'm told, though I confess I don't feel like someone who's doing well. I'm exhausted all the time, but I suppose that's to be expected for a while.'

'You look well,' Lavender said.

'Thank you. I have a good GP on hand, which gives me a head start on most.'

'It must do.' Ottilie smiled as she handed him her bottle. He looked tired and she could see now why Fliss was refusing to let him start work again. He was probably fretting about it – both he and Fliss were committed to their jobs – but he didn't look strong enough to Ottilie to be stressed this soon, even if he did look and feel better than he had straight after his heart attack.

'Ooh, lovely, thank you.'

Lavender did the same.

'Take a seat in the sitting room,' he said, making his way to the kitchen with the wine. 'We'll call you through in a minute. Just got to go and mop the chef's brow.'

Simon was browsing a vast, ceiling-high bookcase when they went in. He turned at the sound of Lavender's greeting.

'Hello, Dr Stokes. Fancy meeting you here.'

'Ah, Lavender! Indeed!' Simon gave a low chuckle. His gaze flicked to Ottilie. 'Hello. You both look lovely.'

'Now I know he's buttering us up for a good reason,' Lavender said with a wink at Ottilie. Then she turned back to Simon. 'So you're being extra nice to us. Is that because you're going to be asking us for lots of favours at work soon? Is there something you want to tell us about staying at Thimblebury surgery more permanently?'

'I don't know what you mean.' Simon smoothed his face into a picture of innocence. 'Can't a bloke give his colleagues a compliment these days?'

'Charles looks well, doesn't he?' Ottilie said as she took a seat on the sofa.

'I thought so,' Simon agreed. 'I'm sure Fliss is making sure he doesn't overdo it.'

'Well, if you can't have a speedy recovery when your wife is a doctor then you've got no hope,' Lavender said, taking a seat next to Ottilie. But if she'd meant to make Simon laugh again, he didn't. In fact, he suddenly looked strangely reflective.

'Yes,' he said, though his gaze went to the window, as if he wasn't acknowledging Lavender's comment at all, but something else.

All three turned at the sound of Charles poking his head around the door and announcing that dinner was finally ready. Ottilie might have been tempted to ruminate on Simon's strange response, but dinner was calling and all else would have to wait.

Fliss was ruddy-cheeked as they filed in to take a seat at the table. Ottilie bit back a grin. She suspected that rather than it just being from cooking, there might have been some wine involved.

'Hello, hello… welcome… Take a seat, everyone – never mind where, no place cards or that nonsense at my house. Wherever you like… Wine, everyone?'

Lavender shot Ottilie a look that told her she'd thought the same, and that Fliss was probably way ahead of the wine game already.

'Thank you,' Ottilie said. 'It smells amazing.'

'Oh, it's nothing special,' Fliss replied, nodding for Charles to take a seat too and then going to the fridge.

'It's your dirty macaroni,' Charles said with a hint of pride in his voice as he sat down. 'It's always special.'

'What's that?' Simon asked. 'Sounds… interesting.'

'Oh, we had it on holiday in Dubrovnik years back,' Fliss said. 'It's actually called sporki macaroni, but sporki means dirty in Croatian so that's what we always call it. It's not exactly the way they cooked it there, but I've been experimenting for years, trying to recreate it. I don't think I'm far off.'

'I think it's spot on,' Charles said.

'That's because you've forgotten what the original tasted like,' Fliss replied, going to the stove. 'You've been eating my version for so long you think that's how it was back then.'

'What's in it?' Simon asked.

'Slow-cooked beef and red wine and other odds and sods.' Fliss stirred the contents of a large steel pan. 'You did say you eat meat, didn't you?'

'Oh yes. Sounds amazing.'

'That's good, because if not that then you'd have to go to the cupboard and open some crisps – I don't have anything else to offer you.'

After one last sniff, a quick taste and a final sprinkling of salt, Fliss brought the pot to the table and set it down on a trivet. Next to it she'd already placed a basket of bread, a butter dish with a fresh pat of creamy yellow butter in it and a large bowl of leafy green salad. She'd also put out olives and breadsticks and other bits and pieces. It was all very informal but elegant – effortlessly so, in fact, a bit like the way Ottilie always saw Fliss. Even when she was trying to be casual she had a sort of class that shone out from her.

'This all looks incredible,' Lavender said. 'We must have done something very good to deserve such a treat.'

'You have,' Fliss said. 'I don't know what I would have done without the support of this wonderful little team over the past few weeks.'

'Me neither,' Charles said. 'Because Fliss was able to have such confidence in you all to take care of the surgery, she was able to take care of me. I'm quite sure I wouldn't be sitting here with you all now if not for her.'

'Of course you would,' Fliss said briskly. 'Don't talk rot.'

Lavender let out a giggle. 'Poor Charles.'

'I know.' He rolled his eyes. 'Pour my heart out, try to give the woman a compliment and what do I get? You see now what my married life is like? People think I must have it made but they don't see this.'

Ottilie smiled. Despite how they teased or reprimanded or chided one another, she knew that there were few more devoted couples than Fliss and Charles. The villagers of Thimblebury gossiped about them often, speculated on the fact that they'd never shared a home, how they appeared to have entirely separate lives. Some saw what Ottilie and Lavender did – that no matter what anyone thought about it, the way they inhabited their marriage worked for them, and it worked brilliantly. Others couldn't understand it, and some were convinced it was a marriage of convenience, though Ottilie couldn't imagine what they thought there was to be gained from such a strange one, where there was no reason to do it.

Ottilie held out her plate and Fliss scooped a ladleful of the pasta onto it. 'More?'

'God, yes, please!' Ottilie grinned. 'If it's not depriving anyone else.'

'There's buckets of the stuff,' Fliss said. 'Eat as much as you like. I'll be happy if you approve enough to eat more than one plate.'

'If it tastes as good as it looks, I might run off with the pan,' Simon said.

Fliss beamed at him. 'I know it's not done to blow one's own trumpet, but I like to think that it does. Should I booby-trap the pot just in case?'

'I think you might have to.'

Lavender had her plate filled, and then Simon, and then Charles. Finally, Fliss served some for herself and took a seat, reaching for her glass. 'Bon appétit.'

A chorus of complimentary and contented voices rippled around the table as everyone tucked in and gave their opinions on the dish. Ottilie had expected it to be good, but she was surprised to find it was incredible. She wasn't sure she could replicate it, and if she tried it would never be as delicious as this, but she quickly decided to ask Fliss for the recipe before she went home so she could make it for Heath.

Despite the relaxed conviviality and polite chatter, Ottilie couldn't help but feel a sense of anticipation hanging in the air. Fliss's decision was the reason they'd all gathered, but as yet, the subject of her retirement hadn't been broached, and Ottilie wondered whether she'd save it until they'd eaten.

As usual, Lavender was less inclined towards tact and jumped straight in with both size sixes. 'So, are you are going to tell us your plans?'

Fliss exchanged a look of amusement with Charles.

He smiled. 'Nothing changes, I see.'

'Sorry, but I thought…'

'Yes, there's an update,' Fliss said. 'I was going to wait until we were on the pudding course and a bit more wine, but as you seem so eager to know, I'll tell you.' She glanced at Simon, who smiled. It was obvious he knew what was coming. 'I've decided not to retire just yet, but I am going to cut my hours. And Simon has kindly agreed to stop on.'

'For how long?' Ottilie asked.

'I'm looking into making him a partner. There are some details to iron out, but…'

Lavender sat up. 'That's brilliant!'

'It is!' Ottilie agreed. 'Congratulations, Simon. I'm so happy you're both going to be staying at the surgery.'

Simon inclined his head, his smile growing. 'Thanks. I'm happy too. I wasn't sure about being in such a small village at first, but it's weird how Thimblebury grows on you. I had to think about it for a bit—'

'For far too long,' Fliss cut in. 'A woman could be offended by that, you know.'

Simon's smile turned into a grin. 'Sorry about that. But now that it's all sorted, I'm really looking forward to getting started properly.'

'When will that be?' Lavender asked.

'Well, I suppose I'll have to serve some sort of notice to the agency, but the good thing is I can do that while I continue to work here, so the transition ought to be so smooth nobody will even notice it. The only thing that will really change is who pays my salary.'

Ottilie reached for her wine. 'That's really good news. Looks as if everything has worked out pretty well.'

Fliss nodded. 'I'll say. Certainly better than I ever could have hoped for.'

Ottilie turned back to Simon. 'So are you still going to commute back and forth? It's a long way to do that many times a week.'

'Well, that's the other big change,' Fliss jumped in again. 'Sorry, Simon, don't mean to steal your thunder but…'

'No, go ahead. It's your news really.'

'This one won't affect either of you,' Fliss added, looking at Ottilie and Lavender. 'But Charles and I have finally decided, after thirty-six years of marriage, that we're going to move in together. I'm sure there will be many in the village who would say it's about time.'

'Wow,' Ottilie said. 'I didn't see that coming. What's changed your mind?'

Perhaps it was obvious really, but Charles was happy to elucidate.

'I think,' he said, 'that she wants me where she can keep an eye on me in case I decide to almost die again.'

'That's a good enough reason as far as I can see,' Lavender said. 'Which house is going up for sale? That's going to be news in itself – nothing ever goes up for sale round here. I think the last one was Wordsworth Cottage.'

'I think so,' Ottilie agreed. 'Lucky for me.'

'Charles is going to move in here.' Fliss topped up her wine and then began to work her way around the table doing the same for everyone else. 'We're going to keep hold of Rosemary Cottage, though. Simon is going to rent it from us for the foreseeable future.'

'A handy escape route, eh?' Lavender said with a wry smile. 'Don't buy, in case you don't settle.'

'Actually,' Charles said with a laugh, 'it's more to do with us wanting to keep hold of it in case our domestic arrangement doesn't work out. We've never lived together before – we might end up hating each other. And you said yourself, nothing comes up for sale around here, so once we've let it go then that's it, gone.'

'But what if that happens?' Ottilie asked. 'What about Simon?'

'Oh, I expect I'll find something,' Simon replied in Charles's stead. 'If not here I could look a bit further afield. Even a couple of towns away isn't going to be as bad as driving back and forth to Liverpool every day like I am now.'

'Quite.' Fliss glugged a mouthful of wine from her glass to make room for the last drops in the bottle. Charles raised his eyebrows meaningfully and she waved it away. 'You're only jealous because you can't have any.'

He picked up his glass to show her. 'I've got some here.'

'You can't have any more then. That had better be the last one. You've barely set foot out of hospital – I don't want you rushing back in there again.'

Charles turned to Simon. 'Actually, I've changed my mind. Can I have Rosemary Cottage back?'

Everyone started to laugh except Fliss, who shot a sour look Charles's way, though nobody was convinced she meant it.

Ottilie's smile lingered even as her laughter faded and she gazed around the table at every face, happy. This promised to be the best possible outcome for the surgery. If she'd had all the powers in the world to make anything happen, she couldn't have made any of this better. She loved working with Lavender and Fliss and she had a feeling she was going to love working with Simon once the post was official too.

CHAPTER SIXTEEN

A couple of weeks after Faith had called to let Ottilie know about the trial date for Josh's attacker, exactly as Faith had predicted, Ottilie received a letter saying it had been postponed. She quickly decided it was best not to work to a date and simply wait and see. When it happened, it would happen, and she ought to leave it at that. And so she went about her days as before, trying not to think about it. There was plenty to keep her busy after all, not only at work but also all the extra things she did in her spare time, like the monthly film club, which was fast approaching.

Heath had always found the notion of Magnus and Geoff's film club a bit ridiculous, and while Ottilie could see it to a point, she sometimes felt his opinion was unfair. She enjoyed it and saw it as a way to connect on a regular basis with Thimblebury's community. Heath rarely approved of their film choices either, but the way Ottilie saw it, the film wasn't important, because it was never really about the film but about them all sitting together and talking about it afterwards.

She always looked forward to their monthly meet-up, but whenever she told Heath this, his expression was more than sceptical. Manchester was far more metropolitan than tiny Thimblebury and there were way cooler things to do there. His attitude to film club made her think that if Heath were to relocate for her, he would miss them a bit too much, and whenever she allowed herself time to dwell on the possibility it worried her. She couldn't leave Thimblebury now, but if Heath felt the same about Manchester then where would it leave them if their relationship ever got to that stage?

Simon, on the other hand, was as keen to settle into village life as she herself had been when she'd first arrived in Thimblebury. 'Or die trying' were his actual words, which had made Ottilie giggle for the rest of the day after she'd heard them. So when she and Lavender had told him about film club and how much fun it was, he immediately wanted to know when the next meeting was and if he would be able to join.

And so Ottilie decided to mention it as she popped into the post-office-cum-general-store for some milk on the way home that evening.

'He's staying on?' Magnus scanned Ottilie's goods into the till with a satisfied smile.

'Looks like it.'

'That *is* good news.'

Geoff was sitting a few feet away at the other end of the counter. He looked up from his iPad. 'You would say that.'

'You get on with that ordering and stop interfering,' Magnus replied mildly.

Ottilie looked from one to the other with a vague frown.

'Fancies him,' Geoff said.

'I don't.'

'Yes, you do. After all these years together you don't think I can tell when you fancy someone?'

'I can appreciate he has lovely symmetrical features,' Magnus said, winking at Ottilie. 'That's all.'

'I suppose he does,' Ottilie said.

Geoff went back to his ordering. Ottilie couldn't tell if he was hurt or if he was joking, but she wondered what else had been said in private between the two of them. They hadn't been getting along all that well – Stacey had said so, and Ottilie had seen it first-hand – but surely it was nothing serious? She couldn't imagine Thimblebury without Magnus and Geoff and their film club.

'Which reminds me,' she added. 'I told him all about film club and he wondered if he'd be allowed to come along one time.'

'Of course,' Magnus said. 'The more is merry.'

'The more the merrier,' Geoff corrected him.

'That's what I said.' Magnus started to pack Ottilie's groceries into a cloth bag she'd given to him. 'Anyone who's interested in movies is welcome to come.'

'That's what I thought, but I wanted to check.'

'It's not often full anyway because not everyone comes every time.'

Ottilie took the bag from him. 'I thought that too. So I'll bring him to the next one?'

'Sure, why not? I'm sure we can squeeze him in somewhere.'

'Great! What film are we doing by the way?'

'*Midnight Run*.'

'Is that the one with Robert De Niro and that comedian?' Ottilie couldn't help a grimace, and Magnus laughed.

'Lavender's choice – what can you do? It was her turn after all.'

'I'm sure a couple of wines will help it go easier,' Ottilie said. 'What a way to introduce Simon to the club.'

'What makes you think he won't like it?' Geoff looked up from his iPad again.

'OK.' Ottilie smiled. 'You've got me there. I'm sure it's just me who's not so keen, and I suppose that is the point of film club, isn't it? Makes us watch things we wouldn't normally choose.'

'That and an excuse to drink lots of wine and eat nibbles,' Magnus said. 'We'd love to see Simon there. What about your Heath? Will he be coming this time?'

'I don't know; I haven't managed to ask him yet.'

'I'm not sure Flo will when she hears what the film is,' Geoff said. 'She can be awkward as anything when she's not keen.'

'What makes you think she won't like it?' Magnus asked, throwing his own words back at him.

Geoff rolled his eyes. 'Because this is Flo we're talking about and she complains about every film we show.'

'And you can't argue with that,' Ottilie said. 'I love her to bits but even I can't stick up for her there.'

'I don't know where you find the patience,' Magnus said as Ottilie made her way to the door to leave.

'Aww, she's not so bad when you understand her.'

'That's the problem,' Magnus said as Ottilie opened the door. 'I don't think I'll ever understand that woman as long as I live.'

Stacey was on her way in as Ottilie left the shop.

'Hey, stranger,' she greeted. 'Where've you been hiding? Haven't seen you for ages.'

Ottilie laughed lightly. 'It's only been about a week.'

'It feels like longer. I should take that as a compliment. So you've been busy. Work, I suppose? I hear a certain doctor is staying on. What do you have to say about this rumour? Is it true? Are my sources correct?'

'I forget how fast things get round this place,' Ottilie said, and it suddenly occurred to her that Magnus might have been pretending not to already know about Simon so as not to steal her thunder. Sweet, but not necessary – Ottilie was under no illusions about the efficiency of the gossip wheel in Thimblebury. 'He is. Who told you?'

'Now, now, you know that's not how it works. I have to protect my sources or they won't tell me anything again.'

'Lavender?' Ottilie raised her eyebrows and Stacey laughed.

'I will neither confirm nor deny.'

'It was Lavender then.'

'And I hear he's going to be relocating to Thimblebury.'

'That's the plan, I think.'

'So we'll be seeing a lot more of him.'

'Possibly.'

'I'd like to see a lot more of him… and I'm not talking about living here.'

Ottilie grinned. 'You're terrible. I'll pretend I didn't hear that. How's everything with you anyway? Any more on Chloe's secret boyfriend?'

'Apart from the fact that she won't tell me anything so now I definitely know there's a boy, not really. It's like something from an espionage film – every time her phone rings she sneaks out with it and she's whispering. It'd be funny if it wasn't so ridiculous. What does she think I'm going to do? Ask for proof of honourable intentions and a copy of his latest bank statement? I don't care who she sees as long as he's a good'un and he makes her happy.'

'I seem to recall I was a bit like that when I was younger,' Ottilie said. 'I don't think my parents ever met a boyfriend until I got serious with Josh.'

'I was like that when I was about fifteen but I'd got it sorted by the time I was Chloe's age.'

'Aww, I suppose she's being cautious after her bad experience with Mackenzie's dad. How is the cutest little man in Thimblebury by the way?'

'Oh, he gets more gorgeous every day. Listen… what are you up to tonight?'

'Not a lot.'

'Fancy coming round to mine for an hour? Chloe will be out and I'm babysitting, but Mackenzie will probably be down by about eight, and he more or less sleeps through the night now. It'd be good to catch up. I wanted to run some ideas for the mum and baby group by you as well.'

'That sounds lovely.'

'Great! Turn up whenever you're ready!'

After a quick shower Ottilie headed back over to Stacey's house. They hadn't arranged to eat, but she had some curry left over and decided to take it with her so they could share it. Even if Stacey had eaten, Ottilie was so hungry she was certain she could manage the entire lot by herself. She was still thinking about it when Stacey opened the front door, the relaxed and fun version from earlier gone and replaced by a face etched with worry. Mackenzie was in her arms, red-faced and screaming.

'What's wrong with him?'

'I don't know. He started with a temperature all of a sudden. He's boiling and he won't stop crying. I've tried to call Chloe home, but she's not answering her phone.'

'Want me to take a look at him?'

'Would you? I was going to call the doctor but I knew you were coming over anyway so I thought I'd wait to see what you said.'

Ottilie gave a brisk nod and followed Stacey inside.

'Thank goodness you're here.'

Stacey went to the living room and sat on the sofa. Ottilie took a seat next to her and opened her arms to take Mackenzie.

As he was passed from his grandma to Ottilie his cries seemed to get even angrier and more desperate. Ottilie put her hand to his back. 'Really hot… Do you have a baby thermometer?'

'Somewhere, but I can't find it.'

'Has he been sick or had a bad tummy or anything?'

'No.'

'Not coughing or anything like that?'

'No.'

'Hmm…' It was then that Ottilie noticed a subtle rash on his chest. Her breath caught in her throat. 'Would you get me a glass?' she asked as calmly as she could.

'A what?'

'A clean glass – a tumbler will do.'

Looking confused, Stacey dashed out into the kitchen. Ottilie looked at Mackenzie, dread in her heart, hoping to be very wrong. 'Oh, little man…' she murmured. 'What is going on with you? Please don't do this – anything but this.'

Her thoughts were lightning fast because she needed to act fast. With a free hand she got out her phone and started to dial Fliss's number. If they'd been in Manchester right now she'd have been calling for an ambulance, but this was Thimblebury, miles away from the nearest ambulance station, and the easiest and fastest course of action was to get Fliss over here.

But the call went to voicemail as Stacey returned with the glass.

'What do you think it is?' she asked, handing it over, though her face told Ottilie that she was beginning to work it out.

'I don't know,' Ottilie lied. 'I'm just checking… Could you get my phone and look for Simon's contact and call him while I…?'

As Stacey dialled the number, Ottilie rolled the glass over Mackenzie's rash. She allowed herself to breathe again as she noticed that it seemed to fade with the pressure. It wasn't absolutely certain, but it was hope.

'Hello…? I'm with Ottilie… I think she wants to ask you about…'

Stacey handed the phone over and took Mackenzie into her arms. Ottilie could hear his cries fade as she took him into the kitchen, presumably so Ottilie could hear what Simon was saying.

'What's the matter?'

'This is a long shot,' Ottilie said briskly. 'I know you stayed behind to do some paperwork and…'

'I left about ten minutes ago. What's wrong?'

Ottilie's heart sank. She'd been pinning her hopes on him still being in the office, but she should have realised he'd have gone by now. She shouldn't have wasted time trying to get hold of him. She ought to have bundled Mackenzie into her car and driven him to the hospital herself.

'Ottilie…' Simon repeated. 'What's wrong? Has something happened at the surgery? Is it Charles?'

'No, nothing like that. It's my friend's grandson. He's about five months old, he has a really high temperature and a rash I don't like the look of at all. I was hoping you'd still be at work. I can't get hold of Fliss. It doesn't matter – I'll run him to the emergency department now.'

'I think it's the best course of action. I could come back, but if it's what you suspect then there's not a lot I could do anyway and every second counts. The best place for him would be hospital. Put him in the car and take him there. I'll come to you.'

'You don't need—'

'Don't waste time arguing. I'll see you shortly.'

Ottilie thought again about calling for an ambulance but in the end decided her way was quicker. They went in Stacey's car, though Ottilie drove because Stacey was in no state and Mackenzie was better with her anyway. The roads were quiet, headlights sweeping through the gloom. Ottilie was aware of breaking the speed limit on several occasions, but if they got a fine then they'd have to deal with it. The most important thing was getting Mackenzie help, no matter what that took. Stacey was silent too, her attention on keeping Mackenzie as comfortable as they could and trying to get through to Chloe. They'd given the little boy something to try to keep his temperature down – Ottilie hadn't wanted to alarm Stacey, but if it went much higher she was afraid of fitting, or even more permanent effects.

Under her breath she muttered vague prayers to nobody in particular and sometimes curse words whenever the road or traffic held them up, eyes fixed on the road, face etched with concentration and purpose.

When they finally reached the hospital Stacey dashed in with Mackenzie while Ottilie found a parking space. She allowed herself a moment to release the worry tensing her shoulders. It wasn't over, but they were here and help was at hand.

As she made her way to the emergency department entrance to find Stacey, Simon approached from the opposite end of the car park.

'They're inside,' Ottilie said. 'We've only just arrived ourselves.'

'That's good.'

'I appreciate you coming but there probably isn't much point, you know.'

'I know. But I wasn't far away and I would have been dwelling on it at home so I might as well be here to help if I can. It might be I need to pull a few strings, have a word with the triage team to get him seen quicker.'

While Ottilie was touched and impressed by his dedication and support, she couldn't help but feel something more was going on here. He'd only been a locum GP in Thimblebury for a few weeks and he barely knew Stacey. He'd never seen her or Chloe as a patient, and Ottilie was fairly sure he'd never seen Mackenzie either. He was making a permanent move to the village and she supposed that might have some bearing on his decision to come here tonight, but it still seemed very much above and beyond his duties, even then. As she'd told him, the emergency team would be dealing with it now and there was very little for her to do here, let alone him.

But even as these thoughts floated vaguely through her mind, she couldn't process them. Stacey needed her and everything else would have to wait. There was no point in arguing with Simon either. Perhaps his influence would have no bearing on Mackenzie's treatment – in fact, it almost certainly wouldn't – but that didn't mean to say Ottilie wasn't grateful for the offer.

Inside, the waiting room of the emergency department was thankfully quiet. There was a woman and a girl who looked about ten and was nursing her arm, sobbing quietly, and a man with his hand in a blood-soaked bandage, though he was alert and joking with his companion, so clearly not too distressed. The walls were covered in posters bearing health advice and slogans about quitting smoking and only using the service for genuine emergencies, and orange plastic chairs were lined up in rows in front of a sweeping reception desk.

Stacey was at the desk now giving some details to a clerk. Mackenzie had stopped crying, his head resting on Stacey's shoulder as he gazed dolefully out. But the fact he was quiet now didn't reassure Ottilie at all. In fact, it made her more worried.

Stacey turned to sit down, but when she noticed Ottilie and Simon she seemed slightly taken aback.

'How's he doing?' Simon asked.

'I don't know,' Stacey said wearily. 'At least he's stopped screaming.'

'We gave him some baby ibuprofen,' Ottilie said to Simon. 'I expect that had something to do with it.'

She didn't really think that, and she knew he didn't either. It was more for Stacey's benefit, to keep her calm and hopeful. The last thing Ottilie wanted to do was scare her.

Simon seemed to understand and he nodded. 'That's good.'

As Ottilie and Stacey sat down, he went to the desk and spoke quietly to the same clerk Stacey had been giving her details to. A minute later, he thanked her and came to join them. Neither woman asked what he'd said, though Ottilie could guess he'd asked for some favour to bump them up the queue. She also suspected it was all rather academic, as their case would have been urgent enough to do that without his input. Mackenzie was a baby and his symptoms would have been concerning enough for that.

Whether it had been down to Simon or whether it would have happened regardless, they didn't have to wait long. Stacey and Mackenzie were called through to a treatment room, leaving Ottilie and Simon to wait.

'Hopefully they'll get to the bottom of it quickly now he's in,' he said.

Ottilie turned to him. He looked tired. 'You didn't have to come, you know. Not that we're not touched by it, of course. But if you wanted to head home, that's all right. There's not a lot either of us can do now and there doesn't seem any point in both of us being here for hours.'

'I know,' he said, nodding slowly. 'I'll stay for a while longer to keep you company if you don't mind.'

'God, no, I don't mind, but I do feel guilty that you're here. You must be shattered and you've got a long drive home yet.'

'It's my choice so there's no need for that. And I'd like to see he's OK.'

'I could let you know when they're out.'

'I know that too.' He glanced across at a vending machine. 'Want a coffee? I'm going to get one to perk me up before I drive home.'

'I thought you didn't drink coffee?'

'True, but sometimes you need caffeine. Do you want one?'

'I don't like coffee either, and the tea from those things is usually disgusting. I suppose if there's hot chocolate it'll probably be OK.'

'Chocolate… right.'

Ottilie watched him punch numbers into the machine. He was restless, up and down on the balls of his feet as he waited for their drinks to be dispensed. It was strange – she'd never seen him like that before. At the surgery he'd always been relaxed, confident, reassuring. They were in a stressful situation, yes, but surely nothing more stressful than he'd encountered before during his career. He must have seen far worse and more worrying cases than this.

As he turned back, she tore her gaze away, suddenly feeling guilty for staring at him. He handed her a drink in a plastic cup.

'It's nice to see they still put this stuff in cups so thin the top layer of your skin is burned off on contact,' she said as she took it, and immediately had to put it on the floor beside her chair.

'Yes, why mess with a perfectly good tradition?'

Simon seemed to be more resistant to the heat of his drink. But even then he winced as he took a sip.

'Is that because it's so disgusting or because it's boiling?' Ottilie asked.

'A bit of both. But it will wake me up, which is the point.'

'I'm sure you didn't need the taste buds on your tongue anyway.'

Simon relaxed into a tired smile. 'It's good Stacey has you here.'

'You too.'

'I didn't do anything except show up and be useless.'

'You didn't need to show up at all. Not many would have done, knowing it was all in hand and not in their remit to do it anyway.'

'I feel as if it *is* in my remit. I am going to be one of Thimblebury's GPs, after all. I owe it to my patients to do what I can, even when that's not much. The only reason I haven't been more involved is because it's out of hours and I wasn't there to see him first.'

Ottilie frowned. They were meant to have an out-of-hours service and someone should have been on call. That was supposed to be Fliss. It would be a difficult conversation, and Ottilie might seem to be overstepping the mark, but she'd have to say something about it when she next saw Fliss, because she wouldn't be able to leave it. She was meant to be available for an emergency like this, and while Ottilie understood that she had Charles to worry about, that fact remained. And perhaps she'd have only sent them straight to the hospital once she'd seen Mackenzie, as Simon had done, but to Ottilie that wasn't the point.

'I'm so glad you're staying on,' she said. 'Thimblebury is lucky to have you.'

'I don't know about that. I feel lucky to have Thimblebury right now. I wasn't looking forward to moving on again. I mean, I know that's part of the deal when you're a locum, but I didn't really want to be a locum long-term. It's a pleasant surprise to get a permanent job so quickly in such a nice place.'

'You don't feel it's going to be too quiet for you then?'

'Quiet is appealing these days. I had a lifetime's worth of excitement in Botswana. I can do quiet for a bit.'

'Was it stressful?'

'Challenging is more like it. I was working in a very cut-off rural area. Not enough equipment and what we had was often unreliable. If you're lucky enough to live in a city there's actually a decent system – the government there have invested hugely in improving it over recent years – but that system is yet to reach poorer areas.'

'I take my hat off to you. It must have taken guts to go.'

'Going was the easy bit,' he said, taking a sip of his coffee. 'What I left behind…'

Ottilie waited for him to finish his sentence, but he didn't. Instead, his gaze went somewhere she couldn't see. What she was beginning to see was tragedy, somewhere in his past, something that had made him run from his old life all the way to Africa. She saw it because she'd lived it herself. She'd been running from her grief when she'd first come to Thimblebury. Everyone had wondered how she'd had the guts to leave everything and everyone she knew behind at such a time, but for Ottilie, staying was so much harder that it was an act of cowardice, if it was anything at all.

After a few moments of silence he turned to her. 'You're a relative newcomer to Thimblebury, aren't you?'

'Last year.'

'Fliss tells me you lost your husband. Is that why you moved?'

Ottilie reached for her drink. It had cooled a little and she was able to wrap her hands around the cup, the synthetic aroma of cheap chocolate seeping into her head. 'I couldn't stay in Manchester. I worked at the hospital where he died. There were too many bad memories everywhere I looked. People would say to me that there would be good ones too, in time, that I'd be able to see them again, but I didn't have the strength to wait for that day. I just woke up one morning and thought: *I don't want to be here*. So I looked for a job and found my house, and that was that.'

'But you've settled? You like it there?'

'I love it. The community has been so welcoming. I arrived under a cloud but that didn't last. Now I couldn't imagine living anywhere else. Thimblebury is home.'

'It's certainly picturesque.'

'It's more than that. It's… well, it sounds cheesy, but I'd say living in the Lake District is almost a state of being. Like the landscape becomes part of your soul. I think I'd always carry that with me whether I stayed or not, and I'd always miss it.'

He raised his eyebrows. 'Wow? It's that good?'

'You'll find out for yourself soon enough. But don't shoot me if you don't end up feeling the same. Did you like Botswana?'

'It's a beautiful place and I sort of see what you mean about getting into your soul. I don't think I'd want to live there again but I don't think it will ever quite leave me.'

'What made you decide to come back to England? You'd had enough or something happened to make you leave?'

'I felt what I'd gone for I'd achieved. It had been a strange time in my personal life, but I felt as if I was coming to terms with that too. It just seemed like the right time to end that chapter and start a new one.'

'And so you ended up in a tiny village in the middle of England.'

'I must admit I never saw that coming. If you'd have asked me ten years ago where I'd be now in my life, I wouldn't have seen any of this coming. Not Botswana, not here, not… well…' He paused and cleared his throat, and then took a huge drink of his coffee. 'Not losing my wife and our baby.'

Ottilie looked sharply at him. 'I didn't know that.'

'I didn't say – how would you?'

'God, I'm… I don't know what to say. I'm so sorry.'

'I think that's why I enjoy talking to you. I know you understand what it's like. I'd like to think we'll become good friends one day.'

Ottilie nodded slowly, uncertain what to make of it all. She wondered if Fliss knew, but he answered the question before she'd asked it.

'I told Fliss about it when she offered me the job the other day. I asked her not to mention it to anyone else. I don't know why really, but… well, it seems silly now to keep it a secret. It happened, and no amount of keeping it to myself will change that.'

'Is it OK to ask what happened?'

'Yes. Kiki is… *was* Japanese. We met when I was newly qualified and it was love at first sight. At any rate, I like to think it was, but she used to tease me about that and said there was no such thing. She definitely took longer to fall for me than I did for her. Iris – our little girl – was five months old when it happened. They went to visit family in Japan and I stayed home because I had to work. There was an earthquake, and her parents' building wasn't one of those shock-proof ones like they have in Tokyo. It was the middle of the night and they would have been in bed. The building collapsed. Kiki and Iris never stood a chance. I blame myself every day for not being there with them.'

Ottilie's eyes filled with tears and she rubbed them away. She didn't want to cry in front of him because it almost felt like stealing his sorrow away, though the story made her desperately sad. The tragedy of losing Josh, that anger and despair it had brought had driven her to the lowest depths she'd been able to imagine, and yet Simon's was so much worse. At least she hadn't lost a child. She'd lost the possibility of children yet to come, of course, but it wasn't the same at all.

'But you couldn't have done anything if you had been there.'

'True, but I would have died with them and in the beginning I think I would have preferred that. Sorry…' he added hurriedly, glancing at her with an expression like guilt on his face. 'That wasn't meant to come out. It's not fair to burden you with—'

'It's not a burden. I mean, I understand sometimes we wonder how much it's OK to share. I can't imagine what it must have been like. I lost Josh and it felt as if my world had ended, but I never...'

She didn't know how to finish what she'd wanted to say. She'd never wished to be dead, no matter how low she'd been. She'd wished for Josh to still be there, that he hadn't gone to work that day, that she'd somehow been able to save him where the emergency doctors had failed and many other scenarios, but not once had she wished she'd gone with him. She had wondered how she could carry on living without him many times, but that was a very different thing.

'How long ago was this?'

'Coming up to six years.'

'So you went to Botswana after it happened?'

'Not straight away. I tried to carry on for a while – threw myself into work and even tried to have some kind of social life. Friends were worried; they were always asking me to go to dinner or whatever, and it was like I was trying to fool myself that I could move on, that I could go back to a normal life. The wheels soon came off that plan. I realised there was no normal life, not any more. And then one of my colleagues told me about the medic placement scheme and I thought I might as well go for it. I thought if I was somewhere totally different and doing things for other people it might help me. Not to forget – because we both know you can never forget – but to stop me from thinking about it every minute of every day. Botswana wasn't the first placement. I also did some work in Central America before that.'

Ottilie knew only too well what he meant. She understood the logic because it was the same logic she'd applied to her own situation. More time had passed for him, that was true, but listening to him now he didn't seem any further in his healing than she was. And she had Heath. She didn't know if that was the answer for everyone, but Heath had helped her do what she hadn't been able to do alone – and that was to see how life could be good again. Second chances did happen, and they might always have a bittersweet joy to them, but it was joy nonetheless. Simon hadn't mentioned a partner and she got the impression there had been nobody since his wife. She knew he lived alone in Liverpool and that he hadn't left anyone in Botswana he'd been close to in that way because she was certain he'd have said so.

'I nearly packed in medicine altogether, you know.'

Ottilie looked around at this new revelation. 'After you lost Kiki and Iris?'

'When I was in Botswana. Now I'm glad I didn't.'

Ottilie wanted to ask more, but at that moment Stacey came out of the treatment area. She looked drained.

Ottilie stood up. 'What's going on? How is he?'

'They've taken him for some tests and they said they'd shout me back in when they were done. I've managed to get hold of Chloe. She's trying to organise a lift to us.'

'I could go and get her.'

'I know, I thought you'd offer and I told her that, but she said she thought she could sort it. I'm sure she'll let us know if there's a problem.'

'I don't mind driving out for her if I can get a postcode,' Simon said.

'Thank you.' Stacey gave him a grateful look. 'That's very kind of you. It's kind of you to be here at all. I think it would be easier to let Chloe sort it. I'm sure she's got something in mind or she would have said so.'

Simon looked at Ottilie. 'So should I stay for a while? Just in case—'

'You must be tired and you've got a long drive home. Honestly, we'll be fine. Thanks so much for being here.'

'You'll let me know when there's news?'

'Of course. The minute we hear anything.'

He looked torn, as if he couldn't quite decide if he ought to leave or not. But then he seemed to come to a decision.

'You've clearly got all this in hand and I don't want to get in the way. But if you need me, call. I'll keep my phone close.'

Ottilie decided right then she wouldn't call. Any circumstance that might require it was unlikely, but even then it wasn't his problem to deal with. And he was right – they had got everything in hand now that they'd reached proper help.

'Thank you,' she said.

Simon gave a brisk nod and drained his coffee cup. 'I'll see you tomorrow then? But if you're here all night let me know and we'll see what we can do about cutting your clinic.'

'I'm sure I'll be fine.'

'Still, don't struggle on if you're unable. Martyrdom isn't in the job description, you know.'

Ottilie gave a tired smile. 'OK, I'll bear that in mind.'

After another brisk word with the receptionist where he appeared to thank her, Simon left them.

Stacey sank into a chair. 'I can't remember a night this bad, not for a long time. God, I hope that little boy is all right. I don't know what I'd do if...'

She burst into tears, and Ottilie threw an arm around her and pulled her close.

'We got here quick and he's in the best hands. He'll be fine.'

'So much for gossiping and ideas for the mum and baby group.' Stacey sniffed, rubbing a tissue over her eyes.

'It couldn't be helped.'

'And poor Chloe. She hardly has a social life as it is.'

'I would imagine her interrupted social life will be the last thing on her mind right now,' Ottilie soothed.

'I know that, but I feel responsible. I said I'd look after Mackenzie and…'

'And you have. These things happen – you couldn't have stopped it. Neither could Chloe if she'd been home. Nobody could. But Mackenzie's being looked after now. Everything will be all right – wait and see.'

Stacey's phone began to ring and she pulled it from her bag. 'Oh, this is Chloe… Hello…'

Ottilie watched Stacey get up and take the call outside. It reminded her that she hadn't checked her own phone since she'd arrived at Stacey's house earlier that evening. She wasn't particularly expecting anyone to call, but she got it out anyway. There wasn't much activity, apart from two messages. One was from Heath – some idle banter. The other was from Simon reminding her that he was only a phone call away should they need him.

That one didn't need a reply, but Heath's did. She was wording it in her head when another came through.

Everything all right?

There was too much to put into a text and Heath would probably have questions, so she dialled his number.

'Hey,' she said as he answered, careful to keep her voice down. 'Sorry I didn't get back to you earlier. Something's happened. I'm at the hospital with Stacey and Mackenzie.'

'Oh God, are they all right?'

'Mackenzie had a raging temperature and a rash. We didn't want to risk it so we drove him straight here.'

'You're still there? What time was this?'

'I can't even remember. I think we got here about half eight.' Ottilie glanced up at the clock to see it was almost eleven. The last few hours had seemed to last a lifetime, and yet she was still surprised to see how much time had elapsed.

'You must be exhausted. Need me to come over?'

'No, there's not a lot you can do.'

'I can support you.'

'I've got Stacey here.'

'I'm sure you're doing more supporting there than the other way around. Who've you got?'

'Well, Simon's only just gone so it's been fine.'

'Simon? You mean Doctor Simon?'

Ottilie detected a subtle shift in Heath's tone. She didn't know what exactly it was, but she didn't think she liked it. 'Yes. We phoned him for advice, and he came over to see what he could do.'

'To the hospital?'

'Yes.'

'But they have doctors there, so what did he—'

'He was following his instincts, I suppose. If you're a caring person, you don't stop caring because you're not on duty.'

'Of course not… Let me come to you. Traffic will be light – I can be there in—'

'Really, it's better if you don't. Thank you, but Stacey is here and Chloe is on her way, so that will be three of us. Four is probably overkill, which is why Simon left.'

'Oh, I see. You'll let me know what happens then?'

'Absolutely. I phoned now because I didn't want you to worry.'

'No, sure. Thanks.'

Ottilie's attention was drawn to the entrance doors. Stacey was back, and she had a strained-looking Chloe with her.

'Chloe just got here,' Ottilie told Heath. 'Sorry, I have to…'

'I get it. I'll speak to you tomorrow maybe?'

'Yes.'

He'd been saying goodbye when Ottilie ended the call. She hadn't really been listening, distracted by Chloe's arrival.

At that same moment, a doctor came from the treatment area and called Stacey over. All three women went to speak to him.

'Our tests have all been clear so far,' he said. He glanced at Chloe. 'Are you Mum?'

Chloe nodded. 'Is he going to be all right?'

'We're going to keep him in overnight for observation. We think it might be a viral infection – nothing life-threatening, but better to err on the side of caution. You're welcome to stay with him, but I'm afraid all three of you can't do that.'

'That's OK.' Chloe gave Stacey a tight smile. 'I'll do it.'

Stacey turned to the doctor. 'Could I stay in here then? I don't want to leave her alone.'

He paused, and then nodded. 'I'll see if I can sort beds out in Mackenzie's room for you both. Bear with me on that.'

Ottilie was wondering how she was going to get home as they'd driven over in Stacey's car, when Stacey turned to her.

'I could run you home and then come back?'

'Don't do that – it'll take ages. I'm sure I can get a cab.'

'Out here at this time of night? You'll be lucky, and it would cost you an arm and a leg. Let me take you home – it's the least I can do after all you've done.'

Ottilie hesitated and then nodded. Much as she wanted to refuse the offer, she could see that Stacey had a point. And perhaps it would do her good to get out of the emergency department for an hour anyway. Chloe was a young mum but perfectly capable of being there for her son. In fact, in many ways Chloe was more capable. Where Stacey had been at her wits' end, Chloe looked worried but calm.

'Only if it's no problem.'

The doctor walked away. Chloe hugged Stacey and then followed him while Stacey got out her car keys.

'Let's go then,' she said wearily.

CHAPTER SEVENTEEN

'I won't come in.' Stacey pulled on the handbrake but left the engine ticking over.

'Oh God, of course not,' Ottilie said. 'I'm sure you're desperate to get back. Thanks so much for bringing me home, but I could have got—'

'No you couldn't. I wanted to do it, but I will head back if that's OK.'

'Let me know as soon as you have news.'

'I will, but it's sounding hopeful, isn't it?'

'Very.' Ottilie gave Stacey her most reassuring smile.

After a brief hug and more thanks, Ottilie got out and watched as Stacey drove away before turning to her garden path. It was dark, but there was a soft light from the solar lanterns she'd hung from the tree that shaded her front door. It was strange to think that not so long ago she found being out here at night nerve-racking. Scary even. But now she couldn't imagine a safer place. A lot had changed since her arrival in Thimblebury, and much of it without her really noticing.

But as she slotted her key into the lock, her eye was caught by a large, upturned plant pot underneath her window. She removed the key and went over to take a closer look.

The rose bush that had been in it was lying on the lawn in a mound of soil. Someone had gone to the trouble of tipping it out so they could use the pot. To do what? To stand on it? If they'd thought to use it to look through her window there was no need because it was low enough for anyone to see in. It didn't make any sense – but that didn't mean Ottilie wasn't rattled by it. Who would do something like this and why? There didn't seem to be any reason for it, but there was no doubt it was a deliberate action – it had to be. If it had been knocked over by a passing fox, the shrub wouldn't have been pulled out in the way it had.

She thought about calling Heath, suddenly feeling she'd be grateful for his presence, but then decided against it. He'd probably be heading to bed by now, and he had so far to drive she didn't want to drag him out for this.

Another thought occurred to her. What if someone had been trying to break in? It seemed unlikely, but it might explain the pot. Had they tried and failed? Or had they succeeded and were in there now?

Ottilie scanned the garden. Her gaze fell on a spade she'd left by the wall when she'd been distracted from some gardening a few days before. She'd kept on forgetting to put it away in the shed. Right now, she'd never been so glad to forget something.

She grabbed it and went back to the door to unlock it. Gripping the spade tightly, she felt along the wall for the light switch and flicked it on.

'Hello?' she called, immediately feeling stupid. If there was a burglar they were hardly going to answer.

Cocking her head like a dog, she listened for a moment. The house was silent, save for the humming of the fridge.

Ottilie moved along to the living room and turned the light on. Satisfied all was well in there, she went to the kitchen and did the same, and then up to the bedrooms.

There was no burglar and no sign that anybody had been in. Ottilie let out a breath and stood the spade by the back door so she'd remember to take it out in the morning. She was tired, wound up and not in the mood to go messing around in her shed.

As she made herself a last drink before bed, she was still puzzling the plant pot. It was such a strange thing for someone to have done, and it seemed to serve no purpose whatsoever.

Perhaps there was a logical explanation – and a non-scary one at that. She supposed the root ball could have been a bit dry and the pot falling had knocked the whole thing free. And she supposed it could have been done by a large fox. Or a badger – they could be hefty brutes, couldn't they?

Ottilie much preferred to believe a more innocent explanation. And so she did her best to make that the one she believed.

Ottilie woke long before her alarm was due to go off despite her late night at the hospital. But Stacey had been up earlier still – proved by the fact that Ottilie's phone showed a missed call from her.

Sitting up in bed, immediately alert, Ottilie dialled her number.

'Morning!'

Stacey sounded bright and relaxed. Ottilie allowed herself to relax too. It had to be good news.

'How was your night there?'

'Oh, it was horrible, as you can imagine. Not a wink of sleep for either of us. But the important thing is Mackenzie is all right.'

'They didn't find anything?'

'Nothing they were worried about. Tests were clear. They think he's picked up some sort of virus, but it's not life-threatening. Probably a forty-eight-hour thing. He's better already this morning – temperature is down, and he's smiling at us.'

'That's a relief.'

'You're telling me! I can't thank you and Simon enough for being there with me. I don't know what I would have done without you.'

'Oh, I'm sure you'd have got through it. It's surprising what we're capable of, especially when it comes to our loved ones.'

'Still, I'm glad you were there. Thank you.'

Ottilie smiled as she ran a hand through her hair. The early sun was moving across the window, sending a shaft of light onto the opposite wall. It probably looked warmer than it was, but it also reminded her that spring had well and truly arrived, and that was cause for celebration. Her second spring in Thimblebury promised to be a lot more certain and settled than her first and she was determined to enjoy it, even if she was also reminded that her first summer in Thimblebury had been marred by a freak flood that had threatened to wreck her house. Best not to dwell quite so much on that one, and everyone had said it wasn't likely to happen again. Even if it did, knowing what to expect, Ottilie would be ready.

'I'm so glad he's OK. I don't mind admitting I was a bit panicked for a while, so goodness knows how you and Chloe were coping. Even Simon was stressed.'

'He phoned me, actually,' Stacey said. 'Wanted to check how things were.'

'When did he do that?'

'First thing – before I called you. I can't get over how lovely he was. I mean, I imagined he was lovely, but he's way, way nicer than I thought. So kind and caring. No wonder he's a doctor – I couldn't imagine him doing anything else.'

'He is,' Ottilie agreed, the tragedy of Simon's past coming back to her now. He'd shared so much – perhaps in the drama of the moment – and he'd opened up in the most unexpected way. She had to wonder if, in the cold light of day, he'd regret that. She decided she wouldn't bring it up again unless he did. In a purely professional capacity, it might be the best course of action for them both. She loved working with people she could call friends, but there was always a limit, even then, and in reality, she hardly knew Simon beyond the few weeks he'd covered for Fliss.

'Thank him for me, won't you?' Stacey said.

'I will, though knowing you I'm sure you've done that about a million times on the phone this morning.'

Stacey gave a light laugh, and following on from their stressful night, it was good to hear.

'Listen, I'll let you go,' she said. 'Chloe's waiting for me to bring back coffee. I'll speak to you later, if that's all right.'

'Absolutely. I'll call on my way home if you're up to a visit.'

'Well, we certainly didn't get much of one last night, but perhaps give it a day or so, just to make sure Mackenzie's back on top form. If he's still a bit grumbly I'd rather concentrate on him.'

'Oh God, yes. Of course – I never thought. Text me when it's a good time.'

'I will. Speak soon.'

Ottilie bid her goodbye and then ended the call. She tapped a thumb on her mobile thoughtfully, her gaze trained on that beam of sunlight slicing across the room. She wondered whether to call Fliss and fill her in on what had happened, but she suspected Simon would have done that already. And perhaps it would wait – she was seeing Fliss in a couple of hours at the surgery anyway.

There was no way she was going to get back to sleep and probably very little point for the good the extra hour would do, and so Ottilie got up and decided to make the most of her spare hour before work by going up to Hilltop Farm a little earlier and spending a bit of time with Ann and Darryl. She hadn't been able to do that for a while, and it would be good to see how Ann was doing – not only as a patient, but as a friend who had a lot on her plate and could use the support.

CHAPTER EIGHTEEN

'Good morning.' Ottilie looked up from her diary as Fliss peered around the door of her office.

'Fliss! Morning.'

The GP sidled in rather sheepishly and closed the door behind her. 'I hear there was some drama last night.'

'Oh, you mean Mackenzie? Yes. We had to take him to the hospital. He's all right, though. Had the all-clear and they're going to be bringing him home. Stacey says he's much brighter.'

'You tried to get hold of me.'

'Oh, yes.' Ottilie tried to make light of it, even though she had initially planned to confront Fliss about the fact she'd been unavailable when she was meant to be around for emergencies. She could see that Fliss felt guilty about it and she didn't want to make it worse. Fliss must have had a pretty compelling reason for not being available, after all, but perhaps she didn't want to be forced to share that either.

'I can only apologise. Whenever I'm on call I sit for hours and hours next to my phone and nobody phones. The one time someone actually needs me and…'

'Honestly, it all worked out. Luckily Simon was around and he advised me to take Mackenzie straight to the emergency department.'

'Lucky for us all.'

'Fliss, you've got no reason to feel bad. You've spent years single-handedly supporting the health needs of this community, no matter what else was going on in your life. I haven't been here all that long, but I can see what that means to everyone. You have things going on in your own life now, and everyone can see that too, and everyone understands.'

'I'm a doctor.'

'You're also a person. I don't need to know and I don't want to pry, but is everything all right at home? I know you've had the thing with Charles…'

'It was Charles I was tending to. He's all right, before you ask, nothing to worry about, but we needed a good long talk about our future and so I put my phone to one side. Of course that would be the one time someone needed me. I won't be making that mistake again.'

Ottilie frowned. 'I thought you'd already sorted out your future. You're still planning to stay on here, aren't you? I thought you and Simon were going to run the surgery together.'

'That's still the plan, but we have other things to think about, things we haven't yet decided on.'

'Like what?'

'Where do I even start?' Fliss gave a wan smile. Ottilie shook her head.

'I suppose there must be tons.'

Fliss nodded. 'You could say that. Mostly legal and administrative tangles, nothing for you to worry about.'

'I'll let you get on. See you in the kitchen for lunch as usual?'

'Lavender has made lasagne, so I don't need asking twice about that.'

With a last nod of acknowledgement and perhaps gratitude, Fliss left her and closed the door softly. Ottilie went back to her diary, but her mind wasn't on the week's appointments as fully as it ought to have been. She'd told Fliss she didn't need to know, but she couldn't help but wonder whether she ought to be worried about whatever Fliss's discussion with Charles had entailed.

The office phone started to ring. Ottilie saw it was Lavender and picked up.

'You'll be pleased to know Mrs Blythe is early and she's asking to be seen.'

'Her appointment isn't for another hour.'

'I know, but she says she needs to go shopping.'

'What?'

'Hey, don't shoot the messenger.' Lavender lowered her voice. 'I'd say no, but I did say I'd ask you. Up to you, my love. I can send her away if you can't do it and tell her to come at her appointment time like a normal person.'

Ottilie glanced up at the wall clock and let out a sigh. She wasn't doing anything else apart from worry about Fliss, and it would be good to have one patient out of the way. If anything it might do her a favour too – she'd be able to get some other things done during that slot. 'Send her in.'

'Sucker,' Lavender said, and as the phone went down Ottilie could hear her chuckling.

Heath opened Magnus and Geoff's side gate and stood back to let Ottilie through before following. It was strange to be here with him – the last time they'd sat in the couple's home cinema it had been because Magnus and Geoff were trying to engineer a romance between them. They hadn't succeeded – in fact, they'd driven things a long way in the opposite direction – though Ottilie had to admit that they'd been right to see the potential.

Most of the members of film club were already there. Flo had decided, as she often did, that she didn't fancy the film and so wasn't coming, but many of the other regulars were in attendance. Simon was yet to arrive, and though Ottilie wanted to think better of Heath, it was telling that the first time he'd been interested in coming along was also the first time Simon would be there. She'd given him absolutely no reason to be jealous, and yet, she sensed it.

'Ottilie!' Magnus came rushing from inside the cinema room to greet them. 'Everyone is inside already. We haven't started yet, so don't worry about that.' He offered a grateful smile to Heath. 'It's lovely to see you here too. I hope you enjoy.'

'I'm sure I will,' Heath said, and though Ottilie tried her best, the look she threw his way was laced with more than a little scepticism. Perhaps it was unfair and undeserved, and she didn't really want to feel that way, but it was hard not to. Perhaps he really had only decided to give it a go, and perhaps it was for all the right reasons.

'I hope everyone hasn't been waiting for us,' Ottilie said. 'You should have got started if you needed to – we could have caught up. I did text Lavender to tell her we were running late and that she could—'

'No, no… we're still waiting for Simon too. I wouldn't dream of getting started without him – seems a bit rude as it's his first one.'

'Oh, right… That's fine then.'

'Not to stress but do you know how long he'll be?'

Ottilie gave him a blank look. 'Me? Not a clue.'

'Only I'm assuming you've seen him at work today and I thought you might have left together.'

'Why would you think that?'

'Um…' Magnus let out a self-conscious laugh. 'I suppose I thought… I don't actually know. I wondered if he might come to your house to eat and get changed in the meantime.'

Ottilie suddenly realised she'd never even asked Simon what

his plans were in that regard. He wouldn't have driven all the way back to his place in Liverpool and then returned and, presumably, he'd have wanted an evening meal and a freshen-up. How did she not think of that? How could she have been so remiss? 'I don't know where he went.'

'Probably went to Fliss's place,' Heath said.

'Oh, right… I suppose he did,' Ottilie replied vaguely, though she had some doubts because she'd waved Fliss off herself that evening, alone and with no mention of Simon planning to follow on.

She resolved to be better than that, regardless of what Simon had ended up doing this time. Next time she needed to be more mindful and to check he was OK. She was settled in Thimblebury now and she had lots of friends here, people who always had her back, but she had to remember that it wasn't like that for Simon, not yet at any rate. And she had to remember what that was like, because not so long ago it had been her.

Magnus was already beckoning them inside when the gate opened again and Simon appeared. Ottilie noted that he hadn't changed his clothes from earlier that day – though that wasn't necessarily any indication of what he'd been doing during the chunk of time in between the end of surgery and now – and he seemed fairly relaxed. At least that was a positive.

'Sorry I'm a bit late,' he said, glancing between all three as they turned to greet him. 'Got carried away catching up on some paperwork and lost track of the time.'

'Oh, don't worry about that!' Magnus hurried over and grabbed him by the hand for an enthusiastic shake. 'We're just glad to have you here!'

'Glad to be invited,' Simon replied with a grin. He glanced again at Ottilie and Heath and gave them both a good-natured nod of acknowledgement.

'Come through if you're ready,' Magnus said. 'There are nibbles out. We usually do the drinks and nibbles after the film, but as we weren't quite ready to go we decided to have some of them beforehand today.'

'Is that my fault?' Simon asked as he followed him to the doors.

'No, we were late too,' Ottilie cut in.

'Oh, in that case happy to accept joint responsibility,' Simon replied, his grin spreading. 'It's good to meet you, Heath,' he added. 'I've heard a lot about you.'

'Likewise,' Heath said, and Ottilie couldn't help but detect a measure of… well, measuring up. She'd never seen Heath go alpha male and she'd never imagined she would, but there was a definite hint of it about him now.

'I hope you're hungry,' Magnus told Simon as he led him inside. 'There's always too much food.'

'Starving!' Simon said.

Inwardly, Ottilie chided herself once more. It sounded as if Simon had simply stayed behind at the surgery once the last patient had left and worked overtime. And he hadn't eaten either. Granted, she'd told him they usually had food at the film club, but she'd also told him it was only nibbles and didn't constitute a full meal.

Magnus strode to the front to remind everyone what their film was going to be and to catch up on general housekeeping, such as when subs were due and special events in the area and that sort of thing. And then he smiled at Simon, sitting in the second row of seats.

'Everyone, I'd like to welcome our new member – Dr Stokes.'

A chorus of greetings rippled through the room and Simon looked slightly embarrassed by the fuss. Ottilie caught sight of Heath and wished she hadn't. The word that came to mind was resentful, though what he had to be resentful about was anyone's guess.

As the end credits rolled, everyone filed out of the cinema and into the house for drinks and more food. As usual, the members had done a fine job of providing various nibbles to share – though Simon offered his apologies more than once that he hadn't realised he was meant to bring something.

Simon joined her and Heath as they sipped at a glass of red.

'How have you found your first film club meeting?' Ottilie asked.

'I've enjoyed it,' Simon replied as he reached for the bottle on the table next to them and poured himself a small one.

'Have you got to drive back tonight?' Heath asked.

Simon eyed his glass of wine and nodded. 'Don't worry, this is the one and only, and I'll make sure I fill up on sausage rolls before I leave to soak it up.'

'It wasn't a judgement,' Heath replied. 'I was only—'

He broke off as Ottilie gave him a significant look. She was beginning to sense something she'd never expected from Heath – and if she hadn't known better, she'd have said it was rivalry, like he saw Simon as a threat.

Stacey came over, and Ottilie was glad of the distraction from her worries.

'So,' Stacey said to Simon. 'What do you think? You think you might come to more film nights?'

'Absolutely,' he replied, and Ottilie noted the warm smile. Did he seem happier to see Stacey than he had been to see her and Heath?

'Simon…' she began after a pause, her tone more earnest now. 'I wanted to say thanks again for—'

'Honestly,' he cut in. 'Please… It was nothing. How is Mackenzie?'

'He's right as rain again. You'd never even know he'd been through all that. I bet he doesn't even remember any of it.'

'I'm sure that's true,' Simon agreed. 'They're resilient, aren't they? Little ones, I mean.'

'Lucky they are,' Stacey said. 'We'd all be very messed-up adults if we let half of what happens to us as kids get to us. Have you got children?'

Ottilie held in a groan. She hadn't shared what she'd learned that night about his wife and daughter with anyone, thinking it was best to respect his privacy, but instantly she realised that her decision might have been a mistake. If she'd given Stacey a heads-up, it would have prevented an awkward situation like this.

'No,' he said in a dull voice. 'I don't. If you'll excuse me, I have to…'

His sentence tailed off as he left them and made a pretence of getting food. At least it looked that way to Ottilie.

'That was weird,' Heath said.

'He has his reasons,' Ottilie replied, and when both Heath and Stacey turned to her with obvious questions in their expressions, she shook her head. 'It's not my place to say.'

Stacey lifted her glass to her lips. 'I can't say I'm not even more intrigued now, but I get what you're saying. I wish I'd known I wasn't supposed to mention a family before I opened my big trap, though.'

'I'm sorry – that's my fault. I probably should have mentioned it, but I wanted to respect his privacy.'

'Can we at least get a clue so I don't put my foot in it again?' Stacey asked. 'I presume there's something bad going on there? Is there anything else I ought to avoid mentioning?'

'I think just steer clear of family for now,' Ottilie said. 'I expect in time he'll tell people himself. All I can say is I imagine it's a painful subject.'

'Is it painful like your past was when you first got here?' Stacey asked, and Heath looked at Ottilie so intently now she felt she might buckle under the scrutiny.

She didn't want to give all this away – certainly not here and now – but Stacey was making it difficult not to. And she had a point – nobody wanted to be the person who put their foot in it and caused Simon distress, and that came from a place of kindness rather than nosiness. She also had a feeling Heath's interest was more selfish than that, which didn't sit quite so well with her. She wished she didn't think it, but she got a strange vibe from him whenever Simon was mentioned. Ottilie knew details nobody else did – nobody in Thimblebury at any rate. That meant they'd shared at least one intense and personal conversation. What Heath might make of that she didn't know, but she had another hunch that she might have to explain it to him sooner rather than later.

'Yes,' Ottilie said and was saved from further interrogation by Magnus coming over to talk to them about the next film club.

CHAPTER NINETEEN

It was Sunday. The week had felt like a very long one, but the bright spot on the horizon was that Simon was doing his final week as a resident of Liverpool and was due to move into the village ready to take up his permanent post. It would make life easier for everyone – not least Fliss because he'd be able to take a lot more of her on-call responsibilities from her, so she was in a very good mood. She had agreed to do the emergency cover for this weekend to allow him to move into Charles's old cottage (and perhaps because she still felt a bit guilty for not being available when Mackenzie had been ill).

This morning, being at a loose end, Ottilie knocked at the door of Charles's old place to see what she could do to help her new neighbour.

After a few moments, and with an expression of surprise, Simon opened the door. Ottilie could see rows of boxes, stacked up and lining both sides of the hallway so that the gap between them was probably only wide enough for one person to very carefully make their way down.

The décor was quite traditional – muted earth tones and dark wood. Ottilie had always thought it looked sort of manly, and she'd often felt it needed a woman's touch – though that woman probably wouldn't have been Fliss, because her decor wasn't all that different. The garden was neat, dense with hardy evergreens for minimum maintenance. It looked nice enough, but Ottilie preferred the more romantic wildness of her own. She wondered if Simon would make many changes.

'I haven't come at a bad time, have I?' she asked.

'Um… no. Of course not.'

'I won't come in,' she added, glancing down the hallway again. 'I can see you're still upside down. I had wondered if you might have been able to get everything unpacked yesterday after your removal van had gone.'

'Sadly not. And quite honestly if I wait until I'm straight in here to ask in a visitor then it might be years before I have company. Please – come in if you can get in.'

'Are you sure? I don't mind—'

'No, please… I'd actually really like it. My parents are always telling me I spend far too much time alone and they're probably right. Some company would be nice, as long as you don't mind the fact there's barely anywhere to sit and the fridge isn't plugged in yet for cold drinks. You're my first visitor here, actually,' he continued as he stepped back to let her cross the threshold. 'I would have been a bit further along with my unpacking by now, but Charles was a bit behind moving out.' Simon turned to her with a wry smile as she followed him down the narrow spit of hallway that was still accessible. 'I got the feeling neither of them actually wanted him to move in with Fliss.'

'God, no, I can imagine,' Ottilie said with a light laugh. 'I don't want to alarm you, but Charles might be begging you to let him move back in with you by the end of the first week. Fliss has always said they get on better apart. The heart attack has really shaken things up.'

As they went into the kitchen, Ottilie saw that there were even more boxes in here, filling corners in teetering piles, spilling out under and on top of the dining table. Charles was reasonably neat but his decor was quite functional, with solid oak units that looked a little dated, magnolia walls and white tiles around the cooker and sink. Ottilie wondered whether Simon would do much to suit it more to his tastes, but she supposed it was early days yet.

There were odd bits of furniture and fixtures and fittings that she recognised as belonging to Charles. She assumed he'd left them here, partly to help Simon and partly because he wouldn't have had much room at Fliss's place to take them with him. She wondered if they were a help or hindrance, because she assumed Simon also had plenty of furniture of his own that he'd brought from Liverpool with him.

Ottilie held up the carrier bag she'd brought in with her. 'You might think I'm interfering where I'm not wanted, but I brought some cleaning bits for you. It's one of those things you don't always think about when you're moving into a new place, so if they're of any use, you're more than welcome to them.'

'That's actually brilliant, thank you. I've got some but probably not enough. The place needs… um…'

'Don't worry.' Ottilie smiled. 'I know what you're too tactful to say.'

'I'm sure Charles has been too ill to worry about spring-cleaning.'

'Well, that's true, but I don't think he was very fond of cleaning before he was ill. I don't think Fliss is either. Their minds are on more… how can I put it…?'

'They'd rather be doing something more fun?'

'Yes.' Ottilie's smile grew. 'Although I was going to say they were occupied by more cerebral things than cleaning.'

Simon raised his eyebrows. 'You mean like wine appreciation? Or sitting down in front of *Celebrity Gogglebox*?'

'Exactly!' Ottilie replied, laughing now. 'I see it hasn't taken you long to get the measure of them. I mean, everyone here loves them to pieces, but they're a nightmare couple – so chaotic. I don't know how Fliss keeps it together long enough during the day to be such a brilliant doctor. And I can totally see why they needed to live apart for so long – imagine how chaotic each of them is living alone and then imagine putting all that in one house.'

'That had crossed my mind too. Lucky for me, if not them, that they decided to pool their resources, because it means I have somewhere to live here without all the hassle of trying to find somewhere. I did have a scan of the local estate agents, but there really was nothing within about a ten-mile radius of this place – nothing suitable, at any rate.'

'Are you thinking you might buy then?'

'I was hoping to. I think there might be a possibility of buying this place at some point if their cohabiting works out.'

'So you're fairly certain you want to stay in Thimblebury long-term?'

'Well, yes…' Simon seemed confused by the suggestion that he might not want to stay long-term.

'No, I mean, I didn't want to assume anything. If you do, I'm really glad. It's not for everyone.'

'The way I see it, if I buy somewhere and then it doesn't work out, there seems to be a healthy market around these parts, so I don't imagine I'd have much trouble selling on again. So it makes sense as far as I can see to buy. But I'm all right at the moment – there's no rush. Charles has done me a very fair deal on the rent here, so I'm happy.'

'I think they're just happy to get you here and in that job whatever it takes,' Ottilie said, putting the bag of cleaning supplies down on the only clear corner of table she could see. 'I know Fliss would never say it, but she's been needing a partner for a long time. It took Charles's health scare to force her to step back and look at what long hours they were both working and how neither of them are getting any younger. If not for that, I'm sure she'd have kept pushing herself until she dropped.'

'That's one of the many occupational hazards of being a GP,' Simon said. He turned and started to search in one of the boxes stacked next to the sink. 'If I can find the mugs, I might be able to offer you a drink.'

'That's all right – don't stress on my account. I've got a few hours spare; maybe I could help you clean and get a bit straighter in here? Not that I think you can't manage on your own, of course. I only wondered if a second pair of hands might make things a bit easier.'

'The company would make them more pleasant, that's for sure. I'd feel as if I were taking advantage of your good nature, though.'

'Don't be daft – that's what friends are for, right?'

'Even so…'

'Honestly, I'm happy to help. If I went home now I'd spend the afternoon feeling awful that I'd left you to do all this alone. I'm sure you've noticed by now I'm not very good at keeping my nose out of things.'

Simon chuckled. 'I wouldn't put it quite like that, but I have noticed you like to get involved. It's an admirable trait. It's a shame more people aren't as community-minded as you are – the world might be a much nicer place.'

'Oh, I don't think it's so bad as people say. I also think more people than you realise do their bit every day, even if it's in small, unnoticeable ways. The millions of little acts of kindness that happen every day are what makes the world tick over, not the grand gestures that everyone notices.'

'Hmmm…' Simon was silent for a moment as he held her in an approving gaze. 'I like that way of looking at it. In which case, who am I to refuse such a generous offer of your time?'

'I was hoping you'd say that.' Ottilie took off her shoulder bag and pulled out some biscuits and a box of teabags. 'I brought provisions too. Can't have a cleaning party without chocolate digestives.'

Ottilie started on what floors she could get to, followed by wiping down skirting boards and door frames and then windows and frames while Simon concentrated on cleaning every cupboard before he filled it with his belongings. Finally they met to do the downstairs bathroom together, and then they broke for tea and biscuits. There was a bit more cleaning, and then Simon shouted up to Ottilie that he was starving and was going to search for the packs of instant noodles he knew were in his boxes of food, and if she wanted some, she only had to say so.

'I can do better than that…' she called back down from the bedroom, where she'd been taking down the curtains to wash at her place because Simon had yet to plumb in his machine. Apparently, Charles had never washed a single load of laundry during his married life, Fliss doing it for him at her place and therefore negating the need of a washing machine in his house until now. 'Hang on…'

She hurried down the stairs and went into the kitchen, where Simon was still searching his boxes, a pan sitting on the stove ready to go.

'Unless you're desperate for noodles,' she began, nodding at the pan, 'I've got leftovers at my house. Plug the microwave in and you can have veggie lasagne. It's a Jamie Oliver recipe – I can't promise I make it like Jamie does, but Heath seems to like it and he hates vegetarian stuff usually.'

'I couldn't—'

'Of course you could! I'm only going to throw it away if it doesn't get eaten, so it's no bother. I mean, if you don't like that sort of thing, then—'

'That sounds wonderful. And if it's anything like the things you've cooked and brought in for lunch over the past few weeks, I'm sure it's going to put my sad instant noodles to shame.'

'Give me two ticks then to run home and get it.'

'You're sure it's no bother?'

'Will you stop being so bloody polite and take the offer!'

Simon laughed as Ottilie pulled on her jacket.

'Don't go anywhere – I'll be back shortly!'

Ottilie raced home, taking Simon's curtains with her. After dumping them in the machine and setting it to wash, she gathered all the leftovers in her fridge, and a few more bits beside to make the meal stretch, and then rushed back. She'd have to be ready for Heath when he came over later, but if she had her wits about her there was no reason she couldn't help Simon too and still get back in time for Heath's arrival.

When she got back to Simon's cottage, the front door had been left open for her and the kitchen table cleared. He was busy fixing the glass plate into his microwave and looked up at her arrival.

'That was quick.'

'Was it? I must have been hungrier than I realised!'

Ottilie began to take all the food from her basket.

A slow, bemused smile spread across Simon's face. 'A few leftovers?'

'Well, I suppose there is quite a lot. But what we don't eat you can keep to tide you over until you have a chance to shop properly. You've got a freezer?'

'Yes, Charles left one.'

'So a lot of this will freeze if you need it to.'

'I don't deserve you,' he said, his smile fixed in place.

'That's not true at all. Never mind that – let's get this stuff in the microwave. Sooner we eat, the sooner we can crack on and finish your cleaning.'

'You really don't have to stay this afternoon,' Simon said, plugging in the microwave and taking a tub from her to put in. 'You've done more than enough, and I can manage.'

'I know. Heath's coming over later so I'll only stay another hour and then pop off. I've got the time to spare and I'd only be messing around at my place.'

'I don't think you ever mess around at your place. From what I can tell you don't have time – you're always doing things for other people. I mean, today is a perfect example. You ought to be enjoying a well-earned day off, not knee-deep in muck at my house.'

'I suppose there's a bit of me that doesn't like being alone too often,' Ottilie said, taking out a bag of chopped salad. 'Too much time to think. I'd rather be occupied.'

'I can relate to that,' Simon said, the mood visibly darkening over the room.

Ottilie forced a bright smile. 'I'm not going to say it gets easier, because you and I know that's not really what it's about. It does get easier, but that doesn't change the facts, and it getting easier only makes your emotions about it more complicated by guilt.'

Simon nodded slowly. 'Couldn't have put it better myself. You don't lose someone and then it's all right. They're always lost, no matter what else comes, no matter who else moves into that space.'

'Exactly.'

'If you don't mind me asking… how does it work for you? I mean, how does it…' Simon let out a sigh. 'I know what I'm trying to say but not how to say it. But you have Heath now. I've never even thought about anyone else and I don't know how I'd deal with a new relationship. But I suppose it might happen. You're there now, so how do you deal with it? The guilt, I mean? Because I'm sure there must be some – I know I'd feel it.'

'Sometimes I don't even know. I try to remember that Heath is not replacing Josh; I'm just making space in my heart for more than one man. I have to stretch it – perhaps that's a good thing. My heart is bigger for having to make that extra space, and perhaps it's easier to love because it's bigger…' Ottilie let out a short laugh. 'That makes no sense to anyone but me, I'm sure. I felt guilty all the time at first. In fact, I tried hard not to like Heath, even though I was mad about him. I couldn't admit that I had feelings for someone else because it felt like such a betrayal of Josh.'

'You don't feel that way now?'

'Sometimes, but not as often. It's like anything – it takes time. It's not much for you to go on, but it's the best I can offer. I'm sorry if you were hoping for something more profound.'

'No, but it's good to see that there's a light at the end of the tunnel. Since the accident, it's felt as if there would never be anyone else – I didn't want there to be anyone else. But since I got to Thimblebury I've started to feel a bit differently, and I don't really know what to do with it.'

'I felt the same. I'm sure it's normal.'

The microwave pinged, making Ottilie jump.

'God, I'd forgotten all about that!' she said with a shaky laugh.

'Me too.'

Simon smiled now, but Ottilie could see he was still troubled, still mulling over their discussion, perhaps deciding how he felt about her advice – such as it was. She hardly felt it constituted advice at all, and it was vague at best. She couldn't tell him how to deal with his grief, how he could move on, because she'd fumbled her own way through it, no clear path, no strategy, no words of wisdom to be gleaned from her experiences. All she could say with certainty was that it had been hard, and sometimes she'd felt she might get swallowed by the darkness, and it was only because the right man had come into her life that she was here at all.

And she couldn't underestimate the support of her wonderful friends and neighbours in Thimblebury either. They'd welcomed her in and given her all the time and patience and understanding she'd needed to help her heal. She was sure they'd do the same for Simon too, but she wasn't going to tell him that. Somehow to say so seemed patronising and assumed that was what he wanted from them. And when she thought about it, his relationship with the villagers was bound to be different from her own. He was going to be their GP, after all, and he probably didn't – or couldn't – allow everyone to get too close to him. Fliss had always kept a distance for exactly the same reason. She was a part of the village, but there had always been a final line of defence that kept her a little detached too.

As they sat down to eat, surrounded by boxes and things in the wrong place, Ottilie was reminded all too forcibly of her own arrival in Thimblebury a year before, and turned the conversation to safer subjects. Simon had a passing acquaintance with some of the things that went on in the village and surrounding areas – the film club, for example – but his knowledge went no deeper than that. So Ottilie filled him in on the ones she knew about and how she was involved.

'Wow,' he said when she'd finished and looked down to see she'd finished her lunch too. 'You never stop. How do you get time to do anything for yourself?'

'I suppose it might sound a bit sad, but I think stuff like the community kitchen and the mum and baby group might count as my hobbies. I love doing them so it's no hardship and I don't feel as if they eat into my spare time at all. I've got a brilliant social life and a huge circle of friends from doing those things, so it's win-win as far as I can tell.'

'I never thought of it like that.'

'Maybe you wouldn't because your job is quite demanding as it is.'

'I'm sure yours must be. Don't you find it draining at times, constantly having to care even when you're exhausted and you don't feel like it? I know I do.'

'I wouldn't be human if that didn't happen from time to time.'

'And yet you still try to fit more in?'

Ottilie shrugged. 'What can I say? I'm a people-pleaser – always have been. I'm far happier when I'm caring for others than doing things for myself. I'm sure there's a good therapist out there who might have something to say about that, but I'm not sure I'd want to fix it, even if I thought it was a fault… which, sometimes I have to admit I do. But it's a fault that I want to keep because I don't think it's a bad one.'

'Me neither.' Simon put his cutlery down and smiled at her. 'And thank you for lunch – it was as good as I thought it would be. Far better than my crappy instant noodles.'

'You're welcome.'

'If the community kitchen's meals are that good I might have to pretend I've got no money and turn up myself to get fed.'

'Oh, it's not only for people with no money. Anyone who wants a meal can come – we get all sorts with all sorts of reasons.

People are lonely, they struggle physically, they might not have good cookery skills and they might be a bit broke that week. We don't turn anyone away.'

'Isn't that open to abuse?'

'I suppose it might be, but I like to think the people of this village are decent enough that they wouldn't want to abuse a service like that. And generally it's true – I've yet to serve someone who didn't need it.'

Simon shook his head wonderingly. 'I can see living here is going to take some getting used to.'

'Wasn't it like that in Botswana? You said it was a small community where you volunteered. Surely villages are essentially the same the world over? At least, I always imagined that to be the case. People are close, they know each other's business, they look out for one another...'

'I suppose it was a bit. But I never expected to find that in England. Especially being from a big city.'

'Pockets of cities can be like that too – you just need to know where to look.'

'Ah, that's clearly where I've been going wrong then. Perhaps I never looked hard enough.'

'You know...' Ottilie paused. 'Actually, I'm sure you're going to be too busy...'

'You were going to ask if I wanted to come and see what you do at one of your projects?'

'I only thought it might be a good way to get to know some of the villagers. I didn't think about how busy you'd be doing other things until I'd started to say it.'

'I am, but I think I'd like to. Maybe when I'm settled in here I'll pop down to the kitchen. Might even get involved – I have been known to make a decent chilli con carne in my time.'

Ottilie broke into a smile as she poured a glass of water. 'They'd love that!'

Ottilie would love it too, and she hoped he truly meant it. To have a newcomer like her fall in love with Thimblebury as she'd done, especially knowing its power to heal someone who'd felt loss as keenly and unexpectedly as she'd done, would make her happier than any treat she could buy or luxury break she was spoiled with. It was true what she'd told Simon – often she'd felt her innate and overwhelming desire to see others happy was as much of a burden as it was a blessing, but it was who she was, and at the end of the day, she couldn't be anything other than that.

CHAPTER TWENTY

Ottilie had enjoyed her morning helping Simon more than she could ever have anticipated, and she felt as if she knew him so much better than she had before. She left his house full of hope for a brilliant working relationship, one that might see them both to their retirements, one that was fulfilling, one that helped many people and one that might eventually help Simon himself too. She'd seen only too clearly a man still struggling, bravely battling his grief and the demons that came with it – she saw it because she'd lived it and had only recently begun to let go. That period of her own life was still fresh and recent enough that the memories were visceral: the way she'd felt, the hopeless emptiness of each day, the desperate need to fill the hours with anything that would stop her dwelling on the past she'd longed for and a future that was lost.

Back at Wordsworth Cottage there had been time for a shower, a change of clothes and a layer of make-up ready for Heath's arrival. They'd planned a quiet night – some food, wine and maybe a film. Heath had wanted to do something fancier, but Ottilie was glad now she'd resisted his suggestions. She was perfectly content to keep it low-key, and she was beginning to feel they were at the point of their relationship where they didn't have to always be on, where they could be relaxed in each other's company and not always feel as if they had to be trying to impress. At least that was the way she saw it, and she hoped Heath was beginning to feel the same way.

He arrived bang on time with a smile, flowers and a bottle of wine, and a warm kiss that left her as breathless as the first one they'd shared. Every kiss made her feel that way, and while she hoped for that familiarity in the way they enjoyed each other's company, she also hoped the thrill of his kisses would never lessen.

Ottilie had eaten so much at lunch that she hadn't been hungry when they sat down to the Thai banquet he'd ordered in from a neighbouring town – something that had taken quite a bit of trouble and a larger-than-usual delivery charge – and so she'd done her best to show her appreciation and eaten as much as she could manage. Far from feeling pleasantly satisfied, she ended up making herself feel sick, so when Heath got close on the sofa while the film was on, all she wanted to do was hold on to her stomach and wait for it to pass.

'I'm sorry,' she said, baulking at the look of disappointment on his face. 'Give me an hour or so… I don't feel brilliant.'

'Was it the curry? I thought you loved Thai food… You said—'

'I do, and it was gorgeous and so thoughtful of you. There was nothing wrong with the food. I think I overdid it. You know, because it was so delicious I couldn't stop.'

'Oh… right.'

He moved away, still sitting close but giving her enough space to spread out and get comfortable. She pulled a cushion to her tummy and willed her discomfort to pass. A walk would have been a good idea, and though they were settled and in the middle of a good movie, she was about to suggest they pause it and go out for a stroll to see if it would make her feel better when there was a knock at the door. Heath shot a faintly suspicious look at her. Or perhaps there was no suspicion. Perhaps that was all in her head.

'You didn't say you were expecting anyone.'

'I'm not.' Ottilie got up. 'I won't be a minute.'

Simon was at the door. As she opened up, he held out the dishes she'd brought their lunch over in.

'Thought you might need them,' he said. 'I washed them up and thought about bringing them into work tomorrow but then decided to have a walk.'

'Oh, right… Thanks so much.'

'No…' He gave a warm smile. 'Thank you so much. I don't know what I would have done without you today. Actually, I do. I would still have been wallowing in Charles's dirt. And please never tell him I said that!'

Ottilie smiled. 'I won't.'

'Anyway, I really appreciate it. Especially the amazing lunch and your company. And I've been thinking about what you were saying about your volunteering. I'm definitely going to get involved. I can see how much you enjoy it and so, well, there must be something in it, right?'

'That's good.' Ottilie cradled the bowls as she glanced back down the hallway. 'So we can talk about it tomorrow at work if that's OK. It's…'

'Oh God, yes, of course…' Simon slapped his forehead in the most comical way. 'You've got company. I remember you said now. God, I'm so stupid… in a world of my own.'

'Not at all, but Heath is here, so…'

'I'll leave you to it. See you tomorrow.'

With a casual wave, Simon turned and walked the path to the gate as Ottilie closed the front door. She turned with a start to see Heath standing at the end of the hallway.

'Who was it?'

'Oh, it was Simon. He was returning these…' Ottilie held up the dishes.

'He borrowed them?'

'Sort of.'

'He doesn't have any dishes of his own?'

'He's only recently moved in, hasn't he? All in boxes still.'

'Yeah, I suppose so. What was that about you having lunch with him?'

'We had lunch. It was only leftovers. Because he couldn't cook anything at his place.'

'But you had lunch with him?'

'I was there anyway so yes. We were cleaning.'

'You were cleaning for him?'

'No, *we* were cleaning. I was helping him. I figured he might need it. I was lucky my place was so clean when I moved in, but it's not always like that and I know what Charles and Fliss are like when it comes to cleanliness. I thought there was a fair chance he'd need an extra pair of hands, and I was right.'

Heath folded his arms. 'So have you been there all day?'

'No.'

'But long enough to want lunch?'

Ottilie narrowed her eyes and made to get past him with her bowls. 'What is this? What does it matter? Why the sudden interrogation?'

'I don't know, but I'm here and you're too tired to do anything and you can't eat the meal I went to a lot of trouble to—'

'I did eat the meal!' Ottilie dumped the dishes onto the kitchen table and turned to Heath, who had followed her in there.

'You said you were struggling.'

'Sometimes you're hungrier than others. That's normal.'

'I'm only asking. Am I in the wrong for asking?'

'For God's sake, Heath. I'm not Mila!'

Heath's expression went from one that was battling suspicion to hurt and anger. Ottilie saw immediately she'd said the wrong thing, but she wasn't about to take it back. If he could speak his mind – and she'd been left in no doubt what was on it – then so could she. So what if he was offended. She was offended too. She'd been under the impression they were beginning to understand each other. Surely he'd worked out by now that she was nothing like his ex? Surely she deserved more of his trust than Mila?

'Do you want to leave?' she asked.

He stood for a moment, still and silent, as if trying to read her, but the expression of hurt never left his face.

'Yes,' he said finally. 'Maybe that would be a good idea before one of us says something we'd regret.'

'I have nothing hurtful to say, but if that's the way you're feeling then you'd better. When you've got your head on straight, I'll be here. Come and talk to me then.'

Heath ground his teeth as he studied her silently again. But then he nodded shortly, got his coat, kissed her briefly on the cheek and left.

At first Ottilie didn't quite know how to react. She stood alone in the kitchen, staring at the dishes Simon had returned, her mind racing. Should she go after Heath? Should she give him space and trust he'd come to his senses? Because whichever option was the best, she was certain of one thing: none of this was her fault. She wasn't about to apologise when she bore no blame. Josh would never have expected her to, and if Heath wanted to be in her life, then that line in the sand was going to be drawn right here and right now for him too. She was upset, hurt at how he could distrust her, that he was still comparing her to Mila even though she'd given him no reason to.

She thought about going to bed early. She was tired and there was no reason to stay up now, but she was so wound up she'd struggle to sleep. Besides, it was still early. She wondered if Stacey was up. Stacey was fast becoming Ottilie's go-to confidante in Thimblebury. If anyone could make her feel better it was Stacey. So Ottilie dialled her number and waited for her to pick up.

She didn't, but as Ottilie made the decision to clear the kitchen and make a cake to take her mind off her bad mood, Stacey called back.

'Hey, sorry I missed your call… Is something wrong? You usually text rather than phone.'

'Oh, it's nothing urgent. Just a bit of… I don't suppose you have an hour free if I come over, do you? Don't worry if not – it doesn't really matter.'

'Sounds like it. I actually have someone here, but I…' She lowered her voice and Ottilie frowned slightly. 'I'm assuming he's not planning to stay for long but I don't know. Would it be a problem for you? If you need me to get rid, I can—'

'God, no!'

If Stacey was entertaining a potential boyfriend then Ottilie certainly didn't want to get in the way of that to grumble about Heath.

'Is it someone I know?' she asked, unable to contain her curiosity despite her own woes.

'Um…'

'You don't need to tell me.'

'Actually, I don't know why it matters. He only popped in to see how Mackenzie was doing so it's not like there's any great mystery. Simon's here.'

'Simon?' Ottilie's frown returned. She wasn't sure why she was surprised either, but somehow she was. But if he was making an effort to settle into life here and make new friends, then of course he'd be visiting people. It was what she'd done. Something about it seemed more unlikely in his case, though. Or perhaps he was genuinely concerned for Mackenzie's well-being. That would make sense, given what she knew about him and the fact he'd been to the hospital with them that night. 'I won't disturb you then.'

'You wouldn't be disturbing. He's been telling me you were there today helping him move in. You should have phoned me – I'd have come over too.'

'I thought you'd be busy.'

'Never too busy for my two biggest heroes. I owe you both for that night Mackenzie was ill. I owe you for the night he was born! You only have to shout up when you need anything; you must know that.'

'You don't, but thank you.'

'So come over, please. If you need it to be just us two I can make some excuse and I'm sure he'd understand.'

'No, don't do that,' Ottilie said, her mind going back to Heath's issues with Simon and suddenly feeling quite belligerent about being in his company. Ottilie got to say who she spent time with, not Heath. She had nothing to feel guilty about and nothing to hide, and she was perfectly entitled to choose her friends. Besides, Simon was going to be a partner at the surgery – it made sense to get along with him for that reason if no other.

'Please come over; it'd be good to see you,' Stacey said.

'You know what, I will. Shall I bring a bottle?'

'Oooh, if you like!' Stacey said with a light laugh. 'Now you're talking my language!'

Ottilie's plans had taken a complete about-turn. Rather than sulking in bed, she was now on her way out to Stacey's with a bottle of red and a determination to put Heath's unreasonable moodiness out of her mind. Stacey and Simon were both brilliant company, and there was nothing quite like a Mackenzie cuddle to cheer her right up. He might be in bed, of course, but with a bit of luck he'd be up for a feed and she'd get to make a fuss of him. Before she left home she checked her phone for missed calls or messages from Heath, but there was nothing. She supposed he might still have been driving. She decided to give him the benefit of the doubt and assume that was the case, and if he was still sulking, she wasn't going to give it a second thought.

When she arrived, Stacey threw open the front door. She was beaming and Ottilie couldn't help a broad smile in return. She wondered if Stacey had made a start on her own wine, because she had a distinct glow about her and she was bouncier than Ottilie had seen her in a good while.

'You didn't mess around, did you?' she asked, kissing Ottilie on the cheek.

'I was already dressed and ready to go. I've left a sinkful of dishes but who cares, eh? Sometimes there are more important things than dishes.'

'Absolutely. I'm glad you decided to come.'

'Me too,' Ottilie said as she went inside and closed the front door behind her.

In the living room, Simon looked very settled on the armchair with a glass of wine at his side and Mackenzie on his knee. Ottilie's smile spread as he looked up at her.

'Hello again! We've got to stop meeting like this!'

'I know.' Ottilie held out the wine for Stacey to take. 'I'm sure we'll see enough of each other at work soon.' She glanced at Stacey. 'Where's Chloe?'

'Out with the mystery man again.'

'So we know it's a man now?'

'I'm making an educated guess. She's being very sneaky. If it was a friend she wouldn't care what I knew about it, but as she's playing her cards close to her chest, it's a boy.'

'Probably.' Ottilie cast a longing glance at Mackenzie.

'Oh.' Stacey laughed lightly. 'Sorry, Simon, I think you're going to have to give him up for a minute. Ottilie can't live without her baby cuddles.'

'Well, I am his godmother, after all,' Ottilie said with mock affront as Simon offered him up. As she lifted Mackenzie to her, he let out a delighted giggle, thrusting a drool-covered hand into her hair.

'I can see he loves you,' Simon said as he watched them.

'I should think so,' Ottilie cooed. 'I'm the first face he saw in this world.'

Simon's confused glance went from Ottilie to Stacey and then back again.

'Ottilie helped Chloe give birth upstairs. It's a long story, but apparently my family is really good at creating emergencies.'

'I didn't do it all alone,' Ottilie said as Simon threw her a look of awe. 'I had you with me, Stacey. And Heath was there too.'

'I seem to recall I wasn't much use,' Stacey said, her tone rueful now. 'Heath was a star.'

'He was,' Ottilie agreed, her mind going to the argument she'd had with him. She'd been determined not to think about it but realised now that these situations were never so simple.

'I'll go and open this,' Stacey said. She looked at Simon. 'You'll stay for another glass?'

Ottilie watched them both carefully, her curiosity piqued once again. Something in her manner was coy, almost shy suddenly. That wasn't so surprising – she'd admitted to Ottilie she found Simon attractive and she'd made no secret that she wanted to find love again. What was more surprising was that Simon's reply sounded almost as shy.

'If you want me to. I don't want to get in the way if you had plans to—'

'We don't,' Ottilie cut in. 'Not at all. I'm the one who crashed the party.'

'Hardly a party,' Stacey said, hurrying to the kitchen with the wine Ottilie had given to her.

'I'd only meant to call for five minutes after I left yours,' Simon said to Ottilie as she moved a pile of toys to take a seat on the sofa. 'But then we got chatting and Stacey opened the wine and here I still am. It beats being on my own surrounded by boxes.'

'I'm sure it does. Stacey's a good host – you were never going to get away with a quick five-minute visit.'

'I can see that now. You know what,' he continued, settling into the armchair and draining his glass, 'it's amazing, but I'm starting to feel settled in Thimblebury already.'

'A couple of glasses of red will do that to you,' Ottilie said wryly. 'I'm assuming you're not on your first one – at least, if I know Stacey you're not.'

'Oi!' Stacey laughed as she came back with the open bottle and a new glass for Ottilie. 'What are you trying to say about me?'

'I'm saying you're always the hostess.' Ottilie took the glass from her.

'Good, because it might sound to someone who didn't know that you were calling me a lush.'

Ottilie laid a hand on her heart. 'I'd never do that! I mean, you can sink more booze than a navvy but that's beside the point…'

'Cheeky cow!' Stacey's laughter grew, and Ottilie glanced at Simon to see him smiling. Not at them both, but at Stacey. She allowed herself an inward smile at the situation. Was there something blooming here? Was she witnessing the beginning of something wonderful for them? She couldn't think of two people who deserved it more, and so with all her heart she hoped so.

Stacey sat next to her. 'You still want to talk?' she asked, lowering her voice while Simon pretended a bit too obviously not to be listening.

Ottilie glanced between the two of them and shook her head. What kind of friend would she be if she dampened the mood here now, not when it all looked so promising for them.

'It's nothing that won't wait,' she said, bouncing a gurgling Mackenzie on her knee. She wasn't about to spoil whatever was going on here; she was only glad not to have to think about how annoyed she was at Heath for a while.

CHAPTER TWENTY-ONE

Heath had phoned while Ottilie had been with Stacey and Simon, and she hadn't noticed until she was on her way home. She wasn't drunk, but perhaps less guarded and less tactful than she might have been had she been totally sober, and so she phoned back with such carelessness that she could hear the shock in his voice.

'Hi… I'm sorry, I thought… Well, I hate the way we left things earlier, and I know—'

'That it's all your fault?' Ottilie cut in. 'I'm glad you can see that because it's true and I'm not going to argue.'

'I'm sorry,' he said again. 'You're right. It's… You have to understand what I went through before—'

'Do I?' she interrupted again. 'What *you* went through? Yes, I need to understand what you went through because clearly that's more important than anything I've been through. We all have a past, Heath, but some of us try not to live the rest of our lives according to it.'

He apologised again, and it was so full of heartfelt sincerity that Ottilie felt guilty for demanding it with such uncharacteristic bluntness. But at least the matter was settled, and they could say goodnight and leave things on a brighter note, and when she went to bed later that night, she was content that things were back on an even keel once again, and so she went straight to sleep with no bother.

. . .

The following morning was Monday and the start of another week. Ottilie's first job, as always, was a visit to Hilltop Farm to check on Darryl and his mum Ann. When she got there today, to her delight she found Corrine sitting at the table sharing a cup of tea with Ann.

'You're out early!' Ottilie said, giving her a hug.

'That's what a farming life does for you,' Corrine said, glancing at Ann. 'I'm right, aren't I?'

'I can't remember the last time I slept in,' Ann agreed. 'And even without the farm I'd still have mister over there waking me up with the lark.' She angled her head at Darryl, who wasn't listening but poring over his two favourite books about trains. Both the one Ottilie had gifted to him and the newer one from Simon were open on the table, side by side, and he appeared to be reading them both at once.

'How's Victor and the girls?' Ottilie asked Corrine as Ann went to pour another tea for her. Ottilie caught sight of her glittering ring, the one Victor had bought for her to show his affection in light of their close call. The sight warmed her.

'Oh, they're all good.'

'And how are you?' Ottilie added in a more significant tone.

'Never better.' Corrine's smile was broad and full of genuine gratitude.

'That's good.'

'How's everything with you?' Corrine asked. 'How's that man of yours?'

'Oh, you know… lovely.'

'You seem to be a magnet for lovely men,' Ann said, offering her a freshly filled mug. 'I hear the new doctor moved in yesterday.'

'He did,' Ottilie said.

'I'm so glad he's staying.' Ann sat down at the table and ruffled an oblivious Darryl's hair. 'He's been brilliant with us. Everyone likes him.'

'I wonder if they'd have liked him quite so much if he'd been taking over from Dr Cheadle and not just going into partnership with her,' Ottilie said, and all three of the women laughed lightly.

'True enough,' Corrine said. 'Nobody much cares for change around here. I remember the fuss they made when you took over from Gwen.'

'So do I!' Ottilie said with such conviction that Corrine laughed again.

'Is the new doctor married?' she asked after it had died down. 'I hear he's moved into Charles's old place alone – is that right?'

'Yes. Not married, and before you ask, because I know you will, he doesn't have any children either.'

'There's a surprise, a lovely man like him on his own. I wonder what happened.'

Ottilie wished people wouldn't wonder – at least not out loud to her. She loved Corrine dearly and she recognised that neither Corrine nor Ann were gossips, but still, she knew things about Simon that she felt she ought to share out of friendship for them, even though her friendship with him deserved her discretion. She half wished she didn't know and then she wouldn't feel the burden of the secret in the way she felt it now. She wondered if he'd told Stacey yet. They'd seemed to be getting on well, and even as Ottilie spent a few hours with them the previous night it seemed to her they were getting closer, right before her eyes.

Corrine shot a shrewd look at Ottilie and then smiled brightly at Ann. 'None of our business, though. I suppose if he wants people to know then we'll know in good time.'

'True enough,' Ann agreed. She turned to Ottilie. 'Now then – bacon sandwich this morning? There's plenty to spare.'

'That sounds amazing. I ought to be a bit more restrained, though. You might start to think I only turn up here to get my breakfast cooked for me.'

Ann laughed. 'Heck of a trek up this hill to get a sandwich! But even if you did, I'd never complain. There's nobody save my Darryl I'd rather cook for.'

'That reminds me,' Corrine said. 'Ottilie, are you down for the community kitchen this week?'

'I think so. Thursday night, if memory serves me. Why?'

'I thought I might lend a hand and it'd be nice to do the same time as you. Give us a chance to catch up. We don't see you so much these days.'

'Too busy being in love,' Ann said.

Ottilie forced a smile. She was in love all right, but she couldn't say the same about Heath. He still hadn't actually said the words, and after their argument the night before she had to wonder if he even felt them in the way she'd hoped and believed he did.

'I'm sorry, I've been so busy time keeps getting away from me. Before I know it, a new week has started and ended, and I've done nothing I meant to do with it. I'll make an effort to come up to the farm and see you and Victor this week, I promise. But if you still want to help out at the kitchen I'm sure Janet would be grateful.'

'I'll give her a tinkle later,' Corrine said. 'Wouldn't be a bad thing to cook for someone other than Victor once in a while.'

'Don't let Victor hear you say that.' Ann wrapped Ottilie's sandwich in some greaseproof paper and put it on the table in front of her.

'Thank you,' Ottilie said. She looked at Darryl. 'Everything all right this morning, Darryl?' she asked. 'Insulin done?'

He glanced up and nodded once, and then went back to his books again.

'Not very talkative this morning,' Ann said apologetically. 'Some days it's like that.'

'That's all right,' Ottilie said. 'As long as he's content and well, nothing else matters.'

'Seems to be. It's nice for things to be on an even keel for once.'

'I'm sure,' Ottilie said, wishing her own keel could be nice and even for a while too.

Ottilie bid Corrine, Ann and Darryl goodbye and headed out to work, her sandwich tucked into her satchel and smelling so good she could have torn it open and devoured it on the spot. But it would have to wait, because she was already running late and if she didn't get a move on she'd walk into a waiting room full of annoyed patients. She often wondered if half of them had anything to do other than visit her, because they always arrived far too early, treating the waiting room like some kind of social club where they could catch up with the latest gossip. On more than one occasion she'd even walked in to find Lavender serving cups of tea to the older ones while they chatted away to whoever else was in there.

As she made her way to her car, her phone pinged the arrival of a text. It was Heath.

My mate has some spare tickets for that band you wanted to see. Thursday night in Salford. A bit short notice but I can buy them from him if you fancy it. X

Ottilie frowned. She couldn't think which band he meant, but even if she'd been desperate to go she'd already committed to helping out at the community kitchen on Thursday evening. She supposed they'd manage without her if she explained the situation, but the idea of leaving them short-handed didn't sit well with her.

Sounds great but I can't. I'm so sorry, I've already told the kitchen I'll help them on Thursday night. X

Can't you get out of it?

Ottilie could have replied, but she really didn't have the time. Besides, she'd said she couldn't go. Heath knew how important her community projects were to her and how she felt about letting people down. But she also understood that perhaps he was trying to make up for his mistake the previous night more than anything else. She'd call him when she got a moment and reassure him that all was well, the incident had been forgotten and he didn't need to shower her with gifts for them to move past it.

She got into the car, tossing her phone onto the seat before she started the engine, and as she did she noticed a follow-up text from Heath. That one was going to have to wait too.

For one reason or another, Ottilie hadn't seen Heath that week. Thursday night arrived, and although they'd spoken on the phone and she'd asked him if he might like to help out at the kitchen and had been perfectly transparent about the fact that Simon had offered his services and would be there, Heath had declined and sounded a bit miffed about it all. She wondered if he was sulking about her refusal of concert tickets or whether he was annoyed she'd chosen the community kitchen over his offer, or if she was simply imagining it.

After some consideration Ottilie decided she might be reading too much into the situation and so thought no more about it, but the fact she hadn't seen him and so she didn't feel they'd truly been able to clear the air nagged at her. She was too busy for it to worry her for long, and when she realised she wasn't worrying enough, that worried her even more. If she could so easily set it aside, what did that say about her relationship with Heath? Was it less than she'd imagined? Was it more fragile? Was it built to last after all?

When she arrived, Magnus and Stacey were already there.

'Hello,' she said, going over to them both as Stacey peeled some potatoes and Magnus chatted to her.

Then the door to the kitchen opened and Simon walked in, immediately greeted with enthusiasm by those closest.

'Am I late?' he asked, looking round. 'Sorry if I am – paper-work, you know…'

'It's never too late here!' Janet, the organiser of the community kitchen, smiled at him. 'Even if you arrived after service there'd be cleaning down to do. Any help is welcome, no matter if it's three minutes or three hours.'

He glanced over at Ottilie with a nod of acknowledgement, but when Stacey looked up, he broke into a warm smile. It was then Ottilie noticed that Stacey seemed to be wearing more make-up than usual. She didn't have her usual jeans on either but wore a flowing dress beneath her apron. Something was definitely going on between these two – there was no denying it now. Ottilie exchanged a look with Magnus. She wondered if he could see it too. Ordinarily he and Geoff had a radar for budding romance and went out of their way to facilitate it, but she couldn't see any signs he'd noticed it yet. Perhaps he was too preoccupied with other things.

'What would you feel comfortable doing?' Janet asked.

Simon turned back to her and cleared his throat; he looked guilty, as if he'd been caught doing something he wasn't meant to. 'I don't know. I can probably handle most tasks. Point me to whatever needs to be done and I'm sure I can get on with it.'

'Brilliant… why don't you help Stacey with the potatoes?'

'Sure, I can do that.'

Stacey looked up and blushed. 'I could do with the help too – there's thousands of these things.'

Janet went to get Simon an apron.

He turned to Ottilie and Magnus. 'What duties did you get?'

'I've only just arrived myself,' Ottilie said. 'I expect Janet will find me something suitably mind-numbing to peel or shell.'

Simon laughed as Janet returned with his apron. 'If you're all right with peeling and chopping then I've got plenty to be going on with. Onions, perhaps?'

'Watch out,' Stacey said. 'If Flo gets here she'll have you sucking on a spoon.'

Simon looked confused.

'It's supposed to stop your eyes from watering when you chop onions,' Ottilie said.

'Oh.' Simon frowned slightly. 'And does it?'

'I'm not entirely sure.'

Simon rooted in a nearby drawer and pulled out a paring knife. 'I won't do the spoon thing, if it's all the same to everyone.'

'While I'm here, Doctor,' Magnus said. 'Geoff and I have been saying for weeks we ought to invite you over for supper. We'd love it if you could come over one night soon.'

'That sounds good,' Stacey said, even though the invite hadn't been for her. 'I'm quite free for the next few days, so…'

Janet had wandered over to another station before the conversation had got underway, and she beckoned Ottilie over now.

'Sorry, I've got to make a start,' she said to the others, more than a little disappointed that she wasn't going to hear where this was going. 'Catch you all later?'

'Absolutely,' Stacey said before turning her quite undivided attention back to Simon.

Ottilie grinned as she walked away. Magnus had to have noticed by now. Much as she loved the idea of Stacey and Simon as a couple, perhaps she ought to have a word with him. He and Geoff had pulled a cupid stunt on her and Heath and it had very nearly backfired. If they tried it again with Simon, it might ruin everything. If anyone asked for her opinion (and they likely wouldn't), she'd say to let things run their course. If Stacey and Simon were meant to be together they'd find a way to make it happen all by themselves.

CHAPTER TWENTY-TWO

Ottilie's shift at the community kitchen had been one of the most fun ones she'd done since she'd begun as a volunteer there. Simon and Stacey had soon settled into banter, and he revealed a cheeky side that Ottilie hadn't known existed. It seemed Stacey brought out something naughty in his nature and it was strangely reassuring to see that not only was he a serious professional but an actual normal human being too, who liked a joke and could be silly from time to time.

At the end of the evening, Ottilie, Stacey, Simon and Magnus had walked through the village together, Ottilie leaving the other three at Magnus's place before going to her own home to settle down for the night. They'd tried to persuade her to go in for one drink, but she'd noticed more than one missed call from Heath and wanted a moment to speak to him, and she didn't feel that a rowdy drinking session (it would turn into that if Magnus and Geoff had anything to do with it) was the place to do that.

The following morning at work, Simon had a look about him she'd never seen before. It could only be described as hopeful. He'd always been pleasant and friendly, but there was something in the way he smiled that was different. What had happened the night before? Ottilie wanted to ask, but she had to remind herself that the best course of action was to leave well alone. But she didn't have to wait long for the first clues.

Her tummy was rumbling, and the last patient had just left. She could hear Lavender moving around downstairs, locking up the surgery so they could have their regular lunch together in the kitchen. Ottilie's would have to wait a little longer, though. She needed to get her afternoon schedule straight before she could join them, otherwise she'd be at sixes and sevens all afternoon without time to catch up. She was busy getting to grips with it when there was a light tap at the door and it opened to reveal Simon poking his head around it.

'Ottilie… have you got a minute?'

Ottilie looked up from her diary. 'Of course I have. Is something wrong?'

'No…' Simon stepped into the office and closed the door. 'It's a bit awkward really, but you're the one person who might understand and I'd appreciate your take on it.'

'OK, so now I'm intrigued.'

He laughed awkwardly. 'Don't be… It's not that exciting. Scary, but not exciting. At least, not to anyone else.'

Ottilie didn't speak this time but nodded for him to go on.

'It's… Well, I know you lost your husband but you've found love again.'

'Right…' Ottilie said, wondering where this was going. She had a hunch, but she couldn't understand what it had to do with her if her hunch was correct. And besides, though she was with Heath, she was beginning to doubt that this was her second true love. The way he'd been lately, she wondered how much longer they could last. 'Yes, I suppose I have.'

'Did you feel… in the beginning, did you feel like it was too soon?'

'A little. But it hadn't been all that long for me since Josh had died – not as long as it's been for you.'

'Hmm…' He cleared his throat, staring down at his feet as he shifted his weight back and forth. 'Still feels too soon. I think it might always feel too soon, no matter how many years go by.'

'I suppose I felt like that too. I almost had to force myself not to.'

'And… I know we discussed this once, but I'm still struggling to see it… How did you deal with the guilt? I assume you felt unbearable guilt, because that's what I'm feeling right now.'

Ottilie shrugged. 'I think you have to accept it as part of the deal. I still have guilt when I think of Josh, but he's not here and Heath is, and I don't want to be lonely anymore. Not for the sake of a bit of unnecessary guilt. And I know what Josh would have said about it. He'd have said it was unnecessary guilt too. Doesn't make it go away, though. I'm sorry, I don't have a magic fix for that.'

Simon shoved his hands in his pockets and nodded slowly. 'That's more or less what I thought. Thank you.'

'I didn't do anything.'

'That's not true. You told me straight, and that was what I needed to hear. I've been trying to dress it up to myself, trying to convince myself there's a solution, that time will put things right, that I'll somehow simply forget about Kiki, find a convenient way to put my guilt aside, but of course, none of that is going to happen. I must find a way to live with it and accept it as part of any new beginning I might hope for. I see that now.'

'Tell me to mind my own business, but do I know this person? I assume there's someone on your mind and this isn't only a hypothetical conversation.'

'You don't need to mind your own business, but I haven't told her how I feel yet. I haven't even got straight in my own head how I feel yet. I know I like her, and I know I feel more relaxed and content in her company than I have in a long time. She's down to earth and practical and funny and… I can't tell yet, but I feel like she might be the right person to try again with. But I don't want to say who it is until I've spoken to her and told her all of this.'

Ottilie smiled slowly. 'I'd say that's a very good idea. Whoever she is – and if it's who I think it might be, then you're right, she's amazing – I hope she feels the same way, and I hope you can see a way to make it work. I didn't sugar-coat the guilt, but I will say, for the right person, it's totally worth going through.'

'You're glad you did it?'

Ottilie nodded. 'Glad I took a chance, yes. I have a feeling that if you take a chance you'll be pleasantly surprised at the response.'

He frowned slightly. 'She's said something? Assuming we're talking about the same person?'

Ottilie's smile grew. 'Why don't you ask her? It's got to be easier in the long run, even if it's scarier.'

He broke into a smile now and began to back towards the door. 'Thanks, Ottilie. I'll do that.'

'And be sure to let me know how it goes,' she called after him as he left the room. Shaking her head, she turned back to her diary. Life could be a funny old thing, but sometimes it threw the sweetest curveballs. She hoped she was right and that he was talking about Stacey, because she knew they'd be great together.

But as she was finishing off, there was another knock at the door and Simon was there again.

'Do you think I ought to have a housewarming?' he asked breathlessly.

Ottilie blinked at him. 'Do you want a housewarming?'

'I don't know – it just occurred to me. Is that what people do here? Did you have one?'

'I didn't. Never even crossed my mind, to be honest. I'm sure nobody would object if you wanted to throw one. Magnus and Geoff are the party kings around here – I'm sure they'd be able to help you, depending on how big you wanted to go.'

'Oh, I think informal ought to do it, don't you?'

'If that's what you want.'

'I don't know. I've never had one before. It feels…' He shrugged.

'Like a time for firsts?' Ottilie asked.

'Like it's about time I put myself out into the world again. Thanks, Ottilie.'

'For what? I really haven't done anything.'

'You paved the way. I can see how you've made this village and the people your new life, and I think if it's been this good for you then it might be good for me too.'

'Still, I haven't done anything special except live my life.'

'Exactly!' Simon beamed. 'And that's what I need to do too!'

A few days later, Ottilie was opening her gate when she heard her name being called. She turned to see Chloe get up from a nearby bench. Baby Mackenzie was in a pushchair and he grinned up at Ottilie, throwing out his arms in delight as they made their way over.

'Hello!' Ottilie said, cooing at Mackenzie before straightening up to see that Chloe looked grave. She had to admit to being surprised by the visit. Stacey was nowhere to be seen, and although Ottilie and Chloe had some pretty huge life events binding them together they'd never been what Ottilie would call close. She always got the feeling Chloe tolerated her mum's friend simply because she was just that. They had very little in common apart from those connections, and Ottilie couldn't remember the last time they'd had a proper deep and meaningful conversation – perhaps never. She couldn't hold back a frown. 'Is everything all right?'

'I don't know,' Chloe said. 'I mean, I'm all right. I don't know if everything is all right for you.'

'What does that mean?'

Chloe glanced around, as if to check they were alone.

'Maybe you'd find it easier to come inside?' Ottilie asked.

Chloe nodded. 'Yeah, I think so. I won't stay long.'

'Stay as long as you like.' Ottilie forced a bright smile. 'I'm always happy to see you and make a fuss of Mackenzie.'

'OK,' Chloe said, following her down the path, but Ottilie didn't imagine for a minute she'd stay longer than she needed to.

Her hunch was proved right as Chloe went into the house with Ottilie but stood awkwardly at the front door, pushing Mackenzie's buggy back and forth in tiny, jerking movements.

'This is going to sound weird, and I don't want to freak you out, but I think someone is stalking you.'

Ottilie's grip tightened on her housekeys. 'What do you mean?'

'I've seen a woman looking in your house. I thought it might be someone you knew looking for you, but then I asked my mum and she said you never said you'd had a visitor or anything. I mean, I know you don't have to tell everyone when you get a visitor, but… I don't know, I got a weird feeling about her. She looked shifty.'

'Oh…'

They were silent for a moment. Clearly Chloe had said what she'd wanted to, and Ottilie didn't quite know what to say in response.

Now that she thought back, it would explain the upturned plant pot she'd found a while back under her windowsill.

But she wasn't quite sure whether that made her feel better or worse.

'I think you should watch out,' Chloe said. 'Maybe you should get Heath to stay over for a bit.'

While Ottilie appreciated Chloe's concern, she wasn't about to do that.

'What did she look like?'

'Don't know.'

'But you must… Nothing? Hair colour? Age? Anything?'

'She had a hat on and she was a bit far away.'

Ottilie was thoughtful. Going on this, she had to wonder if it was even a woman. Could have been a man. Could have been a goblin for all the description Chloe was able to offer. Perhaps there was a far more innocent explanation – a delivery driver at the wrong house maybe. Although, it wasn't like Chloe to be melodramatic.

'Perhaps I could get one of those doorbells with the cameras on.'

'Yeah, that's a shout. You should do that.'

'Chloe, do you want a drink? It's no bother if—'

'Nah, I'm going out later. Mum will be in if you fancy a drink with her. She's babysitting.'

Ottilie nodded. 'Maybe not tonight. Have a good time wherever it is you're off to. And thanks for coming over.'

'No worries.'

Chloe turned and opened the front door, and Ottilie held it for her while she manoeuvred the pushchair out onto the garden path.

'Bye,' Ottilie called after her. 'Bye-bye, Mackenzie.'

Chloe put her hand up in a vague wave and then left with a clatter of the garden gate. Ottilie frowned as she watched her go. While she was grateful for Chloe's concern, she still didn't know what she was meant to do with this new information.

But the fact that Chloe had cared enough to come over without her mum to warn Ottilie, despite the nature of the warning, warmed Ottilie. She'd found Chloe fairly impregnable – difficult to talk to and even more difficult to like – but maybe they'd turned a corner in that respect? Perhaps Chloe was beginning to see Ottilie as a peer rather than an interfering adult she had nothing in common with. Chloe had been the toughest nut to crack since Ottilie's arrival in Thimblebury, but perhaps this could finally be the start of a proper friendship. As long as it didn't turn out to be something sinister, then perhaps the odd stalking incident might be a catalyst for good.

Still, Ottilie needed to do something about that. She didn't feel safe or secure enough to forget about it, though she had no idea what she could do. The camera doorbell – that could be a good start, but it wouldn't reveal people who'd been snooping before its installation. She could ask around the village, though if anyone else had noticed someone hanging around Wordsworth Cottage, Ottilie liked to think they'd have already come to tell her, as Chloe had done. Unless they'd forgotten or hadn't thought anything of it.

She wandered to the kitchen, deep in thought, filled the kettle and switched it on. As it boiled she got out her phone and went online to order one of the camera doorbells she'd mentioned to Chloe. The delivery time was a week, so there would be nothing in place until then, but that couldn't be helped. Who else might have seen?

Her phone pinged the arrival of a message and she looked to see it was Heath. Rather than reply by text, she dialled his number.

'Hello, gorgeous,' he said as he picked up. 'How's your day been?'

'Oh, the usual. Are you planning on coming over tonight?'

'I thought we'd agreed on tomorrow?'

'Oh, yeah, sorry, distracted…'

'What's wrong?'

Ottilie let out a sigh. 'It's probably nothing, but Chloe just told me she'd seen someone, a woman, snooping around my house. Like trying to see in. And the other week there was an upturned plant pot in my garden. Not just knocked over – the plant had been lifted out and the pot turned upside down. I thought it was weird but… well, I couldn't imagine what might have done that. Like who would do that? I'm trying not to freak out but I must admit I'm feeling a bit rattled.'

'Anyone would be. Have you actually seen anything yourself?'

'No. And apart from the pot, nothing else has been disturbed. I don't know what to think. I just ordered one of those doorbells with a camera on it.'

'Good plan.'

'But that's not going to be here for a week. Do you think it will be all right?'

'You want me to come over?'

Ottilie wanted him to come over more than anything, but she didn't want to be *that* woman. She wanted to be the woman who was confident and independent and didn't need a man to protect her. Whoever might be doing this for whatever reason, the one satisfaction she didn't want to give them was to look scared.

But then her thoughts went to Josh's attacker. She'd spent so many of the months after Josh's death terrified that his attacker might come for her next, plagued by irrational fears, that to realise now she hadn't thought about that for months was a shock. But this couldn't be connected, could it? Josh's attacker had been arrested and was awaiting trial. He might be out on bail, she supposed – she'd never thought to ask when the trial had been put back. Even so, as far as she knew, nobody who might put her in harm's way knew where she'd moved to – not even Faith, Josh's colleague on the police force who'd been keeping Ottilie in the loop about the case. Perhaps it wouldn't be a bad idea to call Faith and mention it to her.

'I'm coming over,' Heath said into the gap.

'It's fine,' Ottilie decided. 'It's late and a long drive.'

'I can't say I'm happy about it, but if you're sure…'

'I'm sure. It's going to be something and nothing, isn't it? I'll put the burglar alarm on tonight before I go to bed so I'll be safe enough.'

'Look at you, Ms Oakcroft. All independent now.'

'Is that sarcasm?'

'No! I mean it. When I think back to first meeting you, you were full of nerves.'

'Was I? I mean, my confidence had been knocked, but I had good reason. I suppose I know what you're saying, and I'm guessing there's a compliment in there somewhere.'

'I'm sorry, I know that – it was a flippant comment and I shouldn't have made it. I only meant I'm proud of you.'

'Thanks. So I'll see you at the weekend?'

'Try stopping me.'

'Good. Looking forward to it. Love you…'

There was a pause. Ottilie had said the words in the way she often did now to end a call with him, casually, trying not to attach meaning but hoping for it just the same, but she'd never heard them said back.

'Look after yourself,' he said. 'Call me if there's even a sniff of trouble and I'll be there.'

'I will,' Ottilie said, ending the call, not reassured, as she'd hoped to be, but deflated. Even in the midst of all this, even though she might have bigger things to worry about, the one thing playing on her mind was that those three little words had still to be uttered by him. Why couldn't she get past it? Surely he didn't need to say them when he showed her he cared, and yet, it still mattered to her for reasons even she didn't really understand. Still, that had to be better than being scared, didn't it?

CHAPTER TWENTY-THREE

Ottilie was on her way out for her first call of the day, her usual visit up to Hilltop Farm to check on Darryl and Ann, when the knock came at the front door. With a puzzled glance at the clock to confirm it was as early as she'd suspected, and wondering who might want her at such an hour, she answered it to find Flo on her doorstep.

'Morning, Flo. Everything all right?'

'I'm all right,' Flo replied gruffly. 'I only wanted to check on you.'

'Me?' Ottilie frowned, but then her expression cleared. 'Ah… Heath phoned you last night.'

'Heath?' It was Flo's turn to frown. 'No. Haven't heard from him in days. I had thought I'd find him here, but no car, so…'

'No, he hasn't been over yet this week. Both of us have been a bit busy, you know.'

Ottilie gave a patient smile and allowed a beat of silence in the hope Flo might be inclined to say why she'd come out so early to see her. She wanted to be there if Heath's grandma needed her, but she also had other people to see. But when Flo only shuffled on the doorstep and cleared her throat expectantly, as if she was waiting for Ottilie herself to offload, Ottilie spoke again.

'Um… was that all? Not that I don't appreciate you coming over, but I'm supposed to be up at Hilltop.'

'Well, if that's how it is…'

'It's not like anything,' Ottilie said, keeping hold of her

patience. With Flo, that could sometimes be a challenge. 'I only wondered if there was something specific you needed me for. Because I could call at your house after work if you needed—'

'No, I wanted to see you were all right and I can see that you are. Nothing bothering you, all quite well.'

'Is this because we haven't been over for a few days?'

Flo paused for a split second too long before she nodded. 'Yes, that'll be it. Silly old woman, aren't I? I expect you can both humour me for five minutes at the weekend, can't you? If you can make time in your busy schedule, of course.'

'Flo…' Ottilie tried harder than ever not to frown. 'You know it's not like that. We love coming over to yours but sometimes it's not that easy.'

'I only live down the road,' Flo huffed.

'Yes, but…' Ottilie finally let go of the weary sigh she'd been holding on to. Never mind that she worked all hours and then had volunteer projects too. Never mind that she was still early in a new relationship and that she had things from her past that needed her attention. Never mind that she was entitled to quiet time of her own in between all of that, that she had to sleep and eat and take care of herself too. 'You're right, we've neglected you.'

'I'm not a dog you keep in the yard.'

'Sorry, that didn't come out the way I meant it to. We'd love to pop over, and when Heath gets here tonight I'll make sure we do.'

Flo folded her arms and jutted out her chin. 'I might be out. I might have plans – you can't just turn up when you feel like it.'

'We'll phone ahead to check. Sorry, Flo, but I really have to get to Hilltop before work, so…'

Flo hesitated and then glanced up and down the street in a way that was suddenly so shifty Ottilie had to wonder whether there was something else going on here. Had Flo really come over this early just to complain that she hadn't been visited in the past few days? Reading between the lines now, Ottilie was starting to doubt it. But if not that, then what?

The asking would have to wait.

Flo stepped back, glancing up and down the lane again, and then seemed satisfied with what she saw.

'Tonight, you say?' she asked as she made her way down Ottilie's garden path to leave.

'Tonight, I promise,' Ottilie said.

'I'll make a bite to eat then. Remember, if you don't come it'll be wasted.'

'We'll be there.'

Ottilie shook her head as she watched Flo waddle down the lane towards her own house. She loved that old lady, but boy could she be hard work. You never knew quite where you were with her. But if she knew anything about Flo – and it wasn't much, admittedly – it was that there was more than met the eye to this morning's visit. Ottilie would have to find out what it was at some point, because she felt like it might matter.

Ottilie had to admit she was surprised that Simon's housewarming actually went ahead the following weekend. She'd imagined it was a spur-of-the-moment idea, instigated by his strange mood the week before when he'd come to ask her about new starts and second chances and all that other deep stuff she hadn't quite known how to respond to, but he'd been into her office a few days later to issue the invitation properly. It wasn't anything big or fancy, he'd said, just a few new friends and neighbours being offered drinks and nibbles and an opportunity for them all to get to know each other better.

She was more surprised that Heath had agreed to go with her. Simon had invited him, of course, and while Simon had seemed keen to get to know Heath better, Heath appeared to have other ideas. There was no outright animosity, but Ottilie did get a strong sense of dislike and she couldn't see a reason for it other than silly macho rivalry.

She was standing in Simon's kitchen with Charles and Fliss as they explained why they disagreed with Simon's redecoration, but in the next breath stated they didn't really care what he did with the place because Charles wasn't going to go back there. Clearly they did because they had a critical eye for every little thing he'd done to make it his home rather than one he was borrowing.

Ottilie tried to listen and nodded politely where she felt she ought to, but her attention was very much distracted by Heath's conversation with his grandma to the side of her. He'd been irritable since his arrival, and even though he'd obviously done his best to keep his mood even, Ottilie could tell something wasn't right. She could hear it now in his tone with Flo too, but at least Flo could give as good as she got. They were going to have to battle it out without her because she wasn't in a position to referee right now; she only hoped they'd keep things civil enough that the party didn't get ruined.

Flo had been acting strangely since she'd turned up on Ottilie's doorstep the other morning. They'd been to visit as she'd promised, but Flo had acted as if nothing had ever been wrong. Ottilie would never understand that woman as long as she lived. Even more confusing, while Heath had appeared to be his normal self, Ottilie couldn't help but sense an undercurrent of disquiet, though she couldn't put her finger on what made her feel that or, indeed, what the cause might be.

He turned from his conversation with Flo now, and at the same moment she glanced away from hers with Fliss and

Charles and caught his eye. He forced a smile. She could tell it was a forced one – they were getting to that stage now where she could read him better. She tried to return it with one that was warmer and more reassuring, to silently let him know that whatever was on his mind he could share it when they got a moment and she'd do her best to understand.

Whether he got it or not she didn't know; he turned back to his gran, who was now nudging him and pointing to Magnus and Geoff. Ottilie tried to hear what she was saying, but Fliss and Charles were closer and too loud. In fact, Fliss was on her fourth or fifth large glass of red and they'd only been at Simon's house for an hour. Ottilie had the feeling things were going to get lively later, and the quiet informal gathering Simon had been hoping for would turn into something entirely different.

Unable to prevent herself, her eyes roved the room to see where Stacey was. She was still by the window, talking to Simon. They were both laughing their heads off. Ottilie allowed herself a smug, private little smile. If they weren't a couple by the end of the year she'd be shocked. And Simon had as good as admitted to Ottilie that he was interested. The biggest surprise at this point was that he hadn't yet asked Stacey out. It seemed like he'd made up his mind to do just that when he'd been in Ottilie's office to admit he had feelings for someone, but as far as Ottilie knew he hadn't, and that had been over a week ago. She supposed she could have a word with Stacey and nudge her to do the asking, but she'd vowed to stay out of it and assumed one of them would be brave enough to make the first move. Apparently, she'd sorely overestimated them both.

Magnus and Geoff came over to talk to Flo and Heath, and now Ottilie really wanted to be involved in that conversation rather than the one she was currently stuck in with Fliss and Charles. She did her best to tune in but it was no good – she couldn't make out what they were saying. She cast around for an opportunity to sneak away from her current company. Perhaps it was a bit rude, but she felt like they were both too tipsy to notice. In fact, the way they were going, in half an hour they'd both be too tipsy to notice if she was with them at all. It seemed Charles had forgotten all about his health scare and the fact he wasn't supposed to be drinking, and if his own fully paid-up GP wife wasn't going to tell him off, then it certainly wasn't Ottilie's place to.

Simon's dining table had been pushed up against a wall to make room in the centre of the floor, and it was loaded with snacks and bottles. Victor and Corrine were looking over the plates while Ann chatted to them and Darryl, armed with his train books, was on a chair in the corner, alternately reading and glancing up to check the situation in the room. More often than not his gaze went straight to his mum, who seemed to have a sixth sense for it, because every time it happened she responded immediately by turning to him with a smile and a nod of reassurance. And when she did, he'd go back to his books, seemingly satisfied that his anchor was still close by. Ottilie loved their relationship. They'd weathered so much together; Ann was devoted to her son, and he clearly not only needed her but in his own awkward way adored her.

Corrine glanced at Ottilie and offered a little wave. Ottilie smiled back and spied her chance to get away from Fliss and Charles.

'Excuse me,' she said at the first gap for breath, 'I want to see how Corrine is.'

Fliss shook her head wryly and knocked back the remainder of the wine in her glass. 'Always working, eh?'

Ottilie smiled. 'I promise I'll work some socialising into it.'

'Off you pop then, Nurse Oakcroft.'

As she made her way over, she passed Heath and Flo. Their conversation halted once she was in earshot, and he turned to Ottilie with that forced smile again.

'Everything all right?' she asked, laying a gentle hand on his arm and looking from one to the other.

'Of course,' Flo said. 'Why wouldn't it be?'

'No reason…' Ottilie looked into Heath's eyes, trying to read him. Something was going on, but she couldn't work it out.

Flo looked over at Simon and Stacey. 'Hmm… someone's getting friendly over there.'

'They get on well,' Ottilie said.

'Flirting like mad,' Flo continued.

'Well, they both deserve some happiness,' Ottilie replied. 'I hope…' She let the sentence tail off without finishing. She was meant to be keeping out of it, and that included keeping out of gossip about it too.

Heath looked across to where they'd been approached by Chloe, who had Mackenzie in her arms, and Simon was currently making quite a fuss of the little boy, making him giggle. Heath made no comment on his grandma's observations, but in what must have been an unguarded moment, the dislike was clear on his face. If they'd been alone, Ottilie would have demanded to know what Simon had done to deserve his obvious disdain, because as far as she could tell he'd done nothing at all. They'd barely even exchanged two words, even tonight where Heath was a guest in Simon's house.

The more she knew Heath, the more she saw things that bothered her. She was no fool – she understood as well as anyone that relationships were like that. The honeymoon period was a thing for a reason; the sparkle and fireworks dimmed with time and it required more effort, but while she accepted that, she was also filled with doubt. What if Heath wasn't her second happy ever after? What if she'd got it wrong? What if discovering this new side to him, one she wasn't sure she liked, was the beginning of the end? She'd made herself vulnerable for this man, had taken a chance on him and had invested so much of her emotional energy she wasn't sure she could bear the thought that it had all been for nothing.

'He lives here alone,' Flo said.

Ottilie looked at her. It seemed like an unnecessary statement. Simon had made no secret of the fact, even if he'd chosen not to tell people about his past.

'Yes.'

'Strange for a man of his age.'

'Is it?' Ottilie asked. 'Why's that? There's all sorts of reasons. Heath lives alone.'

'But there's a good reason for that.'

'There might be a good reason for Simon too.'

'Came here from Africa…'

'Yes.'

'And nobody knows anything about him. What on earth was he doing in Africa?'

'Working,' Ottilie said, unable to keep the tartness from her voice now. 'Looking after disadvantaged people who don't have access to proper healthcare. Is that the answer to the riddle you were hoping for, or did you want to hear something juicier than that?'

Heath turned to her now. 'There's no need to get defensive. Gran's only saying what everyone is thinking.'

Ottilie raised her eyebrows. 'Including you?'

'No, but… well, you've got to admit he's a bit too good to be true. Nobody is that good and pure.'

'Aren't they?'

'I'm only saying.'

'Well, don't. It's mean-spirited and it doesn't suit you to be mean-spirited.'

Heath held up his hands and pretended to back off. 'All right…'

'And don't patronise me.' Ottilie's voice had a warning edge now. 'I'm going to talk to Corrine – I might actually get a sensible conversation over there.'

'Ott, wait…'

She didn't wait. She marched across to the table, smoothing her expression as Corrine turned to greet her. She wanted to enjoy the evening, but at the same time she wasn't going to stand by and allow unkind speculation about Simon, even when that came from Heath. She didn't want an argument with Heath, but when he was wrong she was going to say so, even if it did end up causing an argument.

'Hello.' Corrine, Victor and Ann all turned as she reached the table. 'This is all very nice and civilised, isn't it?'

'The party?'

Corrine nodded. 'We don't get invited to many parties these days,' she continued, and Victor gave a short nod.

'True enough.'

'I can't remember the last party I went to,' Ann said. 'It's nice to be out.'

'I bet,' Ottilie said.

Darryl looked up and she smiled at him. 'All right there in your corner?'

He nodded vaguely, glanced once at his mum and then went back to his books.

'When are you coming up to Daffodil Farm?' Corrine asked. 'Seems like we never see you up there these days.'

'You're not the first person to tell me that,' Ottilie said ruefully. 'It's making me wonder if I'm neglecting a lot of people.'

'I expect you're busy,' Corrine added.

'Yes, but also wondering how I ever managed to visit anyone before, because I've been busy from the first day I arrived in the village and it didn't stop me back then. I will make an effort to come up next week. After all, I'd like to see how Alpaca Ottilie is doing.'

'Oh, settling in brilliantly,' Victor said. 'Just like her namesake did.' He chuckled as he reached for a mini sausage roll. 'Good to see the new doctor keeping it simple,' he added, popping it into his mouth. 'None of that rubbish fancy food. You know where you are with a sausage roll, don't you?'

'Hmm…' Corrine gave a sceptical look, and Ottilie couldn't help a little laugh.

'You do,' she agreed. 'Though I don't ever say no to the fancy stuff either.'

'He seems nice,' Corrine said, angling her head at Simon, who now had Mackenzie in his arms as Chloe went to get a drink. 'Ann has been telling us all about when he came up to see to her when she had her infection.'

'Oh, he was lovely,' Ann gushed. 'So kind to me, and Darryl really took to him. That's rare enough as it is – he doesn't say much, my Darryl, but he's a very good judge of character. If he likes you, chances are you're a good one.'

Everyone had only good things to say about Simon, apart from Heath. He hadn't said anything bad, but he hadn't said anything good either, and it was obvious he had thoughts he wasn't about to share with Ottilie because he knew she'd disapprove. Everyone wanted to know what Simon's story was too – and Ottilie was reminded of the secrets she kept for him once again when Corrine aired her curiosity.

'I know he lives here alone, but I wonder if he's ever been married,' she mused as she watched him talk to Mackenzie.

'Must have been — a man like that would have been snapped up by now. Very good with children too, by the looks of it. Do you think he has any? I bet you know, don't you, Ottilie? As you work with him, you must know.'

Ottilie paused to choose her words carefully. 'There's no wife and no children,' she said slowly. 'But I think it's best if people leave that subject alone.'

All three of them turned to her now, and there was no mistaking their intense interest.

'Please,' Ottilie said, knowing she was probably appealing to the three most sensible and considerate souls in the room, 'don't ask me any more about it and please don't bring it up with him.'

Corrine nodded, some kind of understanding seeming to dawn on her. 'Of course.' She glanced over again. 'Poor man,' she murmured, and although Victor seemed confused by her statement, he didn't ask. They'd have plenty of time to speculate together later, and Ottilie didn't doubt for a minute they'd be doing that once they got home. She was certain that they would come to a conclusion reasonably close to the truth of the situation — that Simon had somehow lost his family in tragic circumstances — and as long as she could be confident she'd kept her secrets about it then she was fine with them working it out for themselves.

Ottilie gave a knowing smile as she noticed Fliss corner Chloe at the drinks table. Poor Chloe looked shell-shocked. It was probably the longest social conversation she'd ever had with Fliss, and as Fliss was already tipsy, Ottilie thought she might like to be a fly on the wall for it. Chloe looked as if she wanted nothing more than to run away, but Fliss appeared determined to keep her to finish whatever it was she was telling, or asking, or whatever she was doing.

'Dr Cheadle seems happy to have the new fella on board,' Victor said.

'I think it suits them both,' Ottilie said. 'The timing for him arriving back in England couldn't have been better – he says so himself.'

'Ah yes, that's right. Africa, wasn't it?' Victor sipped at his beer. 'Yes, he…'

Ottilie's sentence tailed off again. She seemed to be doing a lot of that lately. But she'd noticed Simon give Mackenzie to Stacey and make his way over to Flo and Heath. Presumably he was making an effort to get to each guest and have a quick word – as any good host would do. But knowing how they'd both been gossiping about him moments before she wasn't entirely sure she trusted either of them to stay as tactful as they ought to be.

'I won't be a minute,' she said vaguely, already beginning to walk away. 'Just got to see Heath…'

Victor replied, but Ottilie didn't catch it. She'd go back to them later and make it right, but for some reason she couldn't put her finger on, she felt as if she had to intervene in the conversation that was about to take place across the room, if only to make sure Flo and Heath behaved. Somewhere in the back of her mind was the notion that she shouldn't have to do this for two grown adults, and perhaps she was overreacting, but it didn't stop her from going over anyway.

'We were just talking about you…' Simon greeted as she looped her arm into the crook of Heath's and offered them all a smile that was far breezier than she felt.

'Oh? I hope it was to say how amazing I am.'

'Actually, it was,' Simon said with a fond smile that made her heart sink.

She glanced up at Heath. Why was this so stressful? Surely there was no need for her to feel this way?

'I was saying,' he continued, 'how dedicated you are and how much the patients love you and how you've been so welcoming to me.'

'Oh.' Ottilie wafted away the compliment. 'It's only what anyone would do.'

'That's where you're wrong,' Simon said. 'I've done short-term stints at a few other places since I got back to England and I've never enjoyed them like I've enjoyed being at Thimblebury surgery. I certainly wouldn't have wanted to take on a permanent position with them, even though I'd been looking for one. It's great here. I hope I'm here for a long time.'

'We do too,' Ottilie said firmly.

'Where did you say you came back to England from?' Heath asked.

'Botswana.'

'I bet that was different.'

'It was, but I enjoyed my time there.'

'You were working as a doctor? Was it good pay? Better than here?'

Simon laughed. 'The pay was non-existent. God, if I'd done it for that, then I'd have realised what a huge mistake I'd made after the first week and come home.'

'You were there a long time then?'

'A little over a year.'

'What did make you come home if it wasn't the pay?'

'Oh, I felt my time was up there. When you know, you know, right? I woke up one day and felt I'd done what I could there – at least what I'd wanted to do.'

'Which was?'

Simon shrugged. 'It's quite hard to sum it up. How long have you got?'

'But if you had to sum it up,' Heath insisted.

'I suppose I wanted to make a difference somewhere. Earn my place on the Earth, you know? I didn't want to just take up space; I wanted to contribute.'

Flo coughed loudly, and when Ottilie looked she could see some scepticism. Simon's ideals had sounded laudable, and while she totally got him, she could imagine Flo might find it all a bit pretentious.

'Anyway' – Simon smiled warmly at them all – 'help yourself to anything – nibbles or drink or anything that's out. I wanted to come over to thank you for being here. It means a lot to me to be here myself, in this village with such a great team of colleagues and new friends and neighbours.'

'Which reminds me,' Flo said as Simon left them with a good-natured nod. 'Where's Lavender?'

'Good question,' Ottilie replied, searching the room. 'She told me she'd be late but I didn't think she'd be this late.'

'Perhaps she couldn't get in past Simon's halo,' Heath said in a low voice.

Ottilie turned sharply to him as Flo chuckled. 'What was that?'

'Well… you've got to admit he's too good to be true, isn't he?'

'You said that before.'

'And I still think it.'

'There's nothing wrong with trying to do good in the world.'

'Of course there isn't, but there's doing good in the world, and then there's expecting a medal for it.'

'He's never said he wants anything for doing it!' Ottilie squeaked, and then realised how her voice was rising and tried to get it under control. 'What's got into you?'

'Nothing's got into me. I could ask you the same thing.'

'There's nothing wrong with me.'

'I make a bit of a joke and you're down my throat.'

'That wasn't a joke. Jokes are meant to be funny and that was just mean.'

'Come on, you two…' Flo cut in, and she looked concerned now. 'Settle down.'

'We are settled,' Heath said.

'It looks like it.'

'Gran, butt out.'

Flo's mouth fell open and Ottilie scowled at Heath. 'There was no need for that.'

'Sorry, Gran. Ottilie says you should keep interfering.'

'I'm not standing for this!' Flo yelped and marched off in the direction of Janet from the community kitchen, who'd not long arrived and was helping herself to a handful of nuts.

'I don't even know what to say,' Ottilie hissed as she watched her go. 'I don't know why you're being like this. If you don't want to be here, all you have to do is say so. I won't stop you from leaving; not when you're in this sort of mood.'

'I'm not in a mood.'

'Then why do I dislike you so much right now?'

'I'm sorry you dislike me. I haven't changed, and you used to like me well enough before…'

Ottilie crossed her arms. 'Before you started being horrible?'

'Before… Never mind – you'll only take his side anyway. After all, who can compete with all that?'

'All what? What are you talking about?'

'You know what – don't make me say his name here because somebody will hear me.'

'You had no problem saying it five minutes ago.'

'Yeah…' Heath glanced around. 'But people have started to notice that we're having words now. In this village, having words in public means everyone will know what it's about because they'll be doing their best to hear what we're saying.'

'I'm sure we're not that interesting.'

'You mean I'm not.'

'I didn't say that.'

'But I don't volunteer at soup kitchens or fly across the globe to save the lives of poor people.'

Ottilie had no words. For a moment she simply stared at him. Finally, she found them, for what they were worth.

'Is that really what's eating you? All this because you feel… what? I don't even know. I've never asked you to do any of those things. I mean, I invite you to help out if you want to, but I've never judged you for not doing any of it. I totally understood you didn't have the time. You do good in other ways.'

'Like what?'

'Heath, stop it. I don't know what you want me to say. I tell you all the time how important you are to me, how much I care about you. What more do you want? I don't know what else you need from me. Am I supposed to do something to prove it? Because right now I'm really confused about where we are.'

He was silent for a moment as he studied her. And then he shook his head. 'I'm sorry. I don't know why I said any of that, but you're right. I suppose I feel…'

There was another heavy pause. And then Ottilie spoke into it.

'You don't need to feel like anything. I don't love anyone else; I don't want anyone else. I only love you and I want you.'

'And I want you too,' he said, but Ottilie took no comfort from his reply. She was more concerned at what he'd missed out. She'd said it – again, and more directly this time. He'd only told her he wanted her in return. She'd given him the perfect opportunity to say he loved her and he'd ignored it.

He leaned in to kiss her lightly. 'Ignore me. I must be hard work and you're totally right – I'm being unfair.'

'I wish I could understand it.'

'Honestly…' He rubbed a hand through his chestnut waves. 'So do I. Sometimes I feel like I can't believe you picked me.'

'Well, that's silly.'

'But it's not. Everyone loves you. I bet' – he lowered his voice – 'if you were single, he'd be trying to get with you. And I'm not saying that to be weird or jealous or territorial or anything – it's because I see it. I see the way he looks at you, and you'd be perfect for each other, and if you were both single I know you'd be together.'

'Heath, do you have any idea how daft that sounds? Things don't work like that. Just because two people look as if they ought to go together on paper doesn't mean they will. There's no chemistry between us at all – surely you can see that? He doesn't look at me like anything. Or maybe he only sees me as a really good friend who's been through what he's been through, someone who understands him like only a few other people could.'

'What does that mean?'

She shook her head. 'I can't tell you.'

Heath's expression changed again in an instant. He'd been sorry for his words and behaviour and he'd looked it, but now there was distrust in his face.

'I'm sorry,' Ottilie said. 'I'm not trying to be mysterious or anything, but it's not my story to tell.'

'Not even to me? I thought we were meant to tell each other everything?'

'Not this.'

'So it's secrets? We've been together less than a year and there are secrets already. Something is starting to feel familiar here.'

'I don't know what you mean, but it's not my secret.'

'You're the one keeping it from me, so as far as I can tell it is.'

'If you're so desperate to know why don't you go and ask him?' Ottilie fired back, though that was the last thing she wanted.

In a fit of pique it had escaped her mouth, and now she wished she could take it back.

'You'd love that, wouldn't you? I'd look like a tool, and everyone would think so.'

'That's not what I meant—'

'I think I should go.'

Ottilie folded her arms tight across her chest. 'Oh, now, see, that's starting to feel familiar to me. It's your default response these days, isn't it? We begin a difficult conversation and you bail.'

'I'm not bailing. I'm leaving before one of us says something we regret. There's a difference.'

'Looks the same to me.'

'I don't know what you want me to say, but this is hardly my idea of a good night out and I'm sure it can't be yours. I think you'd rather be talking to Simon right now so—'

'Argh!' Ottilie let out an impetuous squeal. It wasn't in her nature to lose her temper, but she was sick of them going round in circles, and even more sick of Heath's digs. More than one conversation in the room halted and they turned to look at her. She smoothed her expression and lowered her voice. 'If you really must know, he lost his wife and young child. There. Happy?'

Heath at least had the decency to look ashamed, but Ottilie was already angry and there was no way back. 'I wasn't keeping secrets; I was being respectful of someone else's past because I know how hard it is to have something like that in it. I don't know how I can make you see I'm not Mila. I'm not a bit like her, and if you can't see that by now then I don't know how we can move forward. It feels as if we'll always be in her shadow. Right now I feel as if I'm in a relationship with the both of you because she's always bloody there!'

Heath was silent for a moment as he stared at her. 'I'm sorry. I didn't know you felt that way.'

'I don't know how you missed it, but yeah, that's how I feel.'

'So what do we do about it?'

'The question is what *you* do about it. I'm not the one with the problem. Maybe you should go and work on fixing that and then come back to me when you've figured it out.'

'You want to end things?' Heath asked, his voice incredulous.

'Of course I don't, but I also don't like the way things are going. If we don't sort this now then it will end, because between us we'll ruin it.'

'I'd never do that.'

'Open your eyes, Heath. You're already doing it, even if you don't mean to.'

He shook his head slowly. 'I don't want to have this discussion. I think I will go, but I'll call you tomorrow when we've both calmed down.'

'Don't patronise me. I am calm; it's you who needs to calm down. You're seeing threats that aren't there.'

'I think you're the one doing that. You keep telling me you're not Mila like she's… She's no threat to you. She's nothing to me.'

'Then why do you take me to the places you took her? Like the spa, and the restaurant where we saw her… Don't lie – it's obvious the reason she chose that place and the reason you chose that place was because you'd both been there together.'

'That's not the reason we went there – I thought you'd like it!'

Ottilie folded her arms tighter still – any tighter and there was a danger she might squeeze herself to death. But she was so tense, so afraid of what might come next, and yet also determined not to let anyone – not even Heath – walk all over her. And it was starting to feel like that. She was agreeable and tolerant and could compromise when the situation called for it, but there had to be a limit – even for her. Where was the point at which a relationship stopped being equal? Was it when things went that way, or when they *felt* that way? Because this one was beginning to feel like it.

They were silent as these thoughts ran through her head. Was he thinking the same thing? Ottilie wasn't going to ask because she feared the answer, but even if she'd intended to ask the opportunity was snatched away by her phone ringing in her pocket. She wasn't going to answer it because it felt like the worst timed phone call in history, but then Heath nodded at the location of the sound.

'Aren't you going to get that?'

Escape route, she thought vaguely, but perhaps he had a point. No matter how important the call might be, she supposed it might diffuse the tension to leave the conversation for a moment.

Taking the phone out, she noted Lavender's name on the caller ID.

'Is everything all right?'

'Not really. I was on my way in and I heard this huge crash. It came from your house, so I ran over thinking you might be in trouble, but when I got here someone was lying on the ground… I think she's hurt.'

'I don't understand…' Ottilie frowned. 'Someone at my house?'

'Outside your house. Like in the garden.'

Ottilie glanced at Heath. They were a long way from being finished here, but if there was an issue at her house she needed to be there.

'OK… can you hang on for me?'

'Sure.'

'Is she OK? When you say hurt, how badly?'

'Well, she's definitely awake because I've had a proper earful from her. But when she tried to walk off she couldn't, so I think she's done something to her leg. You'd better hurry up if you want to talk to her; she's phoned someone to come and get her and I think he's on his way.'

'Is it someone local?' Ottilie asked, and then shook her head. 'Never mind – it doesn't matter.'

'Actually…' Lavender paused. 'Is Heath there?'

'Yes, but…'

'Maybe don't bring him. Or maybe you should bring him – it's hard to say what's best.'

'What do you mean? Is she dangerous?'

Lavender lowered her voice. 'She's definitely a whack job. Ottilie, I may as well tell you because you'll find out in a few minutes anyway. It's Heath's ex.'

CHAPTER TWENTY-FOUR

Ottilie hurried from the party, Heath following.

When they got there, Ottilie could see the lamplit figure of Mila sitting on the garden wall, glaring at Lavender, who stood with her arms folded glaring back.

'Well, here comes the cavalry,' Mila said as she looked up to see Ottilie and Heath arrive.

'What's going on?' Ottilie glanced between Lavender and Mila, inviting whoever wanted to go first to fill her in.

'She won't tell me,' Lavender said. 'I've asked her about five times now.'

'She'll answer me!' Heath said, making a move towards her.

Ottilie held him back. She looked down at Mila's foot. Even in the gloom of the evening light she could see it was swollen. 'Does that hurt?' she asked.

Mila shifted her weight on the wall, but it was obvious from the careful way she moved that it did. 'Why would you care?'

'Because she's a normal human being,' Heath said. 'Why are you here?'

Mila's reply was so cool, Ottilie knew that her answer was genuine. 'You know why I'm here. I'm doing what you wouldn't.'

'How did you even know where I lived?' Ottilie asked. 'Is it you who's been—'

'Yes,' Mila cut in. 'If you're asking if I've been here before then yes, but you're never bloody here.'

Ottilie paused as she eyed Mila with suspicion. Heath's ex

hadn't given an answer to the question of how she'd found Ottilie's house, but Ottilie could guess that it hadn't taken much to figure it out. People around here would give that away without even realising, especially if they didn't know who Mila was. And it wasn't a huge place – Mila would only have to skulk around a bit to work it out for herself.

'OK,' she said. 'I'm here now. So what do you want?'

'I need you to—'

Heath stepped forward. 'No, Mila, don't—'

'I have to. You'd do it if you were me.'

'I wouldn't because there's no point. Ottilie can't… It's out of her hands – surely you can see that. She couldn't do anything to help if she wanted to, and if I were her I wouldn't anyway. Please, Mila, don't—'

'What?' Ottilie cut in, a deep sense of alarm now searing at her guts. She stared at Heath, trying to read him, fearing now what she'd find. They'd clearly discussed something. Something about her. Mila had wanted something from her and she'd gone to him to get it. What?

And then it all made sense. Mila had been here before, snooping around. It had to be her – the time Chloe had seen a woman, the time her plant pot had been upturned. Ottilie's thoughts raced. Were there other occasions? Flo had called one morning early to check on her. And she'd issued a warning before about trusting Mila.

'If she goes' – Mila tossed her head at Lavender – 'I'll tell you.'

'Charming!' Lavender huffed. 'Should have let you rot here with your bad ankle.'

'Well, nobody asked you to stick your nose in!' Mila fired back.

'Lavender…' Ottilie gave her an apologetic grimace. 'Would you mind…?'

'I'm late for the party anyway, so whatever.' She glared at Mila again before turning back to Ottilie. 'Phone me if you need me.'

'I will, thanks.'

Ottilie waited for a moment until Lavender was a way down the lane before returning her gaze to Mila. 'OK,' she said. 'I'm listening.'

Mila shot a look at Heath, and in it was triumph. Ottilie had already been unsettled, but now she was really worried. What the hell was about to come out of this woman's mouth?

'Mila, I'm asking you to think about this,' Heath began, but that only unnerved Ottilie more. He knew what was coming, and it was so bad he sounded scared. What could be that bad? And if he knew what was coming, how long had he been keeping it from Ottilie?

'I have,' Mila said. She looked at Ottilie. 'So I suppose he hasn't told you who my cousin is?'

Ottilie stared at her, forehead creased in a deep frown. That wasn't how she'd expected this conversation to begin. 'Your cousin?'

Mila nodded and Heath groaned.

'Ashton Steele.' Mila allowed a beat for it to sink in. 'You know who that is, right?'

Ottilie stared, unable to form a response. She knew the name all right. That name would be burned into her memory for as long as she lived. The man responsible for destroying all her happiness; the man who'd taken her Josh from her.

'Oh, I know,' Ottilie said, unable to decide whether she felt sicker with fear or rage. 'He's a murderer, that's who he is.'

'Innocent until proven guilty,' Mila corrected, and for the first time her features softened. 'He didn't do it. He was set up.'

'Is that what he told you?'

'The police set him up. They needed a result, and he was a prime candidate.'

Ottilie shook her head. 'You would say that – he's your cousin. Birds of a feather and all that.'

'Are you saying I'm a criminal?'

'I'm saying blood is thicker than water.'

'Is it wrong to look out for your family?'

'When they're bad people, yes.' Ottilie turned to Heath. 'And you *knew* about this?'

'Not at first. Ottilie, please, let me explain—'

'No need. I get why you wouldn't tell me, though I have to admit to being hurt by it. What was that you said about keeping secrets? You know what's worse than keeping this from me? It's being such a hypocrite about it.'

He began a reply but she flung up a hand to stop him. 'I'm talking to Mila now. So what do you want from me? You want me to know this… why? Do you think it will split me and Heath up? Is that what you're doing?'

'No. I want your help. I want you to talk to your friends in the police, put in a word for him, because he really didn't do it.'

'What? You're joking, right? Even if I wanted to – and why the hell would I want to? – I couldn't do anything to help him. I have friends in the force, yes, of course, but I can't change the course of a trial.'

'You can give evidence – say you don't think it was him.'

'But it *was* him. The police have evidence! They told me—'

'You don't know that! You only know what they tell you, and they can stitch anyone up they want. He was nowhere near your fella that day!'

'The police think so and it's good enough for me. Sorry, Mila— Actually, no, I'm not sorry. I can't help you. And even if I could, I wouldn't.'

Mila let out a sigh, and then her features were more cunning again. 'It's a shame. The family will be disappointed when I tell them that.'

Ottilie's temper finally flared. 'You think that's a threat? I've spent the last year being terrified of your family. Yes, your family are so rough, have such a terrible reputation that I've been scared to death of them even coming near me, and you want me to believe that your cousin had nothing to do with Josh's death? You want me to defend him? Even if he didn't do this you can bet he did something worth going to prison for. Testify for him? I ought to testify against him just because it would be a public service! Bad to the bone, the lot of you! Now get out of my garden!'

'I can't—'

'I don't care! Get out or I'll throw you out if I have to drag you by your hair!'

Mila looked to Heath. 'Aren't you going to say anything?'

'Apart from "I told you so"? Not really.'

Ottilie turned to him now. She could barely look at him but forced herself to. 'She can't walk, so please help her out. I'd see to her ankle, but I'm sure the emergency department in Windermere will be open, so you can take her there.'

'Me?' Heath gawped. 'You want me to take her?'

'You might as well.'

'I've phoned Dwight,' Mila cut in. 'He'll be here as soon as he picks up my message.'

'Dwight knows you're here?' Heath asked incredulously. 'He was totally on board with you coming here to stalk Ottilie? I mean, I knew he was wet, but—'

'Of course not!' Mila spat. 'I called him, and he said he'd come to pick me up. He's not going to leave me here when I'm in trouble, is he?'

The way she emphasised the last bit suggested she suspected Heath would.

'No way,' Ottilie said. 'He's not coming here for you – you'll have to call him back and tell him to fetch you from… wherever. I don't care as long as it's not here.'

'You'll be sorry,' Mila said as she pushed herself up from the wall.

'I already am,' Ottilie said. 'Sorry I haven't taken the opportunity to give you a good slap. Don't come here again.'

'So you won't help me?'

'Wow,' Ottilie said, her voice dripping with sarcasm. 'You catch on quick, don't you?'

'Then I can't—' Mila began, but Heath cut her off.

'Don't. You've done enough damage. I told you Ottilie wouldn't be able to do anything, I told you not to do this, but you did it anyway.'

Mila held out an arm for his assistance, but he simply let out a mirthless laugh. 'You think I'm going to help you?'

'I fell over!' Mila flung an arm at Ottilie. 'Her stupid path was uneven. I ought to sue!'

'Try it,' Ottilie said. 'I'm sure you'll enjoy explaining why you were here uninvited when the case goes to court. I can't imagine what you thought you were going to get by coming here anyway. Were you really mad enough to think I'd help you?'

'I must have been. Ashton told me not to bother, but… well, he's family. I thought maybe you'd see that…'

For a moment her tone softened, and Ottilie was almost won over. But then she shook her head. 'He was right; you shouldn't have bothered.'

'You'll regret it,' Mila said. 'I can promise you that if you go to court and testify against him—'

'Don't be a moron,' Ottilie said in a withering tone. 'I wasn't going to testify against him anyway because I wasn't involved in the incident. I was meant to give an impact statement, but, you know what, I'm going to give it to you now and you can let him know. He ruined my life. He killed the man I loved and I can't wait to see him go down. There, that's all I have to say. Now please leave.'

'You'd better go,' Heath said.

Ottilie looked at him. 'You had too.'

'You don't mean that,' he began, but she nodded.

'Yes, I do. I need some time to think.'

'What does that mean?'

'It means I don't want you here. I want to be alone. If you're here you'll try to talk me round and convince me none of this was your fault—'

'It isn't!'

'No, but you—' Ottilie's throat tightened with tears that she refused to let fall. 'You know what Josh's death did to me, and all this time you knew Mila was related to his killer. How could you keep that from me?'

'I didn't at first, and then we were... I was scared it would drive you away—'

'I don't want to hear it! Now is not the time, Heath. Please – take her away and let me think.'

Heath was silent for a moment. 'Don't do anything rash, please. Promise me you'll talk to me before you make any decisions.'

'I'll do what I want. I don't need your approval.'

'That's not what I meant.'

'Huh…' Ottilie swallowed another wave of tears and pulled herself up straight. 'Funny, isn't it? When there's something important to be said you want to bail on me. But when you're at fault and you want to try and get round me… not so keen now.'

'You're right – I'm at fault and I'm sorry. Give me a chance to show you how sorry.'

'Forget it,' Mila cut in. 'Are you going to help me or not? She told us both to leave.'

'I'm not going anywhere with you,' Heath said to her.

'But you are going,' Ottilie told him in reply. 'Because I don't want you here.'

'Ottilie, please…'

'I'm going inside and I don't want you to knock or phone me or try to get in. I want you both gone.'

CHAPTER TWENTY-FIVE

Lavender phoned an hour after Heath and Mila had gone. Ottilie had watched Heath leave without Mila, and though her conscience had started to get the better of her, and she was tempted to go out and tend to her ankle, she was saved the bother by the arrival of Mila's boyfriend, Dwight, to pick her up not long afterwards. It might have represented the first time in her nursing career she'd refused to use her skills to help someone. It went against everything she was, but she decided to cut herself some slack – extreme circumstances could do that to a person, even Ottilie.

'I wanted to check everything is all right,' Lavender said. 'I was worried because you didn't come back to the party. Everyone is worried.'

'Did you tell them about Mila?'

'No, I didn't think you'd want me to.'

Ottilie gave a short nod. She wondered if Flo knew what had been going on and whether – if she hadn't already known – Heath would tell her anything.

She would probably be as worried as Heath about Ottilie's reaction to the news that Mila was related to the family who were responsible for not only Josh's death but lots of other awful crimes in Manchester. She'd perhaps expect Ottilie to drop Heath – and right now, Ottilie would be lying if she said it hadn't crossed her mind. And not even because of the connection – Heath could hardly help that – but because of how he'd kept it from her once he'd discovered it. If he'd come to her with the truth at the start she might have been shocked and wary and it might have taken some getting over, but she would have been able to deal with it eventually. Now? Now she didn't know what to think. She didn't even know if she could trust him, and she certainly didn't know how she felt about him.

The Heath she thought she knew was lovely: kind and funny and caring. But he wasn't that Heath any longer. This Heath had destroyed her faith and trust. It hadn't helped that he'd been unreasonable and jealous over the past few weeks too. When she'd first met him the attraction had been undeniable but he'd filled her with doubt. And then she'd got to know him and the doubt had gone. But now? Now she felt they were back to square one. She was back to not knowing him, back to being filled with doubt, wondering whether she'd ever really known him at all. Had she seen a second chance for love and been so desperate she'd grabbed it, even though it hadn't been the right one? Had she really been so blinded by her loneliness?

'What's happened?' Lavender asked. 'Are they still there?'

'No, I don't know where Mila is – she was picked up by her boyfriend. And I suppose Heath has gone home.'

'So you're on your own? Want me to come over?'

'Thanks, but no. I need some time to think.'

'But you're all right? You're safe? I mean, what was she trying to do? You said before you thought someone had been trying to get in your house.'

'I don't think she was trying to get in, only to see if I was home. She has a really stupid way of going about it.'

'So it was Mila the other times?'

'Yes. But I don't think she'll come over again. And my camera doorbell is installed now, so if she did I'd know it was her. One way or another, it'll be fine.'

'I don't think I could be that relaxed about it if someone had been snooping around my house.'

'I'm so tired of the whole thing, I don't want to keep thinking about it.'

'Well, if you're sure you don't want company…'

'I'm sure. I don't want to be responsible for Simon losing even more guests from his party. I think it's taken quite a leap of faith for him to throw it in the first place. Would you give my apologies, though?'

'What should I say?'

'I don't know – maybe tell him I came down with a headache.'

'He's a doctor,' Lavender said. 'You do realise he'll be straight round to check you're not dying.'

'Oh God, I hope not. Can you put him off if he looks like he might?'

'I'll do my best. Don't forget to call me if you need anything.'

'Thanks, Lavender. I'll see you on Monday.'

'I'll see you before then – I want to check for myself you're all right so I'm coming over tomorrow whether you like it or not.'

After a bit more back and forth about whether Ottilie needed Lavender to check on her, she ended the call. Over an hour had gone by since Ottilie had sent Heath away. She'd had time to calm down but not time to work out how she felt about him. Things had changed beyond recognition. Sensible Ottilie would phone him to talk it through, but she wasn't sensible Ottilie right now – she knew that much for sure. If she called tonight she wouldn't even know where to start. She didn't trust herself to make the right decisions either.

So when his photo lit up her screen with an incoming call, she hesitated for a moment before rejecting it. She supposed he'd expect her to do that, so it didn't worry her too much, but she also realised he would keep calling and eventually she was going to have to answer. And even though it was the last thing she wanted to think about now, she needed to figure out what she was going to say when she did.

Ottilie looked down onto the path from the upstairs window and saw the top of Flo's head. It was early. Flo seemed to be making a habit of knocking on her front door at an hour that was far too early to be polite, but this time Ottilie supposed she had a reasonable excuse. No doubt she'd heard about the goings-on there the night before and had come to plead Heath's case. Since Ottilie had no quarrel with Flo – not really, although she was feeling rather more irritated by her than usual – she decided she might as well hear her out.

'Heath's told me you had… He thinks you might have split up.'

'Not as such.'

'What does that mean? He'll be ever so miserable without you, and I know you're very fond of him too—'

'Flo, I see what you're doing and I love that you're doing it, but this time I don't think it's your place to get involved. And don't get all offended by me saying so. I just think this is for me and Heath to sort out.'

'He wants to sort it out but you won't give him a chance.'

'I will if he gives me time. One way or another…'

Flo looked taken aback at Ottilie's last sentence. Ottilie supposed it might sound slightly ominous, but there was no point in being anything but completely honest. She didn't know if she could simply forget about this and go back to how things had been. And right now, she wasn't sure she wanted to. Heath hadn't exactly endeared himself to her over the past few weeks, especially since Simon had arrived. In fact, precisely since Simon had arrived. It was hard to get over that sort of hypocrisy when she'd had to put up with Mila's looming shadow for months before that, and felt she'd been more than patient about her. Until this point, of course, and yes, perhaps she wouldn't have been so patient had she known who Mila's cousin was, but that was a whole other conversation.

'So you'll talk to him?' Flo pushed.

Ottilie nodded, though part of her was sick of feeling as if everyone else's needs were more important than hers. Heath wanted to talk to her, but what about what she wanted? In the end, however, she knew she'd give in, and that was perhaps more galling than anything. Perhaps it was herself she ought to be angry with rather than anyone else. Circumstances seemed to conspire against her more and more these days, but did that mean she had to let them affect the decisions she made? They may colour them, but she didn't have to let circumstances rule her, did she?

So she made herself a promise, right there and then. She'd talk to Heath. She'd listen. She'd listen to anyone who needed it, but she wasn't going to let their needs be more important than hers. She was going to take control of her destiny for once and make the decisions that felt right to her, not the ones others wanted her to make. Heath could have his say, and then she was going to say how things were going to be. She loved him and she'd be sad if it meant the end of them, but even love wasn't worth saving if it meant sacrificing pieces of herself at its altar. She'd been alone before and she'd survived, and if she had to do it again then she supposed she'd survive that too.

'Right,' Flo said, glancing across at where Ottilie's kettle was plugged in.

Ordinarily, Ottilie would have asked her to stay for tea, but not today, and Flo had seriously misread the room if she thought that was going to happen.

'So I hope you don't mind if I see you out,' she said. 'I need to get a shower and breakfast before I phone Heath.'

'Oh.' Flo looked flummoxed but as Ottilie herded her towards the door seemed finally to take the hint. 'Of course. I'll be off then.'

After she saw Flo out and closed the front door, Ottilie leaned back against it and let out a sigh. All that and it wasn't even eight thirty yet.

CHAPTER TWENTY-SIX

Heath didn't give her time to phone. He turned up soon after Ottilie had showered and dressed, standing hopefully and sheepishly on her step, bouquet in hand. She tried to look pleased, and then remembered her promise to herself and let her face do its natural expression – which at this precise moment was somewhere between annoyance and exasperation.

'I told you I needed time.'

'I know, but you wouldn't answer my calls.'

'That's because I needed time. That was kind of the point of not answering.'

'I'm sorry, I… I couldn't leave it. I've been going out of my mind. I need to know what you're thinking.'

'And I need time to finish thinking.'

'I know, I just…'

'You'd better come in.'

Heath offered the bouquet. It was lovely – huge and obviously expensive, a burst of bright tropical colour on a muted, cloudy day. Ottilie took it from him as he followed her inside. Ordinarily, she'd have arranged it in a vase immediately, but today she took it to the sink and ran some water to dump it in until she was ready.

'Ottilie, I'm sorry. I'm so sorry for what Mila did—'

'I don't care about what Mila did. I could have expected that from her. What I'm upset about is what you did.'

'I'm sorry I didn't tell you. But put yourself in my shoes for a minute. Would you have told me?'

'Yes! I would have had more respect than to assume you'd never find out! If the tables had been turned you would have felt like an idiot. It's not nice being the last to know – even your gran knew more than I did!'

'I didn't want to lose you! I thought if you knew about Mila's cousin, then…'

'It would have been weird as hell but we could have figured it out.'

'Can't we figure it out now?'

'I don't know – you're pushing again. Like I keep telling you, I need time. I don't know how I feel about any of it yet. And it's not only this – the trial is coming up and that's going to complicate things all over again. I'd hoped to have you there with me when I went through all that—'

'I will be! I want to be!'

'But how can you be? For a start, you must know Mila's family, and they're related to—'

'I swear I've never met Ashton. I've never met half of them – it's a massive family and they're not all close.'

'How can I believe you when you've lied to me before? And if they're not that close, why is Mila so hell-bent on getting him off the charge?'

'I didn't lie. I kept it from you, yes, but—'

'It's the same as lying, so don't try to make a fool of me all over again with technicalities. You knew it was huge and you knew it mattered and you didn't tell me. Now you're saying you don't know this guy, and I want to believe you, but surely you can see why I'd have a hard time with that.'

'Sorry, I didn't mean to make a fool of you. But I swear it's true this time. I've never met him, not even once. Mila kept me at a distance from a lot of that side of her family because…' He shrugged.

'Because they were all bad people?'

'Of course they're not all bad. But I suppose some of them are less than saintly.'

'Less than saintly?' Ottilie threw her hands into the air, her voice rising. 'I'd call beating someone to death a lot less than saintly!'

'Sorry…' Heath flushed. 'I didn't mean to make light of— I didn't mean it like that.'

'I know you didn't, but that only proves to me what I already knew. You don't really understand how it is. How can you when it's never happened to you? You think I'm overreacting.'

'I don't!'

'If you didn't then you wouldn't have said what you just said. You wouldn't have turned up here thinking flowers would fix everything. You wouldn't have asked your gran to come and plead your case.'

'I never— Gran came over?'

'It doesn't matter. You can't fix this. You can't change Mila's family ties. I'm sure you regret the way this has all played out, but you can't change that now either. Please, I feel like a stuck record because I have to keep saying this, but I need time, and that's the only thing that can maybe fix this. And I can't even promise that – I won't promise that because then it puts me under pressure to make a decision, and that's not fair.'

'What about me? Is it fair to make me wait for your decision, not knowing how long that might be?'

'Yes,' Ottilie said simply. 'I think it is. You made this problem.'

'I didn't!'

She frowned and whatever words had been about to follow were never uttered.

'If you love me,' she began slowly, still not even certain that he did because he'd never said so, 'then you'll at least give me this. If you think I'm worth it then you'll wait.'

'But… I feel like you'll have time to think and then decide I'm not worth it.'

'If that happens then it was probably going to come to that one day anyway. You know how I feel about you, but things are more complicated than that now, and I don't feel like you get it at all.'

'Then tell me! Explain it to me and I'll try.'

'I shouldn't have to. I've told you it matters and that ought to be enough. I can't explain it to you, even if I wanted to, because it's impossible to explain to anyone what it's like to lose someone you love that much, especially in those circumstances. Only someone who's been through it can understand.'

'So it's not my fault.'

'No, perhaps it's not, but it's not my fault either.'

'What does that mean? Are we…? Are we over? Is that what you're telling me?'

Ottilie shook her head. 'I don't know.'

'You're just going to leave me hanging until you figure it out?'

'That's up to you. Nobody's forcing you to wait for me. If it's too hard, then you need to do what you need to do.'

'That's not fair.'

'I think we've established that none of this is fair.' Ottilie gave a rueful smile. 'Since when did fair matter? If life was fair, we wouldn't even be here right now.'

She realised at once the implications of her statement and Heath's obvious hurt. Because it meant so much more than them having an argument. It meant that in some other universe, where things were fair and as they should be, Josh would still be alive and Ottilie would be living blissfully in Manchester with him, and she and Heath would never have met. She'd never wish Heath out of her life now, but in that world, she'd never wish Josh out of it. In that world she wouldn't have given Heath a second glance on the street. What did that say about what they had now? Was it somehow second best? She'd never believed that and she'd been happy with Heath, but she'd inadvertently presented the question to herself in the starkest way and suddenly everything was different.

'If that's how you feel…'

He backed away, holding her in a gaze that was at once challenging and yet sorrowful, and a little betrayed. She wanted to go to him and tell him she was sorry, but in the end, that would be a bad idea. She couldn't allow her heart to decide what was best this time. It was too easy to think that Heath was the answer to everything, but this was her life and it was about time she took control. If she let him think that what he'd done didn't matter, where would that lead them? To more things that she let slide when she didn't want to? If they were to have a future then she needed to be stronger than that. And if her being strong ruined everything, then perhaps they'd never been meant to have a future.

Josh had always told her to know her worth. He saw the people-pleaser in her, the aversion to conflict, the need for affirmation from others, and he saw how it sometimes led not to the conflict she'd so desperately wanted to avoid with others but to the conflict it created within her own self. 'You don't have to be a pushover for people to like you,' he'd say. 'They'll like you anyway because you're a good person.'

So right now, she was going to know and acknowledge her worth.

'You're right,' she said, taking a deep breath. 'It's not fair to leave you hanging. I think we should take a break.'

'For how long?'

'I don't know. So I suppose that's leaving you hanging too. In that case, maybe we ought to end it.'

Heath stared at her. 'You're dumping me?' he asked incredulously.

'Is it that much of a shock? Considering what's happened? Did you really think I'd just shrug and carry on?'

'No, but—'

'You said you needed certainty, so now you have it. Now we both know where we stand, no more hanging. It's better this way, and in the end you'll see that.'

He was silent for a moment, studying her face intently, perhaps hoping to see some sign that her resolve would give way. In another life, in another time, maybe it would have done, but not today. And then he shook his head.

'OK,' he said. 'I'm sorry I didn't realise how bad this was and that's on me. I suppose all of this is on me.'

'I didn't say that, but you played your part. Maybe it's a bit on me for letting you think you could. I should have made my lines clearer, but there we go. So for that, I'm sorry too.'

'Can't we at least talk about this?'

'We have. Isn't that what we've been doing?'

'But this is a big decision – it's not one we can—'

'The decision's made, Heath. When are you going to start taking me seriously? This is part of the problem – you don't take me seriously. You think because I'm nice and good you can get away with whatever you like. Mila did it too.'

'Of course I take you seriously!'

'That's not how it looks to me. That's not how it's felt the past few days. It's – us – it's been lovely, but I think we've reached the end of the road.'

'You really think that?'

Ottilie nodded. She was oddly calm, considering she was about to cut the man she loved out of her life. It was almost as if someone else was doing it for her while she watched from the sidelines. She had Josh's words floating around in her consciousness: know your worth. Never had they meant more to her than they did now, perhaps because she'd never needed to understand them as fully as she did at this moment.

After another moment of charged silence, while Heath considered his next move and Ottilie waited, he finally looked as if he'd given in.

'If that's what you want. I can't believe you'd throw this away but I'm not going to beg.'

'I didn't ask you to.'

'Goodbye, Ottilie.'

'Bye, Heath.'

She was still calm as he walked out of the front door and let it slam behind him. And she was still calm as she went to the window to watch him drive away.

And then the floodgates opened and the tears began to fall, and she wondered what on earth she'd done.

CHAPTER TWENTY-SEVEN

In the month since she'd last seen Heath, Ottilie had kept herself busier than ever. While she was occupied she didn't have to think about what she might have lost. He'd always said her schedule was too packed to fit him in, and now she was making it so. This had been her decision and this was how it had to be.

He'd phoned a few times, wanting to talk it through, and while she'd listened she hadn't been convinced by a single thing he'd said that her decision had been the wrong one. Flo had marched round demanding she take him back, full of tales of his misery, telling Ottilie she'd never forgive her, expressing amazement and confusion as to how Ottilie could think anything was Heath's fault. Ottilie tried to explain as best she could but soon realised there was no point because Flo wasn't listening. It pained her to lose Flo's friendship, but once Flo realised she wasn't going to change Ottilie's mind it became another casualty of Mila's scheming, because Flo stopped speaking to Ottilie entirely, even crossing the street to avoid her.

Other people were more supportive, even if they didn't quite understand it. Stacey thought Ottilie had gone mad and said so. She could see why Ottilie might want to tear a strip off Heath, but to end things completely – that she couldn't see. Fliss had made no comment on the situation other than to tell Ottilie that she could take whatever time she needed to get her head straight in the aftermath, and although she appreciated the gesture, Ottilie didn't take any time off because that wasn't what she needed. Lavender had heard the news and simply said what a shame she thought it was, but not much else, which was surprising for someone who loved a drama as much as she did. Perhaps she could see how much pain Ottilie was keeping inside and was afraid if she pushed, she might unleash something she wouldn't be able to put back. Ann, Corrine and Victor uttered words of sympathy, but there wasn't a lot else they could say, and so conversation with them quickly returned to the usual topics and Ottilie was glad about that. The people who seemed most upset were Magnus and Geoff, who both looked as if they wanted to scoop Ottilie up into desperate hugs every time she went into their shop for a pint of milk.

So life had been a thankfully endless round of work, visits, volunteering and sleep, and although Ottilie longed for Heath in every spare second, she'd ensured there weren't too many of them to be had. When she walked in the hills she made sure she had company to take her mind off him, and if she went into town she went on the bus to make sure there were people all around her to take her mind off him, and when she visited or volunteered or worked, she made sure every conversation at those places avoided anything that might take her thoughts to him. Not only that, but she'd been recruited to help with the harvest festival and was busy fetching donations of food and money whenever they were offered and planning for the huge celebration at the community kitchen where she and the other usual volunteers would cook a slap-up dinner for everyone.

The summer days began to lengthen, rushing towards the season's end and bringing the harvest festival ever closer. These were the days she'd have been out on her newly renovated bicycle, given to her by Ann at Hilltop Farm and cleaned up by Victor at Daffodil Farm. Heath would have been with her on his – they'd talked about it before. Perhaps they'd have followed trails that hugged one of the vast, glittering lakes that drew people from far and wide to the district, a heat haze on the road and the lazy buzzing of bees in the wildflower hedgerows. Perhaps they'd have stopped for a picnic, lying on the peppery grass of a hill with the sun on their faces, side by side, smiling up at the sky. They might even have trekked the path to the hillside waterfall, the rockpool Flo had taken Ottilie to the year before, the one Flo had swum in as a girl and where Heath had come to rescue them when Flo had fallen ill. Perhaps they'd have taken a dip themselves, the rushing water crystal clear and shockingly cold, laughing as it took their breath away and stripped the heavy summer heat from their limbs.

Instead, Ottilie was working in a stuffy office, or helping out in a furnace-like kitchen with her clothes sticking to her, red-faced and a permanent sheen of sweat on her brow, or sitting in Fliss's shaded kitchen listening to her complain about this thing or that thing that happened at the surgery, or else surrounded by fractious and tetchy babies in the baking room where the mother and child group was held.

She was there on one particularly hot day, watching a bluebottle constantly missing a wide-open window as one of the mums tried to shoo it out when Stacey's voice interrupted her musings.

'What's that?' Ottilie turned to Stacey and shook herself awake again.

'The barbecue. Saturday afternoon is supposed to be good weather so I thought I'd do one. Can you come?'

'I think so. Who else is coming?'

'Well, that's the point – Chloe is bringing her boyfriend. Apparently, they're a thing now. Before they were "talking"' – she crooked her fingers into the air in speech marks as she said the word – 'whatever that means. I said to her, you're either going out or you're not, but apparently, it's not like that now. Couples "talk" for a bit before they do anything else. What was wrong with meeting a fella, having a date and then being an item? Nowadays it's like a raft of interviews for a job. You have to "talk" to them, and then you're sort of seeing them but even then you're not an item.'

'So when does that come?'

'God knows! I don't think there's an actual rule, only when one of them says they're a thing then they are. Anyway, Chloe says they're a thing and she's bringing him over.'

'Wow, she must like him.' Ottilie pushed her damp fringe back from her forehead.

'That's what I thought. So I figured a barbecue might be a nice way to get to know him without it being too intense.'

'Won't it be intense if half the village is there inspecting him?'

'More intense than if the three of us are sitting around a table while I ask him questions that look as if I'm trying to interrogate him and Chloe glares at me and hisses for me to shut up?'

'Since you put it that way,' Ottilie said with a soft laugh.

'This way, even though there are a lot more new people for him to meet, he's not the focus of attention. We can get to know him but there will be other stuff going on too, and if they want to blend into the background a bit then they can do that more easily. Plus there'll be loads of help on hand for Mackenzie, and he loves company these days.'

Ottilie nodded. 'He does seem to be turning into a little social butterfly, doesn't he? Takes after his grandma.'

'He definitely doesn't take after his moody mum,' Stacey said, sending a fond look at Mackenzie, who was sitting on one of the play mats, staring intently at a picture book with textured pages. 'But he's the best thing that ever happened to us, even if we had lots of doubts before he was born. I couldn't imagine life without him now.'

'I bet. He is adorable. You're asking everyone in the village or keeping it to close friends?'

'I thought I'd ask Simon too.'

Stacey flushed, and the fact didn't escape Ottilie. How those two weren't a couple yet was a mystery for the greatest minds of the age, because anyone could see they fancied each other like mad and got along famously too.

'And of course,' she added, as if to take the heat out of the situation, 'some other people. I expect I'll ask most of the film club.'

'Most?'

'I can't… well, I can't very well ask Flo in the circumstances, can I?'

'You can ask her if you want to. I doubt she'd come – not once she finds out I'm going to be there, anyway. She's barely a member of the film club these days; she never comes and I think that's down to me. In fact, I know it's down to me. I feel a bit bad about it, really.'

'It's her choice. She's the one making it weird, so don't feel bad. Relationships come to an end and there's no point in being petty about it. Nobody promised marriage at the end for you and Heath, but she seemed to think the moment you got together it was a given. It's a silly and childish way to look at things.'

'Well, I don't have a problem with you asking her.'

'I'll probably ask Lavender and Dr Cheadle and Charles too, though I doubt those two will come.'

'Lavender will – try keeping her away from a party.'

'It's not really a party. It's a few burgers and a couple of drinks in my garden.'

'Lavender will turn it into a party.'

Stacey grinned. 'If she wants to I won't complain. I just don't want anyone expecting too much.'

'I think everyone knows the score with this sort of thing. Want me to do any food for it?'

'You can if you like, but don't go mad. I'm going to ask Magnus if he can order some meat in from that nice butcher in Kendal. Gets it with a decent discount so there should be plenty there. Maybe you can do some salad if you really want to, and I'm sure you'd make something whether I said to or not, because I know what you're like.'

'I can't turn up to a thing empty-handed – you know that.'

'Yes, I know. So you'll be there.'

'Sounds lovely. I'm looking forward to meeting Chloe's boyfriend too. I'm quite surprised she's agreed to this.'

'Honestly, so am I. Must be love, eh?'

'He does sound like a keeper. What's his name?'

'Oliver.'

'Right. I'll try to remember.'

'I'm looking forward to it. It's ages since I've had a get-together at our house.'

'I'm looking forward to it too.'

Stacey raised her eyebrows. 'Are you?'

'Of course. Why wouldn't I be?'

'It's… nothing.'

'You think I'm still sad about Heath.'

'Aren't you?'

'A bit, but that doesn't mean I have to stop living, does it?'

'No. But still…'

'I'm getting there, Stacey – you don't have to worry about me.'

'I do. You've made this village bearable since you got here. You've been such a good friend and I worry that I'm not as good to you.'

Ottilie smiled and gave her a brief hug. 'You're brilliant. With a friend like you, who needs a man, eh?'

Pushing a smile across her face, Ottilie wanted to believe her own words, but even after all these weeks, she still found it hard. She missed Heath and she thought about him all the time, and she was beginning to wonder if she'd ever be able to stop.

The sun was still high as Ottilie arrived for the barbecue with a basket of potato salad, home-made coleslaw and guacamole dip, but Stacey's garden was north-facing and so shaded by the back walls of her house. It was a welcome relief from the fierceness of the heat, and while Stacey complained that in the cloudier seasons it meant she got hardly any sun at the back, today it made the temperature bearable. It was a far neater, more manicured garden than Ottilie's own, with a square lawn and a decked patio area, dotted with pots containing tidy shrubs. She'd scattered cushions and deckchairs about the newly mown grass for people to sit, and already almost every one of them was occupied.

Ottilie waved hello to Magnus and Geoff, Lavender and her husband, and Simon, who was talking to Chloe while she did her best to hold on to a wriggling Mackenzie. Ottilie smiled at that – it seemed Chloe was finally opening up. She'd been closed and moody when Ottilie had first met her, a teenager struggling to come to terms with the adult world and the huge responsibility she was about to have thrust upon her, but over the past few months since Mackenzie's birth Ottilie had watched her grow and even thrive. Motherhood suited her, and the fact that she had such amazing support and had now found what sounded like a lovely boy definitely must have helped.

'Want me to take those to the kitchen until we're ready?' Stacey asked, holding out her hands for the basket. She peered inside. 'I knew you'd go mad and make too much.'

'What we don't eat today I'm sure someone can finish tomorrow. Or I can take it into work for lunch on Monday. It won't get wasted either way.' Ottilie nodded at Chloe and Simon, and Stacey smiled.

'She really likes him. I suppose it's because he pays so much attention to Mackenzie.'

'It's good she likes him whatever the reason.'

Stacey turned to her with a puzzled look that wasn't really puzzled at all. Ottilie could see through the innocent act and she nudged her with a grin. 'Don't tell me you and him still haven't worked out how perfect a couple you'd be. And now you've more or less got Chloe's seal of approval, I really don't know what you're waiting for.'

'Him,' Stacey said flatly.

Ottilie frowned. 'This is the twenty-first century, right? You can make the first move, can't you?'

'I could, but with my track record I daren't. What if I've got it wrong? What if he's only being friendly?'

Ottilie raised her eyebrows. 'Seriously? It's obvious!'

'Then why…' Stacey lowered her voice and leaned in. 'Why hasn't he asked me? It's like waiting for Godot! What's he playing at?'

'Maybe you should ask him.'

'Are you nuts? I'm not going to do that!'

'I'll ask him then.'

'Don't you dare!' Stacey hissed, and Ottilie had to laugh. 'That would be mortifying. You might as well pass a note along the garden asking him to meet me behind the bike sheds at break.'

'Well, if that's what it takes…'

'That's it – you're leaving. Out!'

Ottilie's laughter grew. 'All right, all right. I won't say a word to him, but I think it's about time you did. I know he likes you.'

'How?'

'He practically told me so.'

'Are you sure? The "practically" bit has me worried. Categorically is what I want to hear, not practically.'

'I'm as sure as I can be, but there's only one way to find out, and you know that.'

Stacey was thoughtful for a moment but then shook her head. 'No. I'm not doing it. I couldn't look at him again if he said no to me. Imagine having piles or whatever and having to go and see him at the surgery knowing what had happened? As if piles wasn't bad enough on its own...'

Ottilie's laughter was so loud at this that everyone in the garden halted their conversation and turned to look.

'Sorry,' she snorted. 'The mental image. I just can't...'

She was laughing so hard she didn't notice the gate opening and a newcomer entering the garden. But Stacey did, and she suddenly looked anxious. Ottilie's laughter died at the sight and she turned to look at what could have bothered her friend, only to see Flo standing by the gate with a cling-film-covered plate.

'I thought I'd come along after all,' she said, clearly talking to Stacey but looking at Ottilie. 'That's if you actually meant to invite me.'

'I asked, didn't I?' Stacey went over. 'Of course it was an invite. It'd be pretty silly to ask if I didn't want you to come.'

'But people do that, don't they? I'll ask such and such because I have to and they won't come anyway.'

'Not in this case. Let me take that plate from you.'

'It's chips,' Flo said, handing it over. 'I made too many for my tea last night.'

Stacey took the plate with a vaguely confused look. 'Thank you,' she said, though she was probably thinking the same thing as Ottilie, that she had no clue why anyone would bring leftover chips to a barbecue, and that unless someone performed some kind of culinary miracle they'd probably taste disgusting by now.

As Stacey took Ottilie's basket and Flo's random plate of chips to the kitchen, Flo made a beeline for Ottilie.

'Hello,' Ottilie said. 'How have you been keeping?'

'As well as can be expected in the circumstances.'

Ottilie didn't ask what those circumstances were. She didn't want to ruin this by reminding Flo of why she'd been avoiding her; she was only glad that finally Flo had seen fit to be somewhere she knew Ottilie would be and she was willing to talk to her.

'That's good,' Ottilie said. She was casting around for something else to say when Flo jumped into the gap.

'Didn't see the point in us being at odds any longer. What's done is done. Heath's all right now. He's getting on with things.'

'Is he?'

'Knows he did wrong and there's no way back. He's made his peace with that, he says.'

'Oh.'

Ottilie was blindsided by the idea that Heath was already over her. It sounded as if that was what Flo was trying to say. She didn't know how she felt about that. On the one hand, it made things simpler, but on the other, the notion saddened her. Had she really meant so little to him? It had been only weeks since they'd broken up and, while she didn't want to hear he was suffering, she perhaps wanted to know that it had taken some getting over.

Ottilie wondered if he might even try to get back with Mila. Surely not? But where Heath was concerned, she couldn't be certain of anything.

Ottilie suddenly felt silly for ever imagining that Heath might still have feelings for Mila. Had that been a factor in her decision to end things? She hated to admit it, but perhaps unconsciously it had been. Of course, Mila had caused enough trouble – even who she was related to was trouble enough – but Ottilie had been plagued by the idea that Heath hadn't quite got over her. Had it clouded her judgement? Perhaps, but even so, it was too late to do anything about it now. Even if Ottilie wanted to try again, it sounded as if Heath had moved on from her too.

Her attention was caught by Chloe leaping up from her seat next to Simon and racing to the garden gate. There stood a young man, with short dark hair and very blue eyes, dressed in jeans and a T-shirt that looked too big for him, the nerves as he surveyed the gathering obvious in his face.

This had to be Oliver, and Chloe confirmed it by squealing his name as she flew over to the gate.

'I thought you'd chickened out!' she continued as she unfastened the gate for him. He gave an uncertain shrug, his eyes everywhere. Ottilie didn't blame him because everyone was looking and he must have felt as if he was being scrutinised like a lab specimen.

Once in the garden and the gate closed again, Chloe wasted no time taking him to meet her mum inside. Ottilie could see them having a conversation through the kitchen window. It looked to be going well – at least, there was a lot of nervous smiling going on. Then she brought him outside, straight to Ottilie, who was nearest the house.

'This is Ottilie,' Chloe said. 'She's the one I told you about, who helped me have Mackenzie.'

At this, Oliver seemed awed as he said hello, and a warm kick of pride grew in Ottilie. Chloe had never appeared to feel they shared a bond over Mackenzie's birth, as she'd done – certainly, she'd never voiced it – but perhaps she'd only been too inward-looking and shy to say so.

'This is Ollie,' Chloe said to Ottilie and then, as a cursory acknowledgement, to Flo too.

'That's going to be confusing if you're hard of hearing,' Flo said.

'What?' Chloe asked.

'Ollie and Ottilie in the same room. It's a good job Mildred Icke isn't here.'

Ottilie smiled at the reference to the bane of her working life. 'Isn't it?'

'Whatever.' Chloe shook her head. 'Anyway, I'll be back in a minute. Just got to get Mackenzie from Simon. Come on…'

She grabbed Oliver by the hand and led him to where Simon was doing his best to keep Mackenzie entertained, though he seemed to be losing the battle. Mackenzie might have been a lot more sociable these days, but when his mum was around, he only really had eyes for her and didn't take his gaze from Chloe the whole time she was talking to Ottilie and Flo. At their approach, his arms went into the air. Chloe swept him into her embrace, and his little face was immediately one huge smile.

'That lad's got his work cut out,' Flo said.

'Oliver? Oh, I don't know,' Ottilie replied. 'He seems a bit smitten. Nothing's hard work when love is all new, is it?'

'I dare say it's so far back for me I can't remember. You'd know that better than me.'

Ottilie turned to look. The statement had sounded barbed, but there was no malice on Flo's face as she watched Chloe introduce Oliver to Simon. The GP shook him warmly by the hand and they struck up a far easier conversation than the one he'd had with Ottilie. In fact, it was one more way in which Simon seemed to fit into this family. Ottilie was growing tired of waiting for him or Stacey to do something about it, and if they didn't soon, she might just break her own rules and start interfering.

She was glad for Chloe, though. Oliver seemed sweet and absolutely taken by her, and considering how badly Chloe had been treated by Mackenzie's father, she'd earned that affection twenty times over. Ottilie hoped that life was going to be kind to her from now on.

'Drinks, you two?'

Ottilie turned to see Stacey behind her. 'Want me to do those? You've got your hands full with the food about now, haven't you?'

'Actually, Simon has offered to man the grill.'

'Ah…' Ottilie broke into a slow smile and Stacey blushed again. 'I'm sure he has. Anything to get into your good books, eh?'

'Stop it!' Stacey said, but she was laughing. 'You're terrible.'

'And you're slow. Stop messing around – the suspense is killing everyone.'

'What?' Flo looked between the two of them, and Stacey shook her head.

'Nothing, Flo. What do you want to drink?'

Ottilie turned back to where Simon was still chatting to Oliver. She wasn't joking – the suspense was killing her if nobody else. And if she couldn't have her happy ending, perhaps it might be nice to make it happen for her best friend.

In the end, alcohol did what Ottilie had wanted to. They were well into the evening, and the barbecue had lasted longer and been more raucous than anyone had anticipated. Simon had done a brilliant job of looking after the grill while Stacey played hostess, and Chloe had encouraged Oliver to come out of his shell. Ottilie, for a short while at least, had forgotten the tough few weeks she'd had and made the most of the moment.

The embers of the barbecue coals were dying and there was litter all over the place, the remains of meals that nobody had yet cleared away. Stacey had decided to put some music on and had started to dance, soon joined by Lavender, who dragged a protesting Simon from his seat. But then Stacey helped her and they got him to his feet, and as he shuffled awkwardly, the track changed to a slower one, and as the pace slowed the heat seemed to rise. Stacey and Simon grew closer, as if magnetised, as if everyone else in the garden had disappeared and it was only those two. They didn't kiss, but they were so close that it was painfully intimate. Ottilie felt she had to look away to give them a moment. But when she turned back, they'd both gone inside.

She could see them now through the kitchen window. They were talking, still close, and Stacey was smiling like it would split her face if it grew any wider. And then he leaned in and kissed her gently, and Ottilie looked away again, a smile almost as big as Stacey's pulling at her own cheeks. It looked as if they'd figured things out at last, and nothing could have made Ottilie gladder at that moment. She wished them luck – better luck than she'd had with Heath. But somehow she felt they didn't need it. If she could be certain about the future of any couple, it had to be them. Something about them told her they were going to go the distance.

She noticed Chloe had seen them go inside and was watching the kitchen window too, and then she caught her eye and smiled. Chloe returned it. It seemed she approved too.

CHAPTER TWENTY-EIGHT

Ottilie handed the prescription to Flo.

Flo eyed it doubtfully. 'I thought Dr Cheadle was supposed to make these out.'

'As I told you, I'm allowed to do certain ones. This is fine; it's only the same as Dr Cheadle would give you, but you'll get it from me a lot quicker. Think about what I said too. You need to slow down a bit. I know you think you're invincible but you're not. Get help with things; get someone to share the load. You know you can always ask me – if I'm not working I'm happy to pick up shopping and things for you.'

'A day out would be nice.' Flo said.

Ottilie smiled. She wasn't green – Flo wanted to be taken out for a daytrip by Ottilie, exactly like they'd done when Ottilie had been new to the village. In fact, Ottilie was pleased. It meant she was forgiven. Flo had put the whole business with her and Heath behind them. Ottilie only wished she could do the same.

The following month would have marked their first anniversary, and as it drew closer, Ottilie found herself thinking of him more and more. To her surprise – because she'd hardly given herself time to admit it – she missed him almost as much as she had in the beginning. But from everything Flo said, it sounded as if he'd forgotten her – or at any rate moved on. She could have contacted him to see how he felt, but she suspected the result would be disappointing and very painful. Perhaps it was best to leave things as they were. In time, she'd get over him, because time saw to all such things in the end.

'A day out would be nice,' she agreed. 'Is that an offer?'

'If you want.' Flo sniffed.

'Kendal? I like Kendal. I liked that little café you took me to last time we were there.'

Flo nodded. 'If I've got time, I suppose we could go there.'

'Well, when you've got time I'd love that,' Ottilie said, her smile growing. 'Is there anything else of a health nature you need to ask me about?'

'Are you throwing me out? Is that my five minutes up?'

'Kind of. It's nothing personal, but, you know, there's a waiting room full of patients and one of them is Mrs Icke.'

'Oh, her!' Flo pulled a face. 'Let her say a single thing while I'm around – I'd give that old bag what for.'

'While I appreciate you sticking up for me, maybe not in surgery hours. Have your punch-up in the pub at closing time like civilised people do. Before you go, though, are you going to the harvest festival celebration at the community kitchen at the weekend?'

Flo clicked her tongue against the roof of her mouth. 'I expect I'll have to. I don't know why they have to do it so early, though. It's barely into October yet.'

'I think it's to do with the community centre diary. Still, we're close enough. I'm not sure the harvest festival has all that much to do with harvests these days.'

'Like everything else – the true meaning is lost. Take Christmas—'

'Sorry, Flo, but… you know, other patients… Perhaps we can have the Christmas chat another time?'

Flo huffed and looked quite put out to be cut off mid-rant, but Ottilie went to open the office door for her anyway.

Grumpy old Flo was back, but if she was honest, it was kind of the way Ottilie liked it. It meant things were getting back to normal.

When Ottilie arrived at the community kitchen, Stacey and Simon were already there, helping Magnus and Geoff set up.

'What can I do?' Ottilie asked Magnus, who looked as stressed as she'd ever seen him.

'Oh, Ottilie, you're a godsend! Would you be an absolute darling and do the vegetable displays?'

'Where do you want them?'

'On the stage. Create' – he was vague, waving his hands dismissively – 'something lovely with them.'

Ottilie couldn't imagine what 'something lovely' meant, and she was even harder pressed to imagine that anything she could do with a few sacks of carrots and onions could be seen as lovely. But she went to investigate the crates, sacks and boxes stacked in the corner of the hall anyway to see what could be done.

Relieved to find that in addition to vegetables there were also bundles of straw and baskets and bits of display stand, she set to work trying to make a respectable display.

She was resisting the silly urge to make a rude shape out of carrots and potatoes when Stacey's voice was at her shoulder.

'You know you could make something quite entertaining out of those.'

Ottilie turned with a grin. 'I was thinking the same thing, but I don't think Magnus would appreciate it.'

'Oh, I don't know about that; he's got a sense of humour, even if sometimes it's hard to see. Perhaps not some of the other villagers, though.'

Ottilie looked across at Magnus and Geoff, who were working together to put garlands of dried flowers along the coving. 'They seem better. Have they sorted whatever glitch they were having?'

'Oh, I think so. You know what old married couples are like.'

'I never think of them like that, but I suppose that's what they are.'

'Been together for almost thirty years, so I'd say that counts.'

'And how about you and Simon?'

'What about us?'

'Things seem good.'

'Has he said anything to you?'

'Not really. Nothing specific anyway, though I can tell he's happy.'

'I'm so glad to hear that. For all my troubles over the years, they're nothing compared to his. You know about his wife and daughter?'

Ottilie nodded.

'I can't even imagine what he went through, and yet I feel as if there's so much more that he hasn't told me yet. I think he wants to, but…'

'It's early days. I'm sure when he's ready he'll tell you.'

'I hope so. I want us to be at that point where we can share things and he feels he can tell me anything. Like you and Heath—' Stacey stopped and flushed.

'It's all right,' Ottilie said. 'I thought Heath and I were at that point, but I suppose I was wrong.'

'You seemed so good together. Is there really no way you can fix it?'

'Doesn't seem as if he wants to.'

'Perhaps he does but he daren't contact you. From what you told me, I don't blame him. He probably feels as if what he did was unforgivable.'

'And I don't suppose my reaction helped.'

'It was a natural one. It seems sad to me that you two had something so good and it was ruined by lots of things out of your control.'

Ottilie was silent for a moment. Had it been good? She'd had her doubts even before the Mila debacle, but perhaps she'd been reading the situation all wrong. Heath hadn't given her cause to doubt him in the beginning. Now that she thought about it, his behaviour change was probably linked to Mila dreaming up her scheme to help her cousin get off his murder charge and him feeling guilty about it. She ought to have seen it. Instead, she'd lost her patience and proved to him that what he'd thought was right – that he wasn't worthy.

Did it matter that he'd never told her he loved her? Whether she heard the words or not, what difference did it make? Surely love was shown through deeds, not said with words. Any old fool, any old charlatan could say they loved her, but that didn't make it true. What made it true was actions. He'd made a stupid mistake covering for Mila but he'd already explained that it had been done out of fear. Ottilie had refused to listen to that too.

Was it too late? It had been so long now Heath would have moved on, wouldn't he? And rightly so. She'd told him she didn't want him, but that hadn't been true. She had some mad notion of not needing him, that she somehow couldn't make compromises and it wasn't like her. She was the queen of compromises – always had been. She'd wanted to shake that part of her personality; she'd wanted to prove to the world that she could be strong and single-minded and that she didn't need anyone – but at what cost? Wasn't the right man worth the odd compromise? And it wasn't as if he'd ever asked her to change. He hadn't been perfect, but then neither had she. He'd been jealous – but he couldn't help what he was any more than she could. She'd had to contend with Mila trying to wreck what they'd had, and in cutting Mila from her life she'd wrecked what she'd had with Heath all by herself. Heath had been keeping things from her, but it had been a mistake, and surely everyone made mistakes. She'd handed Mila the victory and Mila had hardly lifted a finger to get it.

Yes, she'd been horrified to learn that Mila was related to the family who'd been responsible for Josh's death, and yes, it had made things difficult that Heath had history with her and them, and yes, she'd been angry that he'd kept it from her. But he'd done it from fear of losing her, and perhaps – despite what she'd told him – she'd have done the same. If she'd never discovered it, would it have mattered? Would it have made a difference to them if she'd never known?

It was the uncertainty that had done for them – she saw that now. She'd somehow convinced herself that he hadn't loved her, that he still held a torch for Mila, and perhaps that was down to a lack of self-belief on her part. She'd felt less-than, uncomprehending of why he'd want to love her. She'd seen the effect Mila had on him, had heard the stories of how he'd pined for her, struggled to let go when their marriage had ended, and wondered how she could ever compete with a love so epic. While Ottilie and Heath had been understated and gentle, Mila and Heath had been fiery and volcanic, all passion and hatred, and sometimes the two entangled so that they were the same thing. Ottilie was no Mila. She wasn't fiery and she never could be. She wasn't exciting and dangerous and sexy. She was warm and safe and nurturing, and how could Heath be happy with someone like her when he'd had someone like Mila?

'It's done now anyway,' she said briskly, swallowing back a lump in her throat. There was no point in crying about it. Heath was out of her life and too much time had passed to fix things.

'It's funny how we seem to have swapped roles,' Stacey said. 'When you were with Heath I was alone, and now I'm with Simon… I know what Heath did was out of order, but—'

Ottilie turned sharply. 'Where's this come from? Has he been in touch?'

'With me?' Stacey shook her head, but something about it left Ottilie unconvinced.

'Please, if he has…'

'No. It's not that. I want to see you happy, like you did me. That's it, that's all.'

Any further discussion was cut short by the arrival of Flo, Lavender, Charles and Fliss.

'Here she is!' Charles made a beeline for Ottilie to give her a hug. 'Our favourite nurse.' He turned to Stacey and hugged her too. 'And the woman who's put that big permanent smile on the face of our Dr Stokes!'

'How are you feeling?' Ottilie asked with a smile.

'All the better for seeing you two. I take it you've been roped into helping too.'

'I think the entire village has,' Stacey said. 'What's your job?'

'I have no idea yet, simply reporting for duty. I await my orders.'

'Nothing too strenuous, I hope…' Fliss was making her way over with Lavender while Flo, having shown Ottilie that she'd noted her presence, went straight to the kitchens. Ottilie thought it odd, but then when was Flo anything other than odd?

'I'm sure I'll manage,' Charles replied. 'You worry too much.'

Fliss looked faintly incredulous. 'Is it any wonder when you give me far too much to worry about?'

'A little heart attack? All done and dusted now, and you'd never even know I'd had one.'

It was Ottilie's turn to look sceptical. Charles looked older these days, not quite the robust man she'd met when she'd first moved to Thimblebury. Life, or the heart attack, or perhaps living with Fliss for the first time in decades, or perhaps all three… something had taken its toll.

As if to make certain nobody argued with him, Charles turned his attention to the garlands being hung by Magnus and Geoff, who were now being ably assisted by Simon. The hall itself was like many village halls: neutrally painted with a wooden floor and various noticeboards and community art projects pinned to the walls. Magnus and Geoff were doing a good job of dressing it, though Ottilie couldn't help but feel the real star of the show was the view beyond the windows. There were hills in every direction, bathed in a setting sun, casting their dark hollows and peaks in a bronzed glow. Already some of the leaves on the trees that framed that view were turning amber and russet, and soon there would be a carpet of them on every corner of the village and the hills would glow with colour.

'It looks very nice in here,' he said. 'Very festive. Very…'

'Farm-yardy?' Fliss cut in.

'Which reminds me,' Ottilie said. 'Did Victor and Corrine say they'd be coming down?'

'I should imagine so,' Fliss said. 'They don't usually miss the harvest dinner. I expect Corrine is putting the finishing touches to a metric tonne of home-made cake.'

'Probably,' Ottilie agreed with a smile. 'I was hoping Ann and Darryl might come too. I keep trying to persuade her to come and use the kitchen for the odd meal, but she doesn't seem to think it's for her.'

'Today's a celebration rather than a charity thing, though,' Lavender said. 'So perhaps she might decide to come down for that.'

Ottilie nodded. 'I hope so. It would do Darryl good to interact with someone other than his mum and me. I know he's happy enough, but I do worry about him.'

'Of course you do,' Fliss said sagely. 'I wouldn't have expected anything else from you, Ottilie. You worry about everyone and never give a care for what you might need yourself. It would do you good to think about that once in a while too.'

Ottilie floundered, uncertain how to react to Fliss's statement. She was content and she was well and settled – she didn't need anything else… Did she? Did everyone see her that way? Did it matter?

From the corner of her eye, she noticed Flo come out of the kitchen and go to speak to Magnus. And then Magnus called over from where he was holding a set of ladders for Geoff.

'I don't suppose anyone fancies helping with the chopping… Ottilie? You're good at veg prep, aren't you?'

'I'm already doing veg prep of sorts,' she said with a laugh, angling her head at the half-built harvest display.

'Yes, yes, very good.'

'I can finish this,' Charles said. 'I need to make myself useful, and this is…' He cleared his throat very deliberately and looked at Fliss. 'This should be exactly the sort of non-strenuous activity my GP would approve of.'

'I'll go with Ottilie,' Stacey said. 'I think I'm more or less done with the tablecloths anyway.'

'Yes, yes, we can finish that,' Magnus said as Geoff and Simon nodded agreement. 'You go and help with the cooking. I think they're getting behind.'

Ottilie handed Charles the sack she'd been holding. 'Good luck. I hope you can make it look better than I was doing.'

Charles was chuckling as she followed Stacey to the kitchen. When they got in there, Flo was back at her station. They greeted the other volunteers before being set to work. Stacey was making batter mix for Yorkshire puddings while Ottilie had been put on onion-chopping duty again. She could have sworn that Flo had had something to do with that because she was smirking across the room.

Ottilie searched the drawer for a knife and then reached into the bag for the first onion.

'Do you need a teaspoon to suck on?'

Ottilie spun round, her legs suddenly weak. 'Heath! What are you…?'

'Sorry,' he said, his smile immediately slipping to be replaced by a rueful expression. 'That wasn't meant to be— That was a stupid thing to do. I don't know why I thought it would be— Well, I was trying to be witty or cool, but it didn't really work, did it?'

'What are you doing here?'

'Gran said they needed as many volunteers as they could get, and I was at a loose end and I thought… well, I couldn't keep on avoiding Thimblebury, could I? It seemed a good place to start making things right… I mean, not right, but getting things to a place where I don't have to fall apart every time I see you. I know you can never forgive me for what happened, but I'd like to think we could put it behind us enough to get along. For Gran's sake if nothing else.'

Ottilie stared at him. He thought he'd fall apart when he saw her? Did that mean it was happening now? He seemed fine – relaxed, in fact. At least, more relaxed than she was. He wanted to get along… Was that all it was? And really only for Flo's sake?

'It's good to see you,' he added. 'You look well. I mean, is it OK to say so? I'll admit, I don't quite know how to do this.'

'No… I mean it's fine. You too… you look well, I mean.'

Ottilie couldn't deny that he did. He looked more than well; he looked handsome, and it made her heart ache to see the soft brown eyes that she'd been lost in so many times before, the hair she always longed to run her hands through, the chest she'd lain against to sleep and woken up on the following morning, the smile that would greet her and lift her mood no matter what else was going on. She couldn't deny that she'd missed him, though she hadn't realised until this exact moment just how much. She felt as if all the breath had left her lungs and that she couldn't pull in enough air to refill them, as if the room around them – even the world – had fallen away and been replaced by his face.

'I'd better…' He gestured to Flo, who was innocently scoring the skins of some chicken breasts, pretending she hadn't noticed what was going on, though she could hardly fail to. Nobody in the room could have missed it, though everyone pretended to have seen nothing. It was the strangest, most surreal situation Ottilie had ever been in. '… See what Gran wants me to do.'

Driven to distraction simply knowing he was in the kitchen with her, Ottilie's mind worked at a million miles an hour as she chopped. What was going on here? Why had he turned up now, after all this time? Was it really as simple as he'd made out? Or was there another agenda? And if there was and it involved her somehow, what did that make her feel? Pleased? Annoyed? A little hoodwinked? Or did she secretly hope he was there for her because it was only now, seeing him across the room and longing to be closer, that she understood she'd never really been over him at all?

Someone switched the radio on, and Stacey began to sing along to some eighties power ballad. Flo grumbled for her to shut up and then everyone else weighed in, until the volunteers were all involved in friendly banter. Ottilie was silent. Whenever she dared steal a look at Heath, she guessed he'd been doing the same, because his head would go down, back to his task, as if he'd been caught out. In the main hall, she could hear the preparations continuing and then later people starting to arrive.

Magnus came into the kitchen and began to take glass jugs from the cupboard.

'You want some water for the tables?' Ottilie asked.

'Yes, and some other bits too – pop and whatever for the children.'

'I'll do it.'

'I'll help.' Heath dried his hands on his apron and came over. 'I've finished mashing.'

Now Ottilie knew a plot was afoot, but to her annoyance, she couldn't help but feel pleased. Excited even. Whatever happened here, she couldn't let herself forget the reasons they were no longer together because they'd been very good ones, but that didn't mean she couldn't feel the seduction. The fact he was clearly making an effort wasn't helping in that regard either, and it would be too easy to let him get under her skin again.

They went out to the main room together with trays of drinks. Every so often Ottilie would look up to see him turn his face away as if he'd been watching her, and she'd flush in the most frustrating way. At least in a rapidly filling room of people she was safe from herself, wasn't she? She couldn't go and do anything silly in such a public place, could she?

She caught him perhaps four or five times looking her way, and when she searched for him again, not wanting to but unable to stop herself, he was close, working his way down the trestle table she was working her way up. At some point they'd meet, and they did. He smiled uncertainly at her as they both set jugs of water side by side on the table, hands grazing at the same time, a thrill like an electric shock going through her at his touch.

'Sorry…' he mumbled.

'No, I'm sorry…'

Only she wasn't. She wasn't sorry at all. She wanted to do it again. She wanted more than that.

Ottilie, girl, get a grip! You've been on your own too long!

They both returned to the kitchen for more supplies. Ottilie busied herself making up jugs of cordial while Heath fetched bottles of cola from the fridge. The kitchen was beginning to smell divine, roast chicken and beef and potatoes and all manner of vegetables and a nut roast for the odd few who didn't want meat.

'My stomach thinks my throat's been cut!' Flo called out to anyone who was interested. 'I hope we're going to be able to sit down and eat with everyone else, seeing as we cooked it.'

'I'll serve up,' Ottilie said. 'I don't mind waiting for a while.'

'Me too,' Stacey said, echoed by Simon, who was now assisting in the kitchen.

'So you should be able to, Gran,' Heath said.

'You could go and eat with Flo,' Ottilie told him, but he glanced briefly at his gran, and an understanding seemed to pass between them before she answered for him.

'I said I'd go and sit with Victor and Corrine.'

'I can wait too,' Heath added. 'I'll eat later, after everyone else has been served.'

Magnus came back to the kitchen again. 'How are we doing? Nearly ready? We're all ready out there.'

'Yes, yes, stop fussing,' Flo grumbled. 'It's only a bit of dinner.'

'Yes, and there's fifty hungry folks out there,' Magnus replied, frowning.

'Fifty-one, because I'm famished,' Flo said. 'Don't worry — we're dishing up now. Go and sit down.'

'I can't; I've got to do the opening.'

Ottilie tried not to laugh, and then Stacey leaned over and whispered what she'd been thinking.

'Anyone would think it was the Oscars, not a harvest dinner in a village hall.'

'It had crossed my mind,' Ottilie said. 'But it's nice to see he cares, and we shouldn't be too hard on him.'

Magnus hurried back out, and they heard him announce that dinner was arriving and say a garbled sort of grace that wasn't really grace at all, and then he apologised for the grace in case anybody didn't like that sort of thing, and then he put some classical music on and the people in the kitchen who'd wanted to eat earlier went to take their places, leaving Ottilie, Heath, Simon and Stacey to take all the food out to the tables. Ottilie couldn't help but notice a look pass between Heath and Simon, and it was one that pleased her. It seemed as if whatever problem Heath had seen with Simon before had been forgotten. She couldn't be sure, but it looked very much like an olive branch.

'I see things have changed a bit for you,' Heath said to him.

Simon smiled and glanced fondly at Stacey. 'You could say that. Definitely for the better.'

'Congratulations, mate. My gran told me you'd got together. I, um… well, I don't want you to think I've ever been prying, but I know a bit about… Well, I'm glad you found someone.'

Simon gave a short nod of understanding and then began to load terrines and dishes full of glistening, steaming food onto a hostess trolley. Once it was full he went out with it, followed by Stacey with one of her own.

Ottilie was busy filling her own when she heard Heath's voice close by.

'You don't mind me being here today?'

'Of course not. Why would I? I'm never going to complain about an extra pair of hands for a good cause… In fact, I'm pleased you decided to come. You didn't always…'

Her sentence petered out. Perhaps it was better not to bring up old stories again.

'I know, I didn't always want to help. You must have thought I was such a dick sometimes.'

'I told you then the same as I'll say now – I understood it wasn't so easy for you. You don't live in Thimblebury.'

'I've missed it. Didn't realise that until today when I came back.'

'Really? I suppose Flo has missed your visits.'

'She was sick of being dragged out to a neighbouring town every time she wanted to see me, that's for sure. Has she been all right?'

'You'd know that better than me, wouldn't you?'

'Thank you.'

'For what?'

'For still being so kind to her after… Well, nobody would have blamed you if you'd cut ties with her altogether. I appreciate that you didn't – she'd have missed you. She thinks a lot of you.'

'I think a lot of her, and it was never her fault.'

'No, it was mine and I go over that on a bloody loop. How stupid I was, I mean.'

'Look…' Ottilie drew a breath. Much as she wanted to have this conversation, it wasn't the moment. 'I think… well, this lot is getting cold. Perhaps we ought to…'

'Oh, right, sure. Sorry. Making it about me again, aren't I?'

'A bit.'

Ottilie went out with her trolley and he followed. By now the hall was alive with good-natured chatter, the clanking of cutlery on china and the warm aromas of their food on the air.

The sun was lower in the sky and the hills beyond the windows were ablaze with its light. Simon and Stacey were at the far end of the hall serving out the contents of their trolleys, and so she and Heath started at the top end near the stage. Ottilie noted that Charles and Fliss had done a far better job of the harvest display than she could ever have done.

Once everyone was eating, Ottilie took her trolley back to the kitchen and Heath did the same with his. Simon and Stacey had already taken theirs through and had joined the diners. Ottilie began to stack the dishwasher.

'You're not going to eat?' Heath asked.

'Not yet. Thought I'd make a start on all this. And anyway, we've not finished serving yet. Someone's got to clear away the plates when people have finished and put out dessert.'

'And that's got to be you? All by yourself? You don't change, do you?'

She looked up, perhaps a bit too sharply when she saw the regret on his face. 'What does that mean?'

'I didn't mean… I wasn't trying to be funny or offensive. I only meant… you always put others first. It was the thing that I… loved about you most but also the thing that frustrated me most.'

It was a bit too late to be using the word love, even if it hadn't been a direct admission of it, but Ottilie couldn't be bothered to say so. She was sick of this pantomime – it was driving her insane and taking far too much energy to keep up.

'Why have you really come today?' she asked.

'Nothing gets past you, does it?'

'Were you hoping to get something past me?'

'No. I realise I have no right to say this, and you might not want to hear it, but I've missed you.'

'Have you? Because your gran said—'

'That I was OK? I told her to say that. I didn't want to make you feel sorry for me, and… well, it would have been the wrong reason for us to try again. Pity, I mean. There's nothing sadder than a romance based on pity, is there?'

'So what changed?'

'I suppose I realised that maybe I didn't care as much as I thought about whether it was pity or not. The truth is I can't believe I did such a stupid thing to mess up the most brilliant thing I'd ever had, and yes, I'm sorry if it sounds selfish but I want to know if there's a way back. If you say there isn't, I won't ask again, but if there's even the faintest hope…'

'This isn't fair. Why now, after all this time, after I'd got used to life without you? It's cruel.'

'I'm sorry.'

'The worst thing is I want to try again, and it's not pity, but how can I? How can I trust what we had?'

'Surely you can trust what you felt? It was good, wasn't it?'

'At first it was amazing, and I…'

'What?'

Ottilie shook her head. She'd told him she loved him back then and never heard it said in return. She wasn't about to go down that road again.

The kitchen door swung open and Stacey pushed a trolley full of dirty crockery in.

'Oh… sorry, was I interrupting?' she asked with more than a hint of intrigued amusement on her face.

'No,' Ottilie said. 'Let me take those – I was loading the dishwasher anyway.'

'I'll help,' Heath began, but Ottilie stopped him.

'No, go and help Stacey clear the tables.'

He seemed to realise what the subtext was: Ottilie didn't want to be alone with him right now. He nodded and followed

Stacey out, and as she watched, Ottilie fought back tears. Why was this so hard? She knew what she wanted, and yet she felt forced to deny it. Why couldn't she let go and let him back in?

Stupid, sensible Ottilie had struck again. The Ottilie who never took risks, who overthought everything. Why couldn't she just bugger off? Why couldn't she take a chance on happiness? Was it always bound to end in disaster? Couldn't someone change and learn and grow, like Heath seemed to have done? And couldn't she do the same?

Stacey came back in as Ottilie was closing the door on the first load of dishes.

'I've got—' She stopped mid-sentence and peered more closely at Ottilie. 'Are you all right?'

'Of course.'

'Because you don't have to pretend. Heath is here and… what does he want? To try again – is that why he's come? To talk you round?'

Ottilie nodded. 'I think so.'

'And you don't want to?'

'That's the thing, I do.'

'Then I don't see the problem.'

'How can I? It's not only about where we left it, but remember who he's related to.'

'He's not – his ex-wife is.'

'And she's another problem. I think he still has feelings for her; I think he always has done.'

'Don't be daft!'

Ottilie looked up at Stacey's suddenly sharp tone.

'You're being an idiot if you think that's true. Anyone can see it's not and it's you he wants. Seems to me you're finding excuses… Self-sabotaging, Simon calls it. Like you don't think you deserve good things so you ruin them before the universe has a chance to do it for you. Says he's done it ever since… well, you know.'

'Why would Simon feel that way? He…'

Ottilie now recalled a conversation they'd had in the waiting room at the hospital the night Mackenzie had been rushed in.

'Did he ever tell you about the young boy who'd had a viral infection and he'd missed it until it was almost too late?'

'Well, yes, but…'

'Did he ever tell you how badly that affected him? How he'd almost quit medicine? How he'd almost given up on everything… Well, he felt he didn't deserve to forget that, to move past it.'

So much had happened since that night, but now Ottilie thought about it she remembered Simon telling her he'd almost abandoned his medical career. So it had been about more than losing his family? 'But he has now? You seem so happy together.'

'There's more to it than that – I certainly can't take all the credit. He saw what he was doing and he got to grips with it, and he realised that making himself suffer wasn't putting anything right, and it certainly didn't change what had gone before.'

'He told you all this?'

'Yes. And I know he wouldn't mind me telling you if it would do some good.'

'But it's not the same at all.'

'Isn't it? Isn't it the case that you already felt like you were betraying Josh by falling for another man? And then it was ten times worse when you realised that man had a connection to Josh's killer? As far as I can see, that's at the root of all your problems, but none of it is Heath's fault and it's certainly not yours, so what's the point in both of you being punished for it? You love him?'

'You know I do.'

'And he loves you.'

'He's never said—'

'If he didn't, he wouldn't be here today. It doesn't matter what he's said. What matters is what he does, surely. I can bet you'd be saying that exact thing to me if it was the other way round and I was the one having the wobbles.'

'Wobbles…' Ottilie gave a rueful smile. 'Is that what it looks like?'

'It looks like a bloody earthquake from where I'm standing, but I was being kind. I think the world of you, Ott, but my God you're a total nightmare sometimes! Be selfish for once! Take what you want and stop worrying about the consequences!'

It was Simon's turn to walk in and look confused. 'Sorry, am I…? I can leave if you need a minute…'

'No,' Ottilie said, 'it's fine. People have got to use the kitchen, after all, and we'll have to take desserts out soon.'

'And there you go again,' Stacey said, shaking her head. 'Worrying about what everyone else needs. There's no help for you, is there?'

Simon looked more confused than ever as Stacey left the room, and Ottilie fought the oddest urge to laugh. It wasn't funny at all, but that didn't seem to make a bit of difference.

'I wondered if you wanted me to take over so you could have some food. Heath is already sitting down.'

'I'm not hungry, to be honest,' Ottilie said. 'But thank you.'

'Perhaps there will be leftovers to take home,' Simon said.

'I'm sure there will be.'

'I suppose it's strange and difficult,' he added after a significant pause.

'What's that?'

'Having Heath here today. You're dealing with it well, I have to say.'

There was that mad urge to laugh again. Dealing with it well? Many things could be said about the situation, but that wasn't one of them. Perhaps it looked calmer from the outside than she'd imagined.

'I need… I need some air.'

'Are you all right?'

'I'll be fine – just in need of a breather.'

Whatever Simon said in reply was lost as she hurried out of the back door and into the rear courtyard of the community centre. Those majestic hills looked down on her, now falling into shadow as the sun slipped ever lower down in the sky, but for the first time that day she hardly noticed them. Nor did she notice the birds singing their evening chorus or the gnats hanging in the air above her head. What was going on? What did she feel? What did she want? She hadn't a clue and everyone seemed to have an opinion on it, crowding in on her, confusing her even more.

She dragged in a long breath and turned her face to the sky. But her contemplation didn't last long. The sound of the door opening brought her back. Heath was there with a plate of food in his hand.

'Simon told me you hadn't eaten.'

'I wasn't hungry.'

'Maybe not, but I wondered if you just thought you were too busy. So I made you a hot beef sandwich. And there is no double entendre there – it really is just a hot beef sandwich.'

Despite herself, Ottilie giggled. 'Thank you,' she said as he sat next to her with the plate and handed it over. Taking it from him, she put it on the ground.

'I've missed that laugh,' he said.

'I've missed your daft jokes.'

'I've missed you. I don't care if you want me to say it or not because I can't keep it in any longer. I've missed you like crazy.

I am sorry, you know. More sorry than I can say for what I did. I've had a lot of time to think about it, and I realise now how bad it was. I wouldn't blame you if you couldn't forgive me.'

'But you came today anyway.'

'I had to. Even if we never got back together I couldn't leave things how they were. I had to get… closure, I suppose. I wanted us to at least be friends again. Your friendship meant so much to me. I didn't want you to disappear completely from my life. I had hoped you'd feel the same way.'

'I do… I mean, I'm glad you wanted to…'

She was stumped again. She didn't know how to respond because she didn't know what she wanted. Or perhaps she did and couldn't bring herself to say it.

'This is ridiculous!' she exclaimed finally.

'What is?'

'Me! I'm ridiculous! Yes, I want us to be friends – of course I do! It would be crazy to be anything else.'

'Well, that's something. I think. So… now we've got that sorted, how about you eat your sandwich? I did go to a lot of trouble to steal that beef and slap it in between some slices of bread, you know.'

The way she relaxed into a laugh was like magic. He was wearing her down – she could sense it, and she had to wonder again why she was even trying to resist.

'I've hated the past few months.'

'Have you?'

She nodded. 'Because you weren't in them.'

'I don't blame you for that. I was an idiot. I should have told you about—'

'I can't pretend I wasn't hurt by that, but it was no reason to end things. I was being… I don't know. I thought I had to be some feminist warrior.'

It was his turn to laugh. 'You're being a bit harsh on yourself there.'

'Probably. I don't really know what I was doing.'

'You were doing the thing that was right. In a strange way, even though I got the sharp end of it, I'm proud of you for it. You gave me what I deserved. It's partly why I took so long to come and see you… I suppose I was ashamed. What I did was wrong and I—'

'Don't. Don't let's keep going over the same old lines. You should have said and done things differently, but so should I. Let's not keep raking it over; there's no point.' Her mind went back to what Stacey had said to her. 'It doesn't change what's already done, no matter how many times we go over it. I know you're sorry. I know because you're here now and it must have taken some guts.'

'Not really. I only knew I had to see you. After that, I didn't really think about it.'

'I wish I could be a bit more like that. I think about everything too much.'

'That's so you,' he said.

She looked up at him, lost in his eyes, breathless. 'Is it?'

'You don't have to be anything. Be you; that's all I need. That's perfect.'

'Is it?'

'Yes. I should have told you a lot of things, not just about Mila. I should have told you that. I should have told you what you meant to me.'

'You did.'

'I didn't make it clear enough, apparently. Is there a chance… maybe you'd let me try again?'

'Do you want to try again?'

'More than anything.'

His hand found hers, a warm rush racing through her as he wove his fingers between hers. She closed her eyes for the tiniest moment, lost in it, only then realising how desperately she'd missed his touch.

'So what do you think?'

'I think we could.'

He took her other hand now and pulled her close. 'Would it be a bit forward to kiss you? I mean, we've only just met.'

Ottilie frowned. 'What do you mean?'

'I mean, *this version* of us has only just met. Where you're you and I'm honest. I think this is the version that could go the distance. Who knows if I'm right, but I hope so. Because I hated being without you. While we're being honest, I have to tell you, I came today to help but I wanted to see you too. Maybe I wanted to see you more. I hoped we might be able to talk.'

'And we are talking.'

'But now I'm getting greedy because I'm hoping for more.'

His eyes were full of what she now knew was love as he looked down at her. It had always been there, right from the start, and if he'd never said it she might only have looked harder to see the truth. It would have saved a lot of heartache, and she realised that now too.

As his lips touched hers there were fireworks. In the movies they watched at Magnus and Geoff's film club there were always fireworks when the couple finally kissed, but that was only in the movies, surely? It didn't happen in real life. Except it did and it was happening to Ottilie right there.

There was a voice telling her she ought to put up more of a fight but she refused to listen to it any longer. That was the old enemy, the too cautious, too sensible Ottilie, and she was sick of listening to her. She wanted Heath. A second chance at a second chance – days like this didn't come along very often, and if anyone was learning fast to grab happiness as it flew by, that person was Ottilie. And she would – she'd take that happiness, and she would wring every bit of joy out of it whether it lasted a hundred hours or a hundred years. Whatever it was, if Heath was there, she wanted it.

A LETTER FROM TILLY

I want to say a huge thank you for choosing to read *New Dreams for the Village Nurse*. If you did enjoy it, and want to keep up to date with all my latest releases, just sign up at the following link. Your email address will never be shared, and you can unsubscribe at any time.

www.bookouture.com/tilly-tennant

I hope you enjoyed *New Dreams for the Village Nurse*, and if you did, I would be very grateful if you could write a review. I'd love to hear what you think, and it makes such a difference helping new readers to discover one of my books for the first time.

I love hearing from my readers – you can get in touch through social media or my website.

Thank you!

Tilly

🌐 tillytennant.com

📷 tillytennant6000

f TillyTennant

@tillytennant6000

ACKNOWLEDGEMENTS

I say this every time I come to write acknowledgements for a new book, but it's true: the list of people who have offered help and encouragement on my writing journey so far really is endless and it would take a novel in itself to mention them all. I'd try to list everyone here, regardless, but I know that I'd fail miserably and miss out someone who is really very important. I just want to say that my heartfelt gratitude goes out to each and every one of you, whose involvement, whether small or large, has been invaluable and appreciated more than I can express.

I'd like to thank my good friend Paula Chell for her help in writing this book. I've always been impressed by her dedication to the nursing profession – as I am with all the nurses I know – and I've always been interested in her stories about her long career. She and others like her are an inspiration. Anyone who dedicates themselves to caring for others is special and deserves all the thanks we can give. Paula is the very best of these people – kind, compassionate, selfless, tolerant, understanding but also brilliant fun. Her love of people shines through in all things and I count myself lucky to know her. I'm also hugely lucky that she was patient enough to answer my many, many questions about nursing – and let me tell you, there were *many*!

I also want to mention all the good friends I have made and since kept at Staffordshire University. It's been ten years since I graduated with a degree in English and creative writing but hardly a day goes by when I don't think fondly of my time there.

Nowadays, I have to thank the remarkable team at Bookouture for their continued support, patience and amazing publishing flair, particularly Lydia Vassar-Smith – my incredible and long-suffering editor – Kim Nash, Noelle Holten, Sarah Hardy, Peta Nightingale and Jessie Botterill. I know I'll have forgotten others at Bookouture who I ought to be thanking, but I hope they'll forgive me. Their belief, able assistance and encouragement mean the world to me. I truly believe I have the best team an author could ask for.

My friend, Kath Hickton, always gets an honourable mention for putting up with me since primary school, and Louise Coquio deserves a medal for getting me through university and suffering me ever since, likewise her lovely family.

I also have to thank Mel Sherratt, who is as generous with her time and advice as she is talented, someone who is always there to cheer on her fellow authors. She did so much to help me in the early days of my career that I don't think I'll ever be able to thank her as much as she deserves. My fellow Bookouture authors are all incredible, of course, unfailing and generous in their support of colleagues – life would be a lot duller without the gang!

I'd also like to give a special shout-out to Jaimie Admans, who is not only a brilliant author but is a brilliant friend. There's also an honourable mention for my retreat gang: Deborah, Jo, Tracy, Helen and Julie. I live for our weeks locked away in some remote house, writing, chatting, drinking and generally being daft. You are all the most brilliant women and my life is better for knowing you all.

I have to thank all the incredible and dedicated book bloggers (there are so many of you, but you know who you are!) and readers, and anyone else who has championed my work, reviewed it, shared it or simply told me that they liked it. Every one of those actions is priceless and you are all very special people. Some of you I am even proud to call friends now – and I'm looking at you in particular, Kerry Ann Parsons and Steph Lawrence!

Last but not least, I'd like to give a special mention to my lovely agent Hannah Todd and the incredible team at the Madeleine Milburn Literary, TV & Film Agency, especially Madeleine herself. I'm so lucky to be a part of such a dynamic agenting powerhouse!

I have to admit I have a love-hate relationship with my writing. It can be frustrating at times, isolating and thankless, but at the same time I feel like the luckiest woman alive to be doing what I do, and I can't imagine earning my living any other way. It also goes without saying that my family and friends understand better than anyone how much I need space to write, and they love me enough to enable it, even when it puts them out. I have no words to express fully how grateful and blessed that makes me feel.

And before I go, thank you, dear reader. Without you, I wouldn't be writing this, and you have no idea how happy it makes me that I am.

PUBLISHING TEAM

Turning a manuscript into a book requires the efforts of many people. The publishing team at Bookouture would like to acknowledge everyone who contributed to this publication.

Audio
Alba Proko

Commercial
Lauren Morrissette
Hannah Richmond
Imogen Allport

Contracts
Peta Nightingale

Cover Design
Debbie Clement

Data and analysis
Mark Alder
Mohamed Bussuri

Editorial
Lydia Vassar-Smith
Lizzie Brien

Copyeditor
Anne O'Brien

Proofreader
Laura Kincaid

Marketing
Alex Crow
Melanie Price
Cíara Rosney
Martyna Młynarska

Operations and distribution
Marina Valles
Joe Morris

Production
Hannah Snetsinger
Mandy Kullar
Nadia Michael
Charlotte Hegley

Publicity
Kim Nash
Noelle Holten
Jess Readett
Sarah Hardy

Sales
David Murphy
Jess Harvey

Typesetting
Ramesh Kumar Pitchai

Dear Reader,

We'd love your attention for one more page to tell you about the crisis in children's reading, and what we can all do.

Studies have shown that reading for fun is the **single biggest predictor of a child's future life chances** – more than family circumstance, parents' educational background or income. It improves academic results, mental health, wealth, communication skills, ambition and happiness.

The number of children reading for fun is in rapid decline. Young people have a lot of competition for their time, and a worryingly high number do not have a single book at home.

Hachette works extensively with schools, libraries and literacy charities, but here are some ways we can all raise more readers:

- Reading to children for just 10 minutes a day makes a difference
- Don't give up if children aren't regular readers – there will be books for them!
- Visit bookshops and libraries to get recommendations
- Encourage them to listen to audiobooks
- Support school libraries
- Give books as gifts

There's a lot more information about how to encourage children to read on our websites: **www.RaisingReaders.co.uk** and **www.JoinRaisingReaders.com**.

Thank you for reading.